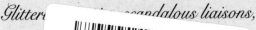

Glittering... scandalous liaisons,

HIGH-SOCIETY AFFAIRS

They're the talk of the Ton!

A *Hasty Betrothal*
by Dorothy Elbury

&

A *Scandalous Marriage*
by Mary Brendan

The Regency

HIGH-SOCIETY AFFAIRS

Volume 1 – March 2009
A Hasty Betrothal by Dorothy Elbury
A Scandalous Marriage by Mary Brendan

Volume 2 – April 2009
The Count's Charade by Elizabeth Bailey
The Rake and the Rebel by Mary Brendan

Volume 3 – May 2009
Sparhawk's Lady by Miranda Jarrett
The Earl's Intended Wife by Louise Allen

Volume 4 – June 2009
Lord Calthorpe's Promise by Sylvia Andrew
The Society Catch by Louise Allen

Volume 5 – July 2009
Beloved Virago by Anne Ashley
Lord Trenchard's Choice by Sylvia Andrew

Volume 6 – August 2009
The Unruly Chaperon by Elizabeth Rolls
Colonel Ancroft's Love by Sylvia Andrew

Volume 7 – September 2009
The Sparhawk Bride by Miranda Jarrett
The Rogue's Seduction by Georgina Devon

Volume 8 – October 2009
Sparhawk's Angel by Miranda Jarrett
The Proper Wife by Julia Justiss

Regency

HIGH-SOCIETY AFFAIRS

Dorothy Elbury &
Mary Brendan

M&B™ and M&B™ with the Rose Device
are trademarks of the publisher.
Harlequin Mills & Boon Limited, Eton House,
18-24 Paradise Road, Richmond, Surrey TW9 1SR

First published in Great Britain in 2004

REGENCY HIGH-SOCIETY AFFAIRS
© Harlequin Books S.A. 2009

The publisher acknowledges the copyright holders of the
individual works as follows:

A Hasty Betrothal © Dorothy Elbury 2004
A Scandalous Marriage © Mary Brendan 2004

ISBN: 978 0 263 87546 1

052-0309

Printed and bound in Spain
by Litografia Rosés S.A., Barcelona

A Hasty Betrothal

by

Dorothy Elbury

For John,
with thanks for his unstinting encouragement
and support

Dorothy Elbury lives in a quiet Lincolnshire village, an ideal atmosphere for writing her historical novels. She has been married to her husband (it was love at first sight, of course!) for fifty years and they have three children and four grandchildren. Her hobbies include visiting museums and historic houses and handicrafts of various kinds.

Chapter One

'*Hell and damnation!*' cursed Robert, Viscount Sandford, as he pulled his horses hard over to avoid a seemingly inevitable collision with the coach that had suddenly appeared from around the curve ahead.

Driven at speed by a reckless youngster with no heed for the safety of either the terrified passengers or any other road user, the vehicle was swinging perilously from side to side as the ageing coachman attempted to wrest the whip from the young blade's hand.

Having eagerly accepted the fistful of guineas from the would-be professional, the driver was now regretting his impetuous gesture and was determined to reinstate himself into his rightful position before they reached the next stage, where the mealy-mouthed proprietor would be sure to report him for this breach of contract. Luckily, the man's skill with the ribbons was still with him and, as the coach swayed on into the distance, Sandford could see that it did indeed seem to be slowing down as he carefully brought his own pair to a sweating, trembling standstill.

'Jump down and hold the heads, Tip,' he commanded. 'We'll have to walk them for a bit until they calm down.

Damned coachmen—I wish to God they'd refrain from giving the ribbons to these young whipsters!'

'Whoops! Guv—looks like he hit something!'

Tiptree, Sandford's groom and one-time batman, pointed to the verge some distance ahead, where a figure lay sprawled in an untidy and apparently motionless heap. Leaping lightly from his seat at the rear of the curricle, he went to the head of the nearside chestnut, talking gently and stroking its nose while Sandford sprang from the driving-seat and strode quickly up the road to see what had occurred. Tiptree followed more slowly, leading the horses and the carriage to where his master was bending over the prostrate form.

'Nasty bump on his forehead, sir,' he offered. 'Wheel must have clipped him as it passed—or maybe he hit it on one of these here stones when he fell?' He crouched beside the viscount and helped him to straighten the crumpled body.

'Why, 'tis only a lad!' he said, as Sandford took the thin wrist in his hand, feeling for a sign of life. 'A stableboy, by the look of his kit! Is he dead, sir?'

'No, he's still breathing—we'll have to get him to a doctor. Dammit! That means more time wasted! Lift him into the curricle, Tip, then we'll see if there are any dwellings hereabouts.'

This feat eventually achieved by Tiptree, Sandford climbed back into the driving-seat, steadying the lad against him with one arm, and, holding the reins loosely in his other hand, commanded Tiptree to walk the horses on. Once or twice, the groom thought he heard a low moan coming from the boy and hoped that the youngster was not going to cast up his accounts over his lordship's driving-coat, for, as sure as eggs were definitely eggs, Kimble would blame him, as usual, for any extra work incurred from this trip. Kimble was his lordship's new valet and prided himself in keeping his lordship 'bang-up-to-the-mark' as the saying went but, luckily, Kimble was still at Beldale, where Sandford had left him contentedly reorganising his master's wardrobe.

The viscount, having purchased his colours some ten years previously, had distinguished himself with honours at the Battles of Corunna and Ciudad Rodrigo and had risen to the rank of Lieutenant-Colonel but, close on the heels of the victory at Waterloo, had received from home the tragic news of the death of his twin brother, Philip, in a carriage accident, and had straight away resigned his commission. His younger brother's death had left Sandford as their father's sole adult heir, so the earl had persuaded Sandford that his army days must, perforce, be over. He must now devote his energies to the Beldale estates and, hopefully, settle down.

The viscount's brother, whom Sandford had always laughingly referred to as 'Farmer Phil' because of his love of the pastoral, had left a young widow, Judith, as well as two little children. During the past year Sandford had become uncomfortably aware that this lady's mother cherished the thought that he must surely now take his opportunity to marry the girl with whom both brothers had fallen in love as striplings, her father's property having neighboured theirs. Sandford, unfortunately for the dowager, no longer carried the willow for his pretty sister-in-law, having long since recovered not only from that particular sickness, but also from several similar afflictions over the intervening years.

Now that Napoleon was safely ensconced on St Helena, many of the viscount's former comrades had also left their companies and returned to England. Sandford had recently been enjoying a spirited reunion with some of his fellow officers in London when he received an urgent summons from Beldale that his father had fallen from his horse and suffered a serious injury. The viscount and his groom were now on their way home with all the speed they could muster.

This present delay would not serve to improve his lordship's frame of mind, thought Tiptree,. as he surveyed the grim expression on Sandford's face. His long military service with the viscount had earned him a special place in his master's affections and he had learned to judge his moods to a nicety.

'Looks like an inn of some sort ahead, sir!' he called, but Sandford had noted the ramshackle building and was already lifting the unresisting victim on to his shoulder and preparing to climb down.

'Bring the carriage into the yard and see to the horses,' he instructed, as he strode to the closed door, at which he kicked violently. 'Landlord! Ho! Open up within, I say!'

Moments passed as he eased his now-groaning burden more securely across his shoulder. Again he hammered and shouted and finally, to his relief, he heard the rattle of door-chains and the screech of an iron bolt being drawn back. The door opened, but only fractionally, to reveal a tousled-headed old woman who regarded him with rheumy eyes.

'We'm closed for business, sir,' she mumbled fretfully, attempting at the same time to shut the door in his face.

'Open up, I say!' demanded his lordship curtly. 'There has been an accident. This youth is injured and I shall require assistance.'

He pushed at the door firmly and the old dame stepped aside fearfully, recognising the Voice of Authority when she heard it, but still she shook her head apologetically as she attempted to grasp his sleeve.

'Sir—sir,' she stammered, 'There baint no one here but mysen. My old Sam—he took ill and died a sennight since and I been waiting for our Jem to come back from the sol-diering...'

Sandford interrupted her. 'Then I shall deal with the mat-ter myself. Get some water heated and show me to a couch of some sort.'

He nudged the old woman firmly along the passageway until, realising the futility of her protestations, she shakily pointed him in the direction of the 'best' parlour where, ducking to miss the lintel, Sandford backed into the room and deposited his once more silent burden effortlessly upon a couch. Then, reaching for a cushion, he gently settled the boy's head on to it and smoothed back the ragged mud-spattered hair from the grimy face.

After some moments the reluctant innkeeper, followed by Tiptree, hobbled into the room carrying a bowl of hot water and a towel.

'My eyesight baint too good, sir,' she wheezed, as she dipped one corner of the linen into the water. She was about to attempt to bathe the boy's forehead when Sandford took the cloth from her and proceeded to wipe the filthy brow himself.

'We're soldiers ourselves, ma'am,' he explained, as he examined the ugly swelling which could now be clearly seen on the boy's temple. 'I've had to deal with many such in-cidents—aye, and worse,' he added, almost to himself. Then, 'Could you rake up some victuals, do you think? Cold pie or bread and cheese will amply suffice.'

He turned to Tiptree, who was examining the patient for broken bones. 'Well, Tip, what have we got, do you think? Is the boy done for?'

'Shouldn't think so, Guv,' said that worthy cheerfully. 'Thing is, though, what we have here ain't exactly a boy!' He pointed to the unbuttoned shirt, beneath which the berib-boned top of a cotton camisole could be clearly seen.

'Good God!' exploded Sandford, stepping back in dismay. 'Cover him—her up, Tiptree, for God's sake!'

He snatched a rug from a nearby chair and together they made a half-hearted attempt to make their patient decent as she gradually stirred and focused a pair of dazed green eyes upon them.

'Wh-what are you doing?' she protested faintly and tried to sit up. 'Oh, my head! Wh-where am I—what has happened—who are you?' She fell back on the cushion in pain and confusion, gripping the rug tightly to her chin as she regarded her rescuers with understandable apprehension.

Sandford stared down at the girl in frowning consternation. No rough serving wench, as he immediately realised on hearing her voice, but surely no young lady of any breeding would appear in public, wearing such shocking attire?

'You must forgive us, ma'am,' he said curtly. 'You were hurt at the roadside—we brought you here—thinking you to be a boy!'

The girl flushed slightly, but a wan smile crossed her face. 'Yes, well—I am in disguise, you see—could you help me up, do you think?' She swung her breeched legs gingerly to the ground and Tiptree grabbed her arm as she swayed forward.

'Oh, dear,' she groaned. 'I seem not to be quite myself—perhaps I should sit for a moment or two.'

Sandford controlled his impatience with difficulty as the girl stared up at him in silent expectation, waiting, he supposed, for him to make the first move.

'Allow me to present myself, ma'am,' he eventually managed. 'Sandford of Beldale at your service—Tiptree here is my man. You must forgive my haste—but I am on most urgent business and I have no time to waste, so I beg you to acquaint me with your destination and I shall see to it that you return home as quickly as possible.'

'Oh, no! You don't understand!' the girl retorted crossly, as she once again attempted to rise. 'I have run away—they were trying to force me to marry— Did you say *Sandford*?' She looked up at him, amazement in her voice. 'Not Colonel Sandford? But yes! I can see that you are indeed he!'

She was, at once, on her feet and staring hard at his countenance.

'I can claim that honour, ma'am,' Sandford replied stiffly, 'but you have the advantage—should I know you?'

'Well, you hardly would—even if you remembered—in this outfit,' countered the young lady, deftly straightening her clothing. 'Allow me to introduce myself—Harriet Cordell—Sir Jonathan was my father—you will not have forgotten him, I'm sure.' She looked at him confidently.

Sandford nodded slowly. 'No, indeed. Our paths crossed many times in Spain. So you are Major Jon's daughter?'

He surveyed the grubby apparition before him and Harriet had the grace to blush.

'But what scrape is this that you are in? Your parents settled in Lincolnshire, as I recollect? How do you come to be in Leicestershire—and in this rig? Is it some sort of wager?'

'No. It is as I said—I have run away from my home. I took the stableboy's clothing and left yesterday morning before the house was up. I have walked *miles and miles* and I slept last night in a hayloft after the owner had put the horses to bed!'

She looked about her in sudden concern. 'Did you recover my bundle? My purse and gown are in it—I don't see it here.'

Sandford glanced at Tiptree, who shook his head. 'We had our hands full with you, miss,' he said apologetically. 'I'll go back down the road and take a look, sir, shall I— but I doubt it'll still be there. It's a busy road.'

At the nod from his master he left the room.

Just then the landlady re-entered, bearing a tray of refreshments, which Sandford, stepping forward, took from her hands, at the same time sending a warning frown to Harriet to remain silent.

'Thank you, ma'am,' he said cheerfully. 'Our patient has recovered. This fare will set us up and we will all be on our way without delay. Here's for your trouble.'

He pressed some coins into her hand, ushered her out of the door and returned to the table. Selecting some of the cold pie and a piece of chicken, he handed the plate to Harriet and instructed her to eat the food.

'And no missish airs, if you please,' he commanded sternly. 'A seasoned campaigner, such as you are, will be well used to eating what's to hand. You spent your youth in the train, I collect?' He helped himself to some food and sat down at the table, regarding her with undisguised curiosity as he ate.

'I admit to having little appetite,' Harriet acquiesced politely. 'And I do have the most throbbing headache, but I shall do my best to take some nourishment. We—Mama and I—learned that lesson in the Peninsula. As you say, we often travelled with the baggage-train, along with the other wives and families. Our quarters were generally quite good, however, and we had our abigail, Martha, with us. Papa went out to Gibraltar when I was tiny and, of course, we went with him, for we had always stayed together...' Her voice trembled slightly and she took a sip from the glass he had poured for her, pulling a face.

'Ugh! Porter! I could never become accustomed to that!'

She was immediately comforted by the sight of his quick grin and covertly studied her rescuer. Throughout her childhood she had listened in awe to the many tales of his daring exploits, so was intrigued and, she had to admit, not a little nervous at meeting her one-time hero at such close quarters. She recollected having been presented to him at a ball in Lisbon, but this had been in her youth and she doubted that the great man would recall such an insignificant incident.

Having cast off both his driving-coat and jacket, Sandford was now in his shirtsleeves, riding breeches and top boots, all of which displayed his good shoulders and strong limbs to advantage. Although not precisely handsome, the viscount was blessed with regular features, crisp brown hair and a pair of steady grey eyes with which he now sat and frowningly surveyed her as she nibbled at her pie.

There was a tap at the door and Tiptree entered, empty-handed. Harriet jumped up and started forward.

'Oh, no! Don't say you could not find it! Now I am in the suds!' She spun round to face Sandford. 'I wonder, sir—could I prevail upon you to advance me some money? I need to get to the staging post, you see. I am going to seek out my grandfather. I am sure he will help me…' She broke off lamely. 'What must you think of me? I will tell you the whole, if you can spare me your time?'

Sandford sighed resignedly. 'My business is most pressing, to be sure, but I cannot just walk out and leave you here. Tiptree, come and eat while I hear Miss Cordell's tale.' He rose from his chair and seated himself on the window settle next to the couch Harriet had just chosen.

'I will be quick, for I can tell that your time is precious,' she said gratefully. 'You may have heard that Papa was injured at Nivelle and we returned to England before Napoleon escaped from Elba, so we were not involved in the Belgian campaign—much to Papa's fury. He had been hit in the chest and never really recovered and he—he died last year, before the victory. Mama was totally to pieces and our neighbour—who farms the land next to ours—was so very helpful to us, arranging the funeral and organising the farm-

workers to carry on and—so many things I shan't tire you
with. Anyway, somehow she grew to depend upon him and
his advice and, just after Easter—three months ago—she
agreed to marry him. Would you believe it, after being married to Papa for more than twenty years! *I* think Sir Chester
is quite the most odious of men and as for his son—words
fail me!'

Harriet clenched her fists and her slim frame shuddered.
'That was it, you see. Sir Chester had married Mama, thinking that she was wealthy—but Papa had left everything to
me, in trust until I am twenty-five or marry. Mama has the
interest from the trust and a generous competence, of course.
Papa was not a rich man, but we were always secure, and
he had also inherited the family farm when his cousin died.
However, to the point; when he discovered that it will be
another five years before I inherit the estate, Sir Chester
started pushing his horrid son at me and throwing us together at every opportunity—he was determined to make a
match, but I was very unco-operative, I can assure you! Two
days ago I overheard them planning to abduct me and force
an elopement, so I knew I had to get away before I found
myself Mistress Gilbert Middleton!'

She was obliged to stop to compose herself and Sandford
took the opportunity to ask, 'You mentioned a grandpar-
ent—he lives in Leicestershire? Perhaps I can take you to
him?' but Harriet shook her head and, after taking a deep
breath, hurriedly continued with her explanation.

'Mama's father—he is a Scottish landowner, but she
eloped with Papa when she was eighteen and she has had
no contact with him since. I understand that he lives somewhere to the north of Edinburgh…'

She then looked hopefully at Sandford, who had risen to
his feet and was reaching for his jacket. Laying her hand
upon his arm, she beseeched him urgently, 'Please, my lord,

will you lend me some money so that I can continue my journey? I was trying to reach Grantham for the staging-post. I believe the coaches leave for Edinburgh at six every morning. We cannot be far away, if you would be so kind as to convey me there?'

'Absolutely not!' retorted Sandford, shrugging into his driving-coat. 'You, my dear Miss Cordell, will accompany me to Beldale where my mother will see to you. You must see that I cannot possibly leave you here alone in this inn. As for allowing you to travel by public stage to some un-known destination—you must be all about in your head still, if you imagine that I will do that! Now, tidy yourself and wash your face while Tiptree sees if the old dame has a cloak or something we can persuade her to sell!'

Somewhat incensed at his lordship's overbearing dis-missal of her project, but suspecting that her protestations would be in vain, Harriet allowed herself to be bundled into the viscount's curricle and, wrapped in the hooded cape pro-cured from the landlady (who had made herself a consid-erable profit from the morning's unexpected activities), re-sentfully succumbed to her fate.

The journey to Beldale was completed almost in silence, with Harriet and Sandford each engrossed in their own thoughts, and Tiptree, seated behind them, wondering if his lordship had allowed his concern for his father's welfare to overset his usually sound judgement.

Sandford was, ruefully, wondering much the same. His mother would have had enough on her plate, he realised, without this additional complication, having hardly had time to mourn her son. Now to be faced with a serious and pos-sibly life-threatening injury to her beloved husband must require all of Lady Caroline's resources. From her hastily scribbled missive he had gathered that Beldale had been thrown, or had fallen, from his horse while returning from estate rounds and had lain helpless in the woods for some hours. His failure to arrive at the stables had eventually alerted the grooms but, although a search party had then quickly located the injured man, it appeared that drenching rain had exacerbated his condition. He had been given the best medical attention available but he had slipped in and out of consciousness as a raging fever had taken hold. His physician had voiced his worst fears and, after a frantic three days, Lady Caroline had reluctantly sent for her son.

Sandford, having lost the precious time he had gained from his headlong dash out of the city, concentrated on his driving and, for most of the journey, refrained from making any sort of conversation until, leaning forward to spring his horses on a straight section of road, he happened to glance sideways and noticed Harriet's white and set face.

'Not so far now,' he announced bracingly. 'We turn off at the next village and then it is a mere three miles to the lodge.'

Harriet nodded glumly. Still feeling the effects of the bump on her head and gradually becoming more aware of other painful areas of her body, she found herself growing increasingly nervous at the thought of the forthcoming interview with the Countess of Beldale. Although her upbringing had been an uncommon one, leaving her with a lack of some of the more usual feminine accomplishments, it had taught her to be very self-reliant. Her common sense now warned her that it was going to be difficult to justify clothing herself in male garb, whatever provocation had led her to do so. Hadn't Mama and Martha frequently been obliged to remind her that she was a lady and that, even in extreme circumstances, she must always endeavour to behave as such?

It had never been her intention to allow anyone of consequence to see her in her disguise. She had supposed that, as a stable lad, she would pass unnoticed on the roadside and that, hidden from view behind some barn or other, she could have changed into her carefully folded good dress and covered her hastily cropped hair with her ample bonnet before boarding the coach for Scotland. She had brought away a purse full of guineas so had expected to travel in reasonable comfort once she reached the staging route. She had not, of course, allowed for this disastrous turn of events.

Having spent her formative years following the army on the continent, she believed that she was well able to take care of herself. She was a skilled and daring horsewoman, having learned her craft under the unforgiving eyes of the grooms and cavalry officers of her father's regiment with whom she had been quite a favourite, with her swinging amber ringlets and her slim, boyish figure. Always willing to attempt the impossible, she had usually managed to remain steadfastly cheerful in the most disheartening conditions.

Not quite so cheerful at the moment however, she saw, with very mixed feelings, that the carriage was negotiating a narrow curve running through a small, picturesque village. The sun was already nestling down into the puffs of cloud above the nearby hills and its light was fading quickly. She held her breath in admiration as Sandford turned his horses into a broad carriage-drive with hardly a check, raising his whip in response to the lodge-keeper's salute as they swept through the high, wrought-iron gates.

She was unable to appreciate the extent of the parkland flashing past her and, in reality, was in no mood to do so for, as the cream stone façade of the elegant house came into view, her apprehension increased.

The great front doors were already on the point of opening as the carriage reached the steps and an elegantly attired lady of mature years was hastening out to meet Lord Sandford who, having cast the reins at Tiptree, had leapt down from his perch and was taking the stone steps two at a time with his hands outstretched.

'Father? How is he?' he cried, anxiously clasping his mother's hands. 'I am not—too late?'

But her ladyship was smiling. 'Robbie—oh, my dear! His lordship has rallied!' she replied joyfully. 'But I'm so glad that you have returned! The physician is with him now—come along, quickly. He will be wanting to speak with you.'

The countess urged her son into the hallway as she spoke and, throwing his driving-coat to a waiting footman, Sandford bounded up the wide, curving staircase. Halfway to the landing he checked, turned and, with his hand on the banister, exclaimed, 'Good grief! I almost forgot—Miss Cordell ! She is still in the curricle!'

She was not. When the groomsmen had taken the horses' heads, Tiptree had handed Harriet down and she had nervously climbed the steps in Sandford's wake, expecting him at least to account for her presence but, with increasing agitation, she realised that she herself would once again be responsible for the difficult explanations. She stepped hesitatingly into the well-lit hall as Lady Caroline turned in puzzlement towards her, then stiffened momentarily as she heard her ladyship's gasp of astonishment.

'Sally! Sally—can it be? But, no! Of course not!'

The countess stepped forward quickly to peer at Harriet's face.

'Please remove your hood, my dear—oh! Your hair! But the colour—and that face! Surely I would know it anywhere—Robbie! Come down at once! Who is this young lady—where is she from?' She drew Harriet to the middle of the hall as Sandford slowly and reluctantly descended the stairs.

'Forgive me, Mama,' he replied, as Harriet agitatedly clutched the shabby cape around her, terrified that her disguise would be revealed both to the countess and to the several impassive servants on duty.

'This is Miss Harriet Cordell. She requires our assistance in a rather delicate matter—shall we go into the salon?'

He took his mother's arm and propelled her gently into a nearby withdrawing-room, signalling Harriet to accompany them. As the door closed, he drew the countess to a sofa and took up his stance by the fireplace, indicating a nearby seat to Harriet, who perched herself very gingerly on its edge, keeping the front of the cape closely about her breeched legs.

Lady Caroline waved her hand impatiently at her son. 'What is this all about?' she demanded. 'This is Sally Rutherford to the letter—I should know! We were bosom bows at our come out. I don't understand!'

She stared helplessly at Harriet, who was herself in total confusion at the older woman's words.

'I am Harriet Cordell, ma'am,' she stuttered. 'My father was Major Sir Jonathan Cordell—my mother Sarah is the daughter of Lord Douglas Ramsey…'

She stopped as Lady Caroline clapped her hands in delight.

'Ramsey! Well, of course! He married Sally—I was her bridesmaid—he took her off to Craigburn and we never met again. We corresponded, to be sure, but she died in childbed—I always believed that her child died with her. Ramsey refused to answer any letters and I supposed him to have gone into a decline. He was much in love with Sally,' she finished sadly.

There was a moment's silence. Harriet cast her eyes up pleadingly at Sandford, who seemed to be studying the pattern on the carpet with great interest. He cleared his throat and his mother looked quickly towards him and smiled.

'Oh, dear,' she said. 'I am being maudlin, aren't I? Do forgive me, my dears.' She turned to Harriet and patted the seat next to her. 'Come and sit by me, my child, and tell me your tale. I can see that Robert is fretting to go to his father and I feel that he will be of little use to us until he has done so.'

Harriet was only too pleased to comply with her hostess's request and waited until Sandford had left the room before reciting her misadventures once more. The countess interrupted her flow only to clarify certain points and then sat, nodding her head in sympathy, until the tale was told.

'—and what I have to do now, ma'am,' Harriet spoke firmly, 'is to ask if you will advance me the money to seek out my grandfather or perhaps…'

'My dear child!' Lady Caroline recoiled in distaste at the very idea. 'I shall write to Lord Ramsey myself. Indeed, I should have done it years ago. Firstly, however, we must see to your dress—Mathilde will find you something.'

She pulled at the bell-rope beside the fireplace and, almost immediately, a footman appeared at the door.

'Oh, March—send for Mathilde and tell Mrs Gibson to have the Rose room prepared for a lady guest.' She turned once more to Harriet. 'I expect you are famished too—have cook send up some substantial refreshments, March.'

The footman bowed and left the room.

'We still keep country hours for our meals, my dear, and had our dinner at three o'clock, but I dare say a hearty supper will be welcomed by both Robert and yourself?'

Harriet nodded. Tired and aching, she was happy for the moment to place herself in her ladyship's hands and, very soon afterwards, she found herself conducted upstairs to a delightful rose-coloured chamber overlooking the gardens at the rear of the house.

Meanwhile, Sandford had hastened to his father's bed-chamber where he was admitted by Chegwin, the earl's elderly valet.

The viscount learned that the crisis had occurred during the early hours of that morning when Beldale had at last rallied and his fever had lessened, although he was still incoherent and weak from the blood-letting upon which Sir Basil, his physician, had insisted.

Chegwin had defied all attempts to remove him from his master's side throughout his illness, refusing all offers of help with either the feeding of the patient or the changing of dressings, resting only when Lady Caroline herself was with his lordship.

'I am glad to see you home, my lord,' he welcomed Sandford softly. 'His lordship is sleeping, but he is no longer as restless as he has been these past days.'

Sandford took his seat by the big four-poster bed and contemplated his sleeping parent gravely. The pale, lined face looked so much younger in repose and his heart softened as he recalled the days of his childhood when he and his twin had accompanied their father around the estate, proudly riding alongside him and always taking his fine example as the pattern-card for their future lives.

He was at a loss to understand how his father, an excellent horseman, had come to take such a toss. The bridleway through the woods on the far side of the estate was a wide and open one and Sandford assumed that the earl would have been riding at a gentle trot. His lordship was over seventy, it was true, but had always been of a hale and hearty disposition and fully active in all outdoor pursuits and had, hitherto, managed his large estate with enjoyment and gusto. Now, the viscount was beginning to wonder if Philip's death had affected the earl more than he had at first supposed.

After his son's untimely death, Beldale had been closely involved with his daughter-in-law's business affairs. To be sure, she had an excellent estate manager in their cousin Charles Ridgeway, but the earl had deemed it his duty to oversee his grandson's inheritance and this was one of the reasons he had felt it necessary to insist upon Sandford's quitting his military career.

During the past year Sandford had become increasingly aware of the fact that his presence at Beldale was likely to be of a permanent nature and that he would have to set about relearning the task of running the estates. He had grown up here, of course, and had dabbled in such matters before the yearning for a military life had sent him on his travels. He had always loved the place and its people, if not quite as wholeheartedly as Philip had done, he ruefully acknowledged, but was gradually coming to realise that there would be few regrets, especially after all the carnage and suffering he had recently witnessed.

The viscount now became aware that his father's eyes had opened and were trying to focus upon the figure at his bedside. A frail hand reached out and felt for Sandford's own and the viscount bent to hear Beldale's whispered words.

'The horse—he fell—something...' His voice tailed off and he sank once more into his drugged slumber.

Sandford drew his head back, puzzled. Chegwin came to the bedside and confided, 'That is how he has been, my lord, and always the same words. Is he worrying about his horse, do you suppose? Smithers tells me that the poor beast had to be destroyed—two legs were broken, I understand.

His lordship has not been informed, of course. Would that be causing such restlessness, sir?'

Sandford shook his head doubtfully. 'I should hardly think so, but certainly it is odd that he constantly dwells upon it.'

He stood up, gently unclasping his father's hand as he did so, saying, 'I shall speak with Smithers myself. You are doing very well here, Chegwin. Please accept my deepest gratitude.'

The old manservant bowed, concealing his pleasure at the young master's words. 'We do our best, sir,' was his reply, but there was a smile on his face as he closed the door after Sandford's departure.

The viscount made straight for the stables, seeking out the head groom who was locking up for the day. Smithers confirmed the valet's story that Cobalt had been destroyed. He himself had attended to the horse immediately after his master had been carried away from the scene of the accident.

'Threshing about in great pain, so he were, sir,' he said sadly, shaking his head. ''Twere a real shame that—a grand old lad, he were. But both his front legs was broke, you see, sir, so couldn't do otherwise.' He looked anxiously at Sandford, knowing that his actions had been correct and wondering where his young lordship's questions were leading.

'Absolutely right, Smithers. I am not doubting your judgement. I just needed to clarify a few points in my mind. Did you notice anything odd about the fall?'

Smithers rubbed his chin and frowned. 'I couldn't see how his lordship came to fall at all on that path, sir, him being such a bruising rider, and Cobalt could have fetched him home blindfolded, as you know. But there it is, sir, his lordship had shot over Cobalt's head—that were obvious from how he was lying—and the horse had gone down on both front legs from the look of the cuts on his knees. Likely a hare or some such startled him is my best guess and I did give it a lot of thought, sir,' he said, shifting uncomfortably. 'Even went back the next morning to have a good look round. Still don't get it, though.' He shook his head again.

'Don't concern yourself, Smithers.' Sandford clapped the groom on the back. 'I'm sure that you did all that should be done in the circumstances. You can show me the spot in the morning, just to satisfy my curiosity. As you say, the fact that his lordship fell at all is a mystery. Now, finish up here quickly and get to your supper.'

Turning on his heel, he left, going at once to his rooms where, with Kimble's disapproving assistance, he quickly changed out of his travel-stained garments before descending to join his mother once more.

The countess was awaiting his return with some eagerness, although she was unable to shed any further light on his father's accident, describing only the injuries he had suffered. A blow to the head causing severe concussion and a broken ankle were the main problems, but the old gentleman was covered in bruises, too, and it would be some time before he was himself again. She was just too glad that Sir Basil, his lordship's physician, was now quietly confident that his patient would make a good recovery and she was overjoyed when Sandford informed her of his intention to remain at Beldale and take over his father's reins until Lord William had fully recovered.

By now, having had ample time to formulate her own ideas for Harriet's salvation, Lady Caroline then turned the conversation to that particular problem.

Chapter Two

Harriet sank gratefully into the luxury of the bath, which had been quickly filled by a procession of maidservants and allowed the last of these, a plump, apple-cheeked damsel, who introduced herself as 'Rose', to wash and rinse her shorn locks.

'Rose?' she asked, in amused curiosity. 'Isn't that the name of this chamber, also?'

The smiling maid nodded, dropping a curtsy. 'Mrs Gibson thought it would be easier for you to remember, miss.' Wrapping a huge, soft towel around Harriet, she helped her from the bath. 'I'm to be your maid during your stay, if you please.'

Rose proceeded to carry out her duties with neat, precise actions, fetching undergarments and a gown from various sources within the room and, finally, taking up a pair of scissors from the dressing-table, set about restoring some sort of shape to Harriet's hair.

''Tis a lovely colour, miss,' she said, brushing back the now shining, red-gold tendrils. 'Who cut it last I can't imagine, but I can just about coax it into that new style they call the "Titus". Luckily you have sufficient curl in it. There!' She stepped back triumphantly to view her handiwork.

Harriet was amazed at the transformation. The curly crop certainly suited her elfin features and, somehow, made her limpid green eyes look larger than ever. The bronze silk gown Mathilde had 'found, from somewhere' accentuated her creamy skin and was of far better quality and design than any she had ever owned. The bruise on her forehead was becoming more obvious and was deepening in colour, but Rose had carefully arranged the curls to disguise it and had woven a spray of artificial lily-of-the-valley through the rest of her hair.

'How very clever of you, Rose,' she said in delight. 'I will be very glad to have you as my maid. It is clear that you have a real talent.'

Rose's ample cheeks flushed with pleasure and Harriet acquired her first loyal friend in the Beldale household. Trained not to ask questions of their superiors, the servants knew better than to query the unexpected arrival of a young lady in strange garb, without luggage or possessions, and, although Rose was bursting with curiosity about her new mistress's background, it was more than her job was worth to exhibit such interest. Mrs Gibson had instructed her to bundle up the dirty, rough clothing and hand it straight to her, and Mathilde, her ladyship's maid, had brought articles from Lady Caroline's own boudoir, although Rose was sure she recognised some of the items as having belonged to one or other of Lord Sandford's young nieces who were often in the habit of visiting with their mamas. The gown was certainly one that had belonged to Lady Sophie, Sandford's youngest married sister, for Rose herself had been set to mend the flounce when her ladyship had discarded it after a recent visit with her young family.

Summoning up her courage, Harriet descended to the hall and was escorted by a patently admiring March to the small salon where her hostess was to be found in deep conversation with his lordship. They both turned at Harriet's entrance and she could not help a feeling of smug satisfaction at seeing the expression of frank amazement on Sandford's face as he took in her transformed appearance.

'My dear,' said Lady Caroline, holding out her hand. 'You look delightful—but I knew that you would. Do please join us and take some refreshment. Robbie—pour Harriet a glass of wine, if you please.'

Sandford complied, taking sidelong glances at his one-time urchin as he did so. He handed the glass to her with a small bow and a practised smile, saying, 'I see I rescued a nymph. No doubt the gods will reward me!'

Harriet flushed uncomfortably at his mocking undertone.

'Who can tell?' she responded dismissively. 'I myself am very grateful for your help, of course, but I must endeavour to carry out my plan. I realise I would have been in great difficulty without your timely assistance but I still need to get to my grandfather.'

She turned to Lady Caroline. 'Please, ma'am, will you give me your help?'

'You may rely upon me to do whatever I can, my child,' said her ladyship, kindly. 'But it will take some time for the mail to reach your grandfather. You will remain in my care until then, of course, but—as I have just been telling Robert—we must concoct a story to explain your arrival. I have already put to him a suggestion that may serve...' She looked towards Sandford and he took up the conversation.

'My mother is concerned that you should suffer no harm to your reputation,' he explained. 'She will be sending to your grandfather, apprising him of your present situation and whereabouts. That, of course, will take several days. Therefore, her ladyship has suggested that, for the time being, it may be useful to engage yourself to me...'

Harriet jumped to her feet in consternation. 'No, no!' she

cried, shaking her head in protest. 'I have not run away from one groom simply to have another thrust upon me!'

Biting her lip, she confronted her hosts. 'I am sorry—but I do not wish to marry anyone. I want to go to my grandfather. If you cannot help me, I must leave...' Her voice trembled.

'Please sit down!' Sandford's voice was curt. 'Perhaps you could do me the courtesy of hearing me out. You mistake the matter. I assure you that there is no question of marriage!'

Harriet looked at him in amazement. 'But you said...'

'He said "engaged", my dear,' her ladyship said gently, drawing Harriet down beside her once more. 'You see, it will save such a lot of talk if Robert is thought to have brought home his new fiancée. It would be quite unexceptional that you should accompany him after his father's accident. We can send notices to the local *Mercury* and to the *Lincoln Post*—for your mother's benefit—then no one will have cause to make unseemly comment. When we hear from your grandfather and know his intentions towards you, you can simply break off the agreement, saying that you found that you did not suit.'

'That, in any event, would be close to the truth,' muttered the viscount under his breath, as he poured himself another drink.

When, during Harriet's absence, Lady Caroline had proffered her suggestion of a mock 'engagement', Sandford was at first horrified and then laughingly dismissive, but slowly began to realise that the scheme would in fact solve a good many difficulties that were certain to arise while they awaited Douglas Ramsey's response to his mother's letter, not the least of which, from his own point of view, was the embarrassing situation in which he always seemed to find himself on his visits to his sister-in-law's house.

Since his return from the Continent he had been a frequent visitor to Westpark, offering brotherly advice and comfort to the young widow and getting re-acquainted with his little nephew and niece, who had grown to regard him almost as a substitute for their beloved father, because of the viscount's uncanny likeness.

He, in his turn, found great delight in their company and had spent many happy hours with Christopher, engaging in those activities so beloved of small boys and grown men alike. Shy little Elspeth had, equally, won his heart with her huge brown eyes and appealing ways and Sandford would gladly have continued this happy association with Philip's family had it not been for Judith's mother, Lady Butler.

This cantankerous old lady had made her home with the young Hursts after her own husband's death three years previously when Judith, having been Sir Frederick's sole heir, had joined her property with Philip's own estates. Although Lady Butler had been left an excellent annuity, she had deemed it more convenient to move in with her daughter, thereby avoiding any of the household duties and attendant difficulties with which she would have been obliged to involve herself had she remained in her own home. She eschewed anything that interrupted the level tenor of her existence and, being an indolent and tediously complaining woman who considered that Life had dealt her a shabby hand, she regarded even the slightest inconvenience as a personal affront. She refused to involve herself in domestic affairs, yet happily criticised their organisation and, whilst she would never dream of offering her daughter any guiding advice on household management, she was always quick to point out where errors had been made. Easygoing Philip had merely laughed at his mother-in-law's eccentricities, even occasionally chaffing her, but Sandford found her both irritating and encroaching and had, in the past, always excused himself from her company at the first opportunity.

Recently, however, the viscount's necessary visits to Westpark had thrown him into Lady Butler's society more often and she had lately taken to pointing out how the children 'loved him so', and how 'dear Judith blossomed' in his company and, worse, 'how comfortably we all sit together'. With increasing dread, he saw clearly where her fancies were leading.

His continuing lack of a bride was being misconstrued by Lady Butler as a sure sign that he was still 'carrying the torch' for her daughter and a second marriage into the Hurst family would simply 'make all neat and tidy' from her point of view, as well as raising her a notch higher in the social scale, for she was very much concerned with her own consequence.

But Sandford was not about to indulge the old woman's fantasy that one brother could simply step into the other's shoes. Judith had made her choice years ago and, Sandford was certain, had never regretted it, so, with this scheme of his mother's, he now saw what seemed to him a perfect solution to his own difficulties. For this reason alone he had finally agreed to the charade.

He was, therefore, more than a little piqued at Harriet's reaction to the suggestion, for he could hardly help being aware that his rank and wealth inevitably classified him as a considerable 'catch' in the marriage mart. He found to his surprise that, although his mother's scheme was clearly meant to be merely a temporary arrangement, he had anticipated a more flattering and appreciative response from this chit of a girl and, considering her present situation, a certain gratitude towards himself.

In his early days as a subaltern in a Rifle Brigade he had found himself fighting alongside Major Sir Jonathan Cordell in several engagements of the Peninsular campaign and had soon learned to respect the older officer's judgement. Conditions were such, during that time, that he had met Lady Cordell very infrequently and her daughter, as far as he was aware, not at all.

Preferring to be in the thick of the action, he was seldom to be found far from the front lines, this enthusiasm earning him rapid promotion, but inevitably he had, during one engagement, received a splinter in the thigh, which had necessitated him being carried off the field and transported to what passed as the hospital area. Here, amidst the sickening carnage and filth, he had witnessed 'Mrs Major', as she was termed, working alongside the wives of the troopers and artillerymen as though she were a mere camp-follower instead of an officer's lady. He had seen that she spoke as gently and compassionately to the roughest infantryman as she did to those of rank and title and he had been equally impressed by her firm efficiency as she tended the most appalling wounds. His own injury had not been severe and his conversations with her had been few and he had soon been transferred to his own quarters but, on other fields and in other battles, he had often recalled the sight of 'Mrs Major' walking quietly amongst the rows of dead and dying, bending to offer what little comfort she could.

Her daughter certainly seemed to have that same indomitable spirit, he now mused, as he watched Harriet deep in conversation with his mother. He had been quite taken aback at her entrance. True, he had not studied her very closely up until that moment, but the transformation from mud-urchin was astonishing.

The dirty, raggedly cropped hair was now a burning halo of soft curls framing a quite delightful face upon which was centred a neat straight nose, lightly dusted with some very unfashionable freckles. And that was a decidedly stubborn-looking chin, he conjectured in growing amusement. The generous rosy lips, unpainted, he would swear, were half open as they exclaimed at some words the countess had uttered, and the eyes—what colour? He could not immediately recall, but was answered as the owner turned her face in his direction. Green as moss and fringed, most unusually, with thick, dark lashes.

The result was breathtaking and, with a gleam in his eye, it suddenly occurred to him that being 'engaged' to this curious little creature could prove to be rather more than just an amusing diversion. Confident of his ability to charm her out of her unwarranted antagonism towards him, his spirits rose as he resolved to take her to visit his sister-in-law at the first opportunity.

Chapter Three

Harriet had suffered a restless night in her rose bedchamber. Her head ached and parts of her body felt very sore as she tossed and turned in the big bed. She was glad that it was not a four-poster, as she had always hated them, slightly fearful that someone may be prowling around beyond the closed bedcurtains.

Having spent most of her youth in Spain and Portugal, she disliked being shut in, preferring open spaces and wide skies. She had discovered, to her surprise, that she loved the lush greenness of England and, even though she had also found that she was expected to conform to the rigid pattern of behaviour required of an English miss, she had eventually settled into her new life as a gentleman farmer's daughter quite contentedly.

However, although occasional digressions still occurred, her stubbornness still had to be held firmly in check, especially if she felt that her wishes were being unreasonably overridden, and her father had often had cause to wonder from whence this mulish streak had come. Her mother could only suppose that it must have been inherited from her Scottish forebears, once reminding her husband that her own father's cussedness had been legend in his lands and who,

Harriet had been subsequently informed, had continued to earn this reputation over the succeeding years.

Harriet wondered if he would respond to Lady Caroline's missive. She had intended arriving, unannounced, on his doorstep, confident of her ability to win round the dear old gentleman she had supposed him to be but, after her conversation with the countess, she was no longer so sure of herself. In fact, he sounded a rather disagreeable sort of fellow, refusing to have anything to do with Mama just because she had wanted to marry darling Papa. He must be slightly touched in his upper quarters, she decided, pulling the quilt around her. Mama had seldom spoken about him and it was only after Papa's death that she had told her daughter that she believed him to be still alive, having read of some Highland clearance dispute with which he was involved. Hearing that he had taken a sympathetic view of the Highlanders' plight had been the main reason that Harriet had elected to seek out her grandfather. She could have succeeded too, she fulminated resentfully, had not that fool coachman knocked her down. Then, that arrogant Sandford! Carting her off like so much baggage! And in the opposite direction, too! And now, she had to pretend to be engaged to him! What a disappointment he had turned out to be! A small tear crept from her eye as she took stock of her situation and, sniffing, she realised forlornly that she would have to make the best of it until a better opportunity presented itself—the words her father had been wont to use if ever he heard her complaining about her lot. She drifted off to sleep, beset by dreams of marching columns, speeding coaches and Viscount Sandford, surrounded by hundreds of tartan sheep!

The following morning at breakfast, Sandford announced his intention of riding over to Westpark to introduce his 'betrothed' to the Hursts. He nodded briskly to Harriet, who glowered at him over the rim of her cup.

'If you could arrange to be ready in half an hour, I shall have the horses saddled.'

'Oh, I'm afraid I cannot accompany you,' she countered. 'I have no habit, although I dare say could wear my breeches, of course,' she offered pertly.

Lady Caroline frowned at her and shook her head. 'Don't be naughty, my child. You must not tease him. He has not yet got out of the way of giving orders.' She turned to her son and smiled. 'I have arranged for Madame Armande to bring her seamstresses to us this morning, my dear. If you could wait until Miss Cordell has some suitable garments I am sure she will be happy to accompany you. You will want her to make a good impression, I know—especially on Lady Butler.' Her eyes twinkled as she saw her words take effect.

'As you say, ma'am,' replied Sandford, rising. 'Then I shall go up to see how Father does and tend to other business instead. Your servant, ladies.' He bowed in Harriet's direction and left the room.

'He's very high-handed, isn't he?' Harriet said, in some surprise at his sudden departure, and strangely disappointed that he had refused to rise to her bait.

Her ladyship patted her hand. 'He has been used to making decisions, my dear,' she said. 'And, like yourself perhaps, he has been out of Society for so long that he forgets how it goes on. You must not mind him.'

Looking at the clock on the mantel-shelf, she rose to her feet. 'Come, now we must attend to Madame. She will be waiting in the sewing-room and we have a lot to get through.'

The next few hours were a test of stamina, with Harriet being pushed and pulled and pinned and measured until her head was in a whirl. Madame had brought several garments ready-made, which were to be altered to fit her at once, in addition to the many bolts of various fabrics that she offered for Lady Caroline's inspection.

At last, the countess took Harriet down for the cold luncheon that had been laid out for them in the dining-room. Sandford was nowhere to be seen. Harriet supposed him to be about his 'other business'. She, herself, was desperate to get out into the fresh air and was about to ask her ladyship's permission to take a walk on the terrace when March entered and announced a visitor.

'The Honourable Mrs Hurst, my lady,' he intoned grandly, and a tall, raven-haired beauty swept in past him.

'Judith, my dear!' The countess rose from her seat. 'I was not expecting you, surely? Not that you need an invitation, to be sure. Sit down, please—you will see we are still at lunch—such a busy morning we have had!'

Judith Hurst took a seat at the table, gracefully arranging the skirts of her black riding-habit and removing her gloves. Her soft brown eyes rested on Harriet with open curiosity as she spoke, her words almost tripping over themselves in her breathless haste.

'I confess to being all agog, Belle-Mere! Mother has sent me over to see how Lord William does and I have just this moment seen Madame Armande's equipage leaving Beldale. Forgive my vulgar curiosity, but I cannot contain myself as to what it is all about!'

Lady Caroline was forced into making an instant decision. Little as she cared to deceive her daughter-in-law, of whom she was very fond, she knew her to be somewhat feather-brained. One of the reasons dear Philip had loved her, the countess supposed but, nevertheless, she doubted Judith's ability to keep the bones of this secret to herself or, more especially, from her mother, which Lady Caroline knew was

Sandford's main objective. Her mind worked quickly and she rose, moving to stand beside Harriet's chair and, placing her hand on the girl's shoulder, she announced, 'Allow me to introduce you to Robert's betrothed, my dear. This is Miss Harriet Cordell.'

Judith Hurst's eyes widened in amazement, then her face became wreathed in smiles as she clapped her hands together.

'Is it true, then? Is he engaged at last?' She, too, rose from her seat and came to Harriet's side. 'How truly delightful! I am so happy for you both. Do say we shall be friends, dear Miss Cordell.'

Harriet, by now full of embarrassment, was attempting to gather her wits in order to make some suitable reply when, to her relief, Sandford entered the room and, striding forward, held out his hands to his sister-in-law.

'How well you look, dear Judith,' he said, with a welcoming grin. 'Still the prettiest girl in the county, I see.'

There was a moment's awkward silence before Judith, laughing, pushed him away in mock dismay.

'Oh, Robert! You devil! Do not tease so!' she chided him. 'Why have you kept such a secret from me? I thought myself your dearest friend and have only just now been informed of your betrothal!'

Sandford shot a glance at his mother and quickly appraised the situation.

'I see I have been forestalled,' he said, with a rueful smile. 'I promise I intended to bring Miss Cordell to Westpark as soon as I was able. We were obliged to quit London in such haste that we had no time to pack our belongings— I believe Madame Armande is attending to some of your more pressing needs?' He cast what he felt to be a fond smile in Harriet's direction.

'I hope the morning's activities have not tired you out,

dearest?' He continued, determined to play his part to perfection. 'I came to see if you would care to take a walk in the grounds—but perhaps you would prefer to stay and talk to Mrs Hurst? I'm sure she is *dying* to hear our story!'

Judith shook her head and laughed.

'Very true, my dear Robert—but I shall not play the gooseberry! And besides, I do want to know how Lord William does. You two lovebirds may run along now if you promise that you will tell me all later?'

Sandford bowed and, taking Harriet's hand on his arm, he led her out through the rear doors on to the terrace. He did not speak until they had descended the steps leading to the gardens.

'I should have foreseen that possibility,' he commented thoughtfully as soon as they were out of earshot. 'I trust that you were not too discomposed?'

'We were caught off our guard,' admitted Harriet, relieved to be out in the fresh air at last. 'Lady Caroline showed great presence of mind. However, it now appears that we have to concoct some sort of history for our sudden—romance.'

Her voice stumbled on the word and he looked down at her flushed cheeks in concern.

'It will not be for long,' he said soothingly. 'We must stick to the truth as far as possible—we could easily have known one another for years. I shall simply say that we met again in London and that I was overcome…'

He stopped, as Harriet came to an abrupt halt beside him.

'Oh, I would prefer that you do not say such a thing, my lord,' she exclaimed, hot with embarrassment. 'I must inform you that I feel sufficiently uncomfortable about this whole charade without having to fabricate even more deception.'

'Judith is no fool,' he informed her bluntly. 'She will

expect ''love'' to be in it somewhere—and how else would you explain such a hasty betrothal?'

Harriet's chin came up and she flashed angry eyes at him.

'I take leave to remind you that it was not my idea, nor was I in favour of it!' she felt constrained to point out. 'Now it appears that we are to be embroiled in yet more deceit. I shudder to think what further complications lie in store!'

'Oh, come now! Surely it cannot be beyond your powers to engage in a little harmless play-acting—you seemed ready enough to dash about the countryside in questionable and, unless I'm mistaken, *stolen* garb only yesterday!'

Tongue in cheek, he was deliberately goading her and knew he had achieved a hit with this sally when he saw her fists clench.

'I did not steal them!' she replied hotly. 'I left a guinea—far more than they were worth!' Then she realised that he was set upon teasing her, which merely increased her anger.

'That, as you perfectly well know, was quite a different matter,' she threw at him, 'and, though I *tremble* to mention it, perhaps it will be your own lack of ability that will bring about the downfall of this ill-conceived plan—especially if you persist in referring to other young ladies as ''quite the prettiest''—even if they are,' she finished lamely, scowling as Sandford laughed outright.

'Clumsy of me,' he admitted cheerfully. 'On that I stand corrected! I promise to remember that you have that honour now and, if you will only play your part with a little more conviction, I'm sure we will hold out.'

He lifted her hand and firmly placed it once more on his arm.

'Shall we say twice around the fountain, my dear? And please endeavour to keep step. I do not wish to seem to be dragging you around the gardens!'

'Then stop striding along as though you were marching

to war,' she protested. 'I cannot walk at such a pace and I refuse to run alongside you. Is everything always done to your bidding?' She swiftly withdrew her hand, as he halted once more.

'You really are the most infuriating young lady I have ever come across,' he said, no longer hiding his irritation. 'And this is fast becoming a bore! Surely you must prefer to be here at Beldale rather than under some hedgerow, or worse. After all your years in the Peninsula, I need not point out what might have happened to you had someone other than myself found you on that roadside…!'

'Yes, well—I do know that and I have repeatedly told you that I am very grateful to you, but that does not give you the right to be always ordering me about. Do you never allow anyone but yourself to have an opinion or a point of view? I am not one of your infantrymen, you know!'

Sandford, highly exasperated, glared down at her.

'I am well aware of that fact,' he said drily. 'In the field one seldom has time for philosophical debate when decisions have to be made. I have learnt to deal with tricky situations in a straightforward manner, without unnecessary roundaboutation or fuss. I fail to see why you should find that so unacceptable.'

'You may make your own decisions as much as you like,' countered Harriet, her eyes kindling, 'but please do not be forever making mine!'

With which remark she turned on her heel and walked quickly back to the house, leaving Sandford wondering, in baffled uncertainty, if this scheme of his mother's was going to be such a good idea, after all.

Sighing, he watched Harriet climb the terrace steps and disappear from his view. He hoped that Lady Caroline and Judith had, by now, left the dining-room, as the girl's singular return would certainly cause a raised eyebrow if witnessed. He hesitated, and then resignedly followed after her.

The room was, in fact, empty when Harriet entered and she stood undecided for a moment, having had time to give some thought to her hasty retreat, and was just about to retrace her steps when Sandford reappeared.

'If I have offended you,' he said, stiffly correct, 'I must apologise. It was certainly not my intention to override your wishes…'

'No, sir, if you please,' Harriet intervened in breathless haste. 'The fault is mine. I—often have—difficulty in curbing my—impetuosity. Father always warned it would lead me to disaster and he was right. It so often does. I beg your pardon, my lord. I shall try to behave as you suggest.'

She looked so much like a penitent child as she stood before him with her eyes cast down that Sandford felt a sudden urge to hold her in his arms. With an effort he turned away and walked to the doorway.

'Then let us consider the subject closed,' he shot over his shoulder as he went out. It appears that the little termagant has learnt her lesson, he thought, with a slightly bemused frown, 'Perhaps we should go and join the ladies?'

Arrogant beast, thought Harriet, immediately regretting her offer of apology but, since no other course of action was open to her, she gritted her teeth and, resolving to try to be on her best behaviour, she reluctantly followed him from the room.

In spite of this somewhat inauspicious start, it did not take Harriet long to find that she really enjoyed Judith Hurst's company, although the young widow was several years older than herself. She admired Judith for the stalwart way in which she had coped at the loss of her beloved husband, remembering sadly that her own mother had not done as well in her grief. Judith seemed truly happy at the news of Sandford's impending marriage and, eager to be involved in introducing Harriet to the local society, at once offered to hold a small party at Westpark House in honour of the engagement. Since Lady Caroline felt that the earl's frail condition must restrict any immediate gathering at Beldale, she readily agreed and, having already taken Harriet's wardrobe requirements into her stride, she was satisfied that her protégée would bring nothing but credit to the family.

Sandford himself had picked out a frisky mare for his betrothed, for he was quite sure that she would be a good horsewoman after her years in Spain, and the first time he tossed her up into the saddle he was gratified to see how capably her hands controlled the prancing bay.

Harriet's eyes had lit up with joy at the sight of the mare, for she was agog to explore the grounds, having waited impatiently for her riding habit to be delivered. Madame Armande had excelled herself in the swift execution of the brandy-coloured outfit, trimmed with military frogging of gold lace down the front of the jacket, along with a pert little shako complete with its own cockade of bronze feathers. Sandford was more than satisfied with Harriet's appearance as they set out on their first visit to Westpark.

They rode through a wooded spinney along the bridleway that joined the two properties and the viscount pointed out various landmarks, which would help her should Harriet choose to visit Judith on her own. When they reached the area where his father had been thrown from his horse, Sandford related the groom's description of the accident.

'I still cannot see why he should have fallen at this spot,' he said, shaking his head. 'He is fairly lucid now and continues to maintain that something caused his horse to go down, but I have scoured the area and can find nothing untoward. He does not recollect seeing an animal on the path or hearing anyone in the vicinity, but swears that Cobalt went down all of a sudden...'

'Perhaps he got a flint in his foot?' suggested Harriet. 'I have seen horses go down in that way. And you say that Cobalt was a veteran—did he suffer from a rheumatic condition which might have caused his legs to fold?'

Sandford considered. 'Smithers didn't mention it, but it is possible.' He studied her curiously. 'You seem to know a great deal about horses,' he said.

Harriet gave a wry smile. 'For a girl, you mean. You are forgetting that I practically grew up in the cavalry,' she replied. 'Being an infantryman, you had only your own string with which to concern yourself, but we had to be horse doctors as well as soldiers, you know.'

She pulled ahead of him as the path narrowed and he was obliged, for the moment, to ride behind her in silence which, as well as preventing him from uttering an indignant rebuttal, gave him ample opportunity both to admire her straight back and elegant posture and to think better of his intended remark.

The bridleway from Beldale opened out through a wide-barred gate into a clearing and Sandford indicated the Westpark gate on the other side of the meadow.

'This is the short cut that the two families use,' he said. 'Carriages have to go round by the lane, of course, which adds five miles to the trip.'

Harriet gauged the distance across the field. 'Race you,' she offered, and was off like an arrow before he had time to reply.

'Watch out for rabbit holes!' he shouted and was after her in a trice, but she had the advantage and reached the far side ahead of him. He reined in beside her, his face wreathed in smiles. Harriet's face was bright with the exhilaration of the gallop and her green eyes were sparkling with delight as she looked at him.

'She's a beauty! Thank you so much for letting me use her,' she said, as she patted the mare's neck fondly. 'Clipper! What a fitting name for her.'

'I'm glad you approve. You ride very well—and don't say "for a girl", for I'm sure I don't mean to minimise your ability. Only, next time, give me fair warning before you challenge me!'

'Oh, I'd hardly take on that boy of yours in fair play,' she laughed. 'I believe in the element of surprise, your lordship. I'm amazed you never encountered the strategy in your battles!'

'Oh, I encountered it, all right, Miss Cleverboots,' he laughed, leaning down to close the gate behind them. 'Now I shall be on my guard—just make sure that you are, also!'

They rode on, side by side, exchanging similar persiflage until they eventually turned into the stableyard at Westpark House, where their horses were handed to the grooms and they entered the house by the rear doors.

'We got into the habit of doing this,' said Sandford, as he ushered Harriet through the entrance. 'Lady Butler doesn't approve, of course, but Phil and I always found it more convenient...' He paused, then continued, '...this passage leads into the main hall. The staff will already have been notified of our arrival.'

He pushed open a green baize door and nodded to the waiting footman.

'Good morning, Finchley. Mrs Hurst is expecting us. Is she in the small parlour?'

The elderly manservant nodded disapprovingly. 'Yes, my lord,' he intoned gravely, as he led the way and showed them into a cheerful sitting-room where Judith was to be found playing spillikins with her two children while her mother was half-heartedly attending to the tapestry on her fulsome lap.

At the footman's announcement, Judith rose gracefully and came towards them, hands outstretched.

'Oh, you came! I'm so pleased. Look, Mother. Robert has brought Miss Cordell to visit us—and what a stunning outfit, I do declare. Do sit down, won't you? Shall I have Finchley bring in some tea—or would you prefer coffee?'

Sandford was already engaged in the game with his niece and nephew and declined refreshment. Harriet, having accepted a glass of lemonade, seated herself opposite the elderly Lady Butler and asked her politely how she did.

'I must not complain,' said her ladyship, pulling her copious shawls about her ample shoulders more snugly, although the day was warm and humid. 'One is beset by so many aches and pains. But I have learned to bear my discomforts with fortitude.'

She leaned forward, peering closely at Harriet. 'You are very young, to be sure. Just out of the schoolroom, I suppose. Do your parents allow you to travel about the countryside without a chaperon? In my day it would have been unheard of.'

Harriet laughed. 'I am not as young as I look, ma'am,' she said, 'and I disremember ever having been in a schoolroom. And as for a chaperon, you must agree that Sandford will serve?'

The old lady sniffed. 'I'm told you met Robert while he was off fighting—a camp-follower, or some such, I hear.'

Sandford stiffened and raised his startled eyes to meet Harriet's. She, however, smiled and nodded her head at Lady Butler.

'We certainly had to follow the camp, ma'am, but we were in excellent company. Several of their lordships' wives and daughters were with us, you know, and it was not fun and frolics quite all of the time!'

The viscount's eyes gleamed with amusement, then became more serious as he intervened.

'Hardly any of the time, actually,' he said, getting up from the floor, 'and as for camp-followers, ma'am, we would have been hard pressed, at times, to manage without their assistance. I must inform you, ma'am, that Miss Cordell's father was a courageous comrade of mine and her mother was well respected for her voluntary tending of the wounded.'

'Oh, do not start to discuss these unsavoury matters again, I beg you.' Lady Butler shuddered, reaching for her vinaigrette and breathing in some of its heady contents. 'Tell me instead of your father. First we are told he is at death's door and now he is quite recovered, I hear? I would that I were blessed with such stamina! What a pity Hurst did not have his father's constitution!'

Sandford winced as he answered, 'Beldale is getting stronger by the hour. Sir Basil hopes that he will be able to come downstairs in a few days but I am afraid that he will be unable to attend Judith's party next week. *We* are looking forward to it, of course,' he finished, gamely attempting a show of enthusiasm.

'Well, it will be a great deal of trouble to arrange, you know, at such short notice, but I am sure we shall try to put on a creditable show. Why it cannot have waited until Lady Caroline could see to it herself, I cannot imagine.'

She folded her untouched Berlin-work and rose to her feet.

'Now, if you will excuse me, I suppose I must see Mrs Walters about the menus.' She trod majestically across the room and left.

There was a moment's silence then Judith laughed, a little self-consciously.

'I hope she does not do such a thing! Mrs Walters would faint from astonishment! Take no notice, Robert, dear. You know how Mama is. I am sure that she means no harm.'

Sandford doubted this, but let it go. 'If this party affair is going to cause you a lot of trouble…' he said hopefully, but Judith looked shocked.

'Trouble? I'm looking forward to it. I have been in mourning for a whole year now, Robert, and this is the first time we will have had any sort of gathering at Westpark since Philip's—funeral—and you know he would not have wanted it so!'

Gathering up the skirts of her black bombazine gown, she began to pirouette around the room, much to little Elspeth's delight.

'Shall we have dancing, do you think? A few country reels, perhaps?' She stopped, flushed prettily and sat down once more beside Harriet. 'What shall you wear, Miss Cordell—oh! Do say I may call you Harriet! I have a gown I have never yet worn. I think it may be just the occasion to bring it out!'

Having only recently come out of mourning herself, Harriet could sympathise with the young widow's feelings and, happy to defer to her hostess's obvious knowledge of what was fashionable and what was not, she was quite amenable to hear Judith's suggestions. She could see that Sandford seemed perfectly content to be entertained by the two children. He pored over Christopher's snail-shell collection with apparent fascination and even helped his little niece to fasten a miniature cape around her beloved doll, with no sign of the self-conscious reticence she expected from most members of his sex when confronted with young children. She noticed, too, that Judith was viewing the scene with a certain fondness and wondered if, perhaps, her own unexpected appearance had interrupted a blossoming relationship between Sandford and his sister-in-law. Judith's words, however, dispelled that thought.

'He is so like Philip,' she said tremulously, bright tears shining in her eyes. 'They do miss him so. Robert has been absolutely marvellous with them and given them so much of his time.'

'I'm sure he loves them dearly.' Harriet laid her hand on Judith's. 'And who would not. They are such sweetly behaved children. Lady Caroline has said that they are a credit to both their parents. She dotes on Elspeth, as you must know.'

Judith nodded, composing herself. 'We were very happy together, Philip and I. I do so wish the same joy for you and Robert. I was afraid he would never meet anyone. He was always so involved with his regiment that it seemed to me that he had no sort of social life at all. You should have known him when he was a boy—he was quite the young tearaway!'

'Do I hear my character being demolished over there?' came Sandford's amused voice. 'I hope you are not about to apprise Miss Cordell of my youthful misdemeanours, Judith. I have worked very hard to gain her approbation, I assure you, and if you are set on ruining all my efforts...'

Both ladies burst out laughing and, seeing Sandford reach for his hat and gloves, Judith rose to see them to the door. Elspeth curtsied shyly to Harriet while Christopher begged his uncle to 'come again soon'. The viscount assured him that he would be over to take him riding the following day and the little boy was allowed to lead the visitors back to the rear exit.

'Grandmama says you shouldn't use this door,' he confided, as they walked out into the stableyard, 'but Papa and

I always did and, as I am now the man of this house, I give you both my permission.'

Sandford took his nephew's proffered hand and inclined his head. 'We are pleased to be so honoured, Christopher,' he said gravely.

Harriet nodded smilingly, adding, 'And thank you for including me.'

The little boy was puzzled. 'But you are to be one of the family now, aren't you? Mama said…' He looked from one to the other.

Sandford laughed and clapped him gently on the shoulder. 'Absolutely right, dear fellow!' he breezed. 'And do you approve of your new aunt? She's a cracking good rider, let me tell you!'

Christopher was suitably impressed. In his opinion girls couldn't really ride, having such stupid saddles to contend with but, if his Uncle Robert said his fiancée was good then, by golly, she must be and that made her fine by him. He watched as Sandford helped Harriet mount, then ran, waving farewell to them as they rode off.

'They are such lovely people—your brother's family,' commented Harriet, as they crossed the meadow to the Beldale estate. 'What a terrible tragedy that he will never see his children grow up. Judith has been so brave in her loss. Am I correct in thinking that Lady Butler cannot have been much help or comfort at the time?'

'None at all, I understand from my mother. She took to her bed with "the vapours", which caused poor Judith even more distress and then she had the gall to preside over the funeral reception wearing black veils and so on. We have very little affection for her, I fear, but she is Judith's mother and grandmother to Philip's children so one must endure her remarks. I have to congratulate you on your forbearance. Another of your famous strategies, I deduce?'

'Just "getting over the heavy ground as lightly as possible" as they used to say,' said Harriet, her face wreathed in smiles at his compliment.

'A veritable fund of manoeuvres! I can see I shall have to be careful not to join battle with you,' he chaffed laughingly.

Fencing companionably in this manner, they rode on for some minutes until a shout from the trees caused them to turn their heads. A horseman appeared on the track ahead of them and a cheerful voice called, 'Home then, Sandford? I'm very glad to see you back. And with a betrothal, I hear. Do I get an introduction?'

The rider was a comely, well-built man dressed in leather jerkin and riding breeches. Sandford greeted him with pleasure and presented him to Harriet as his cousin, Charles Ridgeway.

Ridgeway, as Harriet had already learned from her conversations with Lady Caroline, was estate manager of both Westpark House and Beldale. He lived with his mother, the earl's sister, in the Dower House of the Beldale estate, his own family residence having been sold off many years ago to meet his impecunious father's debts. Baron Ridgeway, having gambled away his wife's fortune, had finally taken his own life when his son was still a schoolboy, leaving them both penniless and, eventually, homeless had it not been for her brother's affection and generosity. The earl had given his sister, Lady Eugenie, lifetime tenancy of the Dower House, along with a generous annuity, as well as funding his nephew's remaining education. When Charles had expressed an interest in land management the earl had arranged for him to work alongside Baxter, his own elderly manager and, upon that worthy's retirement, had handed the office to his nephew. Philip Hurst had also trusted Ridgeway's judgement and had offered his cousin the same post at Westpark. The twins had grown up alongside Charles, of course, he being some six or seven years their senior. He had never married and, although both Sandford and his brother had frequently maintained that Judith Butler had always been the object of his youthful affection, he had never once, during all the years of his employment, treated her with anything but gentle courtesy and respect. After Philip's carriage accident Ridgeway had taken on without complaint the extra load his young master's death had inevitably caused and now, with the earl himself indisposed, his working days were longer still and he was not sorry to see Sandford home again.

'Your servant, ma'am,' he said, smiling as he bent over her hand. 'You will not regret your choice of husband. After his father, Sandford is the finest man I know.'

'Steady on, old chap!' Sandford protested. 'Not quite in the old man's league, I fear!'

'True,' acknowledged his cousin, laughing, 'but you are getting there. I have heard about some of your exploits in Spain, you know, in spite of your efforts to keep them secret. Jimmy Braithwaite's boys came home last month and were full of stories they had heard about you.'

'Mostly exaggerated and of no account, I assure you! These things tend to get blown up out of all proportion. I only did what other fellows were doing all around me.'

'And that was hardly of no account!' interjected Harriet hotly. 'His lordship's exploits were well known when I myself was out there, Mr Ridgeway, so allow me to vouch for the truth of the stories!'

Charles Ridgeway laughed. 'Well, Robert, it's clear that your young lady will defend your achievements for you, however much you care to deny them—which is just as it should be, of course.' He wheeled his horse round and turned to go. 'When you can spare an hour—I must talk to

you about the bottom fences. They need replacing—oh!—
and Potter's cottage caught fire last week. He's staying with
his daughter at the moment, but we really need to discuss
the whole row—when you're ready, of course.' He saluted
them both with his crop and cantered back into the spinney.

Sandford waited until his cousin was out of sight before
turning his head to Harriet.

'Whilst I recognise your need to defend our military exploits, Miss Cordell,' he said, as they continued along the
bridleway, 'I feel I must point out to you that most of our
countrymen have no real comprehension of what went on
over there. I, myself, have increasingly found that is not a
popular topic in polite society and you have already seen
how eager certain people might be to place the wrong interpretation on your presence in the train. I would not want
you to be embarrassed...'

'Oh, pooh to such people!' interrupted Harriet. 'You
cannot think that I am ashamed to have been with the army!
You, of all people! You know that most of the women were
wives of the soldiers and spent their time cooking and for-
aging for their menfolk. The few others I saw were usually
local girls and *very* choosy, so I'm told!'

Sandford raised his brows, stifling his laughter. 'You
shouldn't have been told any such thing. I'm surprised your
mother allowed such a conversation.'

'Oh, don't be so stuffy! When we were surrounded by
death and injury! Some of the men behaved appallingly, it's
true, but hadn't they good reason, at times? Papa never con-
doned their behaviour when they went to extremes, but he
did understand the cause. Most of them will never come
home,' she finished sadly.

'Nevertheless,' counselled the viscount, after a pause,
'none of this is deemed to be a fitting subject for polite

conversation and I must recommend that you endeavour to steer clear of it, if at all possible.'

He had not enjoyed listening to Lady Butler's attempts at giving Harriet one of her infamous set-downs, especially as the girl had won the field on this occasion. From past experience he knew that the older woman would try to find new ways of discomfiting her because there were few things she enjoyed more. Judith's party would provide Lady Butler with an excellent opportunity, he reasoned, and was determined to do his best to safeguard Harriet against public calumny.

'As you wish, my lord,' said Harriet in a small voice, her shoulders drooping. What a pompous prig the hero had turned out to be, she thought in dismay, and wondered if, after all, some of the tales of his exploits had been embellished.

They rode in silence once more, each absorbed in private reflections and, upon entering the house, Sandford excused himself from Harriet, saying that he would go straight up to his father before changing.

Harriet went to her own room where Rose was waiting to help her undress. The girl had laid out one of the new dresses, which had been delivered during her mistress's absence, and Harriet was delighted with the pretty, soft green muslin, its short puffed sleeves just right for the warm afternoon. Rose tied the matching sash high above her young mistress's waist, as was the prevailing fashion, and adjusted the tiny frill that edged the low neckline.

'I hear tell that some of the young ladies do damp their dresses to make them cling to their bodies!' she marvelled, as she knelt to tie the strings on Harriet's slippers. 'And they don't always wear a petticoat either!'

'I don't think I should care for such a fashion.' Harriet assured her. 'This dress is very pretty as it is, don't you think? Is there an evening gown amongst the others? Madame said that it would be ready in time for Mrs Hurst's party.'

Rose showed her the rest of the deliveries, which did, indeed, include the gown for Judith's party. This was a simple but elegant tunic in a sea-green shot silk, which was to be worn over a white satin slip. Harriet's eyes shone with delight when she saw it, immediately taken with its clean-cut shaping, for she was not a girl who cared for too many frills and flounces in her clothes.

'There's slippers to match too, miss,' Rose indicated. ''Tis a pity that you had to leave your jewel-case behind, for a necklace would make all the difference.'

Harriet did not reply. She was beginning to feel somewhat concerned about her increasing indebtedness to her hosts and wondered when she would be in a position to repay them. She hoped that her grandfather would soon be in touch with instructions for her to be sent to him at once as she was still most uncomfortable about the role she had agreed to undertake. A lot of good people were being deceived, she reflected, and was sorry that Judith and her children should be amongst these for she felt that she could easily become very fond of them. Even Sandford's company was surprisingly bearable when he refrained from telling her what she could or could not do, she mused, and she was smiling at the memory of the cheerful raillery they had exchanged during their morning ride when there came a tap at the door.

'His lordship wishes to speak to Miss Cordell if she could spare him a moment.'

Harriet heard March deliver his message and rose at once to her feet. Now what had she done? she wondered, casting about in her mind for possible aberrations as she hurried downstairs to find the viscount waiting in the small salon.

'How very prompt,' he said, surprising her by turning with a smile as she entered. 'Father has expressed a desire to meet you—he knows your story, of course, and he also knew your grandparents in his youth. Do you feel up to it?' He looked at her anxiously.

'But, of course.' Harriet's eyes sparkled. 'I'd love to meet Lord William. Are you sure he is well enough for a visitor?'

'He maintains that he is well enough to look at a pretty face,' Sandford said cheerfully, as they made their way upstairs. 'He is keen to see if Mother's description of your likeness to your grandmother is justified.'

At Sandford's gentle scratch, Chegwin opened the door of the Earl's chamber and placed his finger against his lips to urge their silence.

'His lordship has fallen asleep again, sir,' he whispered, as he ushered them to his master's bedside. 'But he left instructions that you were to remain until he awakes—he drowses off on account of the medicine, but seems anxious to speak with you, my lord.'

His eyes were troubled as they fixed upon the earl's sleeping form. Harriet, too, stared concernedly at the pale and lined features of the white-haired old man in the bed.

Sandford led her to a chair by the bedside and seated himself opposite. Together they watched the shallow but steady rise and fall of the bedcovers at the earl's chest. Harriet felt unaccountable tears pricking her eyelids as she studied the viscount's father. How alike they are, she thought in a flash; the same aristocratic bone structure, straight nose, high cheekbones, firm chin—even in repose. Were his eyes that same clear grey? she wondered, and almost jumped out of her skin when, as if in answer to her question, Beldale's eyes opened and were staring at her intently.

'Don't weep, girl, I'm not gone yet,' came a gruff voice and a hand crept out of the covers to take hers. She held it firmly between both her own and smiled, a gentle flush staining her cheeks.

'And very pleased I am to hear it, sir,' she replied softly. 'Did we disturb you?'

'No, my dear, I was waiting for you, but this infernal laudanum keeps dragging me off to sleep—do better without it.' He glared balefully at his manservant, who regarded him fondly in return.

'Bring a light, man. I want to see the girl properly!'

Although it was daylight the heavy curtains were drawn to keep out the sunshine, making the room quite dark. Chegwin lifted a branch from the dresser and held it aloft so that Harriet's face was bathed in its pool of candlelight. The old man contemplated her steadily for several minutes, his eyes faded but indubitably grey, and she felt no embarrassment at his scrutiny.

Sandford grinned, feeling a surge of respect at such composure. 'Well, sir? And do you approve?'

Beldale gently squeezed Harriet's hand. 'Very fetching, my boy,' he said. 'Your mama was right—image of her grandmother—glad you found her, Sandford—made her ladyship very happy.' His voice faded, then his eyes flashed wide open once more. 'Keep your guard up, Robert—just remembered—something—happened…' His head drooped back on to the pillows and Sandford started up in alarm, but Chegwin put his hand on the viscount's arm and steadied him.

'He's all right, sir,' he said. 'Keeps dropping off like that. Needs the stuff for the pain, you see. Leave him to me, if you please, sir—and ma'am.'

He bowed towards Harriet who, seeing Sandford's agitation, had immediately risen from her own chair but, at the sight of the tears in his eyes, had swiftly bent to tidy the covers over Beldale's recumbent form.

'I know you'll take good care of him, Chegwin.' Sandford's voice held a tremor but, straightening his shoulders, he held out his hand to Harriet and escorted her from the room.

Downstairs, Lady Caroline was waiting in the small dining-room as the dishes were being brought in. They took their places at the table and she signalled to Rothman to begin serving.

'His lordship seems so much better, don't you agree?' she applied hopefully to her son. 'Sir Basil thinks to reduce the medication tomorrow—it has been over a week since his fall.'

Sandford nodded. 'He will be relieved to be off the drug—he dislikes taking it, I know. It seems to make him ramble somewhat, too. I remember having to take it myself on one occasion and had the most awful hallucinations. I'm sure he will be better without it.'

The meal progressed through the various courses, during which Lady Caroline, eyes twinkling at her son, inquired as to the success of their visit to Westpark. Harriet, after describing Judith's plans for the forthcoming assembly, thanked the countess for the garments that had been delivered in their absence, expressing her particular delight with the green silk gown intended for the party and it was in a happy, friendly mood that they all repaired to the salon afterwards, with Sandford opting to take his brandy with the ladies and the evening being rounded off with some rousing games of piquet.

The following day the viscount rode over to Westpark, as he had promised, to take his nephew out riding. Harriet spent part of the morning with the earl, at his request. He was more lucid than he had been on her previous visit and had expressed a desire to hear her story first-hand. He, in turn, was able to tell her more of her family's history and Chegwin was very satisfied to hear, more than once, the sounds of stifled laughter issuing from his master's bedside.

When Harriet rose to leave, having judged that his lordship was beginning to tire, the manservant accompanied her to the door with a smile, saying, 'This has done him a deal of good, miss, if I may say so. He will sleep naturally this afternoon, I feel sure.'

Finding that Lady Caroline was engaged with the housekeeper, Harriet decided to take herself for a walk down to the lakeside, where she hoped that the air would be fresher. The day was warm and very humid and, having been cooped up in Lord William's darkened rooms for some time, she felt that she needed the exercise. She walked sedately across the sweeping stretches of the rear lawns until she was sure she was out of sight of the windows then, running and skipping with pleasure, she reached the waterside.

The lake had been sunk many years previously and its banks were quite steep in parts. Both willow and aspen straddled the water's edge and bulrushes grew in profusion. A small pavilion was situated on an island in the middle of the lake. This was reached, as far as Harriet could tell, by the rowing-boat that she could see tied up outside a boathouse on the far side of the lake and she began to make her way towards it along the path, which meandered around the lake.

Now shaded from the sun by the leafy branches of the trees on both sides of the path, she felt much cooler. Smiling at the sight of the mallard duck leading her almost-grown brood in stately procession across the water, she frequently strayed to investigate the various splashings and rustlings of other small water creatures exploring their habitat. These delays caused her to take much longer than she had intended but, when she eventually arrived at the boathouse, she was still determined to take just a little peek at the pavilion, judging that it would not take her many minutes to row the short distance to the island. She checked that the oars were in place and was beginning to untie the mooring-rope when she heard a cry. Startled, she looked around, fearing that she had, once more, broken some unwritten rule. The cry was repeated, this time louder and she realised that it was a cry of distress.

Someone was calling for help. Her eyes scoured the water and the banks, trying to identify the place from which the sound had come. Then she saw. A small boy, up to his waist in the water, was clinging to the roots of a willow tree that grew at the water's edge. Picking up her skirts, she ran quickly along the path to the spot. She could see that the bank sloped steeply down into the murky water, which was thick with weeds. She could not tell how deep the water was at that point, but did not stop to consider it. Crawling on her knees, she edged her way downwards, stretching out a hand towards the grimy lad.

'Reach forward,' she said. 'See if you can take my hand.'

'Oh, miss—miss—I can't do it,' came the wailing reply. 'I'm stuck fast in the mud.'

Harriet slithered further down, her hands on the roots of the tree and grabbed at the boy's wrist. He suddenly jerked back and pulled himself away and, to her horror, disappeared beneath the surface. Scrabbling to regain her balance, she felt her body sliding sideways down the bank and, although she managed to keep hold of the tree root, she found herself up to her knees in the mud. Frantically, she looked about her for the child, who was nowhere to be seen, but a sudden sound from the water's edge some distance to her right alerted her to the astonishing sight of a small, bedraggled figure climbing out of the lake and disappearing into the bushes.

'What on earth...!' Harriet exclaimed in rage, as she struggled to free herself, but, upon finding that her feeble attempts had merely caused her to lose one of her slippers, she held still and tried to apply her mind to her situation. Her feet were on firm enough ground as far as she could tell, but she could see nothing within her reach that would help her to extricate her legs from the mud's tenacious grasp. She was eyeing the thin root she had managed to keep hold of, weighing up its ability to take any strain, when to her dismay she heard the sound of approaching hooves and then the unwelcome sight of the rider, Sandford himself, appeared on the path. He could not fail to observe her.

'Good God!' he exclaimed, reining in and leaping from his mount. 'How has this happened? Here, take my hand...' and, leaning his weight against the boll of the tree, he effortlessly hoisted Harriet to firm ground. She ignored the glimmer of laughter in his eyes as she tried, ineffectually, to sweep away the thick black mud from her clinging skirt.

'You just can't stay out of mischief, can you?' he said, his grin widening.

'This was not my doing,' she said crossly. 'Someone pulled me in. There was a young boy—I thought he was in trouble—but I slipped and he—he swam off and left me.'

Sandford regarded her with unconcealed amazement. 'A boy? What boy?' he said, looking about him.

Harriet stamped her unshod and mud-encrusted foot. 'How dare you disbelieve me!' she stormed. 'I am not in the habit of telling lies! There *was* a boy, I tell you!'

Tears of fury began to prick her eyes, but she blinked them away and struck out at him with her muddied fists. He backed away quickly before she could touch him.

'Whoa! Steady, there!' He looked at her uncertainly. 'We'd better get you back to the house before anyone sees you like that. Are you cold?'

Harriet shook her head, wearily controlling herself. 'No, thank you. I will soon dry in the sun but—I have lost a slipper and it is a long walk back.'

'I'm sure Pagan can cope,' Sandford rejoined. Pulling a rolled-up blanket from his pannier, he wrapped it around her muddied skirts and proceeded to lift her effortlessly on to his saddle.

How tiny her waist is, he marvelled, holding her steadily as she attempted to find her balance. His senses quickened as he felt the vibrant warmth of her body through the thin muslin fabric. Warning signs immediately flashed in his brain. Abruptly, he withdrew his hold.

'All set?' he asked, with apparent cheerful unconcern. 'See if you can steady yourself against the pommel. Hang on to Pagan's mane.'

Harriet complied with his instructions in silence. Assuming that the viscount would climb up behind her, a mounting sensation of breathless confusion gripped her at the thought of the necessarily close physical contact.

Sandford had intended to ride with her but, for some unfathomable reason, now found that he was unable to trust himself with her tantalising nearness. He hesitated momentarily, then gathered the horse's reins in his hands. 'I'll lead him in,' he said, still feeling somewhat shaken. With a slight frown on his face he started back towards the house.

Harriet registered his hesitation and her heart seemed to shrivel, overwhelmed by feelings of humiliation and rejection. With difficulty she repressed these emotions as she tried to apply her concentration to keeping her seat and her replies to Sandford's searching questions became curt and, for the most part, monosyllabic.

Sandford led his horse into the stableyard and Tiptree came running at the sound of his master's voice. His eyebrows shot up at the sight of the dishevelled figure being helped down from Sandford's mount, but he said nothing as he took the reins and the mud-stained blanket from the viscount.

'Don't put him away,' Sandford instructed. 'I shall need him again. Get Thunder saddled for yourself. I'll be back presently.' He escorted Harriet through the rear of the house to the foot of the staff staircase.

'Come up this way,' he said. 'The kitchen staff will be at lunch. I'll head off anyone who appears.'

Harriet reached her room unobserved and, as soon as she had closed the door behind her, she slumped down on to the nearest chair, regardless of the mess she was making, for she was utterly chagrined. What else could go wrong? she wondered. The morning had started so well and she had enjoyed her time with Beldale. The lakeside walk had been so pleasant until that incident. A puzzled frown creased her forehead. What was the meaning of it? It was no accident, of that she was convinced, but could see no point in what had occurred. Just a malicious prank? But, to what purpose? And, more infuriating, why had Sandford dismissed her story out of hand? Oh, if only her grandfather would reply to Lady Caroline's letter! Harriet felt that she could no longer remain at Beldale under such a cloud and wondered if she could confide her troubles to Judith Hurst. In spite of Sandford's instructions she was tempted to ask her new friend's advice should a suitable opportunity arise.

During the next few days Harriet did her utmost to avoid Sandford's company. She spent much of her time with the earl, who enjoyed her pretty attentions and was making steady progress towards a full recovery. She managed to take one or two rides about the park and to visit Judith, but only when she was sure that Sandford was elsewhere. She was obliged to take her meals with him, of course, but made sure she had a fund of Lord William's stories to relate to the countess so that it became unnecessary to hold a separate conversation with the viscount. Sandford himself appeared not to notice her evasive behaviour and, in any event, always seemed deeply preoccupied with estate business. To Harriet's relief, he made no further reference to the lake incident. Harriet had decided not to tell her hostess the full story of her misadventure, merely saying that she had slipped on the bank whilst trying to untie the boat. Lady Caroline had, at first, been rather shocked that Harriet had not asked a manservant to row her to the pavilion, then she had laughed and said, 'You modern young ladies! You have so much more freedom than we did in my day. I envy you, I do truly!' And the matter was forgotten.

At last the letter for which Harriet had been praying arrived. Rothman delivered it to her ladyship at the breakfast-table and the countess broke open the seal eagerly.

'How quickly he has replied,' she said, as she scanned the contents. 'Yes, he says he has written at once—you are to remain with us—he is actually coming to fetch you himself! He says he is overjoyed—and forever in our debt—what nonsense—but how sweet! Oh, my dear! Your troubles will soon be over!' She placed the missive into Harriet's trembling hand. 'There, my child. You may read it for yourself. Your grandfather will be with us in no time at all if all goes well with his travel arrangements,' and, turning to Sandford, she said, 'Isn't this happy news, Robert? Ramsey will surely come to his granddaughter's rescue now that he knows her whereabouts, don't you think?'

Sandford nodded, but did not reply. He felt a sudden lowering of spirit for which he could not account and stared moodily across the table at Harriet, but she was still deeply engrossed in her grandfather's words. Excusing himself, he quickly finished his coffee and left the room.

'We must go and tell Beldale the good news,' said the countess. 'He will be so happy for you—and glad to see Ramsey again, I dare say—if only to compare the wrinkles!'

Harriet laughed joyfully. She was feeling euphoric, hardly believing that her dream was finally about to become a reality. How long would it take her grandfather to travel to Beldale? Two weeks, perhaps. She could surely hold out until then, now that she knew he was actually coming. Then she was struck by a sudden thought.

'But—Judith's party?' she inquired of the Countess. 'We must inform her before it is too late to cancel. It will not be necessary to pretend an engagement now, surely?'

Lady Caroline hesitated on the stairway, considering the problem.

'On balance, my dear,' she said at last, 'I think it would be wiser to wait until your grandfather arrives—supposing he were delayed? Remember that we conjured up the plan in order to prevent unsavoury gossip. It is still the best protection we can offer you until he comes. Judith's guests will have seen the notice in the *Mercury* and it will not do to start up a hive of speculation so soon after the announcement. Don't worry, dear child. It's only a small local party, after all.'

And with this she continued up the stairs.

Harriet was perturbed, but did not mention the subject again. She knew that the countess had gone to considerable trouble to keep other members of the family away from Beldale House, using Lord William's indisposition as an excuse even to her own two daughters, who had been besieging her with requests to visit their father. Harriet had been relieved to learn that she was not expected to come under Sandford's sisters' scrutiny, as she doubted that her acting ability would pass muster under such close inspection. Casual observation by a few local families at a small houseparty would be much less of a trial, she decided. She determined to put away her fears and do her best to look forward to the forthcoming assembly, reasoning that Sandford was unlikely to accord her anything other than the devoted attentions of the newly engaged man he was supposed to be, especially since the plan seemed to have been concocted with his approval. After that, as far as she was concerned, he could please himself!

Chapter Four

Sandford stood at the entrance to the Dower House with a frown on his face. He was not looking forward to confronting his aunt with his discovery and, on being shown into Lady Eugenie's morning room, he saw that his cousin Ridgeway was also present and resigned himself to an uncomfortable few moments.

Ridgeway saluted him from his seat at the desk and Lady Eugenie smiled at him in welcome.

'Why, Robert,' she said, holding out her hand for his kiss. 'This is indeed a pleasant surprise—but your father—' her voice grew anxious '—he has not taken a turn for the worse?'

The tiny, birdlike Lady Eugenie was a sweet and gentle soul who had suffered a very unhappy marriage to a man who had married her only for her considerable dowry and name. He had treated her monstrously, flaunting both debts and mistresses with total disregard for her sensitivities. When he had finally taken his life she had felt nothing but relief and had dedicated the succeeding thirty years to charitable works. Her brother's pensioner, she had no money of her own, but gave her time unstintingly to any deserving organisation that approached her, from orphans' relief to support for fallen women. The meagre staff she employed at the Dower House consisted entirely of waifs and outcasts rescued from disaster by her ladyship. Ridgeway jokingly predicted that they would one day be found murdered in their beds but, secretly, he was immensely proud of his mother's achievements and her entire household was devoted to both the baroness and her son.

Sandford, having assured his aunt of the earl's continued improvement, stood undecided momentarily, abstractedly tapping his crop against his boot.

Ridgeway, attending to some paperwork, raised his head at the sound and looked at Sandford curiously.

'Problem, coz?' he asked cheerfully.

The viscount nodded. 'Rather tricky, Charles, actually.'

Ridgeway's face grew serious and he rose at once to his feet. 'Let's have it then, Robert—and for goodness sake, sit down. If it's not Uncle Will, what's the trouble?'

Sandford cleared his throat and turned to his aunt with a troubled look. 'It's one of your boys, Aunt Eugenie—he seems to have been up to mischief.'

Ridgeway laughed and his mother's pensive frown vanished immediately.

'The young scamps are always up to something, Robert,' said his cousin. 'Stealing apples, I suppose? You'd think we didn't feed them...' He stopped as Sandford shook his head.

'Fact is, Charles,' he said brusquely, 'two days ago one of them pulled Miss Cordell into the lake and swam off!'

His aunt gasped and put her hand to her throat while Ridgeway started in disbelief.

'You can't mean it, man! Let's have the whole, if you please!'

Sandford related Harriet's tale briefly, then went on to describe how he and Tiptree had scoured the lake area for the culprit, without success. He had then extended his search into the village where every boy of relevant age had been questioned thoroughly.

'I admit I was at point non plus,' he confessed wryly, 'until Tip brought me word that old Mrs Jennings remembered having seen one of your young imps scrambling through our hedge with his clothes soaking wet. She supposed he had been messing about in the lake and thought no more about it. I'm sorry, Aunt Eugenie,' he finished awkwardly, 'but I'm afraid I'll have to follow it up.'

His aunt looked helplessly towards her son, who nodded briskly at Sandford.

'Right, man,' he said. 'Let's get at it.'

Turning to his mother as they left the room, he said, 'Don't worry, Ma. I'll sort it out. It'll be one of Sukey Tatler's young 'uns—you mark my words.'

He led Sandford down the back stairs to the kitchens where a group of Lady Eugenie's reclaimed streetwalkers were to be found chattering merrily as they went about their work. They immediately fell silent at the sight of the two intruders to their domain.

Ridgeway sought out the young woman he had named and beckoned her to the doorway. 'Come outside, Sukey, his lordship wants a word with you.'

Eyes full of foreboding, the young woman complied, while the rest of the group stood looking at one another in consternation. Grateful to have been rescued from the awful poverty and degradation of their former existence, they still lived with the constant fear of being rejected and returned to their old haunts. They idolised their benefactress with unalloyed reverence for her part in their salvation, but were generally resigned to the fact that life had a habit of delivering the most crushing blows when one least suspected them.

Ridgeway ushered the scullery-maid out into the yard.

'Do you know where Billy is?' he asked her gently. 'His lordship needs to speak to him.'

Sukey shook her head.

'Don't never know where 'e is, guv,' she said tremulously. 'But 'e'll be 'ome for supper, that's fer sure. What's 'e done this time, guv?'

'Something very serious, I'm afraid, Sukey,' said Ridgeway.

The woman's face was filled with fear.

'You ain't gonna send us back, guv?' she pleaded. 'I'll skelp 'is 'ide, I swear to God!'

'I hope it won't come to that,' Sandford intervened. 'I have a feeling that he isn't entirely to blame. Do you know who his friends are?'

Getting no further help from the boy's mother, they sent her back to the kitchen where she was at once surrounded by her peers demanding to know whether they were all about to lose their places.

'I'll send one of the men to look for him,' offered Ridgeway. 'If he comes back and hears you were after him, he'll make himself scarce. We need to find out why he did it. Someone must have put him up to it—it makes no sense.'

Sandford agreed with his cousin and reluctantly left the matter in his hands for the time being, but insisted on being notified as soon as the boy was found. He asked Ridgeway to give his regards to Lady Eugenie and took his leave.

Riding back across the fields to Beldale he attempted, for the umpteenth time, to analyse his own turbulent emotions in what he hoped was an objective manner. It had now reached the point where he found himself increasingly reluctant to venture into any of the rooms in his own home for fear of encountering Harriet's stony expression! He was beginning to find it almost impossible to deal with her continued indifference towards him. He had pretended not to notice, of course, and had done his best to stay out of her way while trying to clear up the matter of the missing boy. He was furious with himself for having, apparently, given her the impression that he thought she had been lying, for no such consideration had entered his mind. He had simply been utterly taken aback that such a thing could happen on Beldale lands and had, subsequently, left no stone unturned in his efforts to find the culprit. His constant spur had been the thought of restoring that winsome smile to Harriet's face, but he was still no nearer to any solution and the prospect of another long and wretched evening loomed before him.

He entered the hallway just as the countess was ushering Harriet into the estate office and, as he made for the stairs, he breathed a sigh of relief that at least he would not be called upon to suffer that cool, disdainful gaze in the immediate future.

'Harriet has visitors, my dear,' said his mother, over her shoulder. 'Are you going up to your father? I will join you when I have finished here.'

Sandford frowned as he climbed the stairs, curious as to the identity of Harriet's visitors and wondering why they should be ensconced in the office, which was normally reserved for estate matters. His throat tightened as he considered the prospect of her leaving Beldale sooner than anticipated.

Harriet was also in some apprehension as to who her visitors could possibly be but the initial look of puzzlement was wiped from her face in a flash as she beheld the stocky figure before her and, rushing forward in delight, she threw herself at him crying, 'Ozzy! Oh, Ozzy!—how on earth did you find me?'

Ex-Sergeant Jeremiah Osborne, late of the 67th Cavalry

and her father's one-time batman, took her hands in his and shook his head at her behaviour.

'Now then, Miss Harry, a little more conduct, if you please! What would my Martha say—let alone your mama? Did they teach you to be a hoyden, I wonder?'

He grinned as he spoke and her eyes sparkled in return as she took the seat that Lady Caroline had motioned her into. Standing proudly erect in military manner, the old soldier looked to Harriet exactly as he had done on that day, two years previously when, hard upon her family's disembarkation, he and his wife had decided to part company with them to start a new life of their own.

Harriet turned from Osborne to the countess, who had been smiling at the interchange.

'I don't understand, ma'am,' she said carefully. 'I thought you said a messenger from my mama…?'

Lady Caroline patted her hand and waved Osborne to a chair as she herself sat down at the desk.

'Perhaps we should allow Mr Osborne to relate his own tale, my dear,' she said gently and, nodding to Osborne, 'Please be so good as to begin.'

'Well, my lady, as I was telling you earlier—' Osborne leaned forward, clasping his hands together between his knees '—after we left the family at Dover, Martha—my wife—and I went on to Hampshire, where we'd heard of a little inn we might fancy—you know we'd been keen to try it, Miss Harry…?'

He wagged his bushy head at her and she nodded, hardly able to contain her impatience as he continued with his tale. The inn, it seemed, had been a success and Ozzy and Martha were in a fair way to being quite prosperous and had lately decided to take a much-deserved break, having promised themselves a visit to their old master and mistress as soon as they could manage it.

'We wanted to give you a surprise, you see, but—it was us that got the surprise—or, shock, more like. We only got as far as the Partridge—the village inn, my lady—and the tongues were wagging fit to drop off. Miss Harriet was gone and worse, as far as I was concerned, the Major was dead and Lady Cordell had up and married her next-door neighbour.'

He brushed his hand across his eyes to conceal his emotions, cleared his throat and resumed. 'But I had to go up to the house to see for myself—and what a change I did find in the mistress—her once so brave and feisty! I never knew anything to faze her the whole time we was out there, Miss Harry.'

Tears had started in Harriet's own eyes as she answered him.

'I know, Ozzy. It was Papa dying, you see. It threw her right off balance and it seemed that she couldn't cope with anything at all. That's how she came to marry Sir Chester— for he somehow seemed to take over, dealing with the funeral arrangements, and Mama allowed him to ferret through our papers and all sorts of things. Afterwards, it was very easy for him to persuade her into marrying him. She was just so unhappy and lacked interest in everything. It wasn't until he had moved us up to the Hall that all became clear. He had enormous debts and he was absolutely furious when he found that I would inherit and not Mama. He accused her of trickery, would you believe? Then he started on this plan for marrying me off to his odious son— Mama wouldn't have it, of course, but he made her life unbearable as a result and I could tell he was beginning to wear her down. Then, when I overheard him talking to the ghastly Gilbert—and it appeared that they were planning some sort of abduction—they intended to trap me into marriage—I left a note for Mama telling her I was going to find my grandfather—then—I just left!'

There was a moment's silence. Osborne shook his head and sighed as the countess gave Harriet a little smile of sympathy.

'Don't fret yourself, my dear,' she said gently. 'You will come about, believe me. Lord Ramsey will take care of everything, I feel sure.'

'I am hoping so, ma'am,' Harriet said dispiritedly. 'If only he could come more quickly. You have been very good, your ladyship, but I wish that I, myself, could do something more useful on my own behalf.'

Turning to Osborne, she asked anxiously. 'And you did not see Mama at all?'

'Oh, yes, my pretty, I did that. I crept round to the gardens and gave her the shock of her life, I can tell you! But she was real glad to see me and wanting to hear all my news. We even had some laughs over old times but, as you've said, she wasn't herself although she did tell me much of the tale. Apparently Middleton got hold of your note and had the stagecoach lists checked at both the Lincoln and Grantham offices and your mama was mighty worried until she saw the announcement of your betrothal in the *Post* because she knew then that you were quite safe—and, although it was no easy matter for her to write a letter for me to deliver—here I am, at your service, as you might say. And I also have to tell you that my Martha is a-waiting in your housekeeper's room—fretting herself to bits, no doubt!'

Lady Caroline stood up and motioned to Harriet to remain seated.

'I must go and acquaint his lordship with this news. Robert is with him and I can as easily tell both together. You will want to have more conversation with your old comrades-in-arms. You may use the small parlour—I will instruct Rothman to have some luncheon sent up. Now, pray, excuse me.'

She swept out of the room with a smile for Harriet and a kindly nod to the old soldier.

'A real lady, that one, Miss Harry,' said Osborne in approving admiration after the countess had departed.

As a mere innkeeper and one-time soldier, he was well aware of his status in this sort of Society. Nevertheless, he had a justifiable pride in himself and his achievements. He had served with Harriet's father from the beginning, having been the young Sir Jonathan's groom and then his batman throughout the action in Iberia and he had seen Harriet grow from babyhood into girlhood. He had taught her to ride her first pony, had rescued her from many a childhood scrape and, along with her constant attendant, Martha, had contributed more than a little to Harriet's life and happiness during her unusual upbringing. When his part in the fighting was over he had finally persuaded the worthy Martha to marry him and try for a more settled way of life in their later years.

Harriet understood him well and took his meaning perfectly.

'A real lady, indeed. She has been so extremely kind to me. I wonder if Mama realises that the earl and countess were very well acquainted with her parents and that her ladyship would likely have been Mama's godmother if my grandmother had lived?'

She rose from her seat and, despite his protests, hugged him again. 'You have no idea how glad I am to see you again, Ozzy,' she said, unable to hide the tremor in her voice. 'Now we must go and fetch Martha and then we can all get comfortable—oh, Heavens! I have not yet read the note you brought me!' and, having peeled off the wafer, she began to peruse the missive, alternately shaking her head and frowning in consternation at the hastily scribbled contents.

'I clearly cannot reply,' she sighed, 'for it is unlikely that Mama would ever receive my letter and you will not want to be forever posting up and down the country as a messenger. I hope that Sir Chester has not discovered where I am—but it is a problem what to do. I cannot remain here much longer and there is no knowing how long it will take my grandfather to get here! I have no funds and I do so dislike being a charge on her ladyship.'

She folded the note and placed it in her reticule and, lifting her eyes to Osborne's while forcing a smile, she said, with as much cheerfulness as she could muster, 'Come, let us find Martha.'

Later, as they sat together in the small salon, she related the misadventures that had brought her to Beldale and confessed the deception in which she had become involved. Martha expressed concern and disapproval that Harriet should have become so embroiled in such subterfuge, although she commended the underlying reasons for the duplicity, saying that 'Miss Harry should think herself lucky that it was such a gentleman who had rescued her!'

Privately, Harriet was becoming rather weary of being told how lucky she was and she quickly went on to describe the incident at the lake, which curious event caused both of her old comrades to eye one another in dismay.

Osborne rose to his feet and started pacing the floor.

'Can't have that, miss,' he said, shaking his head. 'That's downright suspicious, if you ask me. Maybe that Middleton has already discovered your whereabouts—and you say his lordship didn't believe your story?'

He stopped suddenly and turned to face his wife. 'What about taking Miss Harriet back with us, Martha? We wouldn't allow anybody to go pushing her into lakes in Ringwood, that's for sure.'

Harriet jumped up and clapped her hands as Martha nodded her agreement.

'Oh, would you? That would be the very thing! Then I needn't pretend to be engaged to Sandford any longer! You can't know what a joy it would be to be able to tell him that!'

She spun round guiltily as the door opened behind her and the viscount entered, his face impassive. Flushing, she wondered if he had heard her remarks but, if so, he gave no indication, merely striding forward to grip Osborne by the hand.

'Good to see you again, Sergeant,' he said. 'Glad to hear of your success. Tiptree will be wanting to swap yarns with you. You'll be staying at the *Fox,* I imagine? He'll be down to join you later, I'll be bound.'

Taking up his stance at the fireplace, he smiled at Martha in cheerful recognition and cautiously allowed his eyes to travel to Harriet's bright cheeks. Although he hadn't actually caught her remarks it was fairly obvious to him that he had been the subject of them. He sighed inwardly.

'My lord?' Osborne was addressing him nervously. 'Mrs Osborne and I were thinking that maybe it would be best if Miss Harry—Harriet—was to return to Ringwood with us, sir—seeing as how she knows us so well and she'd be quite safe…'

He stopped as the viscount put up his hand and shook his head emphatically.

'Oh, I think not, old chap,' he said, experiencing a fleeting moment of self-reproach as he witnessed Harriet's look of stunned incredulity. 'I'm sure Sir Jonathan would have preferred that Miss Cordell remain at Beldale. It's very good of you—and Mrs Osborne, of course—' he bowed to Martha

'—but I really feel that it will be more suitable for her to stay here, at least until her grandfather arrives.'

It was not in Osborne's nature to give up without a fight. 'Miss Harriet has had a fright, your lordship,' he said stoutly. 'And it's not right for you to go doubting her word.'

'Miss Harry couldn't lie to save her life!' cut in Martha bravely, determined to say her piece.

Sandford held up both hands to silence them.

'I am aware of that,' he said calmly. 'The matter is being dealt with, I assure you.' He turned to Osborne. 'Tiptree will fill you in on the details if you care to consult him. Miss Cordell is perfectly safe here, you have my personal guarantee. Now, if you will excuse me.' Without another word he turned on his heel and left the room.

Martha looked anxiously at her husband.

'I hope he hasn't taken offence, Jerry,' she said. 'Maybe we shouldn't have tried to interfere?'

Harriet's brain was in a turmoil of conflicting emotions. She was convinced that Sandford had heard her shameful outburst. He had dismissed Ozzy's suggestion just to punish her, she decided indignantly and yet—it appeared that he had believed her after all and had actually been trying to clear up the mystery all this time while she—she had been treating him with such disdain! What must he think of her? All of a sudden she felt deeply ashamed and looked up to find both Osborne and Martha regarding her with frowning disapproval.

Osborne cleared his throat. 'Seems as if you've done his lordship a disservice, Miss Harry. I'd say he was doing his best for you and, from what I know about him, I'd have been surprised at anything else!'

'And, if you ask me,' Martha scolded, 'it's time you grew out of that impetuous behaviour of yours, miss. I sometimes wonder if we didn't all spoil and pet you too much when you were a little lass. However, you must try to remember that you're a young English lady now and act accordingly!'

'Oh, Martha, please don't be cross with me,' gulped Harriet. 'Everything is so mixed up. I hate living this beastly lie. Lady Caroline has been so kind to me and the earl and I deal extremely well together. It's just Sandford—he seems to be set on finding fault with everything I do and I did admire him so when I was a girl!'

She choked back a sob and Martha, relenting, folded her arms around her one-time charge and held her to her ample bosom.

'There, there, my precious,' she crooned. 'It won't be for long now. Your grandpapa will come and carry you back to his Scottish castle and, no doubt, you will meet some handsome young laird who will sweep you off your feet and you'll all live happy ever after!'

Harriet sniffed and shook her head with vehemence.

'No, I am determined I shall never marry,' she said sorrowfully. 'I shall devote my life to my grandfather's comfort. I intend to be his constant companion and the indispensable helpmeet in the evening of his life.'

'Oh, deary me, Miss Harry!' laughed Martha. 'Then I trust he has a strong constitution.' And gathering up her belongings at a signal from her husband, she said bracingly, 'Now we must be off, so give me a kiss and promise to be a good girl!'

Waving her handkerchief frantically until their hired postchaise was out of sight, Harriet wondered glumly whether she would ever see these two staunch allies again.

Chapter Five

Sandford, meanwhile, had returned to the Dower House in the pursuance of his earlier inquiries. He found that his cousin had, in fact, made some useful progress during his absence.

Ridgeway had eventually tracked down the boy, Billy Tatler who, along with several of his disreputable friends, was discovered attempting to ride some ewes bareback. The terrified sheep had been herded into a corner of a field and Billy was issuing orders to his cronies as to the best way to mount these animals. Needless to say, their efforts were meeting with little success and, at the sight of their master's angry countenance, the urchins scattered and endeavoured to make themselves scarce.

Ridgeway, leaping nimbly from his horse, had managed to grab Billy by the seat of his breeches as the boy tried to scramble through the hedge and, hauling him upright, he had frogmarched him to a nearby barn to question him.

This cross-examination, accompanied by dire threats of the awful punishments and penalties that would be incurred if any lies or omissions were discovered, took both time and patience but, eventually, Ridgeway had managed to extract what he took to be the bones of a very odd tale.

It transpired that Billy and his friend Nick often spent their days larking around the Beldale lake, hopeful of catching a trout or two and, on the day in question, had been splashing about in the water by the boathouse when 'this cove' had appeared and collared them both before they could escape. He had, firstly, threatened to haul them up to the 'big house' then, at their pleas for mercy, he had persuaded them to play a 'little trick' on the young lady who was presently making her way around the lake path. Billy was to pretend he had fallen into the water and, when the young lady leaned forward to help him out, Nick was instructed to give her a sharp push from behind. This was, apparently, to teach the young lady a lesson for some 'bad thing' she had done to 'Lady 'Genie'. Both boys knew that the water was quite shallow on this side of the lake and Billy, when tickling trout, had often knelt upon a large flat stone just below the surface a few yards away from where they had been standing. The 'cove' had then directed Nick to conceal himself in the bushes and Billy had slithered to his place on the stone. They were told they would be being watched by the 'geezer' from behind the boathouse and that he, of course, would go to the young lady's assistance if she got into any real difficulties and, if they carried out the 'job' to his satisfaction, he had promised them a shilling each!

'In the event, Nick got cold feet and scarpered, leaving Billy to do the deed on his own and when he climbed out of the lake and saw Miss Cordell standing up in the water, he didn't think much harm had been done and, when he saw you riding along the path, he made off before the ''cove'' could grab him again!'

'But did he say who this ''geezer'' was?' Sandford demanded of his cousin, at the end of the recital. 'You asked him, surely?'

'Naturally.' Ridgeway was indignant. 'He said he'd never seen him before but thought he must have come from the House. "Tall, thin and dark" was all he could say.'

'Young or old?' asked Sandford impatiently.

'Well, he said "old" but to a child of his age, that could be anyone from twenty upwards,' Ridgeway pointed out. 'Sorry, old chap, back to square one, almost.'

'Not quite,' said Sandford, frowning. 'We know how it happened, but as to why? Miss Cordell has not yet met your mother, so where does she fit into the conundrum?'

'Oh, I figured that one out,' said Ridgeway. 'If the little varmints have any loyalty at all it's to "Lady 'Genie". Billy actually thought he was doing it on Ma's behalf and this chap, whoever he is, must have known that!' He looked squarely at Sandford. 'You want me to lay them off—send them back to London?'

Sandford flushed. 'I hope you know me better than that, Charles,' he said shortly, getting ready to mount his horse. 'Sounds as if you've put the fear of Lucifer into the brats already. The real villain has still to be discovered!'

He wheeled his horse out of the Dower House stableyard and, raising his crop in salute, he galloped back down the lane to Beldale.

Upon his entry into the hall he encountered Harriet sitting on a chair, reading. To his surprise she jumped up and came forward to meet him.

'Lord Sandford,' she said, clearly in some agitation. 'Could I speak with you, if you please?'

Puzzled, he led her into the salon and, closing the door behind them, he turned to face her.

'How may I help you?' he asked, feeling his heart contract at the sight of her downcast face. He steeled himself

for whatever battle of wits he was sure must be about to
follow.

'I—I—want to apologise, my lord,' she said in a small
voice. 'I fear I have misjudged you. I...'

Discomfited, he put up his hand to stop her.

'Please, Miss Cordell, no more!' he protested. 'It is I who
am at fault if I gave you the impression that I disbelieved
your story. Believe me, it was never my intention...'

'But you have found the culprit?' she interrupted eagerly.
'You have solved the mystery?'

'Alas! Not entirely,' admitted Sandford, vexed at having
to disappoint her. 'Sit down please, Miss Cordell. Let me
tell you what I have ascertained.'

Briefly, he related his own investigations and his cousin's
discoveries, deeply conscious of Harriet's eyes on his own
the whole time he was speaking and sick at heart that he
was unable to bring a smile to her face.

'But these boys,' she said, anxiously gripping her hands
together. 'Surely they are in some danger now? The man
must be aware that they could expose him. Who can he be
and what do you suppose it all means?'

Sandford shook his head and laid his hand on hers, to
still the trembling.

'I confess I am at a stand,' he said reluctantly. 'Unless
you know of anyone who would wish you harm? These
Middletons...?'

Harriet shook her head. 'They could not have known of
my whereabouts last week,' she said. 'Even Mama did not,
until the—engagement—notice was in the paper.'

Sandford regarded her silently for a moment then, rising
purposefully to his feet, he became his normal efficient self
again. 'Then we must assume that the whole thing was some
unfortunate mistake,' he said decisively. 'For the present,
however, I must insist that you refrain from wandering off

on your own again and that you always tell one of the household where you may be found...'

He stopped, at her look of astonishment.

'Must you persist in treating me like a child?' she asked in disgust. 'Perhaps you could look out some leading-strings for me?'

He sighed, all at once too weary to engage in the inevitable bout of verbal fisticuffs he had come to expect from their interchanges.

'My concern is merely to ensure your safety until your grandfather arrives to remove you,' he said stiffly. 'I would be obliged if you would comply with my request during the remainder of your stay here. I have wasted far too much time on this wild-goose chase already.'

Wrenching open the door, he left the room, conscious of an overwhelming desire to give Harriet a good shaking or, perhaps, just hold her tightly in his arms. Cursing under his breath, he crossed the hall and climbed the stairs to his chamber, where he curtly dismissed Kimble and attended to his own toilette, much to his valet's chagrin.

Harriet, still angry, paced the floor of the salon for some minutes after the viscount had gone, mulling over both his revelations and his subsequent chastisement. Aware that she had little choice but to heed his instructions, she contemplated the possibility of dashing down to the village the following morning in order to catch the Osbornes before they left for Hampshire. Rejecting this idea as impractical and, ruefully sensible of the fact that Martha would simply return her to Beldale, she wondered once more whether she could confess her situation to Judith Hurst but, oddly, the closer her friendship with Judith grew, the less that idea appealed to her. Reluctant to expose herself to her friend's possible disapprobation, she realised that she had no alternative but to sit tight until her grandfather arrived, however long that might be. She resigned herself to remaining inside the four walls of Beldale House for the foreseeable future, since there was absolutely no way she was going to stroll about the grounds with a footman at her heels and, as for riding with Sandford, she would see him damned first!

Once more an uneasy truce attended their meetings, which Sandford confined to the barest minimum, unwittingly causing his mother deep misgivings, for she could sense his unhappiness and concluded that he was regretting his decision to return to Beldale permanently.

The earl continued to make good progress and no longer seemed to have a compulsion to dwell on his accident. Harriet spent a good deal of her time with him, playing chess and piquet and reading scurrilous articles from the newspapers to him, which latter usually developed into heated debates between the two of them, culminating in paroxysms of laughter.

Sandford entered his father's room on one such occasion and, although the sight brought a smile to his lips, his eyes remained bleak and he indicated to Chegwin that he would return later.

Lord William, however, noticed his son's retreat and speculated upon the cause of it, but was reluctant to broach such a delicate subject with Sandford. Instead, he elected to quiz Harriet during one of their games of Hazard.

'I shall miss you when you are gone, my dear,' he said gently. 'I'm sure you must know how attached I have grown to you—we all have. Her ladyship calls you her breath of fresh air!'

'Sandford would probably say ''whirlwind'',' she said, smiling ruefully as she took her turn at the dice. 'He seems to take such exception to everything I do.'

'You dislike him?' he shot at her, regarding her intently.

Startled, she raised her green eyes to his faded grey ones and sighed. 'There are times when I really do, I'm afraid,' she admitted. 'He can sometimes be so overbearing, you know, and then, just when I could happily murder him—he does something so—so—unexpected.'

Beldale gave a snort of laughter. 'Well, you are honest, I'll give you that—not that I'd expect anything less of you, of course,' he said, looking at her fondly. 'Care to tell me about it?'

'Well, it seems that no matter how hard I try to conduct myself with the dignity and propriety he expects of me,' said Harriet with a grin, 'I find myself involved in some sort of scrape. Papa always used to say it was lucky I wasn't a cat—although I do have the eyes for one—for I must easily have lost all nine lives before now!'

'Curiosity is regarded by some philosophers as a prime virtue,' observed his lordship thoughtfully. 'How else could we acquire knowledge? My throw, I believe.'

Harriet passed him the dice-box and studied her score-sheet. 'That makes about fifty thousand guineas I owe you, my lord,' she laughingly informed him. 'I will have to ask for time to pay, or shall you have me cast into Bridewell?'

'Bridewell? Hmm—that might just be the answer.' The earl answered absentmindedly, as he shook the box.

Harriet looked up puzzled. His lordship seemed abstracted.

'Oh, I have tired you out,' she exclaimed, jumping up in concern and beckoned to Chegwin to clear away the bed-table.

Lord William smiled at her agitation and took her hand in his. 'Perhaps I shall take a nap, my dear,' he said. 'It's Judith's assembly this evening, is it not? Be sure to come and see me before you leave.'

Harriet, bending to kiss him on the forehead, promised that she would.

As soon as the valet had closed the door on her departure, Beldale hauled himself up on his pillows and issued several succinct orders and a request for Lady Caroline's immediate attendance.

That evening, as she stood submitting herself to Rose's final administrations, Harriet felt a pang of regret that she would shortly be losing the cheerful young maid and wondered if her grandfather would allow her to offer the girl a position in his household.

'Don't frown so, miss,' admonished Rose, as she buttoned her mistress's glove. 'You'll get lines on your forehead soon enough, believe me! There, now—a real picture you look!'

Harriet studied her reflection in the pier-glass. Her soft, copper-gold hair had adapted happily to its new shape, its curling tendrils framing her elfin face, whilst her deep green eyes mirrored the colour in the shot silk of the over-tunic. The neckline of the white satin underslip was low but decorous, without ruffle or frill, accentuating the creamy curves of her bosom. The tunic, which was sleeveless, fastened around the waist with a narrow sash decorated in a gold-threaded Greek-key design and Rose, still bemoaning her mistress's lack of jewellery, had fashioned a similar ribbon to weave through her curls.

Feeling enormously pleased with the whole effect, Harriet took the fan and reticule Rose was holding and thanked the smiling girl for all the effort she had made on her behalf, determined that she would find some way of rewarding her for her loyalty before she left.

'You're to go and see the master,' Rose reminded her, as she handed Harriet a dark green velvet cloak. 'He'll be wanting to see you in your finery, I expect.'

Both Lady Caroline and Sandford were waiting in the earl's room when Harriet arrived. The old man's eyes lit up when he saw her and he beckoned her to him.

'Just like a little sea-nymph,' he chortled, beaming with pleasure and nodding at his wife. 'See, my dear? I was right. Hand me the box, please.'

The countess, smiling, passed him a flat leather case from which he lifted a glittering necklace of tiny emeralds strung on a gold chain. Harriet gasped as Beldale passed the necklace to Sandford and bade him fasten it round her neck.

The viscount, whose senses had been considerably affected by Harriet's appearance, found his fingers trembling as he battled with the clasp.

'Oh, Lord William!,' breathed Harriet, as she leaned over to kiss the earl's cheek. 'I promise I shall take the greatest care of it! I shall return it to you personally first thing in the morning.'

'It is not a loan, my dear.' His lordship patted her hand. 'It is but a small token of thanks for the many hours you have devoted to my recovery.'

'But I cannot possibly accept such a gift,' she protested. 'And you know perfectly well that I, too, have enjoyed our tête-à-têtes.'

'Which is why you cannot possibly refuse my gift, I think,' said his lordship gently. He looked at his son. 'Isn't there something else, my boy?'

Sandford cleared his throat. 'Father was concerned that Judith's guests would be sure to mark the absence of an engagement ring,' he said, reaching for the small box which he had previously selected from the assortment on the side table.

'These jewels are all part of the Beldale collection, my dear,' said Lady Caroline conversationally, as Harriet removed her glove. 'They belonged to Lord William's grandmother, the third countess. She was very fond of emeralds, we are told. I myself prefer the sapphire and our girls have always regarded the green stone as unlucky…' She hesitated. 'Oh dear, I trust you have no such qualms, my child?' She looked anxiously at Harriet, who let out a ripple of delighted laughter.

'Not at all, ma'am—it is, in fact, my birthstone so I believe so I believe that to me it must be lucky…' She stopped, as the box Sandford was holding fell from his grasp and bounced across the floor. Chegwin bent to retrieve it and handed it back to the viscount, who was looking at Harriet with an incomprehensible glint in his eyes.

'Perhaps you would do us the honour of wearing this tonight,' he said, executing a stiff bow and handing her the box. 'Certain people are sure to comment—will it suffice?'

Harriet opened the lid and beheld a flawless square-cut emerald, surrounded by diamonds and mounted on a gold ring. Her lips trembled as she slid the jewel on to her finger and, holding up her hand for all to see, 'It fits perfectly,' she observed, in shaky surprise.

'I hoped that it might,' murmured Sandford impassively as, somewhat shaken himself, he picked up the box and returned it to the pile.

'And just one more,' interposed the countess, holding out a bracelet she had selected. 'This matches the necklace, I believe—now you will do us proud.' She clasped the bracelet around Harriet's wrist and stood back to admire the result. 'Your grandmother would have loved you so—I can hardly wait to see the effect you have on Ramsey!'

'I shall be sorry to miss seeing the effect she has on Judith's male guests,' chuckled Lord William, bringing a deep blush to Harriet's cheeks. 'I shall expect to hear all about it tomorrow, so don't disappoint me.'

She threw her arms around his neck and kissed him again.

'Oh, I shan't, I promise—and thank you so much—all of you. I swear I have never looked so grand!'

Sandford's lips twisted in a wry smile as he turned to pick up his cloak. 'A vast improvement on certain of your outfits, I am bound to agree,' he said, failing to register either Harriet's crestfallen expression or the look that passed between his parents. 'Shall we depart, ladies?'

Chapter Six

The August evening was warm and still. Judith had thrown open the doors of her largest drawing-room to allow her guests to walk on the rear terrace, should they desire to take the air. She had also arranged for the carpets to be taken up, determined to encourage 'a little dancing' in spite of Lady Butler's sighing disapproval.

Groups were already assembling around the room when the Beldale party was announced. Conversation ceased as all heads turned to scrutinise Sandford's betrothed and more than one hopeful mother of unwed daughters heaved a sigh of regret at the charming picture that Harriet presented.

About a dozen families had accepted Judith's invitation and Harriet was quickly presented to the most senior of these, amongst whom were the local vicar, the Reverend John Taylor, with his very pleasant wife and two daughters, and Squire Bevans accompanied by his prodigious family. Also present were the earl's family physician, Sir Basil Lambert, along with his wife Patricia and their son Cedric. This youngster considered himself a very bang-up, dashing man-about-town and lost no time in claiming Harriet for one of the sets, which started a minor flurry as other young men jostled to be included in her favours, and Sandford found himself having to take a back seat during these proceedings.

'Making quite a mark, dear coz,' came Ridgeway's amused voice next to him. 'Trust you to win such a prize. Every man in the room is full of envy.'

Sandford forced a smile. He had been studying Harriet's bright and animated expression and wondered how it was that he always seemed to manage to quench her natural liveliness. Other young ladies of his acquaintance had always conducted themselves with elegant composure and dignity, but this one seemed to have little respect for convention—even laughed at it—and yet everyone was drawn to her. His father was obviously entranced and his mother adored her and yet he, himself, constantly found fault with her and could not explain the sometimes violent irritation she aroused within him—especially at this moment, surrounded as she was by laughing admirers.

Harriet lifted her eyes and caught his frown and her eager expression vanished as she excused herself from her court and came at once to his side, acknowledging Ridgeway with a polite and conventional smile while Sandford inwardly cursed himself.

'Oh, I see Eugenie is here,' said Lady Caroline, taking Harriet's arm. 'Do come and meet her, my dear. Charles, do your duty.'

Ridgeway bowed to his aunt and presented Harriet to his mother. Again that lively look of real interest appeared on Harriet's face and in no time at all she was deep in friendly conversation with the earl's sister as the countess brought Lady Eugenie up to date with Beldale's progress. Harriet had been as fascinated by Sandford's aunt's history as Lady Eugenie quickly became with hers and they were soon immersed in a cheerful debate concerning some charitable organisation or other with which Lady Eugenie was involved.

Sandford, all at once discovering a growing hatred of himself, interrupted their laughing exchanges to point out to Harriet that he supposed the company might expect them to dance together at least once. She handed him her card and invited him to take his pick.

'Not a lot of choice, I see,' he said, scribbling his initials in the few blanks that remained. He desperately wanted to tell her how lovely she looked and to compliment her on her success but, realising that he had missed the moment, could think of nothing that sounded neither flippant nor contrived. 'I shall take you in to supper, of course.'

'Of course, my lord,' she replied, without enthusiasm.

He hesitated and was about to begin his speech when one of her young admirers arrived to claim her for the reel that was presently assembling.

Harriet threw herself into the dance with relief, skipping around the circle, changing partners as the movement required and clapping her hands in time to the sprightly tune being executed on the piano by Lady Eugenie, who had been happily persuaded to perform that task.

Judith, looking radiant in her ruby silk gown, mingled gracefully with her guests, ensuring that no one was ignored or left without a partner for a set. She was sad that Philip was not with her to enjoy the success of his brother's betrothal party, but equally determined that she would not shun society because she had been widowed. She had the children's future to consider and knew that Philip would want her to see that they grew up with the same standards and expectations that he would have given them. He himself had not been fond of high-society occasions but had always entered wholeheartedly into the many country dances and musical evenings which had been held at Westpark and Judith was delighted to find that she had not lost her touch.

His vigilant sister-in-law had paired Sandford off with

one of the vicar's daughters, still in the schoolroom, and it required all of his social skills to put the girl at her ease and to rescue her from her many foot-faults. When he was finally able to return her to her parents, having brushed away her stumbling apologies with a melting smile, he looked about the room for Harriet and, as he could not immediately locate her, he strolled outside along the terrace, fearful of being collared once more by his zealous hostess.

Couples were forming for the next set and Harriet had promised this to Charles Ridgeway but, finding herself slightly out of breath from the Circassian Circle she had just thrown herself into, she begged him to take her outside for some air instead. Laughing, he admitted that he was not the most practised of dancers and would be glad of the respite himself.

Lady Caroline, holding court beside the doors, waved to them as they went through and Harriet was embarrassed to overhear her own virtues being extolled at some length as Ridgeway led her down the terrace steps into the garden.

'—even won Cook over by begging to be taught to make almond tartlets and three hours later I discovered her sitting on the table regaling the entire kitchen staff with her tales!' This was received with peals of delighted laughter from most of her ladyship's listeners, but one or two ladies raised their eyebrows at one another.

Harriet glanced up at Ridgeway. 'I suppose I shouldn't have done that?' she said mournfully.

Charles laughed. 'Why not? You are something of an original, to be sure. Robert must be delighted that you have everyone's admiration.'

His own eyes travelled across the room to where Judith Hurst was standing. 'Not that he would care if they took you in deep dislike, I'll be bound,' he continued, absentmindedly.

'Does she know that you're in love with her?' Harriet asked bluntly.

With a shocked expression, Ridgeway swung to face her. 'What are you saying?' he said, as a dull flush crept up his cheeks.

'Well, it is pretty obvious,' said Harriet cheerfully, motioning him to the seat at the foot of the steps. 'You never take your eyes off her. She speaks very highly of you, you know.'

'As her estate manager,' Charles said bitterly. 'What could I possibly offer her? She even pays my salary!' Involuntarily his eyes homed in to their target once more and his shoulders slumped. 'I should leave,' he said. 'I have tried, but I cannot.'

Harriet put her hand on his sleeve. She was desperately sorry for him, realising how keenly he felt the hopelessness of his situation.

'Judith is still young and so beautiful,' she said awkwardly, 'but she is also very lonely and she still has a lot of love to give—someone. Why should it not be you? Do you mean to stand by and watch her turn into an embittered old harpy like—well, you know...' She bit her lip and looked around anxiously.

Ridgeway burst out laughing and his eyes suddenly gleamed with a newfound confidence as he stared at Harriet curiously. 'How did one so young come to be so astute?' he asked.

'Well, I've hardly had the conventional sheltered upbringing,' Harriet answered dismissively. 'I've mixed with people from many different walks of life, which I believe has helped me to appreciate other points of view. I have always been interested in people and—well—travel is supposed to broaden the mind,' she laughed. 'Isn't that why young men were sent on the Grand Tour?'

Ridgeway's eyes crinkled appreciatively. 'I missed that myself, as a matter of fact,' he said. 'So I suppose you must consider my mind to be on the narrow side, since London and the Lake District are the furthest reaches of my travels!'

Harriet flicked his hand with her fan. 'You know perfectly well that is not what I meant and just for that I shall oblige you to stand up with me for the next dance. So, kindly do your duty, sir, and lead me to my place.'

Laughing together, they re-entered the room and joined the set that was presently forming, Ridgeway carefully ensuring that he positioned them as close as possible to Judith and her partner, young Cedric Lambert, and, as Lady Eugenie struck the first chord, Sandford arrived back just in time to see his betrothed swing into the steps of the dance which he had selected as his.

A hot anger filled his throat as he watched Harriet's laughing interchanges with the other members of her set and, turning away, his fury was such that he was obliged to sit down to control his breathing. Unfortunately, he chose the seat next to Lady Butler's.

'Without a partner, my lord? Your little miss is quite the little honey-pot, I see.' Her voice held its customary disapproval. 'She is no doubt used to being the apple of all the men's eyes.'

Sandford's eyes glittered in distaste. 'What makes you think that?' he asked carefully.

'Oh, I see how she tosses her head at them all—it is but a come-on—I was used to do it myself, of course, as a girl— I was much admired. She will have had plenty of practice with the military, I'll be bound, and without such chaperonage as is considered *de rigueur* in our own society. Certain young women nowadays do seem to have the most perfidious disregard for convention, as I am sure you have found. However, I must admit to a certain surprise that you allowed your own betrothed to disappear into the garden with one of her recent conquests—and for so long!'

Sandford rose to his feet and bowed stiffly. 'I cannot say that I have much experience of young *women*'s ways, ma'am,' he ground out between clenched teeth. 'And, since it appears we are about to go in for supper, I am sure you will excuse me if I now make a push to collect my own young *lady* before she bestows that singular honour on one of her many conquests!'

'Your loyalty does you credit and is most touching, I'm sure,' sniffed Lady Butler, also rising heavily to her feet. 'I suppose I must see to my own repast, as usual.'

She waited expectantly for Sandford to offer his arm but he, still seething with indignation, ignored both her remark and her person and turned swiftly away from her just in time to see a smiling Ridgeway leading Harriet towards him.

'Apologies, Sandford,' said his cousin cheerfully. 'I appear to have stolen your dance—Miss Cordell seems to have misread her card—not going to call me out, I trust?'

Sandford swallowed. He had been about to take Harriet to task, but had no quarrel with Charles. He doubted that Harriet had misread her dance-card, for she had made it perfectly clear that she did not care to dance with him. He gave Ridgeway a mock punch in the arm and said, with forced gaiety, 'Pistols at dawn, I should think—I trust you're as much out of practice as I am?'

Ridgeway returned the punch and laughed. 'Quite right, coz. Guard her with your life—she's a pearl beyond price!' He smiled down at Harriet. 'Thank you, dear lady—I think I know what to do now.'

Sandford frowned as he watched his cousin walk away. 'What was that supposed to mean?' he asked suspiciously.

'Oh, nothing,' countered Harriet quickly, not wishing to divulge Ridgeway's confidences. 'I'm truly sorry about the dance mix-up—shall we go in to supper? I see Lady Caroline beckoning us.'

The viscount led her to his mother's table, where the countess and Lady Eugenie were exchanging reminiscences.

'Harriet, my dear. Do join us.' Lady Caroline patted the seat next to her. 'Robert and Charles will fetch us our supper.'

She smiled at her son, who battled his way through the crowd to find Ridgeway already at the supper table collecting a plateful of sweetmeats and comfits.

Charles glanced at his cousin and grimaced. 'Can't stand these things meself,' he said. 'No substance to any of 'em.'

Sandford laughed, nodding. 'A good beef sandwich would suit me—and a tankard of decent ale.' He looked around. 'I suppose it's Madeira or Portuguese for us, as usual?'

Ridgeway pointed to the decanters. 'Brandy too, I see. I wonder how Judith managed to slip that past her ladyship?' Laughing, he made his way back through the throng to his table.

Sandford tossed back one large glass of brandy and indicated to the footman to pour him another. Thus fortified, he collected his glasses of lemonade and delivered them to the ladies who were still discussing the dances.

'Not nearly so graceful as the minuets,' Lady Caroline was saying, 'but a good deal more lively. The young ones look so merry. We always had to be so serious, for the steps were quite intricate, you know.'

'The country tunes are so cheerful, too,' agreed Lady Eugenie. 'Mrs Brewster brought me some new ones from London—and some German waltzes, too. I have been practising all week for this evening.'

Sandford's eyes lit up at her words. 'You play the waltz,

Aunt Eugenie?' he asked, the germ of an idea stirring in his mind.

Lady Eugenie nodded, and then shook her head doubtfully. 'Judith's mother will never allow it,' she said. 'I understand it is still considered rather risqué.'

Sandford, now in a very mellow mood, laughed. 'Not at a private party, surely?' he asked. 'And with such doughty chaperons present? I shall speak to Judith myself—come along, Charles, let us petition her together.'

Ridgeway glanced at his cousin curiously as they sought out their hostess. 'What are you up to, Sandford?' he asked. 'Lady Butler won't be at all amused, you know.'

Sandford stopped and whirled round to face him, his face flushed and his eyes bright. 'Dammit, man!' he said angrily. 'This is Judith's house, and she will decide. What's more— if I want to waltz with my fiancée, I defy anyone to stop me!'

Charles put his hand on Sandford's arm. 'Steady on, dear boy,' he said quietly. 'Surely you cannot be foxed? Judith will not appreciate your making a scene, you know.'

Sandford hesitated. It was true that the strong spirit might have somewhat impaired his judgement, but it had been the exhilarating thought of whirling Harriet around the room that was responsible for the sudden rush of blood to his head. He took a deep breath and flashed a conspiratorial grin at his cousin.

'Ne'er a bit, Charles,' he said. 'Just thought to liven things up a touch. Wouldn't you like to waltz with Judith?'

Ridgeway reddened and looked away. 'Not sure I'd know how,' he said diffidently. 'Not been much of a one for dancing.'

'This one is different. Your feet will soon tell you, once the music starts, I promise you. Come on, let's ask the lady.'

They found their hostess collecting couples for the first

after-supper dance and soon discovered that, after all, she needed little persuasion. Her party was an assured success and, as the guests consisted entirely of family and friends, she felt sure that it was highly unlikely anyone would take exception to this little divertissement.

'Apart from your mother, of course,' pointed out Sandford basely.

Judith pulled a face at him. 'You need not remind me, dear brother,' she said. 'However, Mama will not make a fuss until everyone has left, so do let's—it will be the perfect finish to our assembly!'

Since this had been his lordship's intention, he merely grinned and nudged his cousin who, catching some of Judith's excitement, had grasped her by the hand.

'Will you do me the honour, Judith?' he said breathlessly. 'I can't promise expertise, but I will do my best.'

Judith looked up at him in surprised delight and found herself blushing. 'Thank you, Charles,' she said almost shyly. 'It will be my pleasure.'

As soon as the last chord of the eightsome reel had died away, Judith clapped her hands to gain everyone's attention. She then announced that the very last dance of the evening was to be a waltz and that anyone who wished to try out this new dance was very welcome to take the floor. There was a gasp of excitement from the younger members of the local gentry, most of whom had undergone tortuous instruction from Monsieur Lavette, the local dancing master, but few of whom had ever expected to put their dubious skills into action quite so soon. There was a feverish rush of brothers seeking out the sisters who had been their usual partners when Monsieur had attended them for their weekly lessons and a hasty consultation with parents by those without convenient siblings.

The reels and sets that followed Judith's announcement

were danced with an undercurrent of anticipation. Few of the older guests had actually seen the waltz performed but they were, for the most part, level-headed country folk who liked to make up their own minds about such things and who felt that there were enough chaperons amongst them to curb any excessive behaviour that their offspring might exhibit.

Sandford found that the sets he had secured with Harriet were rather unsatisfactory, insofar as conversation was concerned, and the 'grand chaining' that formed part of the movements meant that he was forever having to change partners. No wonder no one else had initialled them, he thought savagely, as he led yet another schoolgirl under the arches of raised arms.

Eventually he had his moment as they stood together once again waiting their turn to 'strip the willow' and, looking down at her bright and laughing face he said in a low voice, 'You will waltz with me, Miss Cordell.'

'Oh, no! I don't think so, thank you, my lord,' she said, flushing momentarily.

'You misunderstand,' he said shortly. 'You *will* waltz with me!'

Startled, Harriet looked up at him in dismay, but was swung away down the set by her new partner before she could formulate a reply. She completed the rest of the movements in a stunned rage, causing at least one of her young admirers to wonder in what way he had offended her that she should look so crossly at him.

At last the floor was cleared and Lady Eugenie struck a new chord. The first notes of the stirring music were played and there were a few suppressed giggles as the floor remained empty while the local blades dug their friends in the ribs to spur them into action. Their movements were stilled as Sandford led his new betrothed into the middle of the floor.

Placing his right hand firmly on her waist, he pulled her towards him and clasped her hand in his. Holding her breath, she raised her free hand to his shoulder, trembling as she felt herself propelled backwards. Moving together as one, they swung across the floor in time to the compelling beat of the music and all eyes were upon them as Sandford neatly executed a reverse turn at the corner of the room. There came a ripple of applause and Dick Bevans, the squire's youngest son, grabbed his sister by the hand and dragged her on to the floor, to the accompanying cheers of his friends, who quickly found their own partners and joined them.

As the floor became more crowded, Sandford skilfully guided Harriet around the less-practised pairs. So smooth were his steps and the pressure of his hands was so confidently in command of her body that she began to feel quite heady, as though she were skimming across a frozen lake. She had waltzed several times before, at the winter headquarters in Lisbon, but never with such an expert. She glanced up at his face, which was curiously expressionless, his eyes carefully anticipating unexpected manoeuvres from all sides. Like a general going into battle, she thought suddenly and choked back her laughter in a hiccough.

He looked down at her in concern and almost missed his step. The laughter brimmed into her eyes as her lips curved in a wide smile.

'You don't seem to be enjoying this much, my lord,' she challenged him. 'In fact, onlookers might suppose that you were undergoing some sort of penance.'

The viscount studied her animated face and sighed. 'My apologies,' he said wryly. 'I suppose I was trying to impress you.'

He swept her round another untutored pair as he spoke and she marvelled once more at his ability.

'Oh, but I am,' she said. 'Impressed, I mean. You've obviously done this before.'

Sandford laughed and his spirits began to rise. 'A fair bit. It was all the rage in Vienna last year.'

He sidestepped nimbly to avoid a young couple in danger of imminent disaster and, in doing so, drew Harriet more closely to him. This is more like it, he thought with a surge of satisfaction.

'More pleasant than our continual jousting, wouldn't you say?' He tightened his hold around her waist. 'A much better way of ''getting to grips'' with one's enemy.'

Harriet looked up at him in consternation as he swung her around once more. 'I do not consider you to be an enemy, my lord,' she protested, 'and I trust you do not think of me in that way.'

Sandford smiled down into her eyes. 'Better if I don't tell you how I do think of you, perhaps?'

Harriet, flustered, drew her eyes away from his and missed her step. Swiftly, he corrected his to hers and they were once more in time with the music.

Struggling to keep her eyes away from his outrageous gleam, Harriet attempted to devote her attention to her footwork. She refused to look up, but had the strangest sensation that the viscount was laughing at her. She caught sight of Charles Ridgeway quite competently shepherding Judith around the room and both were looking extremely pleased with themselves. All at once her reticence evaporated and, tossing her head back, she relaxed into the haven of Sandford's embrace and abandoned herself to the compulsive rhythm of the dance.

Sandford's cup was full. Holding her in his arms at last made him feel as though he had won a great victory. He wished that the music could go on forever, taking them both into a land where there would be no more bickering, no stand-offs, no contention, just pure unadulterated bliss. Oblivious to all else around them, together they swayed and moved as one, whirling and twirling in perfect harmony. Inevitably, the spell was broken as Lady Eugenie played her last triumphant chord and the roomful of laughing, breathless couples swung finally to a halt.

There was a burst of spontaneous applause from both dancers and audience alike and the younger ones crowded around Judith, begging for just one encore but, shaking her head, she smilingly pointed at the clock, for it was almost midnight and, as she reminded them, the following day was Sunday.

In the darkened carriage Sandford leaned back against the velvet squabs with his eyes closed, only half-listening to his mother's approving comments regarding the success of the evening. He had to strain to catch Harriet's soft replies to the countess's questions, but found himself quite content just to hear the rippling sound of her voice. He was acutely conscious of the sensation of being at the threshold of some lofty precipice where a single false step would send him hurtling into an uncharted ravine. Tomorrow, he thought, tomorrow I shall tread lightly and with great care.

Chapter Seven

'There's a letter for you, Miss Cordell,' said Rose, as she helped her mistress remove her pelisse on her return from the morning service.

'A letter?' exclaimed Harriet, examining the sealed missive curiously. 'Who can have written to me—I saw everyone I know at church this morning!'

'Ned sent it up from the gate lodge, miss,' said Rose, hanging up the outdoor garments. 'Said it had been pushed under the door.'

Harriet unfolded the paper and read the contents with a frown. *Dearest—meet me tomorrow in our own special place—C.*

Puzzled, she turned the note over to check the direction and saw her name clearly written there.

'Well, it can't be meant for me—who do I know with that initial? Charles Ridgeway, to be sure, but I am certain it is not he—and young Lambert, last evening—oh! I see!'

Smiling broadly, she sat down and removed her bonnet. 'It's some sort of boyish prank, I suspect—a wager with one of his friends, I suppose—although I don't quite see—still, it's of no importance.' And she tossed the note aside and allowed Rose to tidy her hair before going to the earl's chamber to keep her promise of giving him a full account of the previous evening's entertainment.

She found his lordship sitting in a large armchair by the window and clapped her hands in delight. 'You are out of bed!' she exclaimed, as she bent to kiss the top of his head.

He held out his hand and motioned her to a footstool at his feet.

'So you've come to tell me of your great success.' He smiled. 'I fear you have been forestalled. Sandford has already been here singing your praises. I hear he had to fight his way through the mêlée to dance with you!'

Harriet blushed guiltily as she recalled the embarrassment she had caused the viscount over her mix-up with the dances, although it would appear from the earl's words that she had been forgiven for her lapse.

'Not quite, my lord,' she said. 'But it was all very great fun and Judith looked delighted. She came out of mourning especially—you do not mind?' She looked at him anxiously, conscious of the knowledge that Philip had been his son.

The earl shook his head and sighed. 'No, poor child. It is time. She has a life of her own to live.' He patted her hand. 'Now, what about this daring exhibition you gave with Sandford?'

Harriet beamed. 'Oh, he must take all the credit for that, my lord. I was completely innocent and taken totally off guard, I assure you! But he does dance divinely, you know!' At her vivid recollection of that episode her heart seemed to skip several beats.

'Takes after his sire, of course,' chortled the earl.

Quickly marshalling her thoughts, Harriet took hold of his hand and replied with an impish grin, 'Then I insist on being privy to these remarkable skills! So you must make haste to get back on to both feet.'

Beldale studied her animated face. 'I doubt I shall be on my feet before you leave, child,' he said, his voice gentle.

Harriet flinched and her vivid eyes clouded over.

'I keep forgetting,' she said tremulously. 'When I am here with you I keep forgetting!'

She bent her head to brush away a tear and the earl laid his hand on her burnished locks and smiled a strange, quiet smile to himself.

'Now, now, no tears today, if you please,' he commanded briskly. 'I demand to be amused. Tell me more of Judith's party.'

Harriet dismissed her melancholia and set about entertaining Beldale in her usual appealing manner and soon they were both laughing at her anecdotes of the previous evening.

'And the oddest thing,' she finished, wiping her eyes. 'One of the young daredevils has actually sent me a *billet-doux* but neglected to sign his name, so I fear I shall never know who my reluctant admirer is!'

'Then he must take his chances with the rest of us,' chaffed Lord William. 'I have no doubt you will now be so inundated with invitations from our neighbours that I shall have to make an appointment.'

Harriet shook her head vigorously. 'Not so, my lord,' she responded, with great seriousness. 'Your requirements would always take precedence. I have come to regard you as—almost—as a—father. Is that very presumptuous of me? I do miss him so.'

The earl was silent for a moment and Harriet was afraid that she had offended him with her impetuous remark until he took her hands in his and said, warmly, 'Harriet, my dear child, you have paid me the greatest compliment. I am well aware of the deep bond that existed between your father and yourself. When you have been with me I have often found myself regretting that I did not spend as much time with my own daughters as I might have done—although I must confess that I do not recall them having quite as lively a nature…'

His eyes twinkled at the blush that appeared as he patted her cheek. 'Do not be so eager to extinguish it completely, dear girl. I am already filled with envy that your grandfather is soon to be the fortunate recipient of your infectious chuckle.'

'I pray that I find such favour with him,' said Harriet fervently.

'I cannot think that you will fail to do so,' his lordship vociferated, 'unless he is blind or deaf or the greatest curmudgeon ever and we know that he cannot be any of these, for he is presently braving the tribulations of long-distance travel to come to your rescue!'

Harriet nodded and rose to her feet, seeing Chegwin approaching with the earl's medication. 'That's true,' she said. 'And my consolation is that the longer he takes the more time I can spend with you!'

'Away with you, shameless hussy,' laughed Beldale. Then a thought struck him. 'Go and practise your beguiling charms on Sandford—I'll warrant he is not so easily moved!'

Harriet smilingly wagged her finger at him and left the room, with every intention of keeping as far away from the viscount as good manners allowed, for she was perplexed to find that his very presence suddenly seemed capable of exercising the strangest effect upon her composure. At the morning service, for instance, he had elected to stand next to her in the family pew and his fingers had (quite accidentally, she was sure) brushed against hers as she had leaned forward to pick up her prayer book. This, for some reason that she could not fathom, had prevented her from finding her place and he had taken her book from her and had handed her his own, open at the correct page. She was not even sure that she had given her responses correctly, so aware had she been of Sandford's own resonant, articulate returns. Worst of all, she was sure that she had detected an undercurrent of suppressed laughter in his voice and a swift sideways glance at him had revealed his amused scrutiny of her discomposure. His eyes had held that same disconcerting gleam, which she had done her best to ignore on the previous evening. When he had helped her into and out of the carriage his hand had seemed to linger on her arm a fraction too long and she had, once more, been conscious of the unrelenting intensity of his gaze as he sat opposite Lady Caroline and herself during the ride home from church.

Mentally shaking herself, Harriet hesitated outside the earl's door, unable to decide whether to return to the safety of her own room and stay out of harm's way or to venture downstairs. The events of the last few days were clearly affecting her brain, she concluded, and turned resolutely to the head of the stairway, only to perceive the object of her reverie emerging from his own chambers nearby.

'Ah, Miss Cordell!'

Sandford registered Harriet's violent start at his appearance but made no comment. He had, in fact, been listening somewhat impatiently for the click of his father's door-latch to signal her emergence; therefore his presence was no accident.

'You have been regaling his lordship with a fuller and more entertaining account of last evening's delights than that with which I was able to furnish him, I imagine?'

He seemed to Harriet to be in possession of some private and amusing intelligence and this added to her sense of confusion.

'Oh, well—yes—that is—I did my best to do so,' she answered, in breathless agitation, at the same time attempting a decorous retreat to her own quarters, but he put out his hand to stay her movements.

'Would you care to join me in a carriage ride?' His voice suddenly seemed almost boyish in its eagerness. 'It is such a lovely afternoon and I have to inspect some cottages. I would be honoured if you would accompany me.'

Harriet's eyes widened in surprise. 'That is very good of you, my lord,' she said cautiously. 'I confess I should be glad to get out into the air. If I may just collect my bonnet…?'

Sandford, watching her disappear into her room, had a sudden insane urge to leap on to the banisters he was holding and slide down them, just as he and Philip had done in their youth. Instead, to March's grinning amazement, he bounded down the stairs two at a time and ordered up the carriage.

Sitting on his box behind the driving-seat, Tiptree wondered dismally if he was witnessing his colonel's last stand. Having been privy to most of the 'guvnor's' intermittent campaigns into 'petticoat territory', he had to admit that he couldn't recall anything quite like this one. There had been that stunning blonde in Vienna, he mused, until Lord Sandford had discovered that the lady was a damned sight more interested in his money than in his manners and a certain contessa in Salamanca had seemed to be streaking to the winning post except for her unfortunate tendency to gamble heavily—not one of his lordship's favourite pastimes, Tiptree knew, considering the anguish such profligacy had brought to certain close members of the family. Other beauties had been guilty of having either no conversation at all or far too much and one memorable dazzler had kept dogs! Tiptree shuddered at the recollection of trying to keep three dribbling lapdogs under control in his lordship's open carriage whilst his master accompanied her ladyship into a milliner's salon. Those boots had never recovered, he thought, scowling at the back of Harriet's chip-straw bonnet, as though she were to blame. So, what was special about this one? he wondered. Her dad had been a real good goer, he allowed, and her ma—well she had been a proper trooper in her time. He'd never heard anything either good or bad about the daughter. She was certainly no beauty, not to his taste, anyway, with her ginger hair and cat's eyes, although she was quite a taking little thing—plucky, too and with a laugh that 'fetched the sun out', so he'd heard Smithers say, not that there was much sign of it at the moment, he observed.

Harriet was doing her best to remember Martha's teachings. Her back was straight, her feet were together and her gloved hands were clasped neatly in her lap. Her eyes she kept firmly to the front, on the road ahead. She had exhausted her entire fund of polite conversation, wondering glumly if the English gentlewoman's lot in life were always this dreary and almost wishing that she had stayed at Beldale. Sandford, on the other hand, seemed to be enjoying himself hugely. Out of the corner of her eye she had caught sight of a wide grin on his face, his beaver hat was tipped rakishly to the back of his head and his whole bearing seemed to be one of carefree relaxation, while she herself felt foolishly stiff and uncomfortable.

'How about the hedges?' His voice was brimming with suppressed laughter.

'I beg your pardon?' She half-turned towards him, and then quickly recovered.

'Well now, let's see,' he continued. 'We've had the weather—yes, it is extraordinarily warm for the time of year! And it is fortunate that the rain is keeping off for the haymaking and, yes, the orchards are full of fruit and, yes, I do consider thatching to be the most skilful of crafts!'

Harriet could feel a chuckle starting in her chest and struggled to suppress its unruly behaviour.

'Wh-what about the hedges?' she asked, holding her breath, but refusing to look at him.

'Let's think,' he said, his head on one side, considering. 'Do they need trimming, I wonder, or shall I have them pulled up, burnt down or simply consign them all to the Devil!'

Harriet put her hands up to her mouth in an effort to maintain her composure, but it was to no avail. Her lips curved into a smile, her eyes began to sparkle and the way-ward chuckle burst into a peal of laughter.

A delighted Sandford reined his horses in to a halt and motioned to the widely grinning Tiptree to jump down and hold their heads. Taking out his handkerchief, the gleeful viscount then proceeded to mop up the tears of merriment that were spilling down Harriet's cheeks.

'Not fair—not fair,' she gasped, pushing him away. Her lips still quivering, she attempted to straighten her bonnet, which had somehow cast itself adrift, and regarded Sandford disapprovingly from beneath her wet lashes.

'Ah, but don't they say ''all's fair…''?' he said, reaching out to take her hand and leaning towards her but, just at that precise moment, there came the sound of horses' hooves on the lane and Tiptree's low warning, ''Ware ''parkers'', guv.'

Harriet looked on with undisguised interest as Tiptree vaulted back on to his seat and the viscount spurred his team once more into action.

The occupants of the oncoming chaise saluted Sandford as the two vehicles passed one another and his lordship, although smilingly lifting his whip in reply, wished them in Hell.

Truth to tell, he was feeling slightly abashed at his conduct. He knew perfectly well that he would have tried to kiss Harriet had it not been for the interruption, but knew equally well that their relationship was far too tenuous to survive such precipitant action. Glancing down at her, he wondered if his rash behaviour had indeed set his cause back still further. He immediately resolved to make up any lost ground without further ado, but found himself forestalled.

'I do believe you were setting up a flirtation, my lord,' said Harriet cheerfully, rearranging her skirts.

Sandford, totally unprepared for this challenge, reddened and could only stammer, 'Not at all—you are mistaken—I must apologise…'

'Oh, come now, sir,' Harriet apostrophised. 'I am not a schoolgirl—you surely do not think that you are the first gentleman who has tried to kiss me? Although, upon reflection, I must confess that I have never before been ravished on the public highway!'

'Ravished, madam!' Sandford was appalled. 'I have never ravished anyone in my entire life—I'll have you know…' He stopped, having caught sight of her laughing countenance, and grinned ruefully. '*Touché*—your hit.'

He drove on in sheepish silence for some minutes until a thought occurred to him.

'Where did gentlemen try to kiss you, may I ask? Not since you have been under my protection, I trust?'

'Certainly not, my lord,' replied Harriet, demurely peeping up at him from beneath the brim of her bonnet. 'There was a very dashing subaltern in Lisbon, I recall—two, as a matter of fact.'

'And did they succeed?' asked Sandford, all agog for her reply.

'Succeed? Oh, I see.' Harriet laughed in delight at his masculine phraseology. 'Well, one did—kiss me, that is—

but then the other discovered us in the alcove and offered to "darken his daylights"—I believe that was the expression…?'

Sandford's lips twitched. 'Sounds about right,' he said carefully. 'What happened then?'

'Well, my first gallant appeared to doubt the other's ability to do any such thing and responded with a similar offer of his own—something about "drawing his cork" and "spilling his claret"—as I recollect.' Harriet said mischievously.

'Your memory serves you well,' said Sandford, grinning as he pictured the scene. 'And then?'

Harriet sighed deeply. 'They then seemed to be more intent on having a mill than making love to me,' she said, in rueful reminiscence. 'So I returned myself to the party!'

The viscount gave a shout of laughter and lightly flicked his whip at the horses' heads, his good humour having suddenly returned.

'I wish I had known you in those far-off days,' he said, recalling some of the headier moments of his own time in Portugal.

'We were introduced on one occasion, my lord,' she offered. 'I doubt you will remember—I was only sixteen at the time—a mere child curtseying to your exalted personage. I fancy that your thoughts were more occupied with the very colourful *señora* two paces to my left…' She dimpled at his look of shocked recollection. 'I see that you recall the lady—a capitano's wife, I believe?'

'Yes—well, perhaps the least said about that particular incident, the better,' Sandford interposed hurriedly, ignoring his passenger's laughing eyes. 'And that was the only time we met?'

Harriet considered. 'My friends and I used to run to watch you ride past at the head of your company—you were something of a hero to us,' she said, her lips curving in memory. Then she collected herself and laughed a little self-consciously. 'We were only children, of course—I doubt if you noticed us.'

'I never thought of myself as a hero, certainly,' protested Sandford, remembering many such scenes. 'But I am sorry that I was not better acquainted with you—I wish I might have doffed my hat to you all as we rode out of town!'

'And what ecstasies we would have fallen into then, my lord,' replied Harriet gravely, although her mouth twitched at the corners.

Sandford's eyes gleamed with amusement.

'If you are trying to provoke me, Miss Cordell,' he said, his enjoyment mounting, 'you would do well to remember that you are no longer a child—and must therefore be prepared to accept the consequences of such fulsome encouragement.'

Harriet laughed out loud and shook her head at him. 'I withdraw all such comments, my lord,' she chuckled. 'And you may be assured that I had outgrown all such adulation well before my teens had ended.'

'Now that is a pity,' Sandford groaned, in mock despair. 'I was quite prepared to accept just a modicum of adulation.'

'Oh, no, sir,' replied Harriet, mirthfully aware that she had won the round. 'You have persuaded me that I must seize every opportunity to discourage such vanity!'

'Hoist by my own petard, dammit!' he laughed, pulling in the reins.

The curricle had reached a fork in the lane and Sandford had slowed the horses to negotiate the narrower of the two ways. This smaller track led down to a row of ramshackle dwellings, the furthest of which had obviously been destroyed by fire.

'Mr Potter's cottage, I collect?' said Harriet, looking

about her with interest as, with Sandford's assistance, she descended from the carriage.

He nodded, surprised but gratified that she had remembered Ridgeway's tale.

'We'd been trying to persuade him to move out for months,' he said, walking over to the ruin. 'The rest of the tenants were rehoused last year in the new cottages by Top Meadow...' He gesticulated back towards the fork in the lane. 'Old Josh refused to go—said he'd lived here since he was first married and he intended to die here.'

'Pretty near did, too, by all accounts,' interjected Tiptree, who, having tethered the horses, had joined them. 'Set fire to his bed with his pipe, so I hear. Lucky for him Jack Rawlings was driving his cart along the top lane and got him out.'

'Was he hurt?' Harriet asked, her sympathy for the old tenant immediately aroused.

'Not really, so I'm told,' replied the viscount, 'superficial burns to his hands and legs. Meggy—his daughter—soon sorted him out, according to Charles, but she's had the Devil's own job trying to keep him away from here.' Sandford indicated the blackened roof timbers. 'Going to fall in any minute, I should say. We'd better get a gang on to it right away. The whole row should be pulled down and rebuilt.'

'Poor old man,' said Harriet, her eyes pricking with involuntary tears as she surveyed the pitiful ruins of Josh Potter's belongings. She bent down and picked up part of the charred remains of an ancient book.

'Oh, look!' She showed it to Sandford. 'It's his family bible—how awful! His whole history written off in a single stroke.'

She placed what was left of the ruined volume reverently on the stone windowsill and, as she did so, a withered blossom fluttered from between its leaves. Harriet caught the faded, almost transparent pressing in the palm of her hand and stared down at it bleakly.

Sandford could see the tears trickling down her cheeks and stepped hastily towards her.

'Please don't distress yourself,' he said, holding out his hands. 'I should not have brought you here—I hadn't real-ised it would be so—you are recalling parallels, I imagine?'

Harriet nodded. 'As you say, my lord.' There was a catch in her throat and she smiled tremulously at him as he once again applied his handkerchief to her face. 'What a water-ing-pot you must think me!'

'You never allow me to tell you what I think of you,' brusquely returned his lordship, resignedly pocketing his damp accessory. 'What have you got there?' He pointed to her hand.

She showed him the pressed flower, then looked at him in sudden inspiration. 'Do you have a card-case with you, my lord?'

Sandford frowned and nodded. 'Of course,' he said, pat-ting his breast pocket. 'Why do you ask—you surely do not require me to leave a calling-card here?'

'Don't be ridiculous,' sighed Harriet patiently, as though to a child. 'I need to keep this memento safe for Mr Potter. You can slip it carefully between your cards until we return to Beldale—then I shall think of something.'

'Yes, I'm sure you will,' said Sandford, eyeing the relic in distaste, but he handed over his card-case as requested and watched in amused silence as Harriet gently placed the ancient favour between its folds and tucked it into her ret-icule.

The return journey to Beldale was accomplished without incident. The interchanges between them were friendly and relaxed and when Harriet mentioned that she would be riding with Judith early the following morning Sandford, anxious to avoid damaging the fragile tenure of their newly forged relationship, forbore from insisting that she should take a groom.

Chapter Eight

The two horses cantered side by side to the top of the hill and their riders reined in together, laughing. Judith dismounted gracefully on to a stone block set there for just that purpose and moved away to allow Harriet to do likewise. Tethering their mounts to a nearby sapling, they seated themselves on a fallen tree trunk and surveyed the magnificent view below them.

Harriet breathed in deeply, savouring the fresh morning air. 'This is such a glorious country, Judith,' she said. 'At first I wasn't sure if I could get used to it—after the heat and the mountains, you know, but now I think I shall never want to leave. I do hope I shall like Scotland as much.'

Judith looked at her curiously. 'Are you to visit Scotland? You have not mentioned it.'

Harriet recollected herself with a start. She had grown to be so at ease in Judith's company that she had quite forgotten that there were still things not to be shared with her new friend.

'I believe I am to visit my grandfather,' she said carefully. 'He has an estate near Edinburgh and he has expressed a desire to—to meet—my betrothed,' she finished, on a sudden inspiration. She pleated the folds of her habit between her fingers, unhappy at having to lie in this way to someone of whom she had grown so fond, but Judith appeared not to notice her discomfort.

'That sounds delightful,' she said, nodding absently and, rising to her feet, she strolled across the grass and sat down under a spreading beech tree and began to pluck the daisies, which grew in profusion around her. Harriet watched her in amusement. Already she was beginning to judge her friend's moods to a nicety and had been waiting for Judith to speak first but now, she realised, it was up to her to venture the subject.

'Did Charles enjoy the evening?' she asked suddenly.

Startled, Judith dropped her miniature bouquet and, flushing, bowed her head as she bent to retrieve the scattered flowers.

'Y-yes—I believe so—at least—I don't really—I haven't...'

She gave up, looking ruefully at Harriet, who grinned encouragingly at her.

'I suppose Lady Butler gave you the expected scold,' said Harriet. 'You haven't committed any great sin, you know, and it was an amazing party!'

Judith nodded, her eyes brightening. 'Yes, everyone has said so. I'm so pleased that it was a success and you were so popular—that is very important, you know, for you will be Countess of Beldale one day and to be well liked by the locals is a feather in your cap.'

Harriet blanched at the thought and quickly changed the subject. 'Will you ever marry again, do you think, Judith?'

'I have no need to,' replied Judith, in a low voice. 'Philip left me very well provided for—we have no financial worries and, of course, it is my—my duty to see that Christopher inherits his father's estates in good order and...'

'And Charles no doubt regards it as his duty to do the

same,' interrupted Harriet. 'What a pair you are—you do like him, don't you, Judith?'

'I have known him all my life,' laughed Judith, self-consciously straightening her stock. 'The twins always chaffed me about him—he used to bring me wild strawberries on a dock leaf when I was a little girl—I never thought of him in—you know—that way—I never loved anyone but Philip—but I get so lonely sometimes that everything suddenly becomes very hard to bear.'

She stared bleakly at the horizon, watching the early morning sun slowly ascending the cloudless blue sky.

'Well, you must have seen that he's absolutely dotty about you,' said Harriet bluntly. 'He'll never say so, of course, because of convention and protocol and—oh, Judith, don't waste the rest of your life! Surely Philip wouldn't want you to be sad forever?'

Judith smiled briefly. 'No, but then we didn't exactly discuss the possibility of one of us remarrying—we were too busy being happy, I suppose.'

She looked down at her entwined fingers and then faced her friend. 'Mother always expected me to marry Robert, you know,' she said, in a rush. 'They were both forever in and out of Staines—my home—and Mother always thought it would be Robert who would offer for me, but I chose Philip. Father liked both Hurst boys and was perfectly happy with my choice, which was why he made over half of our farmland to Philip on our marriage. The earl settled Beldale's western boundaries on Philip and we built Westpark House. My parents remained at Staines until Papa died and then Mother let the house out to tenants and moved in with us, lock, stock and barrel, as they say—she even brought most of the old staff with her and expected Philip to find them positions. He did his best, of course, and organised pensions for those whom we couldn't accommodate. Mother has always held a grudge about that, even though she doesn't concern herself in the least about servants—she just took it as a personal slight.'

She glanced at Harriet. 'I'm being fearfully disloyal telling you all this, aren't I?'

Harriet shook her head. 'No, it explains a lot,' she said. 'I couldn't understand why she took me in such dislike—obviously she hoped that his lordship would come back from the wars and snap you up—I'm only amazed that he didn't!' She burst out laughing at her friend's look of astonishment and Judith found herself laughing in return.

'Well,' she said, in relief, 'it doesn't really matter. I couldn't possibly have married Robert. That would have seemed quite immoral somehow—I love him as a brother. Charles is different altogether but ..it will be terribly difficult...' she paused wistfully '—he is such a proud man.'

'That's true.' Harriet nodded. 'So it is up to you to show him how much you depend upon him—how you can't manage without him, in fact. Gracious me, but aren't you lucky to have all these fellows crazy in love with you—it makes me positively green with envy!'

She got to her feet and began brushing the bits of grass from her habit, thereby failing to see Judith's look of puzzlement at her final remark.

'Now we really must get back,' she said, leading Clipper to the mounting block. 'I told them I would return for breakfast.'

'Oh, dear,' said Judith, scrambling to her feet. 'I promised Mother I would bring you back to have breakfast with the children.'

Harriet paused for a moment to consider this invitation.

'Well, I dare say I could stay just for the veriest minute—it is still very early and I could do with a drink, couldn't you? All this heart-searching is very thirst-making!'

Laughing together, they made their way back down the hill and on to the lane that led back to Westpark.

The two children were waiting with their grandmother on the rear terrace of the house and jumped up excitedly when they saw their mother bringing Harriet through the archway which led from the stables. Lady Butler frowned her disapproval as Christopher bounded down the steps to take his new aunt's hand and sharply instructed her granddaughter to remain in her seat.

'Aunt Harriet, Aunt Harriet,' the boy squealed breathlessly. 'Uncle Robert has bought me a new pony—a real goer, he says, and he's having jumps set up in Top Meadow—and he's going to teach me himself!'

His eyes shone with the wonder of it all and Harriet was enchanted with him once more. She allowed him to lead her up the terrace steps into the conservatory where she could see a small table laid for a nursery breakfast.

'You won't mind the informality, Harriet, I know,' said Judith, removing her gloves. 'The children and I often have our breakfast out here in the summertime and Mother was keen to join us today—as you were to be our guest.'

She handed a little silver bell to Elspeth and bade the little girl ring for Jemima. Harriet watched in delight as the child crossed to the house door and, with great dignity, solemnly and carefully shook the tinkling instrument. Almost immediately the smiling housemaid appeared, carrying her tray of glasses and milk jugs. It was clear that the sound of the bell could not have brought her so swiftly, but that Elspeth believed it had was evident by the stately pride with which she marched back to her seat and took her place at the head of the table.

Judith smiled at Harriet, without apology.

'It is we who are taking breakfast with the children, you

see,' she explained. 'Philip and I liked to think that this was the best way to teach them.'

'Piffling nonsense, in my opinion,' sniffed Lady Butler. 'The place for children's meals is in the nursery with Nanny.'

'Oh, no! It's charming,' breathed Harriet, ready to enter into the spirit of the idea. Passing her cup to Elspeth, she requested her small hostess to pour her a cup of milk and graciously accepted a slice of buttered sponge from young Master Christopher. Judith thanked her wordlessly with her eyes and, once more, Harriet felt deep pangs of regret at the deception in which she had become entangled.

After the meal, during which Harriet had managed to smile her way through several biscuit and cake offerings, she was persuaded to pay a visit to Polly, the new pony, to discuss the best tactics of taking fences. The pleasant minutes slipped swiftly by until she suddenly recalled her promise to return to Beldale for breakfast! Hurriedly making her farewells to her hostesses on the terrace and fairly scooting back to the stables to collect her mount, it was not until she turned for a final gay wave to the two children that she found, to her annoyance, that she had mislaid her gloves. No time to go back for them now, she decided, spurring Clipper into a gallop across the meadow to the Beldale bridleway. Luckily, no one would see her on this private path, but she laughed out loud as she visualised Martha's shocked expression had that stickler for propriety been privileged to see her in such a state of undress!

As the dew-fresh scents of the morning rose about her Harriet breathed deeply in appreciation. She would be almost sorry to leave this glorious place, she mused, as she leaned down to secure the gate behind her and started along the ride back. She wondered if Sandford would be joining

Lady Caroline and herself for breakfast. Until yesterday morning, he had usually sought to quit the room before her arrival, thereby avoiding the strained atmosphere that had prevailed at the dinner table during the previous week. Since yesterday afternoon's eventful ride, however, he had been all attention and she had to admit that she was looking forward with an inexplicable eagerness to their next encounter. Why, the very thought of it was making her feel quite giddy, she laughed to herself, and endeavoured to turn her mind to more sober topics.

The thickets of trees on either side of the path shaded both horse and rider from the heat of the rising sun and, almost drowsily, Harriet slowed to a gentle trot, allowing her mount to make its own pace along what had by now become a well-recognised route. They had not proceeded far in this leisurely manner when, to her irritation, she noticed that the dappling of the sun through the trees on one side of the path seemed to be causing her some sort of problem with her vision and she attempted to pull her hat down to lessen the effect. As she did so she became aware of an insistent thrumming in her ears that grew louder and louder as she desperately tried to maintain her balance. Clipper, ever sensitive to her mistress's touch, tossed her head as the reins loosened and at that sudden movement Harriet lost her grip and felt herself sliding from her mount. She seemed to have no control over her limbs and her head was filled with a swirling mist as she felt her body collapsing into someone's hands! Somewhere in the mist she could hear the mare whinnying and a man's voice, which seemed to came from far-away, was saying: 'Whoa, girl! Well, get her foot out of the stirrup, ninny! Come on! We haven't got all day!'

In a trance-like state Harriet felt herself being half-dragged, half-carried deep into the copse between clumps of briar and gorse. She could offer no resistance owing to the waves of nausea and blackness that were drowning her senses. She was aware of being pushed into a shallow depression in the ground and felt her skirts being bundled about her as branches were heaped upon her body, but her voice could make no protest. As she felt herself falling deeper into the roaring abyss of unconsciousness she heard the man's voice once more.

'The ring! Cripes, man! We forgot the ring—where's her hand?'

With a supreme effort Harriet eased the emerald ring from her finger and feeling for her boot, she pushed the jewel under the front fastenings. Then she passed out.

The cold, dank smell of the earth pervaded her senses. For some moments she remained still, trying to break through the cloying mists of her brain. Her temples were pounding and her mouth was dry and foul-tasting. Cautiously she sat up, pushing aside the mound of twigs and branches that covered her and, after peering carefully about, she saw that she was quite alone. Steadying herself against the tree trunk, she managed to stand. Her assailants had gone and Clipper was nowhere to be seen! Surely she had not been the victim of horse-theft? Apart from some rough handling she had not been hurt and she had nothing of value…!

Gasping, she thrust her hand down into her boot and felt the hard ridge of the precious stone against her fingers and almost wept with relief. That was what they were after! They were just common foot-pads after all—but what were they doing on Beldale property? Gradually, it began to come back to her—they must have been waiting for her—but had they actually pulled her from her horse—what had caused her sudden dizziness? Her head ached so, she was covered in bracken and mud and her hat and cravat were both missing!

As she shaded her eyes against the piercing glare of the summer sun she was suddenly transfixed as she registered its position in the sky. It must be past noon! She had been in the copse for hours! Casting about her for a sign that might help to guide her back to the path, she was eventually able to locate the trail of flattened grass along which she had been dragged and, still very unsteady, she slowly and painfully managed to make her way back to the bridleway. Scrambling in sobbing relief through the final clump of gorse, she fell straight into Sandford's arms.

He thrust her roughly aside and she was shocked at the look of naked fury on his face.

'Where the Devil have you been?' he demanded. 'We have been searching for hours. How dared you go off in such a way. Are you totally without shame? Look at yourself—just look at yourself!' His voice was filled with disgust.

Harriet staggered back. 'What are you saying? I was attacked...'

Sandford's lip curled. 'Again?' he said coldly. 'You do seem to make a habit of that, don't you?'

Ignoring her protests, he turned on his heel and strode up the path to where his horse was tethered. Harriet, grabbing up her skirts, stumbled after him, convinced that she must still be in the grip of some dreadful nightmare and her eyes widened in amazement at the unexpected sight of Clipper grazing peacefully on the verge ahead.

'You found her!' she panted, as Sandford came to a standstill beside the horses. 'I was afraid...'

'Much you cared!' Sandford spun round to face her. 'You left her tied up at the gate while you cavorted with your—your what?' He raised his crop as though to strike her.

Harriet flinched, dumbfounded. 'I don't understand,' she said, her head still pounding. 'What are you accusing me of? I was riding with Judith—I told you yesterday...'

'Spare me the details. I've seen the note—you carelessly left it on your dressing table. Rose brought it to my mother when you failed to return from Westpark.'

'Note? What note? Oh—yes, I see—but that was not intended...'

He turned away from her, his shoulders suddenly slumped and he leaned his head wearily against Pagan's neck.

'It doesn't matter,' he said bleakly. 'I am tired of your tricks. Hopefully, you will soon be gone. I wish to God that I had left you in the ditch—my life has been in turmoil since that day!'

'Oh, please,' exhorted Harriet, laying her hand on his arm. 'Please tell me what you think I have done? I beg of you...' She winced as he gripped her wrist, his eyes suffused with anger as he regarded her unadorned fingers.

'You witch!' he choked. 'Where is it? If you have given it...'

'Stop it! Stop it!' Harriet tried to pull away from him and, finding that she could not escape, she raised her free hand and slapped him hard across his cheek. For an interminable moment he stared down at her, almost unseeingly, then with a groan he crushed her to his chest and buried his face in her hair.

'Oh, dear God! What have I done!' he breathed, but Harriet hardly heard him. She dragged herself away from his grasp and glared at him in rage.

'How dare you! Have you gone mad! I hate you! I cannot wait to get away from this place!' She thrust her hand into her boot. 'See! Here is your precious ring! And to think that I went to the trouble of saving it! I pity whoever has the misfortune to become your wife!'

Casting the jewel at his feet, she burst into tears and swept regally past him. It was more than a mile back to the house she knew, but she had no intention of asking for Sandford's assistance to mount her horse. She trudged resentfully along the path, clutching up the muddied skirts of her riding habit as best she could, fulminating at the unfairness of life. She had been at this beastly place barely two weeks and already she had been dragged into a lake and set upon by brigands, which was more than had ever befallen her in all her years with the military! What else could happen? She couldn't expect her grandfather to arrive for at least another week at the earliest. If only she had insisted on leaving with Ozzy and Martha! What right did Sandford have to dismiss their suggestion? Hadn't she just heard him admit that he would be glad when she had gone? He had left her in no doubt as to his opinion of her—calling her a witch—and a trickster!

She came to a sudden standstill on the path, trying to remember the exact words he had used. He had behaved as though he had been the victim, when it was she who had been attacked and tricked not once but three times, she realised, if one counted the puzzle of the note! Walking on, she deliberated upon that particular enigma. Sandford had referred to it with an anger she considered totally uncalled for. It must have been perfectly obvious that the note was not intended for her. Who on earth did he suppose she would arrange to meet in secret? And why? Then an incredible notion entered her head as she recalled his words—he had supposed that! He had been accusing her of having a clandestine tryst!

For a moment or two Harriet felt quite sick as a cold clamminess swept over her body and she had to press her shaking hands over her lips to control their trembling as she struggled to digest the implication of his words.

While Sandford and his men had been supposedly scour

ing the park she had been concealed inside a bush practically under their noses and then, far from giving her a chance to explain her absence, he had been so convinced of her guilt that he had refused even to listen to her. Worse, he had accused her of having spent hours in some furtive and underhand assignation!

Something else occurred to her. Sandford had said that Clipper had been found tied to the gate, but the only gate was at the end of the Beldale bridleway that, as far as she could judge, was more than a mile from the spot where she had fallen from her horse! Someone must have taken Clipper back to the gate and tied her there! But, in God's name, why?

As she neared the house Harriet's indignation was replaced with apprehension. Who else had been furnished with this untruth? Had Lord William and Lady Caroline also come to the same conclusion as the viscount? What other interpretation would they put on her long absence?

The sound of horse's hooves alerted her to the sight of Tiptree riding up behind her, leading her mare. He dismounted and cupped his hands.

'Up you get, miss,' he said dispassionately. 'His lordship wants you to ride in.'

Harriet allowed the groom to raise her into the saddle. She knew that this would be far better than being seen arriving at the stables without her horse but was still at a loss as to how she would begin to explain her disappearance.

The two horses walked into the yard and were immediately surrounded by the grooms and stable-lads, all expressing delight at 'Missy's' return and clamouring for information. Tiptree waved them aside as he swung down from his mount.

'Miss Cordell got lost in the woods,' he said, in brief

explanation. 'She's very tired. Make way, lads. Let's have a bit of space. His lordship is calling in the others.'

Smithers helped Harriet down and took Clipper's reins.

'Glad to see you safe back, miss,' he ventured. 'We was all worried you'd hurt yourself. Don't need no more accidents, you know.'

Harriet took heart from his remark and gave him a shaky smile. Turning to go into the house, she found Tiptree at her side.

'Beg pardon, miss,' he said quietly, 'but his lordship says you dropped this.' He held out the emerald ring. 'He says to tell you "not to worry".'

Harriet looked inquiringly at him but his face was expressionless. She slipped the ring on to her finger once more and took a deep breath as she entered the hallway.

'Harriet, my dearest child!' Lady Caroline swept forward to throw her arms around her protégée. 'Oh, thank goodness you are safe! His lordship has been in such a torment!'

Harriet didn't inquire as to which 'lordship' the countess was referring. Kissing her ladyship on the cheek, she assured her that she was, indeed, unhurt and merely in need of a wash and a very long drink.

Lady Caroline indicated her requirements to March and tenderly led Harriet into the salon.

'Sit down, dearest, do,' she said, pressing the shivering Harriet down on to a sofa and offering her a rug to put over her knees.

Harriet, eyes brimming, shook her head and smilingly refused the cover.

'Please, ma'am, you must not wait upon me,' she protested. 'I promise you I have suffered no great harm—but I would like to see Lord William, if I may—if he has been concerned about me I must put his mind at rest—and there is something I need to ask him, if he is not too tired?'

'About that mysterious note?' the countess nodded. 'Yes, he told me. Sandford had rushed off in search of you before we could tell him that it was some sort of joke—although I cannot believe he took it seriously...'

'I'm afraid he did, ma'am,' said Harriet miserably. 'He seems to believe I was involved in some secret—tryst—with someone I met at Judith's party!'

Lady Caroline was indignant. 'But that is preposterous! Why should he think such a thing? His father will give him such a trimming when he returns! Come, my dear, finish your drink and, if you feel up to it, we will go straight to his lordship this instant.'

The earl had been furnished with the news of Harriet's return on the moment of her arrival at the stables and was waiting impatiently for her entrance. Running to his chair she cast herself into his arms and burst into tears. He stroked her hair gently, murmuring comforting endearments, at the same time raising his eyebrows questioningly at his wife, who shook her head in response.

After allowing Harriet to cry herself out, Lord William took the handkerchief the countess was offering and set about repairing the damage to her face, tut-tutting as he did so.

'Now, now, my child,' he said softly. 'This will not do. I will not have these pretty eyelids swollen. This redness simply does not go well with that glorious shade of green— and I fear I shall come down with the croup if my dressing-gown gets any damper!'

Harriet, smiling weakly, sat back on his footstool and twisted the sodden kerchief between her fingers.

'I'm so sorry,' she said tremulously. 'It isn't usual in me to give in so easily. But I find myself at such a loss!'

The earl and countess exchanged glances and Beldale motioned to Chegwin to fetch a chair for his mistress. This done, at his lordship's gesture the valet quietly left the room and Lord William took Harriet's hands in his.

'I think you had better tell us what is troubling you and together perhaps we shall make some sense out of your problems.'

'But you have been so ill,' said Harriet, in an anguished tone, 'and I wanted to avoid bringing you more worry!'

Beldale sighed. 'I have a broken foot, my girl,' he said briskly. 'There is nothing wrong with my brain—whatever that fool Lambert thinks!'

And so, tentatively at first, Harriet told her hosts the full story of her lake misadventure and, with increasing confidence, she breathlessly related this morning's extraordinary events.

Lady Caroline's eyes grew round with horror at Harriet's description of her woodland tomb.

'But this is quite dreadful,' she exclaimed in dismay. 'On Beldale lands—how can this be happening?' and she turned at once to her husband to await his conclusions.

The earl was silent for some little while, conscious of both ladies' eyes upon him at they awaited some erudite explanation that he feared he did not have. Eventually, he spoke.

'It is clear that someone has wished you harm from the moment of your arrival,' he said to Harriet. 'That person— or persons—seem to be privy to a good deal of information about your movements. On the other hand, a fair amount of coincidence seems to be involved. For instance, at the lake, where you might not have chosen to walk on that particular morning and today—you say you had left Westpark much later than you intended—and who could possibly have foreseen your fainting attack? The emerald ring that they failed to find—thanks to your swift action—has only been in your possession since Saturday evening and advertised only at

Judith's party and yet, it seems to have been the particular object of the attack—I would not have thought it to be of such singular value.' He shook his head. 'I confess, my dears, I am at as much of a loss as you are, but one thing is very clear—one of this household is involved in passing information outside. How else could Harriet's movements be so well observed?'

He looked at his wife, concerned at her obvious distress.

'This has been a great shock for you, my love,' he said, tenderly squeezing her fingers. 'Most of our staff has been with us for so long, it does not bear thinking about.'

'I cannot bring myself to suspect any of them,' said Lady Caroline unhappily. 'We have hardly any recent additions— Robert's valet and his man Tiptree, of course, and Rose Watts—but she was parlourmaid here long before Harriet's arrival…'

'Nothing of this sort happened before my arrival!' Harriet pointed out despondently. 'It is clear that it is my presence which is causing someone great annoyance!'

'But everyone adores you!' her ladyship protested.

'Apparently not everyone, ma'am,' said Harriet, rising from the footstool and straightening her skirts. And I can think of at least one person who positively dislikes me, she thought, at the same time sadly recalling the previous day's easy companionship between herself and that very individual.

'There is just one thing I must ask of you, Harriet,' said his lordship with a very serious expression on his face.

'Anything you wish, sir,' she replied, uncomfortably aware of what his request was likely to be.

'Please do not leave the house without a manservant— one that Lady Caroline has chosen personally. I do not wish to curtail your movements, but you must know that your safety is our prime concern. Quite apart from the fact that we have all grown to love you dearly, you must not forget that we have undertaken to deliver you to your grandfather undamaged!'

Harriet nodded glumly, unable to dismiss from her mind the irritating thought that had she obeyed Sandford's identical request she would not have found herself in this unenviable position.

Chapter Nine

Young Rothman waited outside Meggy Watts's cottage, immensely proud that he had been chosen to accompany Miss Harriet on the visit. Being only third footman in the Beldale hierarchy, he knew that this was a singular gesture on his employer's part and due entirely to the fact of his being the butler's son.

The elder Rothman had served the Hurst family since his youth and had worked his way up from under-footman to the full prestigious office of butler. He had married one of the ladies' maids and produced three sons, the older two of whom had secured positions in other large houses elsewhere. The strapping young Davy had elected to remain at Beldale, thus gaining the benefit of his father's expert tuition.

He was aware that there was some sort of mystery surrounding Miss Harriet and had heard that she had somehow got herself lost in the copse the other day. Since then he had been appointed to attend her on all of her outings from Beldale, including those from which he derived the greatest pleasure, riding behind her just like a groom! The stable lads had been properly miffed at that, he thought cheerfully, but then her ladyship had wanted someone who could be presentable in both occupations and stable lads just weren't cut out to be footmen.

He peered through the small window, satisfying himself that his charge had not been spirited away, and seated himself once more on the bench outside the cottage, casually wondering as to the purpose of Miss Harriet's visit to the villager's cottage.

Harriet herself was seated on the best chair in the little used parlour, Meggy having dashed around in a flurry after the young lady had requested a few words with her father, flinging open curtains and removing dust-covers from her few precious pieces. The cottager had dismissed Harriet's request to remain in the kitchen, seldom having had such an opportunity to hold court in her own little palace. She had brought her unexpected visitor tea in a china cup and now sat gazing fondly at the sight of Harriet in deep conversation with her father.

Harriet had brought old Potter a gift. In the form of a small, opening booklet, such as was used for needles and pins, it held within its covers the withered rose petal she had rescued from the ruin of his old home. Protected from further ravages by the transparent veil of fine gauze she had stitched over it, the relic was bordered by intricate stitchery that proclaimed the legend 'Joshua and Millicent, 10th August 1769'. On the front cover, depicted in delicate watercolours, was as faithful a representation of number 7, Bottom Meadow Cottages, as Harriet had been able to conjure up from her visits to the site and her further consultations with Rose, the old man's granddaughter.

Josh held the little case reverently in the palms of his calloused and blistered hands and stared down at it with tears in his rheumy old eyes.

'How did 'ee find it, lass?' he whispered, with a catch in his throat. 'I never thought to see it again. I went up there the once but her…' he jerked his head towards his daughter '…her wouldn't let me back.'

Meggy Watts came and stood by her father and lovingly stroked his shaggy head.

'It were dangerous up there, Dad,' she said. 'The roof timbers is falling all along the row and some of them kitchen flagstones have dropped right down into the cellars. You've had one very lucky escape—we don't want no more such accidents, now do we?'

She was studying Harriet's workmanship with admiration.

'It's such a true likeness. But how did you know all this, Miss Cordell?'

'Reverend Taylor furnished me with the details of your parents' wedding day from his parish records,' said Harriet, enormously gratified that her efforts had been awarded such a reception. 'And your own daughter Rose corrected some errors I had made in the painting.'

Turning to Joshua, she laid her hand on his arm. 'I know what it's like to lose treasured possessions, Mr Potter,' she told him. 'My family travelled across Spain in the war years and we had to leave our chattels behind on many occasions—and other times they were destroyed almost in front of our eyes. Your sweetest memories—the ones you keep inside your heart—will never die, I am certain, but sometimes a more tangible memento is needed and I hope that this little token might, in some small way, help you to recover from your dreadful loss.'

'You couldn't have brought me anything in the world that would have pleased me more, miss,' said Josh, slipping the little case into the breast pocket of his shabby old jacket and patting it gently. 'It'll be like having my own dear Milly with me again and I can take it out and look at it whenever I choose! 'Twere part of her bridal nosegay, you see.'

His faded blue eyes twinkled at Harriet from under his

bushy brows and he patted the hand that was still holding his own.

'You'm going to make a fine countess when your time comes, miss,' he said, nodding his head at her. 'We should've known that when his lordship finally made his choice his lady would be worth the wait—and, begging your pardon, miss, we all think he's struck gold!'

'Dad! Really!' Meggy was shocked. 'Excuse him, Miss Cordell—he goes too far, sometimes. Honestly, Dad—what will the lady think of us all!'

Shaking her head, Harriet rose to her feet.

'It's to be hoped that a good many years pass before that day dawns, sir,' she said, picking up her reticule. 'And if I could grow to be only half as good as Lady Caroline I should think myself perfect!'

Meggy showed her to the door and Davy Rothman sprang to attention at their appearance, fingering the neck of his smart, new livery nervously.

'Well, hello, Davy,' Meggy greeted him cheerfully. 'My, aren't you the swell, these days?'

Davy inclined his head gravely towards her, feeling slightly awkward at having to address Rose's mother in such a formal way but, at the same time, anxious to impress Miss Harriet with his impeccable manners.

Meggy, too, knew her place and expected no more from him. She bobbed respectfully to Harriet and, on behalf of her father, thanked her once again for her generosity and time.

Walking through the village, with Davy the requisite two steps behind her, Harriet found, to her great discomfort, that she was having to acknowledge bobs and curtsies from all sides as she passed. This entire charade is getting completely out of hand, she thought crossly, but managed to smile as yet another tradesman tipped his hat to her. All of these good people actually thought that she would, one day, be their 'Lady of the Manor' and it was all terribly embarrassing and, she had to admit, inexplicably quite painful to her.

She had spent most of the past week in her room, pleading exhaustion, and the countess, sympathetic as to her real reasons, had not pressed for Harriet's attendance at the dining table and had generously arranged for her to take her meals in her room. Harriet had forced herself to venture out on two previous occasions, in the furtherance of her project, both times escorted by the stalwart Davy, and was deeply conscious of the interest her appearance always aroused. She admitted, but only to herself, that she was now quite afraid that there might be another attempt to harm her in some way and the greatest fear of all was that she had no way of knowing who her enemy could be.

She had not spoken to Sandford at all since the episode in the copse and had seen him only once when, about to come out of her room later that same day, she had caught sight of him leaving his father's chambers. She had stepped swiftly back into the shadows as he appeared and she was certain he had not observed her, but she had been shocked at his demeanour. He had stood for a moment outside the earl's door, shoulders sagging, his face white and drawn and then, as if in a trance, he had walked slowly to his own doorway and entered his room. Harriet had been intending to visit Lord William herself but, after some deliberation, she had decided that it would be unwise to do so and had subsequently returned to her own chamber.

Judith Hurst had ridden over to Beldale that same afternoon, but Lady Caroline had managed to curb her daughter-in-law's curiosity. Westpark House had been Sandford's first objective when Harriet had failed to return to Beldale and Judith had naturally been frantically worried over her friend's disappearance and had demanded to be kept informed as to any developments, sending Ridgeway to assist his cousin in the search.

She failed to comprehend how anyone as level-headed as Harriet could have wandered off the bridleway and become confused in the copse, until the countess explained that Harriet had felt unwell, possibly suffering from a touch of the sun. It had been particularly warm that morning, as she was sure Judith would recall.

Judith did indeed recall that it was she who had been responsible for Harriet's hasty departure and, at once, felt guilty at having persuaded her friend to stay so long at Westpark, surmising that Harriet's headlong dash had been the cause of her fainting fit.

Lady Butler's contribution upon receiving her daughter's account of Harriet's misadventure was to the effect that 'persons who disport themselves all over the Continent with troops of soldiers could hardly be expected to behave with anything resembling acceptable decorum when they returned to civilised society' and Judith found herself heaving a sigh of relief that Sandford was not present when these uncharitable remarks were uttered.

Both Sandford and Ridgeway had been behaving very oddly since Harriet's mishap, she thought. Neither one of them seemed to have time for anything other than estate business and they were usually to be found with their heads together. When Sandford had, almost grudgingly it seemed, eventually found time to give his little nephew some attention in the paddock, he had appeared distracted and disinclined to linger. Judith found Ridgeway's behaviour strange, too. She had thought that he was beginning to let down his guard a little in her favour, for they had exchanged some very promising conversations since their dance together. Then all of a sudden, his interest in her seemed to have vanished overnight and he had no time for anything apart from riding around the park and hanging about in the stables or disappearing off to Beldale with Sandford.

At the end of the week an impatient Judith paid her second visit to Beldale. She had heard that Harriet was apparently well enough to go walking to the village and was hurt that her young friend had not come to visit her. Leaving her horse with her attendant groom, she deliberately forsook her normal practice and entered the house from the rear. In doing so, she almost collided with Harriet as she was crossing the hall. Both girls started back in surprise but it was Harriet who was the first to lower her eyes. Judith quickly noticed this puzzling reticence and impulsively put out her hand.

'Harriet, my dear,' she said, in rising concern. 'Please tell me what is wrong. I know that something dreadful must have happened to upset you so. Won't you confide in me? I thought we were friends!'

Harriet was sick at heart. She wanted to tell Judith the whole story from the beginning but, by now, the tale had become so convoluted that she felt that it would sound quite absurd. In fact, she suddenly decided, it really was absurd and she reached forward and grasped Judith's extended hands in her own.

'Oh, Judith,' she cried. 'I'm so pleased to see you. You can't think how much I have missed you.'

Judith at once put her arms around the younger girl and hugged her. As she did so she spotted Sandford in the act of opening the door of the nearby estate office. To her amazement, he took one look at her and quickly closed the door again.

'What is going on here?' she said, thrusting Harriet away from her and, still holding her shoulders, gave her friend a firm shake. 'Have you fallen out with Sandford? Is that what this is all about?'

The office door re-opened immediately and Sandford stepped out, eyes averted, with a set of papers in his hand.

'Ah, hello, Judith,' he said, in a poor attempt at heartiness.

Judith registered both the tremor in his voice and the sight of Harriet's flushed face at the same time. She took a deep breath.

'Robert,' she said resolutely, 'you look awful. And Harriet looks awful, too. I can only conclude that the reason for such joint awfulness is that you have had a lover's tiff— and I simply will not have it!' And she stamped her elegant foot. 'Mark carefully what I am doing, Robert!'

'Not now, Judith!' Sandford walked towards his sister-in-law with a warning frown, but Judith put up her crop and prodded it into his chest.

'You don't frighten me, Robert Hurst!' she said defiantly. 'I'm the one who tipped a bottle of ink over your head— remember?'

'I remember, Judith,' said Sandford drily, pushing aside the crop, 'but this is not a bottle-of-ink sort of problem.'

Harriet found her lips curving into an involuntary smile.

'What sort of a problem is a bottle-of-ink problem?' she asked, with an interested glimmer in her eye.

Sandford, with a swift intake of breath, took a step towards her, but Judith moved quickly to stand in front of the girl.

'Leave my friend alone, Robert Hurst!'

Sandford lips twitched and he said, 'But you don't have a bottle of ink, dearest Judith—stand aside!'

'Will someone please tell me what ink has to do with all of this?' Harriet asked, now looking from one to the other in amused exasperation.

Judith gave her friend a quick, appraising glance.

'Harriet,' she said sweetly. 'Would you be so kind as to

go into the office and fetch me a bottle of ink? A large one, if you please!'

'Judith!' warned Sandford, but his eyes were now alight with laughter. He backed sideways towards the office door as Harriet, not sure of the point but perfectly willing to give her friend whatever assistance she required, moved swiftly in the same direction.

They collided in the doorway and Sandford, automatically thrusting out his hands to prevent Harriet from stumbling, found himself with his arms around her and it seemed to him, in that second, that the earth rocked.

Harriet had put up her own hands to save herself and now found herself pressed against him with her hands on his chest. An extraordinary sensation was sweeping through her body and she was acutely aware of Sandford's laboured breathing. If I look up I am lost, she thought weakly and forced herself to maintain a steadfast interest in his waist-coat buttons.

'Well, then?' came Judith's voice. 'Surely this is where you kiss and make up?'

Harriet and Sandford sprang apart instantly. Harriet felt herself blushing to the tips of her toes, but did not fail to register that the viscount had refused to relinquish his hold on her hand and she herself, it seemed, had neither the strength nor desire to pull away.

'Pretty dismal exhibition, I'd say,' said Judith, with a wide smile. 'I've still a good mind to...' and her eyes swept around the office as though in search of something.

Sandford, still holding Harriet's hand tightly, leaned over the desk and kissed his sister-in-law on the cheek.

'Pax, Judith,' he said quietly. 'No need now, I promise. You win.'

'No, Robert, this time you win,' said Judith firmly, beaming at Harriet, and Sandford smilingly nodded his agreement.

'I wish someone would tell me what the joke is,' came Harriet's plaintive voice. 'It's like being in some foreign country where one doesn't understand the language.'

'Well, it used to be a private joke, sweetheart,' said Sandford, reaching out for her other hand and smiling into her eyes. 'But we shall tell you!'

Sweetheart! Harriet couldn't believe her ears. Sandford had called her *sweetheart*! Now what game was he playing at? She had to force herself to concentrate very carefully on his next words.

'Well now,' he began grandly, ducking away from Judith's hand, 'there was once a very spoilt little girl who had no playmates—*ouch! That hurt!*—for she always wanted—and usually got—her own way so no one would play with her. Her father—who was a very wise man...' At this point Judith nodded her head vigorously and Sandford, his grin widening, continued '—arranged for his unpopular little daughter to take her lessons with two charmingly behaved—*pax! I said Pax!*—fairly well-behaved young gentlemen. Well, the sweet child tried her tricks out with these lads and discovered that they were totally immune to her foot-stamping and tears until, one memorable day, she threatened the older boy with a bottle of ink...'

'Why?' asked Harriet, at last beginning to comprehend. 'What had you—he refused to do?'

'He had refused to get off his brother's head!' broke in Judith, laughing. 'The two of them were scrapping—as usual—if I may say so—and Mr Penrose—our tutor—had left the room. Our instructions were to fill in some cities in our map-books and I had persuaded...'

'Huh! Persuaded!' Sandford chimed in. 'Philip, who for some queer reason, was becoming increasingly besotted with this creature, had been doing her geography for weeks—she apparently being unable to distinguish north from south—and probably still can't for all I know—*missed!* Anyway, he was patiently filling in her book as well as his own and I accidentally flicked ink over hers. Philip jumped me, I sat on his head and, well—the rest is history!'

'Judith poured ink over your head?' breathed Harriet in awe, unable to believe that her elegant, well-behaved friend could ever have acted in such a totally undisciplined manner.

'Absolutely! Down my collar—over my hair, face, eyes—whole bottle—the lot!'

'What did your tutor do?'

'Thrashed us both—Phil and me,' Sandford answered dismissively, appearing to be deeply interested in counting her fingers.

'But what about Judith?' frowned Harriet, vainly attempting to extract her hands from his grasp.

'That's the point, you see,' said Judith gently. 'Both boys took the blame and said that I had been working the whole time—I was actually given a box of sugar plums—but I couldn't eat them. I was so ashamed! I never had another such tantrum as long as I lived.'

'Well, hardly ever,' put in Sandford. 'Jolly good sugar plums, too, as I recall.'

'You gave them to the boys?' Harriet smiled at Judith, who looked back at her fondly and nodded.

'And you wouldn't actually have poured ink on Sandford today, would you?'

Judith and the viscount looked at each other and both burst out laughing.

'Well, the thing is, darling girl,' said Sandford, raising Harriet's unresisting fingers to his lips, 'neither of us really knows that, for sure!'

He was watching her closely, desperately trying to gauge her reaction. She, for her part, found that she was unable to meet his eyes, afraid of what she might see. Surely he was still play-acting? At that thought a tiny ache crept into her heart and she knew that she was close to tears.

At that moment Judith bent to retrieve the papers that had fallen from her brother-in-law's hands during the scuffle, frowning as she happened to catch sight of her butler's name on one of the sheets.

'What are these lists, Robert?' she inquired, beginning to peruse them more carefully.

Sandford dropped Harriet's hands and leapt to his feet in consternation, plucking the papers from Judith's hands and thrusting them into a drawer.

'Really, Judith,' he chided, raising an eyebrow. 'Reading other people's private correspondence. What would your mother say!'

Judith flushed.

'Don't be a beast, Robert,' she said. 'That was a list of Westpark staff, as well you know. That is my business, surely?'

The viscount shrugged his shoulders carelessly.

'It's just something that Charles and I are working on,' he said, searching desperately for a brainwave. 'Er—fact is, we're trying to cut back a bit!'

'Cut back!' Judith was astounded, then her eyes grew anxious. 'We're not in any trouble, are we, Robert? I thought Charles had been managing rather well…'

'Nothing for you to worry about,' said Sandford, mentally crossing himself. 'We thought we might try to cut out some duplication, that's all—too many people doing the same job, it seems to me.'

'But you can't be thinking of putting people off?'

'No, no—just moving some of 'em around, perhaps. It's not a problem, honestly, Judith. Please forget about it.'

Only partly convinced, Judith dropped the subject and set about extracting a promise from Sandford to bring Harriet to Westpark for dinner the following evening. Having got the nod from that bemused young lady, the viscount agreed and Judith, kissing each of them in turn, forbade them to quarrel and left the room to seek out her mother-in-law.

Harriet turned at once to follow, but Sandford put out his hand to detain her.

'And where are you off to in such a hurry?' he demanded softly, the dangerous gleam once more in his eyes.

Harriet looked at him gravely.

'You don't have to keep up the pretence any longer, my lord,' she said calmly. 'Judith cannot hear you. But I must commend you on your excellent performance.'

'What the—what absurd fancy has got into your head now?' he groaned, clutching his brow.

'Thanks to your clever subterfuge, my lord,' said Harriet, ignoring Sandford's incredulous expression, 'Judith has returned home in a happier frame of mind than that with which she arrived. Your part was so well enacted that it prevented her from asking any awkward questions about my—mishap—and for that I am deeply grateful, for I find that I cannot lie to her any longer—whatever your opinion of my talents in that direction!' Her voice trembled at this point and she looked away.

Sandford sat on the edge of the desk, carefully contemplating Harriet's averted gaze. Tentatively, he reached out and, taking both her hands in his own, he drew her gently towards him, holding his breath as he felt her initial resistance slip away.

'Look at me, Harriet,' he pleaded.

In trepidation, Harriet obeyed and, raising her eyes to

meet his, was confused to behold, not the confident gleam of amusement she had expected, but a very shamefaced expression.

'I don't know where to start,' he said, his voice low and hesitant. 'You said you hated me—I don't blame you—I hate myself. Please don't punish me any further!'

'You called me a witch!' she said tremulously.

'Oh, but you are a witch!' Half-smiling, he lifted one hand and traced his fingers down her cheek. 'You have bewitched me.'

Harriet dashed his hand away in vexation. 'You didn't believe me,' she cried. 'Twice—no, three times—you didn't believe me!'

'I am a contemptible swine,' he said, his throat tightening at the memory.

'You accused me of—of—dreadful things!' Harriet found that she couldn't bear the look of anguish in his eyes.

'I know I deserve to be horsewhipped,' he choked, his confidence on the verge of destruction.

'Horses shouldn't be whipped,' she whispered, her lips trembling.

'But I should?' A flicker of hope had crept into his voice.

'I didn't say that, my lord.'

'Robert,' he said fiercely.

Startled, she tried to move away from him, but he still held one hand tightly in his grasp and seemed intent upon recapturing the other.

'Lord Sandford,' she protested, weakly, 'please release me. This is most improper!'

'Call me Robert,' he cajoled her, the fire back in his eyes. 'Then maybe I shall let you go.'

'Maybe! That's very poor odds!' Harriet replied spiritedly.

He put his head on one side as though considering this

point, then nodded. 'True. Call me Robert and I promise not to kiss you. How's that?'

Scandalised, Harriet struggled to free herself. 'You wouldn't dare—you told me that you were no ravisher!'

'There's a first time for everything,' he said coolly. 'Call me Robert.'

Harriet stopped struggling and regarded him balefully. 'Well, if it means so much to you—*Robert*,' she said, through clenched teeth. 'Now let me go.'

'Say it again—nicely!'

'Oh, Robert! Robert! *Robert!* Damn you!' she exclaimed, without thought for the consequences.

'Harriet, my love, you are truly magnificent!' Sandford stood up, swept her towards him and wrapped his arms around her, ignoring her squeal of dismay.

'Stop struggling—otherwise I shall forget myself—that's better. Now, listen to me, Harriet—please.'

For a moment he stood very quietly, simply holding her against him and, as her eyes crept up to his face, she could see that he had become very serious once more. She didn't move, somehow content to remain within the circle of his arms, listening to the rapid beating of his heart. At last he spoke.

'I know that nothing I can say will undo the hurt that I've caused you...' He hesitated, choosing his words with meticulous care. 'And it is probably of very little interest to you to know that, far from play-acting, I truly believe that I love you.' She quivered and his arms tightened. 'Yes, I do. I had begun to hope that you might learn to hold me in similar regard—I admit that I was mad with jealousy and so desperately afraid, my darling, I think I was about to lose my reason. I was ready to commit murder—I know that now. You brought me to my senses when you struck me and I knew instantly that I had been wrong—that the whole thing was clearly a well-executed plot...'

He stopped as Harriet pulled away from him.

'Why were you so ready to think the worst of me?' she cried. 'You refused even to listen to me!'

Sandford grimaced, finding the memory of that episode of his behaviour particularly repugnant.

'I had found certain items in a clearing near the gate,' he said, clearing his throat.

'What items?' Harriet demanded. 'And how did they concern me?'

Sandford flushed and shamefacedly fingered his cravat, as though it were suddenly too tight.

'Your hat and a glove—I recognised them both, of course...'

'And?' said Harriet stiffly, aware that something worse was to follow.

'A gentleman's pocket flask—it had contained brandy,' choked the viscount, unwilling to meet her shocked gaze. 'And a crumpled cravat.'

'Also a gentleman's, I take it?' Harriet's eyes glittered.

Sandford nodded in dumb resignation.

'All the signs of a sordid tête-à-tête, in fact?' Harriet inquired in a deceptively sweet voice. 'No wonder you didn't want to listen to me!'

'You had the smell of brandy on your breath!' exclaimed Sandford hotly, in his own defence.

'So that's what that funny taste was,' mused Harriet. 'They must have given it to me after I passed out.'

Chagrined, Sandford reached out for her once more, but she neatly sidestepped him and opened the office door. Swiftly he strode towards it, attempting to block her exit, but she was out into the hallway in a trice.

'No doubt your parents—who have proved themselves

my true friends—have by now provided you with the correct version of that morning's events,' she said in a low voice, not wishing to attract March's attention. 'And your only excuse for your appalling behaviour is to tell me that you think you love me—well, we obviously have a very different understanding of the meaning of the word ''love'', my lord. The man to whom I give my heart will *never* doubt my word, *never* assume my guilt—even if confronted with the *blackest* of evidence—but, most of all, he will be prepared to lay down his life to protect my name and my person and—' here her voice broke '—I shall do likewise for him. You, my lord, are not and will never be that man!'

She turned to leave, but Sandford caught her arm. His face was rigid, his eyes unfathomable.

'I wish you well in your search for this paragon,' he grated, 'although such a pattern of perfection is unlikely to choose you as his mate...' He stopped, aghast. My God, what am I saying, he thought, horrified at his own words. He let go of Harriet's arm and bowed stiffly. 'My apologies, ma'am,' he said and re-entered the office, closing the door behind him.

For a moment Harriet stood frozen with shock. His damning words, which continued to echo in her ears, had shaken her to the core, for she was obliged to acknowledge that he was right. In spite of her high-flown speech, she was painfully aware that it had been mostly her own impetuous and foolhardy behaviour that had brought her to this stand. From the time she had left her home in Lincolnshire, right up to this very moment, she had insisted upon going her own headstrong way, ignoring advice from all sides, interfering in other people's lives—people she hardly knew, she realised, her face suddenly scarlet at some of the memories—and presumptuously assuming that she knew what was best for everyone. No gentleman on earth could be expected to regard such conduct with anything but the deepest abhorrence. What might be considered charming in a wayward child was not acceptable in a full-grown female. Would she never learn? she pondered in despair. Time and time again she had disregarded the warnings and now, it seemed, she had reaped the whirlwind and those rash and arrogant words she had so haughtily vaunted would surely return to torment her.

Hot tears welled up into her eyes as she made her way to the foot of the staircase and the sudden blurring of her vision caused her to stumble on the first step. She was aware of a firm hand on her elbow and an anxious March at her side.

'Miss Harriet?' His voice was gentle. 'Are you unwell? Shall I call Rose? Come and sit down for a moment until you recover.'

He led her to a nearby chair and stood uncertainly by, not wishing to exceed his duties but angry that something or someone had upset his little favourite. Ever since that first evening when she had tiptoed nervously down the stairs in her borrowed finery he had felt that she was something special. Always a smile and a kind word for the servants, quick with her thanks for their services and he, for one, had never heard a single complaint pass her lips. He had watched her change from that laughing-eyed, bright-haired angel into a silent shadow of her former self, all in the space of three weeks. One hardly ever heard her spontaneous and infectious laugh these days, he thought morosely, and if that's what being engaged does for a girl he was damned if he was going to offer for Maudie Hiller. He watched closely, wearing his usual impassive expression, as Harriet composed herself, dabbing at her eyes with the ridiculous piece of lace the ladies called a handkerchief, longing to offer her his own pristine equivalent but knowing that it would be quite overstepping the mark to do so.

'Thank you, March,' said Harriet tremulously, rising to her feet. 'I fear I must be coming down with a cold. I will go up to my room now—if you would be so good as to send Rose to me?'

'At once, Miss Harriet,' said the loyal footman. 'And perhaps a glass of wine—a well-known restorative, so I'm told?'

'Thank you, I would be glad of that.' Harriet nodded, avoiding his eyes.

He watched her walk unsteadily up the stairs and had the most disrespectful urge to 'pop' his lordship 'one on the beak'. Blinking, he moved smartly to the green baize door that led to the lower stairs and delivered his instructions to Rose.

Sandford, meanwhile, had been staring blindly at the sheets of paper in front of him on the desk, unable to believe that he had uttered those unforgivable words.

Any minute now I shall wake up, he thought, praying that he must be in the throes of some dreadful nightmare but, raising his eyes to the window and perceiving the peaceful summer scene beyond, he knew beyond doubt that the whole episode had been only too real.

With a shaking hand he reached for the decanter on the side table and cursed when he saw that it was empty. Damned servants! What did they think they were employed for? He tugged angrily at the bell-rope and waited impatiently for March to appear. Pointing curtly towards the tray, he raised his brows imperiously.

March bowed his head in acquiescence. The fact that the room had been occupied for some considerable time, preventing the carrying out of certain domestic tasks, was no excuse for such laxity, as well he knew and offered no plea in his own defence. He picked up the salver and walked swiftly to the door.

'Your lordship's pardon,' he said, exiting at the double. 'I shall attend to it at once.'

Sandford eyed the closed door sourly. The whole damned house seemed to be going mad, he thought, quite certain he had sensed hostility in young March's demeanour. It's her fault, he concluded savagely, sweeping the papers to one side. She has everybody under her spell, from the lowest boot-boy right up to...

'Me, confound it!' he shouted, leaping from his chair. 'But I won't have it! I shall leave! I shall go back to London—Paris—anywhere! Put it down, man, and, for God's sake, get out!'

This last was to March, who had returned with the full decanters. The footman stared at the viscount in open-mouthed astonishment, unable to believe his eyes and ears. Never before had he been spoken to in this manner, not in this house! He carefully set the silver tray down into its appointed place and bowing, with ill-disguised contempt, he left the room once more.

Sandford was astounded. The man was nothing short of insolent, he decided. He'd have him out of here before he could say...! Suddenly, he checked, took a deep breath and gripped the edge of the desk to steady himself, grimacing with shame at this inconceivable lapse. Collapsing limply into his chair, he buried his head in his hands and shuddered in despair.

'Oh, God, Harriet! Forgive me!' he whispered brokenly. 'What am I going to do? The whole world is falling apart and I'm powerless to prevent it!'

He remained, for some time, slumped at the desk until

the sound of the hall clock chiming the hour infiltrated his brain. Straightening up, his eyes fell on the papers he had been attempting to examine earlier. With very little enthusiasm he pulled them towards him and began to peruse the top sheet.

Chapter Ten

Charles Ridgeway sat pensively on his horse, surveying the landscape below him. To the far right he could just make out the chimneys and parapets of the Beldale mansion, bathed in the late evening sunshine and protected by the mass of woodland and fields that surrounded it. At the foot of the hill up which he had just ridden, on the very edge of the Beldale estate, nestled his own home, the Dower House, with its neat gardens and home farm. To his left lay the more modern structure of Westpark House, close to its own boundary with the larger estate and, still further left, the slate rooftop of Staines, the old Butler property, with only the terraced gardens remaining within its demesne. Beyond the distant village and as far as the eye could see, all Hurst owned, in one way or another. A man without property is surely an insignificant creature, he concluded, once more ruefully censuring his late and far from lamented sire for his weak and prodigal lifestyle. Then, not being a vindictive man, Ridgeway sighed and bent his mind to the more pressing problem that was troubling him as he turned his mount towards Beldale.

It is like looking for a needle in a haystack, he thought. Over a hundred men on the list and more than half of them could be described as 'tall, thin and dark'! Putting faces to the names had taken them all week, Sandford having refused to allow anyone, apart from his man Tiptree, to assist in the covert search. In addition, he had demanded that no one was actually questioned, pointing out that this would immediately put any villains on their guard, reminding his cousin that neither Billy Tatler nor his chum Nick had recognised the man at the boathouse and, therefore, this particular check was being carried out only for the purpose of eliminating the obviously innocent. Their objective, he had said, was to whittle down the total number to just a few men whom he could present to the young lads in the hope that they would be able to identify their tormentor.

'We're looking for a recent arrival or someone who doesn't go about in the village much,' he now said to Ridgeway, having arranged to meet his cousin in the paddock between the two estates, where he knew that their conversation would not be overheard.

'Or a casual worker, who has come and gone,' offered Ridgeway, exasperated that his hands had been so tied. 'Or a passing tinker, tramp—oh, lord, Sandford—any number of itinerants come through the village!'

'He won't be an itinerant,' returned Sandford firmly. 'Billy told you he thought he was from the Big House— that indicates his manner of dress and, probably, speech as well. He would have said, if he had thought him to be a vagrant. No, Charles, I'm convinced that this ''cove'' has to have some sort of status or position within one of the households.'

'Well, I hope to God you're wrong in that! And why should anyone have developed such animosity towards Miss Cordell in so short a time?' asked his cousin. 'As far as I can judge, from my discreet conversations around the village…' He caught Sandford's frowning expression '—very discreet, I promise you, old man—she is well liked, one could say almost revered in certain places. I, for one, can't imagine anyone taking her in dislike. She appears to have no faults, as I'm sure you agree.'

Sandford had turned away, a painful lump in his throat, the memory of the previous day's events still haunting him. 'She can be rather impetuous at times,' he said, struggling to keep his voice level.

Charles regarded him curiously. 'But that is her chief virtue, wouldn't you say, neck-or-nothing—that's your lady, Sandford. No half-measures about her. They're all saying she'll make you a grand viscountess, man, she has a rare understanding of people's feelings—not just their needs, as most of us have. You're damned lucky that she chose you—I wish that I were as fortunate!'

He turned his horse's head towards the Dower House and raised his brows questioningly. 'Coming over for a spot of grub? I'm famished, I can tell you—and Tiptree here is feeling mighty peckish, too, I'll be bound. We've been at it since the early hours without a break—although I dare say you'll be wanting to get back to your sweetheart?'

Sandford, wincing at Ridgeway's unintended irony, accepted his cousin's invitation with alacrity. Having encountered Harriet entering the breakfast room just as he was about to depart, he had stiffly reminded her of their joint promise to attend Westpark that evening and, until the appointed hour, he intended to stay well clear of her frosty gaze. She had informed him that she would, of course, be ready at whatever time suited him and had stonily agreed to his request that they should endeavour to keep up their charade for what would probably be only a few days more, until her grandfather arrived.

While the viscount was doing his utmost to flush out her assailants, Harriet was engaged in a verbal tussle with Lord

William. She had spent part of the morning trying to calculate the extent of her financial indebtedness to the Hursts and had made the mistake of mentioning this matter to his lordship.

'Little girls shouldn't worry their pretty little heads about such things,' he said soothingly. 'I am happy to stand your banker.'

'Yes, but…' Harriet was not at all satisfied at this arrangement.

The earl wagged his finger at her. 'I refuse to discuss the matter with you, Harriet. It concerns only your grandfather and myself—at least, for the moment,' he finished, somewhat enigmatically.

Harriet, loath to cause him any distress, changed the subject. Aware that Lady Caroline, Chegwin, and even Sir Basil himself, had attributed much of the earl's speedy recovery to her earlier cheerful visits and, apart from that single lapse into tears which had occurred after the incident in the woods, she had endeavoured to behave in the usual sparkling and light-hearted manner he had come to expect of her. Lately, however, she was finding it a great effort to keep up the merry repartee that so delighted him and, although she was always quickly diverted by Beldale's own wicked sense of humour, she had occasionally experienced the odd sensation that his lordship was working equally hard to keep up her spirits.

'We are to dine at Westpark this evening,' she now told him. 'No doubt I shall have a fund of "Butlapses" to bring you tomorrow.'

'Butlapses' was an expression the earl had coined early in his acquaintance with Judith's mother and he had often used it during his conversations with Harriet after he had discovered that they shared the same sense of the ridiculous.

'I vow she seems to get worse as she gets older,' he chortled. 'Even as a young woman she was prone to making unfortunate remarks but, having apparently devoted her life to perfecting the art, now that she is practically in her dotage she seems to think that age gives her the unassailable right to be downright rude. A good many of us old ones suffer from that same delusion, of course,' he added, with a twinkle in his eye.

'Oh, not you, sir,' protested Harriet. 'I am certain that I have never heard you utter a truly vindictive remark and dear Lady Caroline sees only the good in everyone, so she is also exempt from your reckoning. I believe…' She stopped and her cheeks coloured.

Beldale, who had been contemplating his move on the chessboard between them, looked up at her hesitation.

'What is it that you believe, my dear?' he asked, his eyes suddenly alert as Harriet dropped her own in confusion at his scrutiny.

'I fear I seem to be growing too opinionated, my lord,' she stammered. 'And, unlike—certain of our acquaintances, I cannot plead the excuse of maturity.'

The earl looked at her in blank astonishment.

'Harriet, my love,' he said sorrowfully. 'You are in deadly danger of becoming ''one of them''.'

'One of whom, my lord?' asked Harried, puzzled.

'One of the great English sisterhood of niminy-piminy milksops,' said the earl, banging down his knight with such force that the rest of the pieces bounced off their squares.

'Oh, dear,' said Harriet, putting her hand to her mouth as her lips twitched involuntarily.

'Oh, dear, indeed,' said his lordship reproachfully. 'See how badly your ''best behaviour'' affects my play!'

Harriet burst out laughing and bent to retrieve the fallen

chessmen. 'I believe you did that on purpose, sir,' she chuckled. 'I was near to victory, you must concede.'

Beldale regarded her fondly. 'Worth a dozen defeats to see you laugh again,' he said warmly. 'And now I demand to know who has been filling your head with this nonsense!'

Harriet was silent for a moment then, turning to look him squarely in the eye, she said, 'I'm afraid that Sandford and I have "come to cuffs" yet again, sir. He disapproves of my behaviour and—and—well, he has given me to understand that others might find it equally unacceptable. I was merely trying to m-modify...'

She caught his expression and broke into a grin. 'Well, if you will make me laugh, how can I possibly hope to improve?'

'Improve at your peril, my girl!' exclaimed his lordship, horrified at the prospect. 'If that young fool can't recognise a diamond when he has one in his hand, then he must resign himself to wearing paste! And I shall tell him so myself!'

'Please don't,' interrupted Harriet hurriedly. 'He would dislike above all things to know that I had been discussing him with you—and you must allow that he has had a great deal to contend with of late. I really do intend to try to conduct myself in the most dignified manner when I am with him but—I promise to save my worst behaviour for your lordship!'

'Excellent!' answered Beldale, with a delighted smile, 'Although I am bound to point out that the contemplation of your most dignified manner is enough to send one into the wildest hysterics!'

Ruefully, Harriet had to agree, although privately vowing that she would still endeavour to be on her very best behaviour that evening.

She dressed with care, choosing a pale turquoise crepe gown in the Grecian mode, with its gently draped bodice gathered under the bosom and its skirt flowing softly to her ankles. She elected to wear no jewellery, other than the obligatory ring, not wishing to be reminded of that other eventful occasion, and Rose, still bemoaning the absence of suitable adornment, brushed her mistress's bright locks into their new style and wove a silver ribbon through them. The result was one of simple but charming elegance.

Sandford, too, paid special attention to his toilette, discarding several neckcloths in his efforts to achieve the perfect knot. Kimble stood in silent reproach as, one after another, the snowy silk cravats were hurled aside until, breathing heavily, the viscount pronounced himself satisfied.

Kimble then helped his master into his exquisitely cut tailcoat, adjusting the lapel fronts carefully over the white silk waistcoat and smoothing away an imperceptible crease on the broad shoulders. Grudgingly pleased with the result, the valet stood back and gave a brief nod.

The viscount eyed him sourly for a moment, then emitted a deep chuckle. 'Oh, I've been a terrible trial to you this past week, haven't I, Kimble?' he said, with a sheepish grin. 'Accept my apologies, dear man—and have a tankard on me!'

He proffered a coin, which Kimble accepted with alacrity, although his countenance clearly displayed his affront at his master's suggestion.

'You know that I never frequent the local hostelry, my lord,' he said loftily. 'However, I shall be pleased to share a bottle of wine with Mr Rothman at your lordship's expense.'

He passed Sandford his fobs and signet ring and watched, eagle-eyed, as the viscount pinned a diamond stud into the folds of his cravat. Then he handed him his top hat and evening cloak and, opening the door for his master to leave, he executed his very correct bow.

Sandford, descending the stairs, perceived that Harriet had forestalled him and, to his intense irritation, he saw March step forward, take the cloak from her arm and carefully arrange it about her shoulders. Neither did he miss her smile of grateful thanks to the young footman, who retreated to his appointed place with what Sandford, gritting his teeth, could only describe as a fawning expression.

Great start, he thought wryly, shepherding the impassive Harriet out to the waiting carriage and handing her into her seat. He had been hoping for a more auspicious beginning to the evening, conscious that this could be his last chance to reinstate himself into her good books.

Seating himself opposite her, he leaned forward and smilingly complimented her on her appearance, which admittedly he had caught sight of only briefly before March's swift attentions.

She inclined her head in acknowledgement, but did not meet his eye, seeming to find the passing view of greater interest.

'I trust that you will find some reserves of your usual good humour before we arrive at Westpark,' he said uncomfortably. 'Judith will expect us to have—recovered from our—lover's tiff, or whatever she called it!'

'I can assure you that I am perfectly aware of my part, my lord,' she replied woodenly, clasping her gloved hands together in her lap. 'You will excuse me, however, if I save my performance until we have an audience. You need have no qualms as to the propriety of my behaviour—I shall be everything that is correct, I promise you.'

'Oh, good God, Harriet!' cried Sandford, flinging himself back into his own corner in exasperation. 'How long do you intend to keep this up?'

Unmoved, she regarded him in silence, her green eyes inscrutable. 'Only for a few more days, I hope, my lord,' she said, again without expression. 'My grandfather cannot be far from Beldale now and I hope that I can prevail upon him to remove me to some—other accommodation—until he is ready to return us to his own home.'

Sandford stared in hopeless frustration at her rigid countenance. 'Oh, that will create a fine impression of our hospitality, won't it?' he said sarcastically. 'I'm sure it will please my parents wonderfully!'

Harriet's face flamed resentfully and she glared at him from under her dark lashes.

'Oh, a veritable hit, my lord!' she said scornfully. 'Although it will probably come as a great surprise to you to know that neither Lord William nor Lady Caroline seem to share your low opinion of me...'

'Stow it, Harriet,' he cried hoarsely, his own cheeks flushing, 'you know damned well that I don't have a low opinion of you!'

'It has improved, then, since yesterday, my lord?' she asked witheringly. 'For I seem to remember that you thought me totally beyond the pale only twenty-four hours since!'

'I'm not proud of what I said yesterday,' he exclaimed heatedly. 'I was angry—you know I was angry!'

'It appears to be a particular failing of your lordship's,' she rejoined. 'However, perhaps you could manage to hold yourself in check for the next few hours, as I see we have arrived at our destination. If I could have your hand, my lord?'

Sandford was obliged to stifle the retort that was forming on his lips and, inwardly seething, he sprang out of the carriage to give her his hand.

Judith swept into the hall to welcome them. Harriet was

delighted to observe that her friend seemed to have put off her blacks for good, for she was wearing a most becoming gown of lavender silk. The two girls devoted the next few minutes to comparing styles and laughingly exchanging extravagant compliments with one another.

Sandford, handing their cloaks to the waiting Finchley, quickly registered the return of Harriet's normal lively disposition and, in spite of the earlier setback, was once more determined to take full advantage of any opportunity that might arise.

'Come along into the drawing-room,' smiled Judith. 'Mother and Charles are waiting for us…'

'Charles is dining with us?' asked Sandford, in some surprise.

Judith nodded, a slight blush staining her cheeks. 'The more the merrier, wouldn't you say?' she said, as they entered the room. 'And, since you have lived in each other's pockets all week, I was afraid that you might begin to feel deprived if you were separated for too long!'

'Very amusing!' Sandford said with a grin, striding forward to present his compliments to Lady Butler. 'Evening, ma'am, I trust I find you in good health?'

Her ladyship gave him a pale smile.

'Glad to see that *you*, in any event, are in such good spirits,' she said, fanning herself ostentatiously. 'I myself find this warm weather quite overpowering—I believe your Miss Cordell suffers from a similar weakness—if we are to believe what we hear?'

She looked towards Harriet, who appeared to be involved in some sort of amusing wordplay with Ridgeway. An expression of contempt came into Lady Butler's eyes as she continued, 'I cannot think what possessed Judith to invite her bailiff to eat his dinner with us. Although, I am obliged to point out that it is all of a piece with her conduct since

you brought your—young *lady* back with you to Beldale. A
certain laxity of standards, you might say—I must suppose
that *she* has been filling my daughter's head with some sort
of foreign egalitarian nonsense!'

'Surely Judith has been far too well brought up by your
own good self to be influenced by the word of a mere soldier's girl?' returned Sandford, who was, as usual, intensely
irritated at Lady Butler's appalling rudeness but, at the same
time, fiendishly interested to see how far on to her own cleft
stick he could pinion her. He was gradually beginning to
understand how Philip had handled the old harridan and why
his father found her so amusing.

She glowered at him in silence for a moment or two,
fidgeting with her fan. 'How very like your brother you are,'
she said diffidently. 'That he should perish on his own doorstep in a carriage accident, while you escaped unscathed
after ten years of war in some foreign land, strikes me as
being grossly unfair—but life is so, as I am constantly reminded!'

Sandford, staggered at her outrageous insensitivity, was
momentarily lost for words. 'I'm afraid that I cannot find it
in me to apologise for my survival, ma'am,' he managed
eventually. 'As to unscathed, I can assure you that I have a
fine scar on my leg…' He gently patted his right thigh.

'Really, sir!' she protested. 'I have told you before that I
will not have such unsavoury topics in my house!'

'My brother's house, I believe, madam,' he corrected her
with stiff politeness, 'Or, in any event, Judith's, to hold in
trust for his son!'

As this rejoinder seemed to have the effect of reducing
her ladyship to an affronted silence, he decided that he had
done more than his share of duty insofar as she was concerned, especially as the uneasy pause allowed him to be-

come increasingly conscious of the sounds of merriment that were emanating from the group at the pianoforte.

'May I bring you a drink?' he forced himself to ask Lady Butler, his natural good manners once more to the fore. 'I see Pinter hovering with a tray and our *Cousin* Charles is always so reluctant to push himself forward—unlike myself. Lemonade, perhaps?'

She shook her head ungraciously, unfurling her fan and fluttering it affectedly to and fro across her fleshy cheeks—looking for all the world like some giant puce porpoise floundering on a rock, he thought ungallantly as he made his way across the room.

Harriet and Ridgeway were seated together at the pianoforte, attempting to construct a duet, the former never having had a lesson in her life and the latter unable to recall many of his. That they were managing to produce anything resembling a tune was due partly to Harriet's excellent ear and, mainly, to Judith's hastily mouthed instructions to Ridgeway. Much laughter ensued and Sandford pessimistically predicted that his appearance would be certain to create a damper.

To his astonishment, however, Harriet leapt at once to her feet as he approached and, taking him by the hand, pulled him over to the instrument, begging Ridgeway to relinquish his seat.

'—for I now have a *much* more proficient partner in *Robert*!' she cried gaily, apparently oblivious to the look in his eyes as he sat down beside her. 'Come now, dearest. Show how it is *perfectly* possible for two to devise a tune between them. I shall choose the chords and you must add all the terribly clever trills and runs that you are so good at! We have done this on *many* occasions so I *know* that it is not beyond your capabilities!'

Not quite out of his depth, for he was a competent pianist,

Sandford waited until she struck her first chord, a C major and, thinking swiftly, he tentatively executed a few notes of a popular tune, hoping that the expected G would follow. It came on the beat without hesitation and so, between the two of them, the little ditty was rendered almost perfectly, to the delight of the two spectators, who clapped most heartily at its conclusion.

'Now that you see how it is done,' Harriet said to Judith, 'you and Charles should do far better than we did, for you both have the benefit of a musical education and you, I know, play beautifully.'

So Judith and Ridgeway took their places and their little piece was performed with more zest than skill, due to the laughter that accompanied its execution, but they jubilantly managed to finish at one and the same time, just as Finchley entered to announce that dinner was served.

Judith insisted that, as their number was odd, formalities would be dispensed with and that they must all go directly to the dining-room without further ado; she herself would accompany Lady Butler. Several of the leaves had been removed from the large mahogany table, which enabled the small group to disport themselves within comfortable speaking distance of one another, and still allowed for the prodigious number of side dishes to be positioned within reach.

Judith took the head of the table with the two men seated, one on each side of their hostess, at the top, Lady Butler to Ridgeway's left and Harriet to the viscount's right.

Harriet, true to her word, gave a dedicated impersonation of a loving bride-to-be in addition to keeping up her cheerful bonhomie. She was momentarily disconcerted, at various intervals throughout the splendid meal, to find Lady Butler's disapproving eyes upon her. However, all through the soup, fish, meat and game courses she continued with her amusing repartee, occasioning Judith to upset her wine glass because she was laughing so much, and her friend's mother to tut-tut even more vigorously at everyone's unseemly behaviour! Ridgeway, alternately grinning at Harriet's witticisms and smiling into Judith's shining eyes, was happy simply to be at his goddess's table.

Sandford, on the other hand, was in a perpetual state of nervous tension. One minute he was laughing along with the others and the next finding himself contemplating Lady Butler's rigid disapproval of the merriment at the dinner table. Most of all, however, he was acutely conscious of Harriet's vivacious and captivating nearness, her deliberate and pointed use of his given name and the constant flashing of her smile in his direction. For which dedicated attentions, he reflected gloomily, he would surely be paying dearly before the day ended so he decided he might as well make the most of them and set about entering into her pantomime with gusto.

At last the desserts were brought in. The lively exchanges had continued through a widely ranging number of light-hearted topics, everyone carefully avoiding the more contentious issues of corn prices, royal scandals and the like, any of which could be guaranteed to depress the spirits. The latest novels were touched upon briefly and, when local matters arose, Sandford, catching the flicker of concern in Harriet's eyes, was quick to steer the conversation away from her woodland escapade, in spite of Lady Butler's prurient curiosity in that event. Instead, he regaled them with the story of his own confrontation with Josh Potter when the old man heard that Bottom Meadow cottages were about to be pulled down.

'Such ripe language as he used is not for repetition in mixed company, of course,' he concluded teasingly. 'But I feel sure that, could he but walk the distance, he would do his utmost to disrupt the entire proceedings.'

Ridgeway and Judith joined in his laughter, but Harriet's face became suddenly serious and she stared at them reproachfully.

'Oh, but I can readily sympathise with his feelings!' she exclaimed.

'That much is clear, for the whole village is agog with your kindness to him.' Judith smiled fondly at her friend. 'It was such a—well—a *Harriet* sort of thing to do!'

Harriet blushed and lowered her eyes as the two men grinned at Judith's choice of words. Lady Butler, however, pricked up her ears.

'What kindness was this?' she asked, in saccharine tones. 'Do tell me more.'

'There is really nothing to tell, ma'am,' disclaimed Harriet hurriedly. 'I merely returned one of his damaged possessions to him. He—he was a little effusive in his gratitude, that is all. Please do not laugh. It is a dreadful thing to lose one's home. I, myself, know this only too well!'

In the ensuing silence Sandford, his eyes full of compassion, reached out to clasp her hand and she made no attempt pull away from him.

Her ladyship studied her thoughtfully for a moment then, turning to the viscount, she reverted to the topic of the cottages.

'You intend to replace them or merely to clear the site?' she asked. 'I was under the impression that the new ones in the upper meadow were already a replacement.'

Ridgeway answered for his clearly distracted cousin. 'That was the idea originally, ma'am,' he said. 'But as more of our lads return from the continent, we are finding that accommodation is scarce, especially for youngsters wanting to get wed and set up their own homes. And you know that Beldale likes to take care of his people.'

'I should have thought it would be difficult to justify such an expense at the moment—I hear that Beldale is threatening to cut back as it is!'

She sat back in her chair, satisfied that her words had hit their mark.

Sandford looked ill at ease and, raising accusing eyes to his sister-in-law's, he encountered her shocked and guilty expression.

'I didn't say "cut back", Mama,' she said, in some confusion. 'I merely mentioned that Robert and Charles were devising some sort of consolidation for the estates—at least—' she turned to Sandford '—that is what I inferred from our conversation?'

'That's all it is, Judith,' he returned, with feigned good humour. 'Just one of several ideas we're considering. I told you to forget about it. You must know that we would consult you about anything that might affect Westpark.'

'But, of course!' Lady Butler was at pains to point out. 'Although it is hardly for our bailiff to be making major decisions regarding our property!'

There was an uncomfortable pause as Judith coloured violently and Ridgeway, eyes fixed on the table in front of him, clenched his fists between his knees.

The meal was completed in subdued undertones, Sandford ruefully conscious of all the effort that Harriet had spent in contributing to the evening's earlier success. Looking sideways at her pensive expression, he had a desperate longing to take her in his arms and soothe away her hurts and fears, in spite of her angry declaration that he was 'not that man'.

Finally, when all the covers had been removed and the decanters placed at the gentlemen's elbows, Judith rose to escort the ladies from the room. Lady Butler, with her usual officious manner, deemed it necessary to linger behind to point out some deficiency or other to Finchley and instructed the two men not to linger over their drinks, before following her daughter from the room.

Left to themselves, Sandford and Ridgeway relaxed and the viscount, pouring his cousin a large glass of brandy, grinned sympathetically and said, 'You look as though you need that, old chum! Get it down you and let's talk!'

'I'd drink the whole bottle if I thought it would answer,' said Ridgeway, with a grimace. 'But it didn't serve my father, so its efficacy is clearly in doubt!'

Sandford contemplated him gravely for a moment or two before taking a sip of his own drink. 'What do you hear about this Potter business—with Harriet?' he asked casually. 'I know she picked up a memento when I showed her the cottages—but I'm damned if I can see why it should have set the whole village on its ears!'

Ridgeway looked up in surprise and, seeing that his cousin was clearly ignorant of the whole matter, furnished him with the details with which Lady Eugenie herself had supplied him, she having got them first-hand from Meggy Watts.

'And you say you didn't know any of this, man?' exclaimed Ridgeway, in amazement. 'What do you do? Walk around with your eyes and ears closed?'

'No need to be offensive, old chap,' said Sandford calmly. 'I don't have a houseful of chattering females to bring me the latest *on-dits* like you do and I've been stuck in the outfields most of the week, don't forget.'

'But you were at Mrs Watts' cottage the other day—you spoke to old Josh himself! Didn't he mention it?'

'Well, apart from damning me to perdition, he did suggest that I wasn't worthy of a certain lady's regard—something about not being ''fit to lick her dear little boots'' springs to mind—but since I'm well aware of that fact, I didn't pay a great deal of—why are you looking at me like that?'

'What's going on, Robert?' asked the older man sharply. 'You and Miss Cordell have been at daggers' drawn all week—any fool could see that. Last week it was much the same, if I'm not mistaken and—I have to say this, old chap—you don't act like a man newly in love!'

'Do I not, indeed?' drawled Sandford coldly and for the merest moment his eyes looked bleak as they studied his cousin's concerned face. Then, with a sudden urgency he leaned across the table and said decisively, 'Fill your glass, Charles. I have a tale to tell you—but it must go no further than this room.'

Chapter Eleven

Judith could not imagine what could be keeping Sandford and Ridgeway so long at the table, particularly since Charles had earlier given her the impression that he would be happy to spend every minute of the evening by her side and she had supposed that Robert must wish to do likewise with his new betrothed, yet the tea tray had come and gone and still the gentlemen had not appeared.

She was perfectly content to sit and chatter to her young friend, of course, but, of their own volition, it seemed, her eyes constantly wandered to the clock on the mantelshelf. Her mother, she observed, must also have registered their non-appearance, for Judith was aware of that lady's continual glances towards the door whenever the slightest sound penetrated from without.

Harriet, too, had marked the long absence but, since she knew that inquiries about her assailants were still in progress, she assumed that this must be the topic that engrossed them. She had no objection to Sandford's absenting himself for as long as he chose, she told herself, for she had found that, having expended all of her energy and resources in keeping up the performance of constant good humour which she had promised him, she now felt quite drained and was perfectly happy to relax into exchanging idle pleasantries with Judith, for this required no false effort on her part.

'The gentlemen appear to prefer their own company, I see,' Lady Butler intoned peevishly.

'I'm sure they will not be long, Mama,' answered Judith, attempting to soothe her. 'I dare say they have become involved in estate matters and forget the time.'

'They must be very deeply involved—for even Miss Cordell's skills at the keyboard seem have to have lost their former attraction!'

Harriet laughed, one of her soft infectious chuckles. 'I know you jest, your ladyship,' she said. 'I do not pretend any skill at the keyboard. That was but a game we played whenever we found ourselves in possession of a piano—which was very seldom, as you can imagine.'

'Do tell us,' begged Judith, as much to pass the time as anything. 'This would have been while you were wintering in Lisbon, I collect?'

'Yes, and I cannot claim to have been the inventor of the game,' said Harriet, nodding in reminiscence. 'Some of the young officers could play, of course—those who had been given lessons in the schoolroom—so they would teach us certain chords, the very simplest of all and, therefore, quite easy to memorise, and our musical game developed from this. One of us would strike a chord and any available pianist would be challenged to extemporise. It was all done to keep the younger ones amused, although we *all* thought it rather fun—I was quite young myself at the time, of course. The more often one plays the game, the better one gets and, although it was never possible for me to be given proper lessons at the pianoforte, Mama did try to teach me some of the basic principles—and we sang a great deal, of course.'

She was silent for a moment, then turned to Lady Butler

with a sweet smile, saying, 'Such a silly game bears no comparison with real music, of course. Perhaps we could persuade Judith to play for us. I love to listen to her—as I am sure you do.'

Lady Butler grunted, temporarily mollified at this request. 'Well, to be sure, she had the best of teachers, and a great deal of money was spent on her education—but it is true that she performs excellently, although she gets little enough practice these days. Yes, dear Judith, do play for us—something soothing, perhaps—I believe we have had more than enough jollity for one evening!'

And so, when Sandford and Ridgeway made their appearance shortly afterwards, they perceived Lady Butler slumped fast asleep with her chin on her chest whilst an envious Harriet, standing beside the piano admiring her friend's virtuosity, was the sole audience to Judith's expensive musical education.

At their entrance Judith immediately stopped playing and rose from her seat. She came towards Sandford anxiously, with a finger to her lips as she motioned towards her sleeping mother.

'What has kept you so long, Robert?' she almost whispered, and he found himself replying in kind.

'Sorry, Judith, we—got chatting and, well—you know how it is.'

Judith's eyes flew to Ridgeway, whose face held a very shamefaced expression.

'*Is* there something wrong? I do believe there is something that you are keeping from me...'

Sandford took hold of her hands and shook his head at her.

'Judith, I promise you there is nothing for you to worry about. I told you that if there was a problem with Westpark—'

'*Problem with Westpark!*' Lady Butler's ringing tones interrupted him. 'What problem with Westpark? Explain yourself, young man!'

Sandford controlled himself with difficulty. 'As far as I am aware, your ladyship,' he said carefully, 'there are no problems at Westpark—as I was just trying to impress upon Judith. Why everyone insists upon inventing problems where none exist, I cannot imagine! Charles and I were discussing something quite other, I promise you—and I—*we* apologise unreservedly for our outrageously bad manners in having deserted you for so long.'

Ridgeway nodded his agreement. 'It's true, Judith—Lady Butler—there was absolutely no mention of Westpark in our conversation and I, too, apologise for our lengthy absence.'

Lady Butler gazed at them both with narrowed eyes, as if by doing so she could read their minds, then, collecting together her various belongings, she got heavily to her feet.

'Hmm, well—I suppose you also wanted a little peace and quiet after that earlier boisterous display—frankly, I'm not surprised you stayed away for so long. However, it is now time for us to wish you goodnight—it is, as you see, very late.'

She stared pointedly towards the clock and Judith, looking at Ridgeway, gave an embarrassed little shrug, as he smiled in sympathy.

'Lady Butler is quite right, Judith,' he said, as he bent over her hand. 'The time has flown so quickly and, indeed, I am very sorry that I didn't spend more of it in your company—it would have been infinitely more enjoyable, I assure you.'

'Couldn't have put it better myself, sir,' laughed Sandford, bowing to Lady Butler and kissing his sister-in-law's cheek. 'Many thanks, Judith. In spite of our prolonged absence, may I pronounce the evening a great success?'

Harriet, having also bidden her adieux, was escorted out to the waiting carriage by both men, but was surprised to find that it was Charles Ridgeway who stepped forward to hand her into her seat.

'If ever you need my assistance,' he said in a low voice, as he moved away from the door, 'remember that I am always at your disposal,' and, bowing, he walked off to collect his gig.

Harriet was still pondering over his words as Sandford climbed into the carriage and took his seat opposite her. It was too dark to see his face.

'Have you told Mr Ridgeway how it was that we met?' she asked him curiously.

'Has he said so?' Sandford sounded taken aback.

'Not exactly—but he seemed—different, somehow, and you were away so long I wondered...'

'I felt that it was time to take him into my confidence,' admitted Sandford. 'I am no nearer to tracking down your assailants than I was a week ago—I thought that he might have some new ideas...'

'And has he?' Harriet asked eagerly.

''Fraid not—he latched on to the Middletons, of course— just as I did—but now we're agreed that everything seems to point to someone from the House.'

They were both silent for several minutes then Sandford spoke again. 'Harriet?'

'Yes, my lord?'

'Oh, God! Not still?' She heard the thud as he struck the cushion with his fist.

'I beg your pardon?'

'Harriet—we have to talk—preferably somewhere I can see your face. Will you come into the library when we get back?'

'I am rather tired, sir,' she said mutinously. 'Can't it wait until morning?'

'No, it damned well cannot!' Sandford exclaimed. 'Do you want me to come over there and persuade you?'

'I would prefer that you remained in your own seat, my lord,' she said shakily. 'If I may remind you that I am under your protection...'

She heard his gasp and waited in trepidation for his reply, but there was only a heavy silence in the darkness. All of a sudden an unaccountable sensation of longing welled up inside her.

'Lord Sandford?' Her voice was hesitant.

'Miss Cordell?' he answered patiently. He was hurt and angry, but determined not to rise to any further strictures she might cast at him.

'I want you to know that I am very grateful for all the trouble you have taken on my behalf—no, please let me finish!' She had heard his attempted protest. 'It's just that I'm sure that it must have crossed your mind that had I never come to Beldale—had you never picked me up—you would not have had to spend all your time trying to extricate me from these other mishaps—I realised this some days ago. What I am trying to say is that I want you to stop wasting any more of your time on this endeavour. My own feeling is that it has all been a series of unfortunate and disconnected incidents—no real harm has been done to me—obviously none was really intended, otherwise it could easily have been achieved...*oh*!'

Sandford had leapt across the space between them and had his arms tightly about her.

'No, don't say it,' he said, his voice muffled in her hair. 'I have had nightmares enough. I do not consider it to be a waste of time to find and punish anyone who has tried to hurt you—they will be lucky to escape with their lives!'

'Sir! You must not say so!' Harriet's heart seemed to be leaping about inside her ribcage and she could hardly breathe. She tried to push him away, but her arms were trapped against him. 'Please release me—I beg you—Robert—please!'

At once he loosened his hold and moved a little way from her, still keeping one arm around her shoulders. She could scarcely make out his silhouette in the gloom, but knew that he had his face towards her for she could feel his warm breath on her cheek.

'You must listen to me,' she cried breathlessly. 'My grandfather will be here shortly—I shall keep Davy with me if I go anywhere, I promise. I know I should have done so when you asked me—but in a few days you will be free of me...'

'Free of you!' Sandford choked. 'I don't want to be free of you—I want *never* to be free of you. What I want is...'

But the viscount was unable to finish his passionate words as the carriage had drawn to a halt and Pritchard, the groom, was opening the door and letting down the steps for him to alight. Barely controlling his impatience, Sandford held out his hand to Harriet and led her into the house.

'Won't you come into the library—just for a few minutes?' he pleaded. 'There is something I must say to you.'

Harriet shook her head resolutely and moved towards the stairs. This is all madness, she thought, in a panic. In a few days my grandfather will come for me. I shall return to Scotland with him. That is what I set out to do. That is what I must do.

Sandford, his heart heavy, saw his hopes crumbling away as he watched her climb the staircase, for he realised that, from now on, she would be very much on her guard in ensuring that she did not find herself alone with him again.

He turned away from the unremitting spectacle of her rigid figure, divested himself of his cloak and hat and, handing them to the patiently waiting March, dismissed the servant for the night.

Much later, sprawled in his father's high-backed chair in the library, he emptied another glass of brandy and reviewed his situation for the umpteenth time.

Trounced by a pair of green eyes, by God! After all his years in the field! Plenty of other fish in the sea, of course—and they'd be queuing up, once he let it be known he was hanging out for a wife—which he wasn't—didn't need one. Beldale's future was safe—Phil's boy was a fine enough heir—Ridgeway would help him run the estates.

Ah, yes, Ridgeway! His lips twisted as he remembered. *He* was being mighty friendly to Harriet this evening—supposed to be in love with Judith, too—very interested when he heard the engagement was a sham. Too interested, perhaps? Maybe I shouldn't have mentioned her inheritance, he thought, but he shan't have her—I'm damned if I'll let him have her—damned if I'll let anyone....

March found him slumped in the chair the following morning when he came into the room to open the curtains. The footman stared down at Sandford in distaste and picked up both the fallen glass and the empty decanter.

'He's had a skinful, I'll be bound,' giggled Lizzy, the young housemaid who had accompanied him, but he frowned at her and motioned her to be silent. She flounced away pertly with the tray he had handed her.

'My lord!' March gently shook the viscount's shoulder. 'Your lordship!'

Sandford's bleary eyes dragged open and he blinked rapidly to focus them upon March's expressionless face. Struggling upwards into a sitting position, he groaned as his head roared out its protest.

'What—time—is—it?' he croaked, carefully and slowly.

'Six o'clock, my lord,' March's answer came back smartly. 'Shall I bring you a pot of coffee, sir?'

Sandford started to nod, then quickly changed his mind as the battery of cannon exploded violently across his temples. He flapped a slack hand at the man and closed his eyes once more as March bowed and, with a very unsympathetic grin on his face, walked towards the door.

His lordship breathed deeply for several minutes, trying to remember why he should have chosen to sleep in the library, in such a damned uncomfortable chair when he had a perfectly good bed upstairs. His eyes were still closed when he heard the sounds of the door opening and footsteps approaching.

'Just put it on the table, March, thank you,' he murmured weakly.

'I shall do no such thing,' came a bright and well-known voice.

His eyes flew open in shock and he tried to rise, but Harriet's hands pressed him firmly back into his seat.

'Sit still,' she said, calmly pouring out a cup of coffee and, to his surprise, taking a sip of it herself.

'This is for you.' She indicated and handed him a tall glass full of an evil-coloured liquid.

Sandford sniffed at it and pulled a face. 'What is it?' he asked plaintively.

'It is vinegar and raw eggs—and it is quite horrid,' she said, with a laugh in her voice that woke him up immediately. 'Drink it!' she commanded and came down on her knees beside his chair.

'I can't—it would make me—that is—I should...'

'Yes, I know—you would be sick! Well, my lord, you

will either bring it up or keep it down—whichever way, it will still cure your hangover.'

Manfully, he struggled to down the contents of the glass, hypnotised by the laughing gleam in her green eyes. She removed the tumbler from his shaking hand and put it carefully on the side table, but remained on her knees studying his face with a very serious expression upon her own.

'I came down early, to see if I could catch you before you left,' she said, after a minute or two. 'March told me you had spent the night in here—and that you were feeling somewhat…under the weather!'

'Did he, indeed—blast him!' gritted Sandford, who was fighting a desperate battle with the contents of his stomach and determined to win. 'I suppose that foul concoction was his idea?'

'No,' she said sweetly. 'It was mine!'

He blinked in astonishment at her answer and discovered at the same time that his head was indeed beginning to clear.

'Set on poisoning me, are you?' he asked roughly, his eyes engrossed with the nearness of her face.

'Of course.' She started to get to her feet, but when he beseechingly put out his hand she smiled and remained at his side. 'You'll survive, I'm sure.'

'Only with the right treatment, I think—and it may take a very long time.'

She laughed softly and the explosions in his temples were reduced to mere firecrackers. Tentatively he took her hand in his.

'Why were you hoping to catch me before I went out?'

'I thought you might allow me to ride with you—but I fear you are not up to such vigorous exercise just yet. Perhaps in an hour or two?'

'And until then?' Sandford asked hopefully, but Harriet thrust his hands aside and jumped to her feet.

'*You* will go and lie down on your bed.' She dimpled at him. '*I* shall go and eat a substantial breakfast and, perhaps, take a walk on the terrace—with the faithful Davy, of course—and await your return.'

'With bated breath?'

'There is always that possibility!'

The viscount rose gingerly, holding on to the back of the chair with great deliberation. He certainly felt a good deal better than when he had been woken by March, but perhaps a short rest and a change of raiment would be the best plan to follow at the moment. He looked at Harriet, trying to make sense of her mood.

'You have had a change of heart, perhaps?'

She shook her head at him and pointed to the door. 'Go now and have your rest—I shan't say another word on the subject until you return!'

Somewhat perturbed, but too confused to argue, he allowed himself to be shepherded to the foot of the staircase where he found Kimble waiting in frowning disapproval.

'Your arm, my lord,' said his valet stiffly and proceeded to help his young master slowly up the stairs.

Harriet watched until the pair had disappeared from sight, then turned and smiled at the ever-present March and said, 'Is Davy Rothman about, March? I should like to go for a walk after breakfast, if he is available?'

She still wasn't totally at ease with the idea that Beldale's servants were there for her to command and she regarded the idea of one wasting his time just walking along behind her as perfectly ridiculous, but since she had agreed to it she was prepared to fulfil her part of the bargain.

March's face creased with concern at her request. 'Young Rothman, Miss Cordell? I'm dreadfully sorry, but his father sent him down to the village just five minutes ago—we didn't expect you to be rising this early, miss—after being so late last night and all.'

Harriet laughed and put her hand on his arm. 'Don't look so worried, March—it isn't the end of the world. I shall have my breakfast and, if Davy hasn't returned, surely you have another youngster who is prepared to give up his duties to be my shadow for an hour?'

'Of course, miss.' March's face cleared. 'I know just the lad. You would like your breakfast now, miss? I shall inform Mr Rothman.'

With that, he bowed and left the hall and Harriet strolled into the breakfast parlour where the early morning sunshine was just beginning to filter its pale light through the rear windows of the house.

She stood for a while, watching the gardeners tidying the terrace flower-beds, and marvelled at the amount of work that had to be done in a great house before the occupants rose. Dusting and polishing, sweeping, cooking and even gardening—and so many people involved, so many people dependant upon so few for their daily bread. A terrible responsibility, she realised, and was no longer so sure that she had come to the right decision, after all.

For, after a sleepless few hours, she had at last made up her mind. Sandford's continued protestations of love certainly seemed genuine and she was almost sure that he had been about to ask for her hand when they returned from Westpark last evening. Having searched her conscience thoroughly, she could see no good reason for refusing him. There were times when she actually *liked* him, although she found him very disconcerting too—and very high-handed, but that was to be expected in someone of his rank and position. He had been used to dealing with hundreds of men from different walks of life, many of them rather unruly and very badly behaved, as she well remembered. He would have had to be very strict and autocratic with some of them, she felt sure and, after so many years, it had probably become second nature to him. He wasn't always like that, as she herself could testify and he was often very amusing to be with. She was sufficiently level-headed to realise that refusing an earl's son would be considered absolute folly by the bastions of English Society and, although she knew none of these worthies, she felt that even her unknown grandfather would view such a refusal as somewhat puzzling from a girl with her unusual background. Besides which, she had to admit that the idea of immuring herself in a Scottish castle in a lonely glen was growing less appealing by the day, especially after having been in this glorious Leicestershire countryside for these past weeks.

She was not, she had to own, completely comfortable with the idea of marrying for the aforementioned reasons, especially after her high-flown speech about love and chivalry, and she was uneasily certain that Sandford would not be at all impressed to have any one of them offered to him as her justification for accepting his hand.

However, she was sure that they could learn to deal perfectly amicably together, which was more than a great many married couples could claim. She was well aware that her own parents' marriage had been most unusual in having been a love match and, in contemplating such a union between Sandford and herself, her cheeks grew hot and her heart seemed to skip several beats. Her lips curving in anticipation, she allowed herself to visualise the wicked glint that would appear in his eyes when she gave him her answer. Ridiculous! She admonished herself for her foolish thoughts, vowing to concentrate on only the practical aspects of the matter.

She finished the rolls and coffee that Rothman had

brought to her and went into the hall to see if young Davy had returned from his errand to the village.

March shook his head. 'Sorry, Miss Cordell,' he said. 'He's not back yet—but young Cooper would be glad to accompany you—he's not that keen on polishing silver!' He grinned at her and she smiled in return.

'I can sympathise with that—a thankless task!'

March went to the back stairs to call Cooper up. Harriet walked through the small parlour out to the rear terrace, where a blushing young footman joined her a few minutes later.

At this early hour the dew was still wet on the grass and Harriet was glad she had pulled her riding boots on before coming downstairs. Having dressed with a view to being ready to ride at moment's notice should Sandford have been available, she was still wearing her riding habit. Not the most suitable skirt for a walk on the grass, she realised, but since she would have to change later to attend the church service she elected not to waste any more of the beautiful morning worrying about a damp hem and set off across the park with Cooper in train.

After some moments, the increasing absurdity of the situation brought a smile to her face and she motioned to Cooper to come alongside. 'I hear that you are not fond of silver-polishing.'

Cooper grinned shamefacedly and nodded.

'Will you enjoy being a footman, do you think?' Harriet persevered.

Cooper looked at her in surprise. Enjoying one's work had never been a question that any of the staff had given a great deal of thought to as far as he was aware. 'I think I should like Mr March's position, miss,' he ventured shyly. 'But it has taken him more than ten years to get to be first footman and I'm not sure I'd want to wait that long—or even if I'd be that good at it!'

'I suppose you didn't really have a lot of choice in the matter,' Harriet mused, more to herself than to the youth. 'What would you have done otherwise?'

'I suppose I could have gone in the stables—or the gardens, like my dad, but I'm not that keen on an outdoor life,' said Cooper. 'What I'd really like, miss, is to be a carpenter—but I'd have to go for apprentice and it's not that easy these days.'

Harriet nodded sympathetically. The country had been in a state of unrest since the war ended. Prices had risen sharply and wages had fallen; returning soldiers had been unable to find work and, in many areas, marauding gangs were set on inciting riots amongst the discontented and mob rule frequently prevailed. Beldale had, so far, escaped involvement with these crises, mainly because of the earl's policy of care for his tenants and servants—his 'people', as he called them. This was why Judith had expressed such concern over the possibility of laying men off and why young Cooper was grateful to have a job at all.

They strolled through the knot gardens, with Harriet pausing every so often to admire particularly attractive floral displays. When her young escort ventured to point out which of the gardeners was his father, she stopped to compliment the older Cooper on the magnificence of the late summer roses he was pruning.

'We've had a good year, miss,' he said, knuckling his forehead to her. 'Plenty of sun these last few weeks—although I shouldn't be surprised to see rain before the day's out.' He indicated the clouds gathering over the hill. 'If you're going riding, miss,' he warned, having observed her costume, 'you'll be wise not to venture far afield, if you'll pardon my saying so.'

'How very good of you to mention it.' She smiled at him and, much moved, he bent to clip a perfect specimen from one of the bushes and offered it to her.

'For your buttonhole, miss—almost matches your pretty hair,' he said, ignoring his son's impudent grin. 'It's called ''Beldale Sunset''—one of our own varieties.'

Harriet was deeply touched. 'How lovely!' she exclaimed, inhaling the delicious perfume before carefully tucking the flower into the braiding on her jacket. 'Thank you—for the compliment as well as the rose—I'm honoured that you should clip one for me.' She bestowed another of her captivating smiles upon him and was about to turn away when she happened to catch young Cooper's low and hurried parting words to his father.

'—news of young Tatler?'

She saw the older man's frowning shake of the head as he knelt to resume his work. An odd premonition overcame her and, as they walked on through the gardens, she questioned the young footman.

'Were you referring to Billy Tatler? Has something happened to him?'

Cooper shuffled uncomfortably. Visiting gentry didn't usually concern themselves too much in local problems and he was unsure of the wisdom of passing on rumours, but Harriet's eyes were fixed upon him in such a steadfast way that he found the words tumbling from his lips before he could stop them.

Harriet's eyes grew round with horror as his tale unfolded. It appeared that the lad Billy had gone missing two days previously but, because of his errant lifestyle, his mother had not begun to worry about his absence until late the previous night when she had expressed her concern to Ridgeway on his return from Westpark. He had, it seemed, chosen to regard the boy's disappearance as a much more serious matter than the rest of the household would have expected and had immediately set several men on to searching Billy's known haunts. Mr Ridgeway himself, Cooper told Harriet, had been out most of the night.

'But has no one informed their lordships?' she asked, walking quickly back towards the house.

'Mr Ridgeway wouldn't have them woken up, miss,' panted Cooper, hurrying to keep up with her. ''Tisn't usual for any of the family to be up this early—he'll have left a message with Mr Rothman, I'll be bound.'

Harriet hesitated, and then turned towards the stables where she found quite a flurry of activity. Apprehending a passing stableboy, she instructed him to saddle up her horse at once, while Cooper looked on in dismay.

'But I can't ride, miss,' he stammered. 'That's why Davy—Rothman was picked. Shall I go and see if he's back, miss?'

Harriet nodded. 'Yes, do, Cooper—and tell him to follow me to the Dower House. I shall take the back lane—and tell March to give the same message to Lord Sandford when he wakes,' she called over her shoulder as she mounted.

Wheeling Clipper in the direction of her proposed route, she headed for the short bridleway that led to the south of the Beldale estate, where the Dower House was situated. She had not gone far, however, when she was halted by one of the large group that was milling around the courtyard. A young groom, by the look of him, he signalled urgently to her to stop and she reined in beside him.

'If you're wanting Mr Ridgeway, miss,' he volunteered, 'he's just gone up to Top Meadow along North Lane. You'll soon catch up with him if you take a short cut through the copse—shall I tell Davy when I see him, miss?'

'Oh! Yes, please, would you?' Harriet swung Clipper in the opposite direction and, spurring her mount into a gallop, headed for the woods that led out to the north side of the estate.

Chapter Twelve

Urging Clipper swiftly through the woods, Harriet soon arrived at the dry-stone wall that bordered the estate. Clearing this without difficulty, she cantered up the lane that led, firstly, past the gated entrance to Westpark Manor, then past the old Butler property, Staines, and eventually towards the forked track that separated the crumbling cottages of Bottom Meadow from the newer dwellings in Top Meadow.

There was no sign of Ridgeway as yet, but she supposed that she could not be far behind him. She assumed he was making for the ruins—such buildings being a magnet for small boys. She hoped that Billy had not fallen and hurt himself, but this fate would be infinitely more preferable than her present thoughts concerning a more sinister explanation to the lad's disappearance. Like Ridgeway, she had straight away connected his absence with the mysterious stranger at the lake and was afraid that either Billy or his friend had somehow discovered the man's identity, which would have placed the two boys in serious danger, especially if this was the same man who was involved with her attack in the copse.

However, the track to Bottom Meadow was deserted and, although she could tell that there were stirrings of life in the new cottages further up the lane, she could see no indication of Ridgeway's presence—nor any sign of his big, raw-boned grey. Momentarily undecided, she stared down at the derelict buildings, remembering that Meggy had warned Josh Potter to stay away from the dangerous ruins and, conscious of the fact that she had once again broken her promise never to leave the house without a groom, she reluctantly started to pull Clipper's head up from the dew-sweet grass which the mare was presently enjoying.

Then she heard it. The faint sound of a cry of distress. Hesitating no longer, she dismounted and, throwing Clipper's reins around an overhanging branch, she kilted up her habit skirt and sped down towards the ruins. Again came the cry—from the back of Potter's cottage, she could swear. Gasping for breath, she rounded the end of the buildings and saw that the small cellar hatch at the rear of the cottage had been lifted from its mountings.

Kneeling at the portal, she called down into the gloom, 'Billy? Billy—are you down there? Are you hurt?'

If there was any reply she did not hear it, for something very hard caught her a stunning blow on the back of her head and she felt herself tumbling down and down into the depths of unconsciousness.

Small hands were shaking her. She was dreaming about Billy Tatler. How strange! Her head hurt badly and one of her shoulders felt rather sore. She opened her eyes, but darkness still prevailed. She tried to sit up, but waves of concussion overcame her and she sank back on to her hard and lumpy mattress, insensible once more.

'Miss! Oh, miss—do wake up—please don't be dead, miss—oh, miss!'

The sobs cut through her clouded brain. Small hands *were* shaking her! Very gingerly Harriet reached out towards them. They were real enough! As was the pain in her head! The darkness was only too real.

'Is it you, Billy?' she ventured weakly, as her fingers were grasped tightly.

'Oh, miss!' came the child's relieved cry. 'I fort you was dead—I were that scared, miss! Will we get out, miss? Mister Ridgeway will find us, won't he, miss?'

Harriet drew the boy towards her and put her arm across his thin shoulders. His whole body was shaking and, although she herself was experiencing the same terrors as he was, she knew that he was depending upon her for his salvation.

'Everyone will be searching for us, Billy,' she said, with as much calm as she could muster. 'They have been searching for you all night—I found you first, it seems.' A thought occurred to her. 'Was there someone here with you when I—fell—into the cellar?'

'You din't fall, miss—he whacked you one! I saw him behind you with a bit of wood! He pushed you in and fixed the trap-door back!'

Harriet tentatively put her hand up to the back of her head. There was a sticky, wet mess of hair around a considerable contusion. Grimacing at the pain, she supposed she had better fashion some sort of a bandage for herself. She wriggled uncomfortable as she felt the lumpen mass beneath her.

'What are we sitting on?' she asked her companion. 'It doesn't feel like coal or logs.'

'It's turnips, miss—put down last year, I should think. Maybe potatoes, too, somewhere.'

'I'm going to stand up for a minute, Billy—stay where you are. I just want to wrap something around my head—it seems to be bleeding a bit.'

She slipped off her petticoat and, tearing it into strips, set about padding and binding her wound in the well-remembered procedure that she had learned from her mother. She wondered just how long she had been unconscious and whether Sandford would have recovered sufficiently to come in search of her. She was reasonably confident that it wouldn't be long before somebody found them. Then she remembered, with a tremor of fear, that *somebody* already knew where they were and that *he* would be doing everything in his power to ensure that they were *not* found!

'The man at the lake, Billy,' she said, as she seated herself next to him once more. 'Who is he—and how came you to be in the cellar?'

'Well, miss—' Billy was feeling much more cheerful now that he was no longer alone in the cold and the dark '—me and Nick—him as was with me at the lake—fort we'd better find him before he found us, miss, but he took some finding, I can tell you! Turns out he's one of the gardeners—but he's a right queer cove and no mistake. Never goes down to the village—not even to the *Fox*. Probably drinks them queer potions and things he makes…'

'Queer potions?' interrupted Harriet, suddenly alert.

'Yeah—he's got bottles and bottles of 'em all on the shelves of his hut—sort of a tool-store place at the far end of the gardens at Westpark. Grows all these herbs and things—and works in the kitchen gardens, too. Anyway, we seen him talking to the old butler bloke and we followed him to his hut.'

'That was a very silly and dangerous thing to do. You should have informed Mr Ridgeway at once!'

'Yeah—I know that now, miss.' Billy wriggled uncomfortably. 'We just fort it were a bit of a laugh, see? Only—well, he saw me and came after me. I weren't even that scared then, you know, 'cos I'm pretty quick on my heels—as they'll all tell you…'

Harriet smiled sadly into the darkness as the young urchin attempted to puff up his consequence.

'Yes, and I seem to recall that you're a slippery little eel, too!' she said in a matter-of-fact tone. 'However—go on with your story.'

'Well, we didn't know who you was then,' said Billy, much affronted. 'An' it was 'cos we found out *who* you was that we went looking for him in the first place.'

Harriet managed to persuade him that she was not at all angry with him over his part in the lake incident and pressed him to tell her the remainder of his tale.

Both boys had escaped the strange gardener's clutches, it seemed, and had hidden themselves in the shrubbery of the old Butler property until nightfall when hunger pangs had tempted Billy to venture out. His friend Nick, it appeared, was a somewhat more cautious adventurer and had said he would remain hidden until he heard Billy's 'owl-hoot' from the lane before he elected to join him.

'Only he never heard it—'cos "matey" grabbed me when I jumped down off the wall. He must have been waiting there all the time!' said Billy indignantly.

Harriet patted his shoulder. 'Poor Billy,' she said sympathetically, 'and after all that time in the shrubbery.'

Billy snuggled up to her, his eyelids beginning to droop. After almost two days without proper sleep he was exhausted and, now that there was an adult present and a gentry-mort at that, he felt reasonably sure that all would be taken care of, for no harm would be allowed to befall the viscount's new lady, he was certain. Harriet interrupted this cosy reverie.

'Just one thing, Billy,' she said, gently shaking him awake. 'Did he hurt you? How did he get you into the cellar?'

'There was two of 'em, miss—his dafty friend was there

wiv an 'orse,' he said drowsily. '*He* was the one what brought me up here, threw me down the hatch—but I fell on the pile of bracken so I weren't hurt…' His voice tailed off and he was fast asleep.

Harriet's arm was beginning to go numb with the effort of holding the boy and she was eventually obliged to lay him down upon the sacks of turnips or whatever they were. Her head ached abominably and she too would have been glad to close her eyes and go to sleep, but she knew that this would be a very foolish thing for her to do in the circumstances.

In the circumstances! Good heavens! How could she have forgotten? She had been shut in a cellar before! Voluntarily, of course, and Mama had been with her as well as Martha— when the French were sacking the village near Badajoz where they were quartered. The thing to do first is to acquaint oneself with one's situation, she recalled her mother's words.

Carefully she rose and felt to her right, moving slowly until she made contact with the wall, which was only a foot away on that side. The sacks of vegetables seemed to be piled up in a corner, so she elected to work her way clockwise around the walls until she returned to them. This she did, cautiously and very nervously feeling her way and counting her steps until she could gauge the size of their prison, which appeared to measure approximately eight feet by twelve. This would be directly below the scullery, she surmised, desperately trying to recollect the layout of the cottage. The hatch, she knew to her cost, was at the rear of the property and there was certainly no other way out of the cellar—the log-ladder, as she quickly ascertained, having been removed. The pile of bracken or brushwood just below the hatchway must have been stored there for kindling, she thought, her brow furrowing. Although that in itself was odd, since it smelled fresh and, surely, none would have been brought since Josh left?

The floor of the cellar was quite dry and for this mercy, Harriet was very thankful, for, she suddenly realised, it was becoming very cold and, remembering old Cooper's warning that a storm was brewing, she wondered if rain would seep into the cellar and make their incarceration even more miserable.

Surely she had been missed by now? She had no way of reckoning the hour, but knew that by the time of the morning service somebody would have noticed her absence. Sandford, if he had recovered from his night's libation, would certainly have expected her to keep her promise to meet him on the terrace. Young Davy would have been sent up to North Lane after her, for the young man had assured her that he would pass on her message...

She stopped her conjecturing at this point as a chill disquietude overcame her. The young man who had directed her to the cottages—who was he? Could he be one of the men who had attacked her in the woods—and possibly the same one who had brought Billy to this place? He had been eager to suggest that she went through the woods to North Lane—perhaps there was a quicker route which he had used to arrive here without her knowledge. He could have travelled over the fields, she realised, so that she would have remained unaware of his presence until he was upon her and, as she had learned from Billy, he had an accomplice who might already have been here!

Sandford would not be best pleased with her actions, she admitted to herself ruefully, and he was, of course, right as usual. Her irresponsible and impetuous behaviour had really dished her this time and his lordship, she was sure, would be forever bringing it up for the rest of their lives—given that he found her and still wanted to spend the rest of his life with her! All at once, the thought of any alternative filled her with the most terrible heartache.

A rustling came from the turnip sacks and Billy's voice cut across her dismal thoughts. 'Miss! *Miss*—are you there?' He sounded terrified and she went to him immediately.

'It's all right, Billy,' she said, with a confidence she was far from feeling. 'I was just trying to work out the size of the cellar.'

The boy started to weep. 'I fort I was dreaming, miss,' he sobbed. 'Why ain't nobody come for us? I fort they'd come for you—even if I weren't important!'

'You are important, Billy,' said Harriet, gathering him to her, with tears in her eyes. 'Your mother must be in an awful state of worry.'

'Well, I'm hungry, miss,' came the snivelling reply. 'I ain't had nuffing to eat since Friday morning!'

Glad of the change of topic, Harriet set her mind to Billy's present problem and quickly came up with a solution.

'We are sitting on a bed of vegetables, Billy,' she reminded him. 'We shan't starve.'

'Turnips, miss—and not even cooked!' Billy was not impressed.

'Let me tell you, young man,' said Harriet, unmoved by his cavalier attitude to such largesse, 'that when I was in Spain, such bounty would have kept a whole brigade in fodder for a week—including the horses, probably, so I beg you not to turn your nose up at it!'

She felt in her skirt pocket for the 'necessaire' which she had, in her youth, learned to carry at all times. This particular little roll, containing scissors, needles, pins and thread, she had constructed as a replacement to her own long-serving lost one as soon as she had been able to collect the required items from the housekeeper at Beldale House, regarding it as a vital accessory, for it had proved its worth many times in the past and was like to do so at present. She carefully unrolled the strip of cotton and, feeling for the scissors and a nail file, she extracted them and returned the 'necessaire' once more to the safety of her pocket.

'Now,' she said, with a feigned cheerfulness, 'we have the tools—so we can eat our dinner!'

Billy attacked the turnip sacks with misgivings but once opened, it was clear that their contents were still in good condition and quite edible. Harriet had eaten worse things in her time and entertained Billy with several stories of much more inferior provender she had been obliged to consume when she was not much older than he was now. Highly impressed, he tucked into sufficient of the vegetables to stay his hunger and begged for more anecdotes of her Peninsular experiences.

In this way Harriet managed to allay the boy's fears, although, as time passed, she found herself growing more and more concerned at the absence of any rescue. Where are you now, my reluctant hero? her heart cried out forlornly, but her battered head responded immediately with the sure and certain belief that Sandford would not rest until he found her. Clinging to this knowledge, she found some comfort of her own.

Chapter Thirteen

The first clap of thunder penetrated Sandford's brain and his eyes flew open with a start. Just for the merest moment he had believed it to be the sound of cannon-fire. Then, smiling and relaxing with a lazy yawn, he sat up and stretched and wondered where the devil Kimble had got to, for surely his valet should normally be busying himself about the bedchamber at this hour. He had to shake his head once or twice to clear away the remaining cobwebs and, as he did so, the night's events came rushing back to him. Leaping out of bed, he hastened to the window, which over-looked the rear terraces. It was pouring with rain. He sighed. No sign of Harriet, of course, she must be waiting in the salon. He glanced down at his pocket-watch on the dresser.

Good God! It was almost three o'clock! Why had no one woken him for morning service? Chagrined, he now had vague recollections of Kimble trying to rouse him from his stupor. She'll be furious, he thought, angrily pulling at his bell-cord for the third time, and we'll be at daggers' drawn again, just when it all seemed to be coming about. He cursed his own stupidity.

The door opened and Kimble entered. Sandford was about to give him a piece of his mind when, to his astonishment, he saw his sister-in-law following the valet into his bed-chamber.

'Judith?' he said, somewhat taken aback at this unex-pected invasion.

'Harriet's missing,' said Judith, without preamble.

'M-missing? How do you mean?' Sandford gripped at the bedrail to steady himself.

'Wake up, Robert, for God's sake!' said Judith angrily. 'We've been searching since eight o'clock—the whole vil-lage is out looking for her!'

Sandford sank down on to his bed weakly and stared at her in uncomprehending horror.

'I don't understand,' he said at last. 'She was going to wait on the terrace—she *promised* she wouldn't go any-where without Rothman—where the hell *is* Rothman? So help me, I'll *kill* him!'

'That will be a great help, I'm sure,' said Judith unkindly. 'Just get yourself dressed, man, and come to Lord William's room as quickly as you can!'

Sandford looked down and realised with a shock that he was clad only in his dress pantaloons. Glowering at Kimble, he grabbed the proffered dressing-gown and covered himself in one swift movement.

'Save your blushes, Robert,' said Judith, turning to leave. 'We have more important things to think about.'

After quickly splashing cold water over his face and scrambling into the garments Kimble passed him, Sandford was ready in minutes and hurried to his father's chamber where the astonishing sight of a great crowd of people met his eyes.

'Father? Mother?' He walked forward anxiously. 'What is it—what has happened?'

The earl eyed him sourly. 'You picked a fine time to take

to the bottle, my boy,' he said. 'The whole village has gone mad—and no one is in charge, it would seem.'

Sandford looked around the room, hardly recognising half of those present. 'Where's Charles?' he said heatedly. 'Surely he—'

'Charles has disappeared, too,' said Judith, her voice shaking, and immediately the rest of the group started to add their various and unconnected pieces of information until Sandford could stand it no longer.

'Enough!' he roared. 'Not another word until you are asked!'

The hubbub ceased at once and Sandford's eyes swept quickly amongst the expectant faces, desperately searching for Tiptree, and it was with overwhelming relief that he saw his stolid groom step forward.

'Tip? What's going on, man?'

In his clear but unhurried fashion, Tiptree related the events that had preceded Harriet's disappearance, culminating in Cooper's return to the kitchen and Davy Rothman's setting out, as instructed, for the Dower House.

'He couldn't have been more than five minutes behind her, guv—but there was no sign of her. He searched the bridleways on both sides of the lane and went to the top of Bell Hill—nothing, sir. He's taken it real bad, too,' finished the groom.

'Go on,' said Sandford grimly, caring less than a jot for the inadequate Rothman's finer feelings, but realising that nothing would be gained by losing his temper.

'Mr Ridgeway came back from Westpark and when he heard what had happened he set everybody from the yard and out of the gardens to search the copses—even some of the footmen went into the hayfields to look. When word got down to the village, they *all* turned out and the Reverend had to cancel the service because there was no congregation!'

He studied his master's face anxiously. 'We've been everywhere, my lord,' he said gently. 'The whole place has been combed over twice or more. One of our stable-lads thought he had seen Miss Cordell heading in the opposite direction—up towards the Top Meadow—but we've had searches going on up there, too. They're refusing to stop, guv—even though it's pouring with rain, as you see, sir.'

Sandford shot a cursory look out of the window, then turned once more to face Tiptree. 'You said Mr Ridgeway came back.' He frowned. 'Then where did he go?'

'He took two men down to search the lake area, sir—Beckett and Hinds, from Westpark—but he left them to it and said he was going up to Staines—nobody had looked there, apparently.'

'And he didn't return?' Sandford was finding it difficult to breathe.

'No, sir,' said Tiptree, shaking his head. 'And I went there myself, guv, and searched the place from top to bottom and inside out—the tenants were very co-operative.'

'And no sign of the horses—Mr Ridgeway's big mare?'

'He wasn't riding Bess, guv—she'd been out all night. He'd picked up one of our two-year-olds, but nobody can remember which one.'

'And no sign of Clipper?' demanded Sandford hoarsely.

Tiptree was silent for a moment. 'Miss Cordell's mare has just been found in West Wood, sir—during the second search there. She's been given something, guv—can't tell what, exactly, Smithers is seeing to her—and her saddle was missing.'

Sandford, white-faced, had collapsed on to the empty chair beside his mother, who leaned forward to put a tentative hand on his knee. Her eyes were full of tears for she could find no words with which to comfort him.

'The men are waiting for new orders, my dear,' she said softly. 'You must take charge now.'

There was a tense silence as the expectant assembly now focused its attention on the distracted viscount. The minutes dragged on until a violent clap of thunder suddenly reverberated above the roofs. Everyone in the room started with shock and, at the same time, Sandford leapt to his feet.

'Everyone—downstairs, into the hall,' he commanded, in a voice of steel. 'Tip—on my desk in the office, the lists and the maps—fetch them. And I want to see the lad who saw Miss Cordell ride off.'

He turned to his parents and his face softened momentarily. 'We'll find her—try not to worry. I'll keep you posted and—*forgive me*, Father!' This last was uttered on a low, choking breath just as he turned and left the room.

Chegwin closed the door behind the last of the visitors.

'He'll do it, my lord,' he said. 'He'll find her—you mark my words.'

Lady Caroline clasped her hands together tightly. 'Please God, may you be right, Chegwin—but where can she be? Oh, where can the poor child be?'

Downstairs, the same question was occupying the minds of the now increasing throng, which had gathered, not only in the hallway, but also on the steps and at the front of the building.

Sandford was issuing orders in a sharp staccato manner. 'All Beldale men to my left and Westpark to my right. Mr Ridgeway's men on the steps here in front of me. I intend to have a roll call. When you hear your name, step forward and identify yourself and form into lines of six—Tiptree will call the Beldale staff, I shall deal with Westpark and...'

Who could he trust? he wondered, and felt a hand on his arm.

'You can depend on me, your lordship,' came March's steady voice. 'May I take the Dower House roll-call? I am acquainted with most of the staff there.'

Sandford, without hesitation, handed the shortest list of names to the young footman.

'Quick as you can, March,' he said gruffly and turned to deal with his own group.

Much moved by everyone's eagerness to assist in the search, the viscount was impressed at the speed with which the lines of men were formed. Some of them had been with the military, of course, which helped a great deal, but even the very young and quite old men found their places with alacrity, and in less than ten minutes the division was complete.

'Who's missing?' Sandford wanted to know.

Tiptree's list of Beldale absentees consisted mainly of Davy Rothman and the young grooms and stable-boys who had gone out with him, Rothman having refused to give up his search. Smithers was in the stables, having suggested that his time would be better spent attending to any problems with the horses and Chegwin was, of course, upstairs with the earl.

Ridgeway had only a few men working at the Dower House and they were quickly accounted for. Sandford studied his own list carefully as Judith, who had been watching the procedure in silence, came forward to offer her assistance.

'Who's missing from your staff, Judith?'

She cast her eyes down the list and over the assembled ranks of the Westpark men.

'Finchley and Pinter—they're still at home, of course.'

'Why "of course"?' demanded Sandford suspiciously.

Judith flushed. 'Mother said she needed them,' she said defensively. 'But they're both quite old men, Robert, they wouldn't be much use to you.'

'What about these others—Freeman, Hinds, Purley and Beckett?'

'Freeman—he's Head of Stable—I imagine he's doing exactly as Smithers is. There are a lot of very tired horses, Robert—he'll be trying to keep them on their feet. Purley and Beckett—I believe they work in the gardens—and Hinds—I'm not sure...' She looked towards her head gardener for guidance.

'Jack Hinds—works in the stable, ma'am,' came the answer. 'Came from Staines—along with Matt Beckett—bit of a slow top, but no real harm in him, I'd say.'

Sandford digested this information for a moment then, turning to Tiptree, he asked, 'Didn't you say that Hinds and Beckett were with Mr Ridgeway before he went off to Staines?'

Tiptree nodded, a deep frown furrowing his brow. 'They *said* he had gone to Staines, guv—I'm just wondering...'

'So am I, Tip. So am I. They need to be found...'

Just then a commotion at the back of the village crowd caught their attention and, as the group parted, the wet, bedraggled figures of the two men in question came forward. Beckett hurried up the steps and removed his soaking cap, while the other, younger man stood nervously below.

'Just got back, your lordship,' he panted. 'Been up North Lane again—searched all the ditches right up as far as Top Meadow—then crossed over and came down the south side. Still no word, sir?' His expression was full of concern.

Sandford shook his head wearily, and then faced the assembly once more. 'I want each and every one of you to know how grateful his lordship and myself are for your dedication and hard work. The search will begin again, but first you must all have something to eat and change your coats, if you can—leave your wet things with the laundry staff, they will deal with them. Food and drink will be provided here in the kitchens until further notice—extra help from your wives will be very welcome. Your horses will be fed and watered in the stables. Search parties will go off at regular intervals to comb specific areas and return—this way you will all have time to dry out and take some sustenance. And, please, don't forget that we are looking for three people—Billy Tatler has still not been found.'

There were some caustic mutterings at his last remark, for many of those present believed that Billy Tatler was the root cause of the whole mystery. Although how he could have spirited the young lady away no one was prepared to guess, but most were in agreement that a good thrashing might have served him well.

Sandford had collected the boards with the large-scale maps of the area from the estate office and had set them up in the hall, where they could be studied by all. With Tiptree's assistance he had divided the estates into small workable sections and he had only one stipulation to make as to the composition of the search parties. He insisted that each party must comprise of an equal number of staff from both houses, with the men from the Dower House fitting in wherever they could, along with any volunteers from the village. Only in this way could he feel confident that any possible subterfuge would be immediately exposed. With this, Tiptree was in total agreement, recognising the military precision with which his guv'nor was masterminding the vast operation.

As darkness began to descend over the woods, Sandford felt his spirits lowering in keeping with the dusk. He had been obliged to remain at Beldale, in order to co-ordinate and structure the searches and to keep his parents informed, although he desperately wanted to be the one who found Harriet.

Lady Caroline had insisted upon throwing open all the ground-floor rooms as rest areas for the volunteers and, as night approached, Mrs Gibson had willingly released so many candles from her precious store to light up the huge reception rooms that the house had become the beacon which lit the last returning searchers home.

It seemed that almost the entire village population was gathered in Beldale House and yet there was very little noise. Weary men, in old felt jackets, leaned their backs against pale damask sofas as they sipped at their tankards of ale. Some were too tired even to drink and fell asleep on the Aubusson rugs. Others conversed in hushed, whispering groups in various parts of the hallway, while a never-ending stream of maids and volunteer matrons replenished and removed plates and mugs.

It had been agreed that the search would be renewed at first light and that those who were able to do so would continue with their efforts. Very few of the volunteers had chosen to quit and those who had been obliged to go to their homes to attend to their own domestic matters had promised to return without delay.

Sandford stood watching a group of sleeping youngsters and his heart turned over as he recalled similar watches before dawn offensives in a far-off land. Who could have imagined that this lovely, sleepy Leicestershire village could ever resemble a foreign battlefield! He turned away from the poignant sight with a lump in his throat and was about to go up the stairs to report to his parents when he felt a tug at his sleeve.

'Your lordship.' Davy Rothman was at his elbow, his

dark eyes red-rimmed from both weariness and the tears he had shed.

At the sight of the young footman Sandford had great difficulty in controlling the surge of rage that threatened to overcome him. The boy had been missing all day although every group had been on the look-out for him.

'Where the devil have you been, Rothman?' The viscount's voice was curt.

'Everywhere, sir—anywhere.' Davy's voice broke. 'I'm sorry, sir—sorry I wasn't here—I should have been with her—I know…'

Sandford's eyes searched the boy's face and Davy returned his master's gaze without flinching. Sandford sighed and put his hand on the boy's shoulder.

'Have you been out all day, lad?'

Davy nodded and his eyes filled with tears. 'Yes, sir—but I'll go out again—whenever you're ready.'

'Go and find something to eat, Davy and try and get some sleep,' said the viscount wearily, 'You'll be no use to Miss Cordell in your present state. I'll have you called as soon as it's light, I promise you—you'll be the first.'

The youngster bowed and turned to go to the kitchens, but was stopped in his tracks by Cooper, the gardener, who was staring intently at Davy's uniform cap.

'Where'd you get that flower, young man?' he said fiercely, pointing to the withered blossom tucked into the boy's maroon hatband.

Davy coloured as several interested faces turned in his direction. 'I picked it up on the lane—what's it to you?'

'That's a "Beldale Sunset" that is,' Cooper said mulishly. 'I want to know how you came by it.'

With a heavy sigh, Sandford started back down the stairs. Surely we can do without an altercation about staff filching flowers, he thought in frustration.

'What's the trouble, Cooper?' he asked, with a patience he was far from feeling.

The elderly man pointed at Davy's cap. 'It's the flower I gave her, sir—the ''Beldale Sunset''—on account of it matching her hair. I gave it her just before she went missing—I saw her tuck it into her buttonhole. Where'd he get it from—that's what I'd like to know!'

Sandford approached the scarlet-faced footman and all conversation ceased as everyone within earshot turned towards the little group at the foot of the stairs.

'Well, Davy?' the viscount spoke very softly.

'I told him, sir,' gabbled Davy almost hysterically, terrified at finding himself in this spotlight. 'It was up at the fork—I picked it up because—it was…' His voice tailed off.

'The colour of Miss Cordell's hair?' Sandford could hardly bring himself to say the words, but the boy nodded eagerly.

'I thought it was a sign, you see, and I started searching the derelicts, but somebody else was already there and hadn't found anything, so we came away together, but I kept the flower—for luck.' He stared defiantly at the gardener.

Sandford chewed at his lip. Another dead end, he thought, helplessly, but just then Tiptree stepped forward.

'Begging your pardon, sir,' he said, in his slow careful manner. 'I wonder if young Davy here would be able to point out the other party he was mentioning—the man he met at the cottages?'

Davy stared helplessly around the hallway at the dozen or so men now sitting with their backs to the wall or leaning their weary frames against the great pillars which held up the ceiling.

'It wasn't anyone from our house, sir,' he said, with a shaking voice, as Tiptree drew him into the largest drawing-room and led him amongst the rest of the volunteers. He gazed from left to right with meticulous attention as he made his way through the sleeping groups. Eventually he shook his head. 'Can't see him, sir,' he said, with obvious reluctance.

Tiptree took Sandford to one side as Davy was motioned off to get his much-needed refreshment.

'We kept a list of the men who left, sir—shall I get it?'

Sandford nodded bleakly and sat down on the stairs with his head in his hands. It's hopeless, just hopeless, he thought, in misery. Where are you, my love? Are you hurt and all alone in the dark? Are you thinking what a poor sort of hero I turned out to be? He closed his eyes, willing his brain to convey a message through the darkness—I'll find you, my darling! I promise you I'm coming to find you!

'There's something keeps nagging at me, guv,' came Tiptree's voice at his elbow.

The viscount opened his eyes and frowned questioningly at his groom.

'Well, sir, it's these two blokes from Westpark—Hinds and Beckett. They seem to be everywhere—and nowhere—if you get my drift?'

'Keep talking,' said Sandford grimly, as he rose to his feet.

'It's like this, sir—we know that Mr Ridgeway went down to the lake with them and they sent us on a wild goose-chase to Staines. Thing is, guv…'

'—we haven't searched the pavilion!' Sandford finished, clapping him on the back. 'Get some lanterns, Tip. We'll do it now!'

Striding through the rear salon, over more sleeping villagers, the two men hastened out on to the terrace into the pouring rain, which was still lashing down in a relentless torrent. Sandford raised his lantern and looked down the steps at the pools that were forming on the grass below him.

'Quicker to walk, wouldn't you say?'

Tiptree agreed that horses would be useless in these conditions and, hats down and shoulders hunched against the drenching downpour, they had just started to make their way across the park towards the lake when the viscount's attention was caught by a pale movement on the lawn in front of him. In the meagre glow of his lantern he beheld a sight that stopped him dead in his tracks.

A gasping Charles Ridgeway lay at his feet, his clothing soaking wet and caked with a thick, black mud!

'Sandford?' came his choking voice. 'Help me up, old man—I'm done in.'

Together Tiptree and his master half-dragged and half-carried the exhausted Ridgeway back up into the house, laying him carefully down on to one of Lady Caroline's best damask sofas—a passing thought which did cross Tiptree's mind but knowing better than to mention it, he motioned instead to a nearby footman to bring some brandy.

Sandford himself held the glass to his cousin's trembling lips and gently allowed some of the restorative to dribble into his mouth. Ridgeway was struggling to sit up, his panic-stricken eyes flashing from side to side as he attempted to take in his surroundings. The viscount pressed him firmly back against the cushions.

'Wait just a moment, Charles,' he cautioned. 'Take your time—another sip.'

'No—time, Robert,' rasped out his cousin. 'Beckett and Hinds—they're our men—took me by surprise—knocked out—the pavilion—swam back...' He swooned away once more as Sandford stood up.

Several of the searchers were now beginning to rouse themselves, having heard the commotion, and word quickly circulated that Charles Ridgeway had returned. A crowd began to gather around the couch.

Sandford beckoned to Tiptree. 'Where does this Beckett live? He's a gardener—does he reside at Westpark?'

Tiptree shook his head. 'Dunno, guv. Hinds lives over the stables there. Some of the gardeners live out—Top Meadow, maybe…?'

'No, he don't, sir,' interposed an eager voice and Cooper senior stepped forward. 'Matt Beckett—he's Finchley's nevvy—shares a room with his uncle over at Westpark— got a hut out behind the shrubbery at Staines.'

'A hut?' said Sandford in exasperation. 'What the devil has that got to do with anything?'

'Grows things, your lordship,' replied Cooper, unmoved. 'Herbs—for horse liniment and such. Saw him put an old dog to sleep once—knows a thing or two about sleeping potions, I'd say…' Other heads nodded and wagged in agreement behind him.

'Has the hut been searched—for Billy—or Miss Cordell?' Sick with apprehension, Sandford turned to Tiptree, who assured him at once that it had.

'Couldn't hide anyone there, sir,' he said. 'Full of bottles and pots. Seem to remember that Beckett showed me himself—very keen that I marked it off, now that I recall.'

'Get the horses saddled, Tip,' said the viscount curtly. 'I'm going up to Westpark myself…'

'It's pretty dark, guv. Might be better to take a carriage round the lane—we'd have the lamps.'

Sandford considered this for a moment, then shook his head. 'Take too long,' he said briskly. 'And they'd hear the carriage coming.'

On the couch beside them, Ridgeway stirred and his eyes flew open in shock. 'You don't think Judith is involved in all this, for God's sake?' His voice cracked with horror as he struggled to sit up. 'I'm coming with you!'

Sandford regarded his cousin frowningly. 'If you think

you can sit a horse,' he said without expression and turned to leave. 'Better change out of those things, too—you've got five minutes. We'll be in the stables!'

Apart from a single lamp which hung above the rear entrance, Westpark Manor was in darkness when the three men arrived. Tiptree, still carrying the poled lantern that had guided the riders along the bridleway, swung himself down from his horse and hurried to assist Ridgeway, who was near collapsing with exhaustion.

'I told you not to attempt the journey,' said Sandford unsympathetically, as he himself dismounted. 'You can hardly stand!'

'I'll be fine,' gasped his cousin, leaning against his mount. 'I had to come—you must see that!'

Tiptree glowered at his master. 'Give him another drop of that brandy, guv,' he suggested. 'That'll sort him out for a while.'

Sandford complied, handing his flask to Ridgeway who, after taking a hefty swig of the restoring spirit, took a deep breath and straightened himself up.

'I still think it would be better if you were to wait out here, Charles,' said the viscount, preparing to open the door.

'Not a chance, thank you, coz,' replied Ridgeway indignantly. 'Judith might need—somebody.'

The three men entered the silent house and made their way to the hall, which had the customary single candle burning in its holder on a side table.

'Do you intend waking the whole house?' asked Ridgeway, in a hushed voice. 'The children…?'

Sandford shook his head. 'I expected to find Finchley here,' he admitted. 'If he is involved, along with his nephew, it's unlikely that they will have gone to their beds!'

'That's true.' His cousin nodded. 'Shall we go back and

try the kitchen?' He turned to retrace his steps along the passageway that led to the servants' quarters but, just as the other men were about to follow him, a voice came from above their heads.

'Who's there? I warn you, I have a pistol! Come out where you can be seen!'

It was Judith. Standing at the top of the stairs in her night attire, she was firmly brandishing one of her late husband's duelling pistols in one hand and a branch of candles in the other.

Sandford immediately stepped forward into the shallow pool of light.

'It's me, Judith,' he called out in a soft voice. 'Put down your weapon.'

'Robert!' she gasped. 'What are you doing here? You have found Harriet?' She hurried down the stairs, gaping in astonishment as she beheld her other uninvited guests.

'You, too, Charles? Where have you been all day? And what are you all doing, creeping about the house in this manner?' She spun angrily round to face Sandford. 'Robert? Are you searching Westpark for Harriet? You cannot think that she is hidden here, surely?'

'It appears that some of your men are involved, Judith,' said Sandford uncomfortably. 'We are looking for Beckett. I understand that he sleeps here with his uncle—Finchley.'

Ridgeway reached out to take the pistol from Judith's shaking hand at the same time as Tiptree relieved her of the candlestick. She sank down on to a nearby settle and looked at Sandford in distress.

'Are you certain—Beckett? But he's only a gardener— why would he…?'

'They left Charles for dead in the lake pavilion, Judith,' replied Sandford awkwardly. 'They are clearly dangerous men—and if they've got Harriet…!' His voice trembled and Judith's shocked eyes travelled to seek Ridgeway's.

'You are injured?' she inquired anxiously, but he shook his head.

'Bruised—tired—I'll survive,' he said, dismissing his pain. 'Finchley's room, Judith?'

She rose at once to her feet and pointed to the steep stone stairway that was situated beside the door to the kitchens.

'The men's rooms are on the top floor—second or third door—I'm not sure…'

'Tip—check the rooms,' instructed Sandford. 'Try not to wake anyone.'

Tiptree ran lightly up the stairs and disappeared from view as Sandford and Ridgeway turned back in the direction of the kitchens but, once again, they were stayed by a voice from above. This time it was the harsh, stentorian command from Lady Butler that stopped them in their tracks.

'Stand still, whoever you are!'

'Mother!' gasped Judith, running back into the hall just as Lady Butler, swathed in a massive purple dressing gown, began to descend the stairs.

Sandford, raising his eyebrows in despair and swearing fulsomely under his breath, reluctantly stepped forward to reveal himself. Judith's mother blanched at the unexpected sight of the viscount coming out of the shadows.

'Judith! What is the meaning of this?' she hissed. 'In your nightwear—go to your room at once, miss!' and, turning to Sandford, 'You, sir, how dare you come creeping…' but Sandford had had enough.

'Be silent, madam!' he uttered curtly. 'You are wasting precious time. Come down, if you must, but kindly keep your comments to yourself! Light some more candles, Judith!'

Lady Butler, silenced by the viscount's tone, clutched at

the banister as she trod heavily down the stairs, then, shakily seating herself on the settle, she watched mutely as Judith hurried to fulfil Sandford's request. The hall was soon adequately illuminated and, upon perceiving that Sandford was not the only night visitor, her ladyship started with undisguised dismay.

'Ridgeway…?' she began, but Sandford gave her a quelling glance and she was once again silent, staring apprehensively at the estate manager as he assisted her daughter in the lighting of more candles.

'Nobody up on the top floor, guv.'

Tiptree had returned from his mission and Sandford, nodding, motioned Judith to one side.

'Look after your mother. I didn't mean to frighten her but we don't want the whole house woken.' Then, to Ridgeway, 'You stay on this side of the door in case one of them comes through—Tiptree, behind me.'

The two men sidled along the passageway and pushed open the heavy oak door that led into the kitchen. They were at once confronted with the unappealing sight of Finchley and Pinter lashed to their chairs with clothes-line, both totally unconscious, but snoring loudly. A sniff at the contents of the tankards on the table in front of the servants provided Tiptree with all the information he needed as to the reason for the old men's condition.

'Strong ale, sir—been doped, too, I shouldn't wonder, if "matey" has had anything to do with it.'

Sandford tried slapping the men's faces in an attempt to wake them, but to no avail, and Tiptree had to restrain his now furious master from delivering a more violent punishment to the old servants.

'Leave it, guv,' he insisted, pulling the viscount away. 'We don't know that they're to blame.'

Breathing heavily, Sandford sank down on to a chair and closed his eyes, his shoulders sagging in defeat.

'It's hopeless, hopeless,' he groaned. 'He's ahead of us at every turn—he'd probably left before we even arrived. What now, Tip?'

'Back to Beldale, sir—can't do anything until it's light. At least we know who's behind it all.'

'Do we, Tip—but do we?' His lordship's voice was weary as he led the way back into the hall, where another distasteful sight met his eyes.

Judith was on her knees, attempting to pacify her distraught mother who was now moaning loudly and rocking herself from side to side, demanding to know what was to become of them all. Ridgeway stepped forward to meet the viscount, thankfully leaving the old woman to Judith's administrations.

'What is it, old man?' he said, quickly taking note of his cousin's dejected air. 'You did not find them?'

'Finchley...' began Sandford, his tone heavy, then he staggered back in surprise as a suddenly upright Lady Butler elbowed Ridgeway aside and all but threw herself at him.

'He lies! Whatever he has told you—it is all lies!' she panted, clutching at his lapels.

Ridgeway gripped her roughly by the arm as Sandford wrenched himself away from her clawing hands and Judith stared at her mother in shock.

'Wh-what are you saying, Mother?' she gasped. 'Do you know something about all this?'

'Nothing—nothing!' wailed Lady Butler, vainly trying to pull herself away from Ridgeway's grip. 'I tell you the man lies—he's an incompetent old fool—you cannot believe a word...'

Her voice trailed away weakly as Sandford, eyes glittering, reached out and took hold of the neck of her night-rail.

'You despicable old woman!' he ground out. 'It was you! My God, it was you all the time! What a fool I've been—where is she? If you've hurt her I'll kill you—I swear I'll kill you myself!'

'Robert! For God's sake!' came Judith's voice in protest, as both she and Ridgeway leapt to extricate Lady Butler from the viscount's furious grasp while Tiptree struggled to hold his master back.

'It's your own fault!' spluttered the woman, from the comparative safety of the settle where Ridgeway and Judith had finally managed to deposit her. 'You should have married Judith—I didn't mean any harm…'

Judith stepped away from her mother in dismay, her hands covering her trembling lips.

'What are you saying?' she whispered. 'Are you to blame for Harriet's disappearance?'

'No, I am not,' rejoined the old woman obstinately. 'I didn't tell him to take her away. I only wanted to put Sandford in dislike of her—make her look cheap and common—which she is!' She stared defiantly at the grim-faced viscount who was still fighting to remove himself from Tiptree's iron hold.

'Have done, guv, do,' said the groom, in exasperation. 'You've the whole night to spare. If you want to find out where Miss Cordell is, you've got to hear her out.'

At these words Sandford ceased his struggles and Tiptree at once released him.

Lady Butler shook her head. 'I don't know where he has taken her. I never intended anyone to get hurt—Beldale was a mistake. Beckett should never have…!'

'You were responsible for Lord William's accident!' Judith, horrified, collapsed into Ridgeway's outstretched arms. 'Mother! What have you done?'

'*I* didn't do anything—I merely pointed out to Finchley

how much better off we would all be once you became countess—Beckett took it upon himself to feed Beldale's horse with one of his potions and Beldale went down. No one expected him to recover—well, he is very old.' Lady Butler shrugged, as four pairs of eyes stared at her in shocked incredulity. 'When Sandford came home with *her* I could see that I would have little difficulty in showing her up for what she is—having her fall into the lake was just a lucky chance. Beckett happened to see her on the path, but the fool let the whore's brat get away—*and* he told me that his lordship here only *laughed* when he saw her appalling state—so you must see that it was necessary for me to think of something else.'

'I can't believe I'm listening to this,' groaned Sandford, with his head in his hands, as Lady Butler nodded at her audience in cheerful unconcern. '*You* arranged Miss Cordell's mishap in the woods?'

'Well, it *is* true that I wrote the note—rather a clever idea, I thought.' She shrank back as Sandford moved angrily towards her. 'And I did help Elspeth to give her the pink biscuits. That was *very* tricky—because Elspeth...' At these words Judith gave a frightened gasp. 'I would never have allowed *her* to eat one, my dear—surely you do not think that?'

Her daughter gave a strangled moan and buried her face in Ridgeway's chest as her mother coolly continued her incredible tale.

'Hinds picked up the gloves *she* had dropped in the stables—another lucky chance—and it proved very useful in my clever little tryst scene. Beckett failed to get the emerald ring, of course—that was a puzzle to me for I had seen her wearing it—but I knew that the whole thing had succeeded when I heard that you had taken each other in such dislike!'

Judith, who had known nothing of these events, was staring at Sandford in consternation. '*That* was why you had quarrelled,' she said weakly. 'But you made up—I saw you—and when you came to dinner…!'

'That was when everything started to get out of hand,' cut in her mother, calmly straightening her nightcap. 'Finchley told me that Beckett had caught the trollop's brat and was waiting to know what *I* wanted him to do. Well, I told him that it was their problem and nothing to do with me— which, of course, it isn't, for *I've* done nothing wrong at all and…' she glared resentfully at Sandford '—you can shake me all you like, but I still don't know where he is or where he has taken her!'

'Do you really believe that you will go unpunished for your part in these events?' asked Sandford incredulously. 'People have been hanged for less! You must be insane!'

'Robert!' Judith's face was white. 'She is my mother!'

'For which you have always had my sympathies,' said her brother-in-law tartly, ignoring his cousin's angry look. 'What time is it, Tiptree?'

'Close on one, sir—at least three more hours before dawn.'

'We'll get back to Beldale then,' said the viscount wearily. 'I'm leaving you in charge, Charles—make sure *she's* still here when I get back. See to those two in the kitchen— and for God's sake don't let any word of this get out!'

'Now, look here, Robert,' exclaimed Ridgeway, in protest. 'Judith is very upset about all this—her mother, dammit!'

'What would you have me do, Charles?' said Sandford icily. 'Offer her a viscountcy? Apparently none of this would have happened if I had done so!'

'That is very true,' said Lady Butler, unperturbed at her daughter's obvious distress. 'You see how you have brought the whole thing upon yourself!'

'I think not, your ladyship,' rejoined Sandford softly. 'Although it pains me to have to say this, it appears to be entirely thanks to you that I have other plans for the title.'

Lady Butler frowned. 'Why "thanks to me"?' she asked 'I have explained that I had nothing to do with any of this business!'

The slightest flicker of a smile crossed Sandford's lips as he prepared to leave. 'You tell her, Charles,' he said, 'although I doubt that the lady will appreciate the irony.'

'Aye.' The older man nodded, holding Judith's hand firmly in his own. 'I'll willingly do that for you, man—and mebbe add a few words on my own behalf!'

Sandford, hunched in his damp riding-coat, did not utter a single word on the homeward journey and, since Tiptree's whole attention was dedicated to keeping the poled lantern low in front of his horse's head to guide the two beasts along the bridleway, the groom kept his thoughts to himself.

Chapter Fourteen

In the cellar time passed interminably, for Harriet and Billy were unable to tell whether it was day or night, being aware only of the endless waiting in impenetrable darkness. They could hear the persistent and ominous rumble of thunder, even within their earthen cave, although the torrential rain that accompanied it they could only imagine, until intermittent dripping of water from various parts of the roof indicated its overhead presence.

'You would think that a cellar would be watertight,' observed Harriet crossly, as she moved their now bracken-filled sacks for the umpteenth time. 'One does, after all, expect to keep logs and certain perishables throughout the winter.'

'Yeah, but you have to remember that the roof has gone on this cottage,' Billy pointed out. 'And some of the other wooden bits must have dried out in the fire—them that didn't burn, I mean.'

Harriet considered this. 'Meggy Watts told me that the flagstones had fallen through to the cellars in some of the other cottages. I hope the ones above our heads don't take it upon themselves to come down on top of us!'

She regretted having given voice to these thoughts as

Billy at once let out a loud wail and clung to her like a leech. She was obliged to sit him down and pet him for some time until his terror abated. She dashed away the tears that persisted in forming in her own eyes and leaned her still desperately aching head against the now dank and streaming walls. The thought of falling flagstones kept recurring, however, and eventually gave birth to an idea.

She settled the fitfully sleeping child down on to the damp sacking and felt her way back to the corner where the rest of the vegetable sacks were heaped. Carefully climbing on top of them, she raised her hands and realised, to her joy, that she could feel the underside of a large flagstone. The cellar was hardly more than six feet high! How stupid of her not to realise that this would be the case!

Moving her fingers across the under-surface of the stone until she felt the floor timber that supported it, she widened her search until she could feel another. Twelve inches apart, she judged, and the joists probably nine or ten inches wide. The flagstones must be about twenty-one inches square and heavy enough to rest on the oak timbers without moving— two or three-inch-thick quarry stone, probably—would she be able to move one upwards?

She sat down upon the turnip sacks to weigh up the possibilities. She was no weakling, in the ordinary way, but thought that it was likely that she had lost quite a bit of blood as she had twice felt it necessary to renew her make-shift head-bandage—in addition to having subsisted on raw turnips for who knew how long.

The problem was one of leverage, she supposed, and she had no tools available. She had scoured the floor of the cellar on hands and knees, with Billy's assistance, to scavenge for anything that might have come in useful to them but, unfortunately for her cause, Potter had proved to be an inordinately tidy housekeeper and none of the usual debris of broken shovels or brooms had been found in his underground storeroom.

Harriet made up her mind. Hoping that the sounds of activity would not penetrate the sleeping urchin's brain, for she was reluctant to raise his hopes unnecessarily, she began to rearrange the sacks of turnips into a more stable platform for herself. This was heavy and cumbersome work, for the sacks were unwieldy and unco-operative, in addition to being very wet, and she was forced to stop frequently to rest and recover from the attacks of swimming fatigue that overcame her. But her perseverance was finally rewarded when, some immeasurable time later, she found that her solid pile of sacks would raise her three feet closer to the roof.

She could only crouch at the top, of course, but this had been her intention for she knew that this was the only way in which she would be able to apply any upward movement to the slab, given that her arms could sustain the weight. Where would be the best place to push? she wondered, not wishful of having a quarry-stone come crashing down on her fingers to add to all her other miseries. If she could lift one at its junction with a neighbouring slab, would it be possible to slide it over the top in the same movement? She was well aware that, even with all the will in the world, she had no real hope of holding up such a heavy weight for more than a moment or two, but if she could just get one into position on top of its fellow it would surely be possible to slide it along the timbers and out of the way. Then, even if she could not make her own escape through the aperture, there might be sufficient room for Billy to do so.

She gnawed at the unappetising turnip in her hand, wondering if she would ever be able to bring herself to face the taste again then, smiling at her foolishness, remembered having had the self-same thoughts about stewed rabbit many years ago—what she would not give at this moment for a dish of that delicacy!

She drew a deep breath, at the same time feeling in her pocket for her riding gloves and, pulling them on so that she could get the best possible grip, she positioned herself carefully and, with all her might, she strained her muscles against the unyielding object.

Nothing! A sob of wretchedness escaped from her lips and her eyes filled with tears. Please, God—oh, please, dear God, she prayed, give me the strength—please help me! She applied herself once again and, gritting her teeth with anguish, she heaved at the slab above her head until her arms began to give way and her head swam.

Then she felt, or rather, heard the movement and either her prayers or her desperation must have given her some sort of divine power for, with a grating lurch, the flagstone did indeed lift and move away from her, only a fraction but enough to balance its front edge precariously on top of its neighbour.

She slid down on to the sacks in a half-swoon, her ears pounding, choking for air and was unable to move for several minutes. She heard Billy stirring and his anxious voice calling her, but could not answer him for she had no strength left in her body.

'Miss? Miss—where are you? Did you hear a noise? Where are you, miss?'

He had found her platform of sacks and was clambering up to reach her. Weakly she put out her hand to reassure him and he huddled himself as close as he could get to her limp body.

'What you doing up here, miss?' he asked in shocked amazement.

'I—think—that—we—may—be—able—to—get out!

she gasped, her voice rough with exhaustion. 'But I—must rest—for just a little while—before I can go on.'

'Is it your head, miss?'

Billy couldn't imagine what had happened to Miss while he had been sleeping. This surely was not his stalwart saviour, who had been so strong and resilient up until now. If she folded, he was ready to believe that they were doomed to remain in their underground prison forever and that they would fade away and die—if 'matey' didn't come and finish them off first!

But Harriet was at last beginning to recover from her Herculean efforts and was gradually able to sit up and explain, in simple terms, what she had achieved.

'And I do believe,' she said, trying to make her voice sound bright and cheerful, 'that if we can push the slab from this end, we might slide the whole thing back and make good our escape!'

'Ooh, miss—let's do it. I can help—see! I can easily reach if I stand up next to you! Both of us should be able to push hard enough!'

Harriet fervently hoped so, but begged him to allow her to get her breath back before they attempted the task. She gave him a turnip to nibble while she closed her eyes for a few minutes in a concentrated endeavour to mobilise her few remaining resources. Her arm muscles felt as though they were made of water, the back of her head was causing her considerable discomfort and she knew that she would be able to summon up sufficient effort for only one good push and, after that, how long would it be before her strength returned, in these conditions?

Resolutely, she positioned herself again and gave Billy explicit instructions as to where to put his fingers, even going so far as to insist that he wear her gloves to cushion any impending damage. Curiously, she also removed the

Beldale emerald ring and wrapped it safely in her 'necessaire' before proceeding—a future Hurst bride might not
care for a scratched or chipped ring, she told herself sadly,
should their endeavour fail and any other rescue prove to
be in vain.

'One good push, Billy,' she said. 'Then we must rest.
When I say "now" you must push straight forward with
me—are you ready? Take a deep breath—*NOW*!'

With their combined weight they heaved at the slab together. It did indeed move but, sadly, only an inch or so,
and both Harriet and the boy collapsed weakly on to the
sacks beneath them, neither of them capable of rational
speech for some time.

Gradually, however, Harriet became aware that the deep
blackness of the cellar had lightened. Only to a dark grey
gloom, it was true, but light was actually penetrating
through the small slit. Was it grey dusk or grey dawn? she
wondered despondently, then sat up in rigid shock as she
heard the unmistakable sound of a man's voice almost directly above them. She reached out towards Billy and placed
a warning finger against his mouth as her ears strained to
catch the words.

'I told her, old girl—if I want to come up home I will—
I don't need her to tell me what I can do. Look what's
happened to our little nest, love—all your dear things—
gone. Soon be gone meself, shouldn't wonder—but I'll be
with you, my Milly…'

It was Joshua Potter! In defiance of his daughter's instructions he had come back to his old home again and was
muttering away to himself as he ferreted amongst the remnants of his possessions.

Harriet pulled herself back up to the flagstones above her
head and placed her mouth to the gap. 'Josh! Josh!' she
called urgently. 'In the scullery! Come into the scullery!'

There was a deathly silence, then all of a sudden the sound of stumbling footsteps came towards their corner.

'Milly?' came a breathless voice. 'Have you come for me? Where are you, lass—can you show yourself? I'm ready to come with you!'

Harriet experienced a momentary pang at having to disenchant the old man of his simple belief in his late wife's visitation but, since he was likely to be their only hope, she resolutely dashed this feeling from her thoughts.

'It's me, Mr Potter—Harriet Cordell!' she cried through the slit. 'I am imprisoned in the cellar—with Billy Tatler. Can you see the raised flagstone in the corner of the scullery?'

Please God he has a light of some sort, she thought, and found herself sobbing with relief as she saw the stump of candle in his hand as he bent towards the gap. The flickering light was sufficient for him to see the reflection in her green eyes, now brimming with tears as she recognised his wrinkled old visage.

'It is you, indeed, miss!' he gasped in amazement. 'Everyone's been looking for you—how'd you get down there, miss?'

But Harriet had no heart to indulge in an explanatory conversation from her present uncomfortable position and begged the old man to open up the cellar hatch and, with some difficulty, eventually persuaded him to shuffle off to comply with her request. Presently, however, he came back to inform her that, unfortunately, a large mass of timber was wedged against the trap-door and that, try as he might, he had been unable to remove it.

Harriet beat her fists against the roof timbers in impotent frustration. 'Can you not find something with which to lever up the slab?' she called out in anguish but, as with a growing sense of hopelessness she listened to the old man stumbling about amongst the debris above them, she soon realised that this task would be equally beyond him.

'Josh!' she called out again, unable to bear the tension any longer. 'You must go for help—but *only* to Lord Sandford—do you hear? On no account tell anyone else of our whereabouts and—please—I know it will be difficult for you—but, *please*—hurry!'

'I'm on my way, miss,' came the wheezing reply. 'I'll fetch himself—don't you worry, miss.'

But Harriet was extremely worried and wondered how quickly a tired old rheumatic with chest problems could possibly cover the four miles to Beldale House—even supposing that Sandford was to be found there!

'Will he get back, d'ye think, miss?' asked Billy in a plaintive voice. 'He can't walk proper—it'll take him forever!'

'Well, Billy,' said Harriet grimly. 'We seem to have forever—we certainly aren't going anywhere—so we'd better think of new ways to pass the time.'

She dwelt on this problem for a moment, then brightened. 'Do you know "Black Jack Ladderback"?'

'Can't say as I do, miss. What is it?'

'It's a round song we used to sing as we rode or marched along. I'll teach it to you. It goes like this...'

> *"Black Jack Ladderback*
> *Took the acorn that he found*
> *Dug a little hole and put*
> *The seed into the ground*
> *And the sun it shone, and the rain it rained*
> *And in time it came to pass*
> *There grew beside the wishing-well*
> *An oak tree on the grass."*

And in this way she kept him happily entertained for a full hour as he learned how Black Jack saw first a branch, then a twig followed by a leaf until, inevitably, he found another acorn and the whole song was repeated ad infinitum. This revelation caused Billy great amusement and he insisted on frequent encores. Harriet, for whom the song was less of a novelty, steadfastly put away her tedium and encouraged him to sing out with gusto, all the while wondering for how much longer she would be obliged to keep up his spirits.

By way of their little gap in the flagstones the cellar had slowly lightened sufficiently for each of them to just about make out the other's person in the gloom and this in itself was cheering. They were boisterously chanting out the words of the song for possibly the fifth time when they heard the sound of the trap-door being swung away. Harriet held her breath as she pulled Billy back into the furthest corner.

A sneering voice fell on their horrified ears.

'Sing-song, sing-song! What a pretty sound! Here's a little present for you!' and a load of brushwood and bracken was thrown through the opening, followed by a considerable quantity of dry straw.

With a sinking heart Harriet realised immediately what their captor's intention was. He meant to fire the cellar and leave them to their fate! Frantically scrambling down from the makeshift platform, she dealt firmly with her initial terror at the thought of being burnt to death and, with Billy's help, set about dragging as much of the scattered brushwood and straw as far away from immediate incineration as was possible.

Fear and the deep-rooted instinct for survival had instantly renewed her strength and with a determined obstinacy she then started pushing all the damp and sodden sacks directly below the cellar hatch, reasoning that should their assailant be about to hurl a firebrand into their underground prison, there was an evens chance that it would land on the not-so-readily-combustible pile of vegetables. Although only a few extra minutes might be gained from such a diversion, it could be enough to make all the difference to the outcome.

She held her breath as the trap-door re-opened and, with mounting horror, she saw that the shadowy outline above them had, indeed, set fire to a tarry faggot, for its flickering light enabled her to register the man's grinning countenance just before he tossed the kindling into the cellar and, with a snigger, slammed down the door once more.

She was certain that she had seen him somewhere before—but where? He was not the man who had directed her to ride up here—but she had no time to dwell upon this puzzle as another, far greater problem was facing her.

Sparks from the firebrand had ignited some of the scattered straw that still lay on the cellar floor and she had to engage her whole concentration in stamping out the various pockets of flame as they took hold. Billy, too, was thrashing his wet sacking at the defiant flickers that were creeping towards the dry brushwood at the far side of their prison.

Above them they could hear the sound of debris being piled once more against the trap-door and, at the sight of flames licking around the cracks in the framework, Harriet's heart sank, for she knew that as soon as the flimsy wooden structure burned away the whole mass of burning timber would fall through and, if that happened, nothing could save them.

Thick, acrid smoke was pouring from the faggot that had fallen beside the turnip sacks. The combination of wet earth and damp vegetables had caused the flames to expire, but the glowing, tarry embers that remained were eating their way along the edges of the sacks, causing choking palls to rise up and, mingled with the smoke and stench from all the other sources, the cellar was soon filled with an atmosphere in which no one could hope to survive for long.

Harriet grabbed at another of the empty, wet sacks and wrapped the choking Billy into its folds, pushing him into the corner furthest away from the burning hatchway and ordered him to keep himself rolled up. She dragged off her smouldering boots and, lifting up her riding-skirt, she threw it over her head, sinking down on the cellar floor beside the howling urchin and prayed as she'd never prayed before.

Chapter Fifteen

Sandford stood at the window of the drawing room, watching intently for the first faint streaks of dawn to break across the dark sky. Never in his whole experience could he recall having lived through a longer night. With his brain in a whirl from Lady Butler's revelations, he had been unable to rest without recalling the disasters that had occurred during his earlier torpidity and, like a demented wraith, he had paced the crowded and bedimmed rooms, inwardly cursing his stupidity, weakness and every other fault or failing he could attach to his own ineptitude. Tiptree, dozing in a corner, had continually roused himself to point out in his usual blunt manner that Sandford would be as much use as a tinker's reject by the morning and that he would do better to harness his thoughts for an hour or two, but the viscount found it impossible to attend to this excellent advice.

His eyes were ragged from staring out into the darkness for any perceptible lightening of the black landscape before him until, all of a sudden, his senses quickened as he realised that he could, indeed, separate sky from land. As the pale dawn began at last to spread its pearly pink glow across the low horizon, he turned in relief to give instructions for the first searchers to be wakened.

Very soon a crowd had gathered both inside and outside the yellow drawing-room and Davy Rothman stepped forward in some urgency.

'It's light enough, sir,' he said to Sandford. 'Can we go out now?'

The viscount nodded and Tiptree began issuing new directions and commands to the waiting groups, but his orders were suddenly interrupted by the sounds of a violent altercation issuing from the hallway.

Sandford frowned impatiently. 'Now, what the devil…?'

The crowd in the doorway parted to reveal the sight of Joshua Potter struggling with his son-in-law Seb Watts, who was attempting to prevent the old man from entering the room.

'I *will* speak to him—I *will*!' croaked Potter, who was in a state of near hysterics. 'Get your hands off me, young Seb. I *gotta* speak to himself—*she* said only *himself*!'

Sandford ripped through the crowd that divided him from the contentious pair and frantically grabbed at Potter's arm.

'Who?' he jerked out roughly. 'Speak up, man—for God's sake!'

'She's in the cellar, sir,' gasped the old man, collapsing to his knees. 'Along of Billy Tatler. I come as fast as I could—she said *only you*, sir!'

'He wouldn't tell me what it was, your lordship,' said Watts, screwing up his face. 'Meggy sent me up the lane with the cart, to see if he'd gone up to the cottage again, and I found him half-dead on the verge. He made me bring him—but I wasn't sure…' His voice tailed off as he saw Sandford making for the door, at the same time exhorting every man with a mount to get saddled and ride at once to Bottom Meadow.

Please, God, let me be in time, he prayed, as he gave Pagan his head along the bridleway that was the short cut to both Westpark and to the lane that led to Bottom Meadow. Tiptree and some of the men followed the viscount whilst the rest of the riders had been instructed to take the longer route along the lane.

It was almost full dawn by the time Sandford wheeled his stallion across the meadow that separated the two estates. He did not turn towards Westpark, however, but took his mount at a gallop over the stone wall into North Lane and on towards the fork at the top where, to his utter shock and horror, he could clearly see the thin column of smoke that was spiralling viciously from the vicinity of Potter's cottage.

From the sound of the shouts behind him, it was obvious that the others had also registered the sight. He spurred his horse on furiously, raising his arm in order to thrash down his crop against Pagan's sweating rump when, somewhere inside his head, he could hear Harriet's voice: 'Horses shouldn't be whipped—shouldn't be whipped!'

'Come on, boy,' he urged, as his arm dropped. 'Give me everything you've got!'

Ears flattened and tail streaming, Pagan positively flew the final half-mile and at last the derelicts came in sight and every one of the horsemen could see that the end cottage was aflame! Timber and debris had been piled up against the cellar trap-door and it was a raging bonfire! In one swift movement Sandford had leapt from his mount and, with Tiptree at his side, he had rounded the cottage and was tearing at the flaming brands with his gloved hands.

'Harriet! Harriet!' he called out, ignoring the searing pain in his fingers. 'Can you hear me?'

'Lord Sandford, sir,' came an urgent voice from inside the ruined building. 'We can get in from here—lift the flagstones, lads.'

Coughing and spluttering as the acrid smoke rose from the cellar, willing hands hoisted the flagstones from the scullery corner as Sandford dropped the smouldering branch he was holding and dashed into the cottage. On to his knees he fell, clutching at the sides of the floor timbers, peering desperately into the gloom of the smoke-filled interior.

'Harriet!' His voice was hoarse. 'Are you there?'

A faint moan from below was the only reply. Without hesitation, Sandford swung himself down into the suffocating smog and, as he landed, he narrowly missed falling on a soft, curled-up bundle. It was Billy Tatler, wrapped in damp sacking! He was conscious and groaning, his breath coming in ragged gasps. In one swift movement Sandford had lifted the bundle and thrust the boy through the opening to the outstretched hands above him before crouching and feeling his way around the immediate vicinity. His eyes were streaming and he could scarcely breathe and the heat from the hatchway was growing intense. Through the smoke he could just make out the eager flames licking through the cracks in the old timber and realised that the trap-door would soon disintegrate and drop its burning embers into the cellar. Suddenly his fingers made contact with a wet, stockinged foot and, with his heart almost at bursting point, he threw himself down to examine the motionless form beneath him. She was still breathing! Quickly he raised her in his arms and called for assistance and many eager hands reached down to help lift Harriet's limp body out of his grasp. Gasping for air, he took hold of the joist to pull himself out of the choking atmosphere when, with a roaring explosion, the burning trap-door fell into the cellar and immediately set the straw alight. The force of the blast threw the viscount to the ground where, for several interminable moments, he lay completely stunned. It was only when the sound of Tiptree's voice screaming at him from above finally penetrated his fading senses that he managed to right himself sufficiently to enable the horrified groom to haul him from the inferno. Then, for the first time in his life, he swooned dead away.

Chapter Sixteen

Lord William was very troubled. The extraordinary events that had overtaken his household during the past few weeks were becoming quite beyond his comprehension and, following the recent and most terrifying episode, there appeared to be no one with whom he could discuss the situation for, apart from his son's groom, there was no man in whom he was prepared to put his trust. Even his loyal nephew Charles had refused to answer his summons, sending to say that he had more pressing matters to attend to at the moment and would come as soon as he could.

Tiptree was aware of his lordship's difficulty and, although flattered that he had been chosen to be the earl's confidante, his only concern at the moment was for his guvnor's recovery and he was barely interested in what he thought of as a 'local skirmish' for, in spite of having been a witness to Lady Butler's breakdown, he still had the feeling that Miss Harriet was really to blame for all of this turmoil and the sooner her grandfather arrived to remove her the better it would be for everyone.

The earl had been obliged to hold court in his bedchamber, owing to his inability to manage the stairs without the assistance of two sturdy footmen but, since he had vehemently protested against that particular system of conveyance and scathingly pointed out the awkwardness and inconvenience it would cause all round, all conferences were henceforth held in his room.

Mrs Gibson despaired of keeping the carpets in any sort of order as a succession of muddied footwear beat a path to his door but, with two other invalids in the house, she supposed she must cope and, as her concern for his young lordship was greater than her concern for the carpets, she instructed the housemaids to do the best they could under the difficult circumstances and to be sure to be extra quiet outside the poor viscount's door.

Tiptree had helped to carry his master up to his room himself and had curtly told Kimble to 'clear off, if he knew what was good for him'. Since Kimble had always known what was good for himself and, moreover, had never been able to stand up to Tiptree, he reluctantly complied and betook himself off to the boot-room, where he spent much of his time in tearful but dedicated drudgery, polishing and re-polishing his lordship's Hessians and top-boots until the leather was like to wear away. Apart from Sandford's parents and the physician, whom he was powerless to prevent, Tiptree mulishly refused to allow anyone to enter the viscount's chambers.

'He never needed anyone but me for nigh on ten years,' he said stubbornly, when Sir Basil had suggested that it might be better to send to Market Harborough for a pair of nurses.

Lady Caroline was too wise to allow the two men to argue across her son's sickbed and had gently persuaded the physician that Sandford could not hope to get better care from anyone other than Tiptree. Everything that the groom required was, therefore, provided without question and, apart from insisting that they be given regular reports on the vis-

count's condition, the earl and countess forced themselves
to remain as much as possible in the background.

A whole day and a night had elapsed since Sandford and
Harriet had been carried back from Potter's cottage and his
lordship was still in very poor shape. He had suffered a mild
concussion in his fall and one of his hands had been badly
burned, but it was the problems brought about by the smoke
inhalation that were causing Sir Basil the gravest concern.

Harriet had managed to avoid breathing in great quantities
of smoke, owing to her final inspiration of throwing her
damp habit skirt over her head before crouching down beside Billy, and the wet sacking in which she had wrapped
the boy had protected him from the excesses of both heat
and smoke.

Sir Basil had bound up her head and, in spite of her protests, had insisted upon her remaining in bed until, with
nourishing broths and custards, her strength should return.
She desperately needed to go to Sandford, to talk to him, if
possible, or even just to see him, but Rose had informed her
of Tiptree's adamant refusal to allow the viscount any visitors. Harriet, her heart filled with despair, was constrained
to wait for her share of the all-too-infrequent reports on his
lordship's welfare.

Now, glumly supping some of the restorative chicken
broth that Cook appeared to be making by the cauldron-
load, she contemplated her sadly ravaged hands, which had
suffered greatly from her exertions in the cellar. Cracked
and broken fingernails, blisters, grazes and callouses—a
very unlovely sight, she sighed, putting down her bowl and
tucking the offending objects beneath the bedsheets, wondering whether Sir Basil would allow her to get up and take
a bath.

Rose had sponged away most of the filthy grime before
putting her mistress to bed, but Harriet was still conscious

of the unpleasant stench of smoke and burning timber and felt an overwhelming need to wash her hair. She was busily speculating on the possibilities of this delightful prospect when Rose burst into the room.

'Oh, miss!' Her eyes were shining. 'They're here! Your grandfather has arrived! Her ladyship is taking them into the drawing-room this very minute!'

'Them?' Harriet was confused, but not for many moments as the door was suddenly thrust open and her own dear mama almost ran across the floor to her bedside.

'Dearest girl!' her mother cried, holding her tightly. 'I was so worried! Let me look at you! Oh, heavens! What have they done to you?'

Little by little, in between the tears and the exclamations of shock and horror, Harriet unfolded her tale and when it had been brought up to date she begged Lady Middleton, for, sadly, this was now her mother's title, to account for her own presence at Beldale.

'For I was expecting only my grandfather,' she said, still gripping her mother's hands. 'I can hardly believe that you are really here!'

Her mother smiled in recollection of the momentous day when her father had descended upon Middleton Hall to extract his long-lost daughter from Sir Chester's clutches and she related her own story with undisguised relish.

'It was quite amazing—he burst in—literally! Swathed in his cloak and tartan kilt—Middleton was terrified! *I* recognised him immediately, of course, and he simply *ordered* me to get my cloak and bonnet and get into the carriage!'

Harriet stared at her mother, wide-eyed. 'He sounds very high-handed,' she said, thinking of such another.

'There was no other way to deal with the situation,' said Lady Middleton, laughing at the expression on her daughter's face. 'Father told Sir Chester what he thought of him,

and—oh, Harriet, it's so wonderful—he says he can probably have the marriage annulled—because he's a Lord of
Court or something—isn't it marvellous? We're to go back
to Craigburn with Father as soon as you are well enough to
travel!'

Harriet took a deep breath. 'I'm afraid I cannot do that,
Mama,' she said, her voice firm.

Her mother stared at her in consternation. 'But of course
you can, dearest,' she said. 'Her ladyship will not expect
you to remain here now that we are come for you!'

'I cannot leave until I know that Rob—Lord Sandford is
recovered,' said Harriet obstinately. 'He saved my life,
Mama—you must see that I cannot go until I can thank
him!'

Sarah Middleton stared closely at her daughter in frowning curiosity, then a sudden smile lit up her face. 'Yes, of
course, dearest,' she said, almost absent-mindedly. 'I do see
that—and we must all thank his lordship!' She looked about
Harriet's bedchamber and beckoned to the waiting Rose.

'I think Miss Cordell might have a bath, Rose—could you
see to it, please?'

The smiling girl curtsied and went below to make the
necessary domestic arrangements while Harriet's mother examined her daughter's wounds, exclaiming sadly at the loss
of her pretty ringlets.

'Papa so loved your hair,' she said, her eyes suddenly
glistening, and Harriet reached forward to clasp her hand.

'I know,' she said gently, 'but this is so much easier to
deal with—in fact, you might like to try it yourself,' she
added teasingly. 'Lord William says that I remind him of a
marigold! Oh, Mama! You will love him—he has such a
sense of humour and he is so wise!'

'The whole family has been very good to you, Harriet,'
said her mother, beaming again. 'Lady Caroline did not stop

singing your praises until I begged to come and see whether this paragon was indeed my own girl—for it seems that the entire local population has called to deliver flowers or to wish you well! How we will ever be able to thank them, I cannot imagine!'

With Rose and her mother both vying in their efforts to assist her, Harriet soon found herself bathed and dressed in her favourite primrose muslin. Sarah agreed that the now shining mop of curls did indeed suit her daughter and decided, after some deliberation, that the head-bandage was an unnecessary ornament, and elected instead to dress the wound with a light dusting of basilicum powder. Standing back to survey the finished effect, she heaved such a heavy sigh that Harriet was immediately filled with apprehension.

'What is it, Mama?' she said anxiously. 'You think that Grandfather will not approve of me?'

'Oh, I am sure he will, dearest.' Her mother tremulously smiled. 'I was merely wondering how long we would—but no matter—we must go down. Father will have been waiting with such impatience!'

As Harriet descended the stairs, gripping Sarah's hand tightly in her own, she was filled with very mixed emotions but she need not have worried, for as soon as she approached the door of the salon a huge giant of a man came bustling out and clasped her to his chest.

'Child, och—child,' was all he seemed able to utter, as he rocked her against him. Then he held her away and stared down at her with such affection in his eyes that she almost wept.

'Grandfather?' she whispered timidly.

'Och, you're a sight for an old fool's eyes—that's for sure,' he said, as he led her to a sofa and sat himself down beside her, gently holding her damaged hands in his own huge ones. 'You've the looks of your dear grandmother—

same wicked eyes, I see!' And he let out a great bellow of laughter at her shocked look. 'Och, now—that's a good thing, believe me, lassy—your grandmother broke a few hearts with hers, I can tell you! But she chose me—and I'm gey thankful that she stayed long enough to produce the two of you!'

Harriet looked up at her mother in blushing consternation, but both Sarah and Lady Caroline were regarding Ramsey with such fond amusement that she at once relaxed and began to warm to the old gentleman.

'It was very good of you to come so quickly,' she began, but he brushed aside her attempts at gratitude and berated himself for having been such a stubborn old fool to waste so many precious years and promised that he intended to do his best to make up for his past obstinacy.

'For I can be a bit of a block-head, as your mama will confirm,' he confessed, twinkling his blue eyes at Sarah. 'I sometimes canna bear to admit that I'm wrong, you see— and I'm a great one for digging my toes in!'

'Oh, but I'm exactly the same!' exclaimed Harriet, in astonishment. 'I do try to curb my impetuosity, of course, but it usually gets the better of me,' she finished, somewhat shamefacedly recollecting the most recent disaster.

Lord Ramsey patted her hand. 'There, there,' he said comfortingly. 'Ye can hardly be blamed for what you've inherited from your grandsire—as long as you're not such a fool as to allow it to blight your life. And remember, lassy—obstinacy can be regarded as a great strength as well as a weakness. Ye just have to learn to judge when to use it—and I'm mebbe not the best teacher!'

They all laughed and Harriet leaned forward and kissed him on his cheek.

'I'm so very glad to have met you at last,' she said, with a catch in her throat, for she could hardly help thinking that if only her other hopes were realised it was possible that she would not be returning to Craigburn with him as he obviously expected.

With this thought now uppermost in her mind, she turned to the countess and inquired as to the latest reports from Lord Sandford's sickbed and learned that the viscount was improving, but that Tiptree had continued to deny admittance to visitors for, as he had said, 'Seeing as he can hardly breathe, my lady, there's not much use expecting him to hold a conversation.'

Harriet's mother, noting the shadow that had crossed her daughter's face at this news, tentatively put forward her own suggestion.

'I wonder if Sergeant Tiptree would allow me to assist him with his patient,' she said. 'He knows that I have had a good deal of experience with this condition—he may be willing to trust me.'

The countess was perfectly agreeable that Sarah should petition Tiptree and, leaving a fretting Harriet to relate her misadventures to her grandfather, the two ladies left the room.

'Dinna fash, lassy,' said Ramsey, soon noting her distracted air. 'Your laddie is in good hands—and he's no weakling, so I'm told.'

Harriet, blushing, shot him a look of startled gratitude. 'I feel that his injuries are my fault,' she confided in him. 'If I had not been so hot-headed—if I had waited for Davy…'

The old man shook his head and placed his finger on her lips to silence her. 'Life is full of "ifs and buts",' he said, 'and it does no good to dwell on them—what's past is over—look to the future. Having wasted years meself, I'll not be happy to see you do the same. Now tell me the whole tale—for you must acknowledge that these have been gey queer happenings!'

He listened intently to her story from its wayside beginning to its fiery conclusion and, apart from frowning and nodding and occasionally shaking his head, he chose not to interrupt her flow of words. When she had quite finished he closed his eyes for a moment or two before he spoke.

'Ye've had a lucky escape, lassy,' he grunted. 'But I don't doubt that ye have your father's courage in ye—aye, I'm prepared to own he was a fine man—fer all he stole my daughter!'

However, his bright blue eyes were teasing her as he said this and, delighted at his words about her dear papa, Harriet beamed back at him as he stood up and held out his hand to help her to her feet.

'I think we might go and pay Beldale himself a visit,' he said. 'I fancy I've a few questions that I'd like to put to him. He'll be eager to take a good look at you too, I shouldn't wonder.'

The earl was, of course, delighted to see that Harriet had suffered no great ill effects from her misadventure, and insisted that she sit on his footstool, close beside him, where he could stroke her head and hold her poor ravaged hands at one and the same time.

'For I am constantly reminding myself,' he told Ramsey, 'how near we all came to losing her and I swear I shall have nightmares for many weeks to come!'

Ramsey sat down on the chair in the embrasure next to them, his huge bulk almost blocking the light.

'Aye—ye'd have had some explaining to do,' he grinned. 'But put away your dismals, man—we have her here safe with us—and I hear that your boy is improving by the hour—so all's well that ends well, as they say!'

'If, indeed, it has ended,' said Lady Caroline, who was also present, having recently deposited Sarah with a surprised and grateful Tiptree. 'We are still no wiser as to the reasons behind this man's abduction and—attempted *murder*—for that is what it was, dear child!' She had seen Harriet's shocked expression. 'He is still at large—I, for one, shall never feel safe until he is captured!'

'I cannot believe that he would dare to show his face anywhere in the vicinity,' cried Harriet, trembling at the thought. 'Everyone in the village would surely lynch him after what he did to Billy!'

'I doubt it would be Billy they had in mind while they were stringing him up, lass!' Ramsey's eyes met Lord William's in some amusement. 'I hear that some of them have a bit of a fondness for yourself!'

'Goodness me, yes,' said her ladyship. 'They have been coming to the doors—both back and front—in droves. The vicar, Squire Bevans, young Cedric Lambert—and most of *his* friends—not to mention old Potter's family and Lady Eugenie's "ladies"—it will take you a month to go round and thank them all for their good wishes!'

Harriet beamed. 'I shall be pleased to do it,' she said. 'They will have been concerned for the little boy, you know—he was so afraid. It was a dreadful thing to do—to put such a small child in a dark nasty place like that—he must be a very evil man and Lady Caroline is right! How can we go on as normal when we do not know why he did these things? If he is a madman on the loose, then surely Judith and her children could be in very grave danger?'

Ramsey was scratching at his beard and nodding his head at his granddaughter's words.

'That's true,' he said. 'I've been pondering on this very thing and a thought occurs to me. This Lady Butler I keep hearing about—your daughter-in-law's mother—she wouldn't have been one Ernestine Carr, I suppose? Married Freddy Butler—you remember him, Beldale—very serious sort of fellow—got a knighthood for some Egyptian relics he dug up?'

'Yes, of course.' Lady Caroline clapped her hands. 'Fancy you knowing Sir Frederick—and Lady Butler too. We knew her name was Ernestine, of course, but we would never have dreamt of using it—she wasn't our most favourite person—I always felt so sorry for Judith.' She turned to Harriet. 'Her father persuaded us to let her study with the twins' tutor—her governesses were totally incapable of controlling her. Her mother spoilt her so dreadfully—it's amazing that she turned out so well, although her father was such a dear sweet man—how he can have married…!'

'Aye—I was coming to that,' interrupted Ramsey. 'I wondered if ye possibly didn't know the whole story—it was quite well hushed up, as I recall.'

'Well, don't keep us all in suspense, man,' said Beldale, leaning forward in eager anticipation. 'I knew she'd committed some unpardonable sin—or crime—out with it!'

Laughing, Lord Ramsey shook his head. 'Nay, Will,' he said. 'She was quite a wee peach, if my memory serves me right—just out of the schoolroom at the time and in her first Season. Anyway, her family managed to get her engaged to Jack Fellowes—Viscount Moffat, that was…'

'Moffat?' asked Lady Caroline wonderingly. 'But surely he…?'

'Aye—I see ye remember—he eloped with an opera-dancer and went off to the Americas—jilted the Carr lass at the altar.'

'I never heard that part of the story,' exclaimed her ladyship. 'How dreadful for her—but I collect that she was well into her twenties when she married Sir Frederick…'

'Well, no doubt she was holding out for a better offer—her mother was mighty keen for her to be a countess, as I recall!'

'Poor Lady Butler,' said Harriet, who had been listening to her grandfather's tale with her eyes full of sadness. 'No wonder she always acts in such a grand manner—it must have been an awful shock for her to have her sweetheart…!'

'Sweetheart!' Beldale hooted. 'I cannot imagine the Butler in love with anyone but herself!'

'Do not be so unkind, William,' chided Lady Caroline. 'We do know that the Butlers lost two babies before Judith was born—that was why *she* was so spoilt, of course,' she added, in explanation to Lord Ramsey. 'Apparently Lady Butler insisted upon travelling abroad with Sir Frederick when he was involved in those archaeological diggings— even when she was with child. As a result, she lost both of Judith's brothers at birth, which must have been quite unbearable for her!'

'Oh, poor lady!' Harriet was greatly moved by this tale. 'No wonder she is always saying that Life is unfair—to her it must seem dreadfully so! To lose two babies, her husband, then her son-in-law…!' She stopped in dismay, remembering that Philip had also been the Hursts' son. 'I'm terribly sorry, ma'am,' she said to Lady Caroline. 'How thoughtless of me!'

The countess gave her a gentle smile. 'But it is true, my dear,' she said. 'Philip was her son-in-law. I believe she grew quite fond of him—although Robert would have been her first choice, I suspect!'

Harriet nodded. 'Yes, Judith has said so—and I believe that Lady Butler still has aspirations in that respect—although Judith has confessed to me a certain fondness for Charles Ridgeway— Oh, dear! I should not be telling you this!' Her hand flew to her mouth in confusion.

Three pairs of eyes looked at her.

'Judith and Charles!' exclaimed Lady Caroline. 'But of course! That would be perfect!'

Harriet laughed at the countess's obvious delight, but then her face became more serious as she continued, 'I'm afraid that Charles does not think so, my lady. He is very concerned at his lack of fortune. He says he cannot offer for Judith. Perhaps *you* can persuade him otherwise?'

Beldale regarded her in some amusement. 'Still determined to right the world's wrongs, little one?' he said, patting her hand gently. 'I can see we shall have to keep a tight rein on you until Sandford recovers. As to Ridgeway's lack of fortune—it has always been my intention to leave him well provided for. He is my sister's son, after all, and has earned his share of the estate—although it is odd in him not to have answered my summons. He must know that I need to talk with him!'

'I hear he has his hands full,' Ramsey consoled him. 'He'll still be looking for the Beckett chappie—as well as trying to oversee all the estates—and I'm told that he took a bang on the head himself! Would ye care for me to ride over and see if he needs anything—I've four big lads of my own with me who have always proved very handy in an emergency!'

It was agreed that Ramsey should go to Westpark. Harriet did her best to persuade her hosts to allow her to accompany her grandfather, but Lady Caroline was adamant in her refusal.

'Until the man Beckett is safely under lock and key,' she said, 'we cannot think of letting you out of our sight and, in any event...' she cleverly played her trump card '—supposing Robert were to ask for you?'

'Oh, yes, of course!' Harriet nodded in instant agreement. 'He will surely be himself soon—Mama is the *best* nurse!'

'Tiptree might argue with that,' laughed the countess, 'but I'm sure that between the two of them they will soon have him on his feet again.'

Chapter Seventeen

Sandford was sure he must be dreaming. He could see Mrs Major at the foot of his bed. She was calmly rolling bandages and was in deep conversation with Sergeant Tiptree, who seemed to have given up wearing his uniform!

The viscount tried to struggle upright, but found that one of his arms was encased in strapping, added to which was the desperately uncomfortable sensation of burning inside his chest every time he tried to take a breath.

'Tip?' he groaned. 'What's happened—the men…?'

As the two heads turned towards him, his brain cleared in a sudden flash and he threshed his limbs in a frustrated effort to lift himself.

'Harriet! Oh, dear God!' he gasped, fighting to get some air into his lungs.

'Keep still, your lordship,' came Sarah's voice, and his eyes widened in alarm as he realised that it was indeed Mrs Major standing beside him. If Harriet's mother was here at Beldale, it could mean only one thing! Harriet had not survived the fire!

He sank back on to his pillows in weary defeat and screwed up his eyes, unable to prevent the unmanly tears from welling up. Locked inside his crushing misery he ignored the cool, damp cloths that were being applied to his face, but was eventually forced to respond when he felt Tiptree's strong arms reaching behind him to raise his shoulders from the pillows. He was startled to observe the wide smile on Sarah's lips.

'Another pillow, my lord,' she said. 'The more upright you are, the easier you will find it. In a little while we will get you into a chair by the open window where the air is fresh and clean. Will you take a sip of water?'

Sandford shook his head, his eyes on her face as she held the glass to his lips.

'Harriet?' he croaked, dreading her answer.

'Harriet is very well, my lord,' said Sarah, with a gentle smile at Sandford's hoarse gasp. 'We are all extremely grateful to you—you undoubtedly saved her life.'

As the waves of relief flooded through him, Sandford allowed himself to take a sip of the cooling draught. Thank God, oh, thank God! She was safe! He had not failed her. All would be well! Dismissing his pain, he tried to rise.

'Where is she?' he demanded. 'I must see her.'

'She is resting, my lord,' replied Sarah, soothingly. 'She, too, needs to recover from the dreadful experience.'

For a moment Sandford was silent. Then, 'The boy? Was he hurt much?'

'Right as rain, sir,' came Tiptree's assurance. 'Strutting round the village fit to burst, I hear!'

Exhausted, Sandford lay back, eyes closed, as he digested this piece of information until another thought flashed into his mind.

'Tip! The man—Beckett—you have him?' he shot out anxiously.

Tiptree shook his head. 'Gone to ground, sir,' he said glumly. 'Hinds—the stable-lad—he's been collared but he's refusing to talk—not too bright, you see, sir. Mr Ridgeway's holding him at Westpark, but what with his lordship out of action and yourself, sir…'

'Good God, man—let me up!' protested Sandford, as both Tiptree and Sarah held his shoulders back against the pillows. 'How long have I been here?'

'All day yesterday, sir—and coughing fit to die, if I might mention it,' replied Tiptree calmly. 'It's now Tuesday noon and Miss Cordell's mother and grandfather arrived not two hours since. You can't get up, sir, not until you can breathe proper—and you will no doubt be pleased to know that I stopped the quack from bleeding you—so if you could just keep still for a bit longer, you'll be as right as rain.'

The viscount ceased his struggles and glared truculently at his man.

'Well, get me over to the window—I can't stay here forever—and what's the damage to my hand?' He waved his left arm at them.

He learned that, although his riding gloves had taken most of the punishment from his ruthless handling of the burning timbers, the left one had finally disintegrated, leaving him with suppurating blisters on the palm of his hand.

'You need have no fear, my lord,' said Sarah comfortingly. 'You will not lose the use of your hand, for we have applied goose-fat and its healing powers are well known in such cases.'

'But I need to see Harriet now!' rasped their patient petulantly. 'Why can't I see her?'

Tiptree shook his head. 'Question is, sir—if I might be so bold—whether you would want Miss Cordell to see you, sir—seeing as how you're not exactly in your best looks…!'

Sandford cast him a baleful look. 'What the devil do you mean by that, damn you?'

'Oh, a bit of a singe here and there, guv,' returned Tiptree cheerfully. 'Nothing that Kimble won't be able to deal with—soon as it grows back, of course!'

Groaning, Sandford threw himself back against the pillows. 'I have to speak to my father,' he said weakly. 'There are things to be done—the man is still out there!'

'And Harriet is quite safe here, my lord,' said Sarah soothingly. 'Just take a sip of this, it will help your throat.'

'No drugs,' he slurred, as his eyes closed. 'No drugs, Tip...' and he was asleep, once more.

'He has an aversion to opiates and such, ma'am,' said the groom, straightening the sheet which covered his master's form. 'And he won't be cupped, neither—regular pig-head, sometimes.'

'Well, he's a strong, healthy young man—he shouldn't need any of those things,' replied Sarah, putting down the glass of lemonade that the viscount had refused. 'Perhaps when he wakes up again we could get him into a chair by the window—I wonder if the earl has one of those wicker chairs they use on the Bath promenade—the ones with wheels?'

'Not that I know of, ma'am—but I'm sure they'd soon get one if we asked—Lord William could have done with one of them himself these last few weeks.'

They settled themselves comfortably beside a table at the window, Sarah engaged in some sewing she had brought with her and Tiptree immersed in the latest broadsheet from London. She applied herself to her stitchery for some minutes, then looked up and said to him, 'Harriet seems to think that you hold her responsible for Lord Sandford's injuries.'

Tiptree flushed, and looked uncomfortable. 'I'm sure I've never said so, ma'am,' he replied, frowning.

'But you do think so?' Sarah persisted.

'Well, I will say that his lordship has been behaving very

strangely these last couple of weeks—forever losing his temper and drinking—quite out of character, ma'am—and the hours he's spent looking for these chaps…!'

The groom stopped, remembering Sandford's warning that Lady Butler's disclosures were not to be repeated.

Sarah regarded him silently for a few minutes. 'These two—Beckett and Hinds, isn't it?' At his sudden start, she smiled. 'Lady Caroline has only repeated what I suspect everyone in the village knows by now, sergeant, and you cannot prevent servants gossiping. The story is that his lordship and yourself found two of Mrs Hurst's elderly menservants attacked and left for dead, as a result of which Lady Butler suffered some sort of seizure and was taken to the Dower House and placed under Lady Eugenie's care. Mr Ridgeway, it appears, has apprehended the—minor—culprit, who he has under lock and key—am I correct, so far?' She studied his reaction keenly.

'No keeping secrets from house staff, it seems,' replied Tiptree, shrugging his shoulders and picking up his newspaper again. Behind its sheets he was privately congratulating Ridgeway on his quick thinking—the story was quite credible!

'The stable-boy—Hinds—is, apparently, a little—how shall I put it…?'

'Feeble-minded,' finished Tiptree shortly. 'Wouldn't say "boo" to a goose, so they say. Can't get anything out of him, apart from "Matt'll sort it out"!'

'Matt?'

'Matt Beckett, ma'am—seems he's the real villain of the piece—the one who fired the cellar!'

Sarah shuddered. 'How close she came to death!'

Tiptree cleared his throat. 'They all three did, ma'am,' he reminded her, then, after a pause, 'We once had this old colour-sergeant who used to believe that everyone is born with an allotted time-span—quite a comforting thought for a soldier, I used to think—nobody goes before his time is up, whatever happens!'

'Barring accidents, surely?'

'No such thing as an accident, he used to say—all part of a great big masterplan—everything connected to something else—all pre-determined!'

'So we all have a part to play in everyone else's destiny— and they in ours?'

'Ah, well,' grinned Tiptree sheepishly. 'I admit it gets a bit deep.'

'No, I'm fascinated—did you agree with him?'

The groom shuffled uncomfortably under her thoughtful gaze. 'Well—I dare say it sounds a bit high-flown for a soldier, ma'am, but I suppose I've been inclined to go along with it. I'm still here, at any rate—though what my destiny might be is anyone's guess!'

'Would your sergeant have said that someone who saves a person's life is helping them to fulfil their destiny, I wonder?' Sarah mused, as she poured herself a glass of lemonade.

'Doubtless, he would, ma'am,' said Tiptree, girding his own thoughts as he looked towards the now peacefully sleeping viscount.

Sarah studied his pensive face. 'Do you recall, I wonder,' she said gently, 'our retreat to Corunna?'

Tiptree frowned at her. 'I'm hardly likely to forget it, ma'am,' he said, in some surprise. 'Pretty much the worst days of my life, I'd say.'

'Yes, it was a terrifying time,' agreed Sarah. 'You may recall helping to get the baggage wagons across the River Duoro in full flood?'

'Aye—I do that. We lost most of it, if my memory serves me right—and a host of good men in addition. Freezing cold water right up to the saddles…' He shuddered in sudden recollection of that awful night. 'Eight years ago that was—December '08—right?'

Sarah nodded. 'One of the wagons was carrying children,' she reminded him. 'You were riding alongside.'

He stared at her, taken aback. 'Funny you should think of that, ma'am,' he said. 'I hadn't realised you were with that train!'

'Do you remember what happened, sergeant?' she asked softly.

He lowered his eyes. 'I don't like to think of it, ma'am,' he said. 'Them poor little ones…!'

'You and Lieutenant Sanders saved almost all of them—and, if you really believe in your colour-sergeant's Destiny theory, you have no reason to reproach yourself—you were not responsible for the dreadful torrent that swept the two youngsters away.'

He pondered gravely over this, and then his face brightened. 'Do you remember that little lass—the one who jumped in after the baby's basket? She was a plucky bit and no mistake!'

Sarah's lips curved. 'You pulled them both out—half-drowned, they were, the pair of them! Were you fulfilling your own destiny, sergeant, or helping them fulfil theirs, I wonder?'

'Bit of both, wouldn't you say?' Tiptree grinned at her. 'I wonder what became of them?'

'Oh, the baby was Lord Chadwell's son—I believe he's at Eton, now.'

'Fancy that—and that girl must be a young woman by now—nineteen or twenty, perhaps? Probably married, with babies of her own!'

'Twenty years old last May, sergeant,' she said, her eyes twinkling, 'and no—not yet married.'

For a moment he stared at her in shocked disbelief. 'Miss Harriet?' he stammered. '*That* was Miss Harriet?'

Sarah nodded. 'Her father used to say that he hoped she had a cat's nine lives to go with the eyes—and, since you have now been closely involved in saving at least *three* of those lives, sergeant—what do you think Harriet's destiny might be?'

Tiptree swallowed and his glance travelled once more to the figure on the bed. 'I'd say that it's becoming clearer by the moment, ma'am,' he replied gruffly.

Chapter Eighteen

Patience was not Harriet's forte. She had resigned herself to remaining quietly in the library while her grandfather paid his visit to Westpark and her mother attended Sandford. Disconsolately picking up one book after another, she found it impossible to give her full attention even to her most favourite authors and the onerous ticking of the wall-clock merely served to emphasise how slowly the minutes dragged by.

She had paid a lengthy visit to the kitchens to offer her grateful thanks to the smiling staff and both young Rothman and Cooper had insisted upon accompanying her to the stables where her tributes were gently brushed aside by the grinning Smithers and his men, who were all delighted to see her 'up and about' again.

'Don't you worry about him, miss,' said the head groom, in answer to Harriet's questions about Beckett. 'He'll not dare show his face round here again. My guess is he's left the country—probably signed up on one of His Majesty's ships and gone to one of them there voodoo lands—suit him just about right, we're all thinking!'

'Leaving young Hinds to shoulder all the blame,' Harriet

pointed out, as she stroked the now recovered Clipper's nose. 'I do pity him—he must be so confused, poor boy!'

Smithers regarded her in astonishment. 'But there's no doubt he was involved, miss,' he said, in some consternation. 'He was with Beckett when Mr Ridgeway was attacked—we all know that!'

'Yes, I know, Mr Smithers,' replied Harriet awkwardly. 'It's just that—well, you know everyone agrees that he isn't very bright—perhaps he didn't appreciate what Beckett was doing?'

'Aye, well, you may be right,' said the man, shaking his head. 'I doubt we'll ever know what was behind it all, what with Beckett sloping off and Hinds playing mummer. We're all sorry that you got caught up in their shenanigans, miss, and that's a fact. Please God their lordships will soon be back on their feet taking charge again and we can all get back to normal.'

'Amen to that, Mr Smithers,' replied Harriet fervently, as she turned to leave.

Now, sitting in the heavy silence of the library, flicking idly through the pages of *Chesterfield's Letters*, she wondered how long it would be before her mother could persuade Tiptree to allow her to visit the viscount. Sarah had left her patient briefly to join Lady Caroline and herself for a hurried repast and had assured them both that Sandford had not been badly damaged and that as soon as she and Tiptree had seated him by the open window of his room his breathing had rapidly improved. He had taken some nourishment and was, apparently, impatient to 'get back in the saddle', as Tiptree had put it, and, whilst Harriet was overjoyed to hear this news, she was somewhat disconcerted that his lordship had not asked for her.

She was beginning to fear that the outcome of her latest escapade must have given the viscount such a violent dislike of her that he could not bring himself to face her and this lowering thought was unendurable. During her incarceration in the cellar she had suddenly realised, with a terrible clarity, that Robert Hurst was, indeed, the only man she could ever love. Now she was miserably certain that any passion he may once have felt for her must have been utterly quashed by his recent horrifying experience caused, he would surely have realised, by her wilful disregard of his instructions. It was no wonder he was refusing to see her!

She had been reluctant to voice any of these fears to her mother because it would have involved revealing certain unflattering particulars about her own conduct, which she had been careful to omit from her earlier narration. She shuddered as she once again recalled the foolish and defiant words she had thrown at Sandford and, with equal distaste, shrank from the memory of her cold-blooded resolution to accept his expected offer of marriage. How could she have considered herself suitable for such a position? she wondered, now amazed at her own arrogant presumption.

A tap on the door disturbed her melancholy reverie and she looked up to see March ushering Judith Hurst into the room. Harriet sprang to her feet in delight.

'Oh, how glad I am to see you!' she exclaimed, holding out her hands with pleasure. 'How is Lady Butler? And Charles? He has recovered?'

'Sit down, silly girl,' responded Judith, with a little smile at her friend's exuberance. 'You are supposed to be resting—I promised not to get you excited!'

'Oh, pooh to that, Judith—I am bored to distraction and in such a fit of the dismals! But, what are you doing here? No one can see Sandford—Tiptree's orders!'

'I came to see you!' said Judith. 'Your grandfather said that you were up and dressed, so I came as soon as I could.

What a charmer he is, to be sure—he is still deep in con-
ference with Charles at the Dower House.'

'But Lady Butler? What happened?'

Judith's face at once became serious. 'Mama has had a
stroke,' she said quietly. 'Two of our menservants were
overpowered—I don't know how much you already know?'

The young widow was still badly shaken by the events
that had occurred and had readily agreed with both Sandford
and Ridgeway that the shocking revelations were not for
public broadcast. Her mother's involvement in the conspir-
acy had horrified her, especially when she understood the
futile reasoning that lay behind the scheme, namely that
Harriet's being sent packing would be bound to bring about
a match between her brother-in-law and herself.

Following Sandford's return to Beldale on that fateful
night, Judith had railed long and hard at her mother and,
after informing the hysterical Lady Butler that she had every
intention of accepting Charles's hand, should he still care
to offer for her, she had stormed off to the kitchens to assist
Ridgeway with the two elderly servants, neither of whom
could recall a great deal of what had befallen them. After
rousing other members of staff, she and Charles had managed to get the stupefied pair to their bedchambers where
Charles had ordered a watch to be kept on them at all times.
Both he and Judith doubted that either of the old men were
capable of giving any trouble, but feared that their accomplice might try to contact them for some reason.

On returning to the hall where she had left her mother,
Judith had found the said lady surrounded by a bevy of
maids and footmen, in the throes of some sort of apoplectic
fit. Charles, at once taking charge, had sent for Sir Basil and
also for his mother who, being the first to arrive, had recommended that Lady Butler should be removed to the

Dower House immediately, where she herself would be pleased to look after the poor woman.

'For 'tis clear that she has had a paralytic seizure,' asserted Lady Eugenie, taking one look at Lady Butler's twisted countenance. 'You will never get her up to her room—she must be brought to the Dower House—a flat conveyance is all it requires. Don't worry, Judith, I shall take care of your mama—these dreadful events must have been too much for her!'

At Charles's warning glance, Judith kept her counsel and Lady Butler had been carefully conveyed to the Dower House, where she presently lay, paralysed down one side and able only to offer a savage gurgle in response to Lady Eugenie's kindly inquiries as to her feelings and requirements.

Judith had, naturally, suffered agonies of guilt over her mother's condition, believing her own outburst to be the cause of the seizure and she was only partly mollified by Charles's gentle suggestion that Lady Butler had already worked herself up into a fever pitch well before her daughter's intervention. As the news of Harriet's imprisonment and rescue gradually found its way to Westpark, Judith's feelings of guilt and sympathy for her mother dwindled to those of shame and remorse.

'How can I face them all?' she wept, upon hearing of the unfortunate trio's brush with death. 'My own mother! It is too awful to contemplate!'

Ridgeway's arms were around her in an instant. 'No one is to be told. Sandford was quite specific,' he reminded her. 'This is a family affair, Judith. Let's keep it that way.'

But now, face to face with Harriet, and having been furnished with the truth behind the girl's presence at Beldale, Judith was undecided as to how much of the story Sandford would wish her to know and, indeed, how much she already knew. She was aware that Lord Ramsey, a highly discerning landlord, had not been fooled for a moment by Ridgeway's ingenious tale about Lady Butler's seizure having been brought on by her shock at hearing of her servants' complicity in Harriet's disappearance.

'Try again, my lad,' he had said, frowning at Ridgeway. 'There's more in this than you're letting out. Don't take me for a fool—that old woman is somewhere at the bottom of this—I can feel it in my blood!' And, eventually, he had drawn the whole history from the reluctant Charles.

Judith realised that it was going to be equally impossible to spin Harriet a Banbury tale. She steeled herself to the prospect of the once-respected Butler name being dragged through the mud for some time to come and to the knowledge that dear Philip's children would have to bear most of the ignominy. Nevertheless, she bravely set about providing her young companion with a brief explanation as to her continual misfortunes during the past few weeks.

Harriet heard her out in silence, her green eyes, dark and unfathomable, fixed intently on Judith's face throughout the exposé. Judith's voice trembled as she reached the conclusion of her confession and her own soft brown eyes were filled with tears.

'Apologies are not enough, Harriet,' she choked. 'I do not know what to say to you!' She delved into her reticule for her handkerchief and turned her head away from Harriet's impassive face.

'And you say that Sandford instructed you to hush the matter up?' Harriet's voice was cool.

Judith nodded, dismayed but hardly surprised at the girl's offhand manner.

'He told us—Charles and myself—not to speak of it. Tiptree was present, of course and, apart from your grandfather, you are the only other person who knows. Even Aunt Eugenie believes that my mother's seizure was brought on by—other things.'

'Their lordships would not care for a family scandal,' said Harriet, standing up and carefully straightening her skirts. 'Please do not worry yourself on my account, Judith. You must know that I will not breathe a word about Lady Butler's involvement if that is what Sandford wishes.'

Judith also rose to her feet and, laying her hand on Harriet's arm, she said pleadingly, 'Are we not to be friends any longer? I know how angry you must be and I do so beg your forgiveness! Harriet, please speak to me!'

'I'm very sorry, Judith,' returned Harriet evenly. 'I realise what it must have cost you to come here and tell me this and—I do admire you beyond measure for your courage in doing so—but, as you are probably aware, I shall be travelling to Scotland with my mother and grandfather shortly, so it is unlikely that our paths will ever cross again. Now, if you will excuse me...'

Turning her back on her visitor, she walked quickly through the open doorway on to the rear terrace, leaving the stunned and white-faced Judith to see herself out.

Shaking with anguish, Harriet hastened along the terrace, running almost blindly down the steps that led into the gardens, where she came to a sudden halt, uncertain as to her next move. With weary resignation she leaned against the stone balustrade and stared bleakly across the rolling lawns towards the lake, from where the sparkling reflections of the late afternoon sunshine glinted through the trees.

Of course he would wish to keep such information to himself! His family name and reputation, she knew, were everything to him. Was that why he had striven so desperately to save Billy and herself from the burning cellar? For of course, murder would have been impossible to withhold from the guardians of the law! But to allow everyone to

believe that the villain was still at large when all the time
he knew that she was safely imprisoned in her bed! And to
think that she should have been so foolish as to believe that
he had raced to her rescue for quite other reasons! Tears
started into her eyes and she brushed them away angrily.
No! She would not weep over him! The sooner she put him
out of her thoughts the better, she decided, straightening her
shoulders resolutely. She determined that she would return
to Craigburn with her mother and grandfather as soon as
they were ready to undertake the journey; in the meantime,
perhaps she could persuade them to stay somewhere other
than Beldale.

Drearily retracing her steps, she found herself unable to
resist the temptation of casting a swift glance up towards
Sandford's window, but she recoiled in shocked dismay as
she saw that the viscount had observed her, for he was rising
to his feet and appeared to be shaking his fists at her! Her
face flaming with mortification, she quickened her pace
along the terrace towards the library doors, frantic to remove
herself from his wrathful gaze.

With a pounding heart she careered through the doorway,
only to find herself immediately pinioned in the very strong
clutches of a young man who was determinedly propelling
her into the room. He must have gained entry from the
shrubbery below the parapet whilst she had been standing
out there! Her furious struggles proved futile and his hand
over her mouth prevented her from crying out. He kicked
the terrace doors closed behind him before thrusting her
down on to a nearby sofa.

'Please don't make a sound, miss,' he warned her softly,
as he sprang towards the hall door and turned the key in the
lock. 'I have nothing to lose, it seems.'

'What do you want with me?' cried Harriet, shakily realising that her assailant must be the elusive Beckett. 'I have done nothing to harm you!'

As if undecided for a moment, he walked slowly towards her and stared down at her frightened face.

'I haven't come to hurt you,' he said heavily. 'I just wanted you to know.'

'I don't understand!' Harriet tried to rise, but he held her back against the cushions with one hand while his other delved into his coat pocket and brought forth a ragged sheet of paper.

'I have to make you understand...'

'I rather think not!' came Sandford's haughty drawl from the terrace. 'Move away from the lady, if you please! I have a pistol levelled at your head!'

Beckett spun round in fright, the paper fluttering from his hand and, as he sidled nervously away from her, Harriet was able to perceive the astonishing sight of the viscount lounging, apparently nonchalantly, against the door-frame, his good hand holding a pistol which was pointing steadily at the intruder.

'But how on earth...!' she exclaimed, as she leapt to her feet and rushed towards him.

'Down the ivy,' Sandford responded dismissively, not taking his eyes from the cowering Beckett.

'Down the ivy!' Eyes wide with shock, Harriet rapidly took in the viscount's appearance. His unbuttoned shirt was hanging loosely outside his breeches and he was in his stockinged feet! Patches of his soft brown hair had been trimmed close to his head, his face was ashen and through the unshaven stubble she could see beads of perspiration forming on his upper lip.

'Done it dozens of times,' he croaked, pressing his shoulders against the door-frame to support himself. 'Now, be a good girl and tie the fellow's hands—use a curtain cord—and don't put yourself between us!'

Harriet complied, with all the speed she could muster, having realised that Sandford was about to collapse at any moment. In a very few minutes she had whipped one of the curtain tie-backs from its hook and bound Beckett's hands behind him, motioning him to a chair, to the back of which she then secured the cord. He offered no resistance and seemed to be accepting his fate with calm indifference.

'Looks like he could do with a drink,' he said, nodding towards Sandford, as Harriet stood away from her endeavours. 'Better give him some brandy before he passes out!'

Harriet shot a startled glance at the viscount and saw that he was, indeed, having great difficulty maintaining his stance. She pulled a chair towards him and, after carefully helping him to lower himself into it, she hurried to the table to pour a generous measure of brandy from one of the decanters, returning swiftly to his side, where she knelt and gently held the glass to his trembling lips.

'I tried to warn you,' he gasped, after sipping some of the contents. 'Why did you ignore my signal?'

Harriet flushed. 'I thought you were shaking your fist at me!' she said, in a small voice, avoiding his eyes.

'Shaking my—what are you talking about, for God's sake?' His strength was returning and he dropped the firearm to the floor in order to grasp her hand in his good one.

'Take care! It could go off!' she admonished him, retrieving the pistol at once and, carefully pointing it away from him, attempted to defuse it. She raised her eyes to his in shocked astonishment. 'But it isn't loaded!' she exclaimed. 'You climbed down the ivy in *your* condition with an empty pistol! Are you mad?'

'Probably,' he nodded, with a weak grin. 'I couldn't manage to load it with only one hand—and I could hardly come unarmed, now could I? Why did you think I was shaking my fist at you—and why have you been refusing to come and see me?'

She stared at him pensively for a moment before sudden enlightenment dawned. 'Ask Tiptree,' she said sternly, getting to her feet. 'I thought that *you* didn't want to see *me*! He said you were too ill—thanks to this blackguard here!' She spun round to face their prisoner, having almost forgotten him in her concern for the viscount.

'Why are you still persecuting me?' she demanded of him. 'How could you let yourself be persuaded to do such awful things? What had you to gain from these devilish tricks?'

Beckett raised his head wearily. 'Nothing to gain, miss,' he said evenly. 'Plenty to lose, maybe—and—not that it makes a hap'orth of difference—it wasn't me who fired the cellar.'

'Quite right,' interrupted Sandford, finishing his brandy. 'It makes not the slightest difference—you're in it up to your neck—which will end up in a noose, if I have anything to do with it!'

Beckett regarded his captor impassively. 'I realised *that* as soon as Jack told me he'd knocked Miss Cordell into the cellar,' he said wryly. 'I hadn't reckoned on him being that foolish!'

'Save your story for the magistrates,' said Sandford curtly, getting to his feet and heading towards the locked door, but Harriet forestalled him and, clutching at his sleeve, she shook her head and said, in some urgency, 'No, wait— *I* want to hear his story—it does concern me, after all— please, *Robert*!'

Sandford paused, his lips twitching. 'Minx!' he said, as he sat himself down in a more comfortable armchair. 'Very well—ask away, if you must. But be prepared to have the

entire household trying to break the door down any minute—as soon as Tiptree gets back from his dinner and finds
me gone!'

Harriet pulled up a stool in front of Beckett and sat down
to face him. 'I know why Lady Butler wanted me out of the
way,' she said, ignoring Sandford's start of surprise. 'But
you made no attempt on my life on either of the first occasions—you simply set out to make me look foolish and
ill bred—why did you alter your—designs?'

Beckett stared back at her, biting his lip as she carefully
studied his expression. Suddenly her eyes softened and she
briskly commanded him to tell her the whole.

'From the beginning and with no lies, if you please!'

His mouth twisted momentarily. Then, 'The old missus—
Lady Butler—threatened to put us all off if we didn't come
up with something, miss,' he said, in a matter-of-fact tone
'I could probably have got work somewhere, but who would
have taken Uncle Eddie or old Pinter on—not to mention a
simpleton like Hinds? In the first place, she said that if Lord
William was to have a "little accident" his lordship here—'
he nodded towards Sandford '—would be sure to come back
from London and keep up his visits to Westpark and that
would be that. So I gave Jack—Hinds, that is—something
to slip to the earl's horse when he left him in the stables.
only his lordship fell awkwardly and he was out on the path
in the rain for such a long time before they found him—I
never intended him to be hurt so bad, sir,' he blurted out,
flinching at the murderous look on Sandford's face.

Harriet turned her head and frowned a reprimand at the
viscount before resuming her questioning. 'So Lord Sandford returned home—but with an unexpected complication
in tow,' she said encouragingly. 'What then? Lady Butler
told you to push me into the lake?'

Beckett shook his head. 'No, miss—that was my idea—

spur of the moment, really. *She* told us—Uncle Eddie, Hinds and me—that it would be easy to find ways of making you look ridiculous—and it wasn't. Jack tried loosening your saddle girth after your first visit to Westpark but—like he said—it turned out that you're too good a horsewoman not to check your own straps before you mount, so that didn't work.'

'Cut out the compliments,' said Sandford frostily. 'Get on with it.'

Beckett shrugged and continued. 'Well, I thought if I gave the Tatler lad a shilling he'd be sure to keep quiet, but he ran off without it so I knew I'd have to find him before he put the finger on me—but he's a wily little monkey and he just kept out of the way. Her ladyship was getting really het up because by then everybody was full of admiration for the young lady and—it was actually old Pinter's idea—we all rigged up the pantomime in the copse. I gave Pinter the herb to put into the icing on some of the biscuits and her ladyship organised the breakfast. By the time you got to the bridleway the dope had taken effect—the rest was easy.'

He stopped, eyeing Harriet speculatively. 'Could you loosen this cord a bit, miss? My hands and arms are going numb.'

'Serves you right if they drop off,' grated Sandford savagely, recalling the wood episode with distaste, but Harriet was already on her knees busily untying her knots.

She studied Beckett uncertainly as he sat chafing his hands. 'You won't attempt to escape?'

'Where would I go, miss?' he replied in a tired undertone, wincing as the blood returned to his fingers. 'I know when I'm beaten!'

Harriet waited for a few moments before asking him, 'What did you intend to do to Billy when you found him?'

The young man shifted uncomfortably on his chair.

'There's lots of ways of frightening an eight-year-old boy, miss—*I* should know—I've been there.' His lips trembled momentarily, then he looked her full in the face. 'It was when I found out who you were, miss,' he said, with a tremor in his voice. 'I sort of lost control for a bit and Jack—well, he's not too bright, see—he thought he was doing me a favour—'

'How do you mean?' interrupted Harriet. 'You found out who I am?'

'Your father, miss,' came the astonishing reply. 'He had my dad shot and—I wanted you to suffer like my mum had!'

'Had your dad shot!' cried Harriet indignantly. 'What nonsense! When was this, pray?'

'It was in Ireland—my dad was a trooper in your father's company—they were garrisoned in Dublin—1798, it was—I was six years old.'

'I *was* there,' said Harriet wonderingly. 'I don't remember—I was only a baby—about two, I should think.' She collected herself. 'My father was only a captain then—how could he have had your father shot?' she demanded fiercely.

'My mum got the letter from him.' He indicated the crumpled sheet of paper on the floor beside the sofa. 'I wanted you to read it. It says that my dad was shot for—desertion in the face of duty, it says, and there'd be no more pay for her. I'll never forget how she cried and then we were put out of our lodgings—we were destitute until Uncle Eddie got her some skivvying in the kitchens where he worked. Eighteen years I've carried that letter—and I swore I'd get even one day—now it turns out I'm just a coward—like my dad.'

His chin drooped on to his chest and Harriet, after retrieving the faded missive, looked at Sandford in confusion.

'Vinegar Hill, I should imagine—before my time,' he explained, with a frown. 'A local rabble attacked the garrison—only a bit of a skirmish, if I recollect my history. It isn't likely that your father could have had the man shot, though—needs to be a general or a colonel at the very least to issue that sort of order.'

Harriet nodded vigorously. 'That's what I thought—and Papa would only have written a personal letter to a next of kin if he had liked and admired the man!'

She unfolded the paper and stared down at the faded remnants of her beloved papa's well-remembered handwriting before turning once more to Beckett. 'My father probably didn't even believe in your father's guilt,' she cried accusingly. 'He must have written to your mother out of sympathy—and you have held a wicked grudge against him for all these years! I doubt that your father was a coward,' she said, and then added unkindly, 'He certainly wouldn't be very proud of his son!'

The man stiffened and his face turned scarlet, then he shrugged again. 'Likely you're right, miss,' he said, without expression. 'What are you going to do with me?'

'You still haven't told us why Hinds fired the cellar,' Sandford reminded him curtly. 'Or how Mr Ridgeway came by his injuries. You might as well finish the story.'

'Jack got into one of his panics when the whole village turned out,' said Beckett. 'After I'd told Miss Cordell that Mr Ridgeway had gone up the North Lane I sent Jack up the shortcut—he took one of the horses that were being saddled up. I cut across the hayfield on foot, but by the time I got there he had already pushed Miss Cordell into the cellar and boarded up the trap-door again. I didn't know then that he'd actually hit you, miss, I swear!'

His voice shook again at this point then, swallowing, he continued, 'Jack went over to the stables at Westpark to change the saddles while I went to find out what her lady-ship wanted us to do—she washed her hands of the whole thing, of course,' he added bitterly. 'By that time all our men were over at Beldale, so we both rode back.'

'You rode Clipper back here!' Harriet was astounded. 'Weren't you afraid someone would recognise her?'

'The whole place was swarming with horses by then,' Beckett pointed out, 'and it had started to rain quite heavily, too. When Mr Ridgeway said he was going to search the boathouse I made sure everyone knew we went with him so that it would seem as if we'd been there all morning.'

'But why on earth did you attack Mr Ridgeway?' demanded Sandford. 'If he was your alibi…'

'Jack and him had rowed over to check out the island and the guv'nor remembered that no one had been up to search the cottages. Trouble was, Jack lost his head and hit him with one of the oars—then he locked him in the pavilion. I was waiting by the boathouse and when he came back and told me what he'd done I knew there was nothing for it but to clear out. We told one of the gamekeepers that Mr Ridgeway had gone up to Staines and then we cut across to Bottom Meadow and took turns in putting off any other search parties that turned up.'

Only the ticking of the wall clock disturbed the silence that followed this confession until Sandford cleared his throat and asked, 'This Hinds—I heard that he was a harmless sort of fellow?'

Beckett nodded. 'He is, sir—mostly. He gets a bit beside himself sometimes, when the youngsters torment him—hide his things and call him names and suchlike but, until now, I've never known him get violent—that's my fault, too,' he added swiftly, 'because I told him I was going to get even with Miss Cordell—only I didn't mean to kill her!'

'What did you…?' Harriet and Sandford spoke as one and Beckett shifted uneasily.

'I was waiting until the coast was clear—I was going to

drug the two of them—you and Billy, miss—and take you to the city on a cart and leave you there!'

Harriet gazed at the man in a stunned rage. 'But why?' she wanted to know. 'What would have been the point of that? We would have woken up and explained and we'd have simply been brought back to Beldale!'

Sandford cleared his throat. 'Probably not, my dear,' he said, glowering at Beckett. 'I imagine you were thinking of leaving them in—how shall I put it—a certain area where Miss Cordell's protestations would be of less interest than her charms?'

Beckett nodded, keeping his eyes from Harriet's rosy blush. 'I wanted her to know the sort of life we'd been forced to lead—what it's like to starve and freeze in a filthy slum—and suffer as my mother suffered just to put bread in my mouth!' He put a hand to his lips to control the trembling and, in spite of her anger, Harriet felt a sudden surge of pity for the young man.

'I have had a little experience of the conditions you describe,' she told him gently. 'Not in the same way or for the same reasons, but enough to understand what you must have suffered. How old were you when you first came to Staines?'

'Eleven, miss. Uncle Eddie got the footman's job and mum was taken on as a kitchenmaid at first, then she became cook and I was given work in the gardens. I used to gather herbs for her to use and when Sir Frederick found out I was interested in such things he gave me some books and pamphlets from his collection. He taught me to read and write…' His voice tailed off and he sat slumped on his stool, his hands clenched between his knees.

Sandford stood up. 'None of this makes any difference, you know,' he told Harriet. 'The fellow's a criminal and he must be punished—along with all of his accomplices!'

'But I thought that you wanted to hush it all up!' exclaimed Harriet, in some surprise. 'Judith and Charles have been inventing all sorts of stories to keep Lady Butler's name out of it!'

'Damn!' Sandford sat down hurriedly. 'I'd forgotten about that! But that was before the fire—it's all too serious now, Harriet. Attempted murder and all that—you surely cannot mean them to get off scot-free?'

'Lady Butler has already paid dearly for her part, it seems,' Harriet reminded him. 'Hinds, if I understand correctly, cannot be held responsible for his actions—Lady Eugenie will know of a place where he can be safely housed and looked after, I'm certain—which leaves the two old servants.' She turned to confront Beckett, who had been listening impassively to her words.

'How did they—Pinter and your uncle Finchley—come to be bound and drugged on Sunday evening? Was that your doing?'

'I didn't want Uncle Eddie to be involved,' admitted the young man nervously. 'It was partly Pinter's idea. As soon as we realised that it was pretty well all over for us, he got me to drug the ale and tie them both up—as if they'd been attacked, he said, but I didn't hit them so I'm not to blame for the bruises they suffered.'

Sandford reddened and he leaned forward in surprise. 'How did you hear of their bruises?' he demanded truculently. 'Do you have another accomplice?'

Beckett shook his head. 'I was hiding in the oak settle,' he said, to the viscount's astonishment. 'When I heard you coming, there was nowhere else to go—I had to stay there until you left—and, when Mrs Hurst left her ladyship in the hall by herself, I knocked on the lid for her to let me out, but she started screaming fit to wake the dead and keeled off the settle in some sort of fit. All the servants came rushing in so I stayed there until everybody had gone. I heard Mr Ridgeway describing my uncle's injuries to the other servants.' He eyed Sandford pensively. 'I didn't hit them, sir, as you well know. I'm not a violent man!'

'Not a violent man!' Sandford gave a hoarse laugh. 'I take leave to argue with that!'

'Oh, but I don't think he is, Robert,' Harriet chided him. 'Oh, yes, I know he has given his potions and concoctions out rather indiscriminately, but he was rather *trapped* into it—surely you see that? I really don't see what good it will do to give him to the magistrate!'

'Very well, Harriet,' replied his lordship, with a sigh. 'What would you have me do with him—pat him on the back and give him the head gardener's position?'

'No, of course not—Mr Cooper would not care for—oh, I see! You were funning!' Having registered the smile that followed Sandford's remark, Harriet wrinkled her nose at him, then directed her attention to Beckett once more.

'You weren't intending to drag me forcibly from this room, I take it? You could have made your escape—why did you come back? Were you so determined, still?'

The young man shook his head emphatically. 'No, miss, I swear to God it wasn't that. I came to tell you—to show you the letter—I wanted you to know that I was sorry. I was going to ask you to help Jack—for there was no way that I could get to him!'

Harriet slowly rose to her feet and stood looking down at him for some moments before turning to Sandford. 'He's telling the truth, you know. I've had an idea.'

Without waiting for his reply, she laid her hand gently on Beckett's shoulder.

'Have you ever thought of training to be an apothecary or a pharmaceutist?' she asked him. At his look of amazement she smiled. 'It is possible, you know, and it is, perhaps, time your skills were put to the use Sir Frederick intended. We could make enquiries—perhaps there is somewhere in Bristol near your mother?'

'For God's sake, Harriet!' protested Sandford, clutching his head in despair as Beckett's eyes brightened and looked towards him hopefully. Heaving a great sigh, the viscount finally nodded, then motioned Harriet to unlock the hall door, outside of which they could hear the sounds of growing commotion.

'Better let them in,' he said in weary resignation.

Chapter Nineteen

Tiptree thrust open the library doors, angrily jostling Harriet to one side in spite of Sandford's attempted warning. He marched to the armchair in which his master was slumped and glared down at him in a fury. The viscount gave him a shamefaced grin.

'I know, Tip,' he said. 'But it was an emergency—and you weren't available—so I had to do it for you!'

The groom gave a puzzled frown. 'What, guv?' he said. 'Do what for me?'

'Well, I hear you seem to have made a bit of a habit of saving Miss Cordell's skin,' said Sandford, getting slowly to his feet and leaning on Tiptree's arm. 'Sorry to rob you of your fourth notch, but I had a fancy to even scores with you!'

'Young fool,' berated his man with a slight flush, then gaping as he recognised the third individual in the room. 'What's he doing here? What's been going on?'

'Tell you upstairs, old chap.' Sandford swayed momentarily and Harriet started forward in concern as Tiptree steadied his master. 'Just one thing—Beckett here is to be taken down to the kitchen for a hot meal but no one—and

I mean no one—is to speak a word to him. Get young Roth-man to watch him.'

He had observed the footman standing with the group of servants in the doorway, from where Lady Caroline and Harriet's mother had also been watching the proceedings in concerned silence. 'Now, if you will excuse me—I must go and lie down for a moment. Come along, Harriet!'

'I don't think so, guv!' protested Tiptree, helping the vis-count to the stairs, but Sandford ignored him and held out his good hand towards Harriet.

'You're not moving out of my sight for an instant, my girl,' he said, quite firmly, smiling at her startled look. 'Bring a book—or your tatting—or whatever will keep you in the same place for more than ten minutes. Lady Cordell is welcome to join us if she can prevent you from disap-pearing!'

Sarah stepped forward at once, beaming with pleasure at the viscount's use of her former title.

'I think I can manage that, your lordship,' she said, mo-tioning Harriet to follow the two men up the stairs, while the bemused countess gave orders for the remaining assorted members of her household to return to their duties and a jubilant young Rothman silently prodded what he subse-quently referred to as his 'prisoner' through the baize door into the servants' quarters.

Sandford gingerly lowered his aching body on to his bed and finally closed his eyes, having assured himself that Har-riet was, indeed, safely seated at the table by the window. Sarah, having exclaimed in horror at the state of his lord-ship's bandages, immediately set about replacing the ivy-stained rags with clean linen, while Tiptree stood sullenly to one side, waiting for his master's explanation.

The viscount, remembering his promise, opened one eye and registered the man's affronted demeanour. His mouth twitched as he said, 'Come on, Tip. Don't squabble over me—there's plenty to go round!'

'It's not funny, guv.' replied his servant mulishly. 'You could've killed yourself! Climbing about in your condition—what were you thinking of!'

'You know damned well what I was thinking of, Tiptree,' rejoined Sandford in weary good humour. 'And you might as well get used to the idea for it's quite permanent, I assure you! Now, go and make friends with the lady and I am sure that she can be persuaded to give you a good account of her latest adventure!'

With which advice he turned his head on the pillow and fell asleep.

His man, still bristling, stared down at him in brooding silence for some minutes until, raising his eyes and finding Sarah contemplating him with some concern, he gave a rueful grin and turned to leave.

'Looks like you can manage without me, ma'am,' he said with an obvious effort, indicating the neat bandage on his lordship's hand. 'Dare say he'll do pretty well now—I'll just take myself off to the *Fox* for a tankard or two—there'll be plenty of gossip to catch up on, I'll be bound!'

Harriet jumped up in alarm and hurried to block his exit. 'Oh, no, Tiptree—please don't go. His lordship would be so cross with us—you know he cannot manage without you! How can you say such a thing—tell him, Mama—*no one* can take his place!'

Sarah laughed at her daughter's consternation, but at the same time helped her to steer the unwilling Tiptree towards the window-seat.

'Harriet is quite right, sergeant,' she admonished him gently as he reluctantly sat down. 'Indeed, it would be a very foolish woman who imagined that she could—and I assure you that my daughter is no fool!'

'I never thought she was, ma'am,' said Tiptree morosely. 'It's mebbe me that's the fool! Reckon I'm getting too old for all this domestic brouhaha—it's set me thinking that mebbe it's time for me to be moving along—if the guv'nor's mindful to settle down here—well, he'll be needing a younger man than me!'

Ignoring his listeners' protesting denials, he went on, 'Then there's Kimble—now his lordship's got himself a "top-o'-tree" valet he won't have much use for an old bat-man—different sort of work, entirely. I'm no houseman, ma'am, been a soldier all my life…'

'Stop that at once!' interrupted Harriet crossly, drawing her chair towards him and, to his intense embarrassment, taking both of his hands in her own. Gazing earnestly into his startled eyes she said, 'You must not think such things! His lordship has terribly important work for you to do— something that he would never entrust to anyone else! If you forsake him, how will he manage? You must know how much he values your opinion! He certainly doesn't regard you in the same light as he does his—dresser!'

Tiptree scratched his head and frowned, regarding her in brooding silence for a moment before giving a resigned shrug. 'I'm sure I've never been one to shirk my duty, miss,' he said with a heavy sigh. 'I'll stay to do whatever his lordship requires—it's to do with that blackguard down-stairs, I suppose?'

'It's for his lordship to give you your orders, of course— but if you will allow me to furnish you with the details of this afternoon's events? It has to be kept secret, Tiptree— but you already know that?'

Tiptree nodded, his curiosity immediately aroused, for he was as keen as anyone to know what had occurred in the library and, by the time Harriet had finished her discourse he was, at last, beginning to understand what Smithers and the rest saw in this seemingly indomitable young lady. She appeared to believe that there was good to be found in everyone! Even villains like Hinds and Beckett—who, apparently, was now not such a villain, after all—and that vicious old harpy! How anyone could extend sympathy to that one was beyond his belief! And to have persuaded the guv'nor to set the lot of them up all comfy and tidy-like—now that really was something to be marvelled at. Although, upon further reflection, he had to concede that it was probably the best way to keep such an unsavoury story out of the newspapers.

'It could work, miss,' he said, in grudging admiration. 'There aren't many who know the full truth—except that surely folk hereabouts will be expecting Beckett to get his come-uppance?'

'I thought of that!' Harriet assured him. 'We can tell them all he's been transported—which will be perfectly true, if he's transported to Bristol! Pinter and Finchley will be more than happy to be pensioned off to Mrs Beckett's boarding-house after this, I'll be bound, and poor Hinds…'

Sarah laughed at the man's shocked expression 'A little charity, sergeant?' she said, chastising him gently, as her daughter sought Tiptree's eyes pleadingly. 'The lad cannot be held entirely to blame—in his simple way he must have believed that he was following orders—which is all he is really capable of. When he heard Beckett say that he intended to "get rid of" Harriet and the boy, he must have thought that he meant precisely that!'

'And think how he must have suffered all his life!' Harriet put in. 'Forever teased and bullied by everyone—then finally to have found one friend who did not misuse him! No wonder he feels such loyalty towards Beckett! But punish him? I do not think so!'

'Well, I can't say as I agree with you,' said Tiptree, shak-

ing his head doubtfully, 'but if that's what his lordship
wants, then so be it. I dare say there are plenty of suitable
places where the lad can be sent to see out his days, but it
still seems downright odd to me that none of them are to
be punished for what they did to you, miss!'

'No good would come of it, Tip,' Harriet tried to explain
to him. 'It wouldn't achieve anything but more misery and
unhappiness and surely we've all seen quite enough of that!
I am convinced that none of them will do any more harm—
they no longer have reason to do so—and I cannot forget
that revenge and envy were the underlying forces behind
their actions. For me to perpetuate those feelings would win
me something of a Pyrrhic victory, I feel—I should lose
more than I could possibly gain!'

'If you say so, miss,' he said, after mulling these words
over. 'And truth to tell, I can't see a better way to deal with
it—the guv'nor wouldn't take kindly to being involved in
any sort of scandal—so, if you're willing to "forgive and
forget", as they say, we'd best get it all cleared up as fast
as we may!'

He then looked at her with a curious expression on his
face, 'And if you'll pardon me saying so, miss, I must say
that you certainly seem to have collected a fair bit of wisdom in your short life!'

At this, Sarah nodded in agreement. 'I've often thought
so, myself, sergeant,' she said, smiling fondly at her daughter. 'Although it's clear that she doesn't always use it to her
own advantage!'

Harriet blushed prettily, causing a broad smile to suddenly appear on Tiptree's face.

'I dare say you won't be sorry to get back to normal,
miss?'

'I'm not sure I know what "normal" is in these parts,
Tip,' she returned with a soft laugh, then put her hand over

her mouth as the sound of a deep chuckle came from the vicinity of the viscount's bed.

'Oh, dear! Have we woken you, my lord?' Her voice was full of concern as she rose from her seat and hurried to his side.

'No, my little crusader, I've been awake for some time—still putting the world to rights, I hear,' he teased her, his heart leaping in hope as he registered the expression in her eyes.

'And you are feeling quite well?'

He thought he detected a tremor in her voice. 'Fitter than the proverbial fiddle—truly,' he assured her softly, reaching out his undamaged hand to take hold of hers.

'Ahem! If I might make so bold, sir,' came his groom's distinct tones.

'Tiptree!' Sandford's voice held a dangerous note.

'Sorry, sir.' His man was unrepentant. 'It's just that I see Lord Ramsey has returned—he's below on the terrace with Mr Ridgeway—and Lord William has been waiting for some time to speak with you.'

The viscount gave Harriet a rueful smile and swung his feet to the ground. 'Better get on with it, then,' he said, swaying very slightly as he stood up. 'I'm afraid I shall have to ask you ladies to excuse me while I attend to my toilette and—' turning to Sarah, he bowed '—my deepest thanks, ma'am, for—everything.'

His eyes held hers for a moment until a tiny smile appeared at the corner of her mouth and she gave an almost imperceptible nod.

'Come along, Harriet,' she said. 'We must also go and change. Her ladyship will have postponed the dinner hour to suit our convenience. We must not keep her waiting any longer than necessary.'

As her mother led her from the room Harriet cast a de-

spairing glance towards Sandford, but he was already involved in selecting articles from his wardrobe.

Back in her own bedchamber, undergoing the cheery
Rose's ministrations, Harriet wondered miserably when she
would get an opportunity to speak to Sandford alone, for
how, otherwise, could she discover his true feelings towards
her?

True, he had climbed out of the window to come to her
rescue, but he obviously felt that he had no choice—he had
told Tiptree that it was an emergency. And he had needed
very little persuasion regarding her suggestions as to Beckett's redemption—could that have been because he was tired
of the whole matter and simply wanted rid of her!

Harriet trembled at the thought, and then her eyes brightened. He had called her his 'little crusader' in a very fond
tone, but then she recalled that he was, in all probability,
only half-awake at the time and her heart sank once more.

'If you don't keep still, miss,' chastised Rose, as she tied
Harriet's hair ribbon for the third time, 'I shall have Mrs
Gibson putting me back in the parlour—I'm making such a
pig's pie of this!'

'I'm sorry, Rose,' said Harriet, endeavouring to comply
with the girl's request. 'I'm still in the fidgets—it's been
such an extraordinary day. Tell me what's happened to
Beckett? Has he been taken away?' She wondered if Sandford's orders had been carried out.

'Davy has him under lock and key, miss—and won't allow nobody near him. Made me shiver just to see him walk
past, it did, miss—wicked devil. Just think, if Granfer hadn't
gone up to the cottage…!' Her eyes grew round.

Harriet nodded vigorously. 'It was terribly brave of him
to come all the way back in the dark, Rose, and lucky for
all of us that your mother sent your father out looking for
him—I shall never be able to thank them enough!'

Rose's cheeks flushed with a combination of pride and pleasure.

'That's all right, miss,' she said airily. 'Granfer always says that good deeds usually find their way back home and isn't the Reverend forever telling us that "as we sow so shall we reap". You must have sown a lot of good deeds in your life—we all think so, anyhow!'

'Everyone has been so kind,' said Harriet, her eyes moistening at the girl's words, but then her own cheeks flamed in guilty recollection of her earlier treatment of Judith and she was, once again, deep in dismal self-reproach when Rose's voice intruded upon her thoughts.

'Shall you wear the emerald set, miss? It looks so well with this gown—and seeing as it's a special occasion—what with your mother and grandfather here and— Oh, miss! I nearly forgot to tell you! His lordship—Lord William, that is—he's going downstairs to dinner!'

'Oh, that's wonderful! I must go down at once!'

In her excitement Harriet barely noticed that Rose had already fastened the emeralds around her neck and wrist. She stood up hurriedly, hardly pausing to glance at her reflection, then, suddenly conscious that she had omitted to thank the girl for her efforts, she turned back to the mirror and said, with a sincere smile, 'Thank you Rose. Perfect, as usual.'

Rose's beaming face told Harriet that her instincts had not been wrong. 'You look that lovely, miss. It's such a pleasure to dress you!'

Sarah, arriving at the door just as Harriet was about to leave, was initially somewhat taken aback at her daughter's new finery. Then, secretly rather thrilled to see her one-time scamp looking so delightful, she studied the elegant figure before her with very mixed emotions.

'Papa would have been so proud of you, my dearest,' she said, holding the blushing girl at arm's length, her eyes moist. 'You have grown into such a lovely young lady—he would hardly recognise his romping girl!'

'I'm afraid she's still there, Mama,' laughed Harriet ruefully, 'underneath these fancy furbelows I'm the same impulsive hothead that I've always been—and I do not seem able to do anything about it! One minute I think I have succeeded in curbing my impetuosity and the next thing I know, I'm thick in trouble again!'

Sarah's brow furrowed. 'I do not think you can hold yourself entirely responsible for these extraordinary events,' she pointed out. 'Lady Butler would surely have held her grudge against any potential bride whom Sandford brought home with him?'

'Yes, but that lady would never have behaved as I did—I always have to get involved—with Billy, old Potter—even interfering in Judith's affairs!'

Harriet swallowed hard and turned anguished eyes to her mother.

'Do you think that Lord Sandford holds me in disapproval, Mama?'

Sarah hesitated and Harriet mistook her silence as a reluctance to proffer a blunt answer. Forcing a light laugh, she feigned a devil-may-care attitude as she ushered her mother towards the staircase as the sound of the dinner-gong reverberated throughout the hall below.

'No matter,' she said with seeming nonchalance, as they descended the stairs. 'It is of no real consequence. It is Grandfather's approval I must seek to gain.'

'I doubt you need have any qualms on that score, dear child,' laughed Sarah, as March threw open the dining-room doors.

Chapter Twenty

In spite of Cook having surpassed herself in the variety of dishes she had sent up to the table, Harriet found that she had very little appetite for any of the carefully prepared dishes.

Beldale, resplendent in full evening dress and back, once again, in his rightful place at the head of his table, exhorted her to 'take a little more of this' or 'a morsel of that' as each subsequent course appeared and, to please him, she accepted small servings of food, which she discreetly moved around on her plates in an effort to seem as totally absorbed in her food as her companions were.

Most of the leaves had been removed from the huge mahogany table in order to reduce it to a more convenable size and Lord William had insisted upon Harriet sitting at his right hand with her mother at his left. Lady Caroline, at the foot of the table, had chosen to sit Lord Ramsey on her left, next to his granddaughter. This arrangement had placed Sandford diagonally opposite Harriet but, since a large silver epergne graced the middle of the table, its branched bowls of fruit and flowers had the effect of obscuring him almost totally from her vision.

Because of the lateness of the hour and the difficulties

involved in getting his lordship to his place, the initial greetings and social conformities had been dispensed with and they had come straight to the table and so, apart from the smilingly courteous bow she had received at her entrance, Harriet had been reduced to seeing little more of the viscount than the occasional wrist or elbow although, as she could clearly hear, he was obviously enjoying spirited conversations with his immediate neighbours. 'I have hardly seen you all day,' Lord William was laughingly scolding her, 'and Sandford tells me that you have settled this whole matter almost single-handedly!'

'Oh, no, sir!' Harriet was abashed. 'I merely put forward some suggestions to his lordship—I hope you do not think—it is not for me to decide…!'

'Oh, but I think it is,' said the earl, twinkling at her. 'You have been the chief victim of these dreadful wrongdoings and yet your heart is still full of forgiveness—you put some of us to shame, my golden girl. I have to own that I would have sought to wreak the usual revenge had you not petitioned on those devils' behalves—for I myself suffered considerable discomfort, as you know—and there were moments when I seriously considered that my brain had deteriorated!'

He guffawed at his listeners' horrified expressions. 'But enough of that! We will all hopefully learn something from the experience. And, thanks to you, my child, much good has been gained! Following your excellent suggestion, we have arranged for Tiptree to escort the penitents to Bristol at first light, with Pringle and Garvey—Ramsey's men—as outriders. I have a man of business at the port and I shall provide him with the necessary instructions as to their future welfare. I think we need give that particular matter no further thought.'

'Young Hinds won't be left to shoulder the blame, will

he, sir?' said Harriet, her green eyes wide with anxiety. 'Even Beckett was most concerned that he should not suffer—that was his main reason for returning.'

'Don't worry, little marigold,' his lordship assured her. 'Eugenie has it in hand—the lad will be properly looked after, I promise you—but,' and here his expression grew very stern, 'before you even think of it, I flatly refuse to fulfil any pleas you may be contemplating on the Butler's behalf!'

'She has already been dealt her punishment, I fear,' said Harriet, with a deep sigh. 'Judith is so distressed—and I was so beastly to her when she came to see me!'

Ramsey, who had been listening to this exchange, smilingly patted his granddaughter's hand. 'Don't fret, sweetling, yon Ridgeway has already assured the lassie that you'd soon be back to your own sunny self! He's feeling pretty pleased with himself—these events won him a rare prize— he'd likely still be casting sheep's-eyes!'

Harriet looked towards the countess in delight. 'You mean that Charles has finally…?'

Lady Caroline nodded happily. 'Yes, my dear. They settled it this afternoon. He and Judith are to be married next month. Beldale's man of business is already working out the settlements. Lady Butler is to remain with Eugenie—Sir Basil is hopeful of a partial recovery.'

The room was suddenly silent and Harriet's eyes filled. Sandford, sensing the changed atmosphere, damned the entire guild of silversmiths to perdition and made to rise from his seat, but his mother laid a restraining hand on his arm and threw him a warning frown as Sarah began to speak.

'I believe Sergeant Tiptree would say that it was all meant to be,' she said, smiling across at her daughter, 'and a good many philosophers have agreed with his Destiny theory. If it is really so, it somehow helps to reduce the—horror—of these recent events, wouldn't you agree?'

'Well, I'm eternally obliged to any Destiny that saw fit to restore you to me,' laughed Ramsey, adding, as he twinkled at Harriet, 'A double bonus, which I'm sure I've done nothing to deserve!'

'I think Lord Sandford must claim some of the credit for that,' she said with a blush, glad that the viscount could not see her face. 'He was the one who rescued me from the ditch!'

Beldale, flicking a surreptitious glance at his son's furrowed brow, leaned forward and stretched out his hand to cover Harriet's. 'And we can only be thankful that he had the sense to bring you to us, my dear—such a pretty bonus—but I cannot help feeling that Fate has been dealing you some pretty poor cards lately. I pray that she intends to look more kindly upon you in the future—although I do not care to think of you quitting my house with such unpleasant memories!'

Sandford, rising at once to his feet, observed Harriet's downcast eyes and trembling lips.

'You have teased Miss Cordell quite enough, Father,' he said firmly, vacating his place. 'I believe I can manage without further assistance! I shall withhold on the port, if you will excuse me.'

He strode quickly round to Harriet's side of the table. 'And now, with everyone's permission, I must take it upon myself to remove the lady. She appears to be in need of a little air—would you care to step on to the terrace for a few moments, my dear?'

This last was to Harriet, who rose from her seat in silent relief and allowed the viscount to lead her to the dining-room doors. Four pairs of eyes watched in unconcealed amusement as Sandford gently shepherded her out on to the terrace, now bathed in moonlight.

'You were a little hard on her, William,' said Lady Caroline, signalling to Rothman to close the curtains. 'And Robert was beginning to look distinctly edgy!'

'I wondered if I was going too far,' agreed the earl, taking out his handkerchief and wiping his damp brow. 'But he's been taking so long to come to the point that it was making me nervous. Just thought he needed a bit of a push—maybe they both do! Don't remember being such a slowtop myself!'

The countess raised her brows in surprise. 'Then your memory serves you very poorly,' she chuckled. 'I recall very clearly how long you took—that's what made me think of the epergne—do you remember…?'

Her eyes twinkled at him and he returned a reminiscent grin.

'That I do, my lady,' he nodded. 'Nothing like an insurmountable barrier to raise a man's fighting spirit! Will he ask her, do you think?'

'Aye, he will,' interposed Ramsey. 'He's already spoken to me—and he received Sarah's blessing earlier, I ken.'

Beldale regarded him pensively. 'How will you feel about losing your granddaughter as soon as you've found her?'

Ramsey's smiling eyes travelled to his daughter's face. 'I've won one major prize, man,' he said gruffly. 'It'd be a might greedy to demand two, and besides—' he lifted his glass and tossed off the contents '—I've no intention of losing her. I got yon laddie's promise that he'd make a yearly trek to Craigburn!'

Out on the terrace Harriet was leaning thankfully against the parapet, contemplating the moon's reflection in the lake across the park. Deeply conscious of Sandford's presence beside her she did not speak, afraid that her voice would betray her emotions. His remarks to Lord William had confused her and she still was trying to make sense of them when he spoke.

'I'm not sure that I wouldn't prefer to wrangle with you, O Silent One!' His still husky voice sounded nervous. 'Have you nothing to say to me, Harriet?'

'Wh-what would you have me say to you, my lord?' she stammered.

'Don't start that again, for God's sake!' he exclaimed impatiently. 'I'd have you say plenty of things to me, Harriet, but that isn't one of them!'

Confronted by her further silence, he took a deep breath. 'You can't keep doing this, you know—you must make up your mind!'

'M-make up my mind?' she repeated. 'I'm afraid I don't follow you.'

'You can't keep reeling me in and throwing me back, Harriet,' he said drily. 'Am I such a poor fish?'

She gasped. 'I haven't—I wouldn't...!'

Gently he turned her to face him, raised her chin and gazed searchingly into her eyes. Then, sighing, he removed his hand from her face.

'You really do have no idea of the effect you have,' he said, with a crooked smile. 'I keep forgetting how young you are!'

'Is that why you're always so angry with me?' she asked in a small voice. 'I shall get older, I promise! Some people say I'm very mature for—'

With a strangled groan he pulled her towards him, burying his face in her hair as his good arm tightened about her. She could feel the unruly beating of his heart against her cheek and was conscious of a burgeoning sensation within which was threatening to overwhelm her. As her hands crept up to curl themselves involuntarily around his neck, she raised her head until her eyes locked shyly with his and at his expression her own heart almost stopped in its tracks.

'Harriet?' he breathed hoarsely, afraid that the moonlight must be playing tricks with him, for he could not allow himself to believe what he was seeing.

'Robert?' came her soft reply as her fingers caressed the hairs at the nape of his neck and, with a little gasp, he possessed himself of her lips in a most ungentle manner, crushing her to him in an embrace so tight that she could scarcely breathe until, revelling in the sweet bondage of his arms, she found herself returning his kiss with a passion that equalled his own.

With difficulty, he forced himself to break away from her lips, but only to rain further kisses upon her brow, her eyelids and her cheek, whilst murmuring foolish endearments into her ear, all of which were pure delight to her.

'Do I take it that you still consider yourself betrothed— *my lord*?' she said mischievously, when he at last paused to take breath. 'Surely our arrangement is no longer necessary?'

'Necessary?' He gave a shaky laugh. 'Absolutely imperative now, my little warrior, unless you have a fancy to see your grandfather take his whip to me!'

'But it was agreed that one of us would cry off as soon as he arrived,' she reminded him, her bright eyes dancing.

'Well, let me assure you here and now that it won't be me!' he said fiercely, as his arms closed around her once more. 'Dearest heart, I fell totally in love with you the moment I rounded that corner and saw you rising like a naiad out of the waters, with your irresistible eyes and your flaming mop—and that was the really "unexpected complication'' which dished Lady Butler's plans—and why I shall be forever indebted to her and her incompetent henchmen!'

'I said such awful things to you!' she cried, contentedly snuggling closer to him. 'I said you were not the man for me—and I know now that you always have been!'

His arms tightened convulsively and he pressed his lips to her hair. 'I was damnable to you! Can you ever forgive me?'

'If you promise that you never *will* be a pattern of perfection!' she teased him, her cheeks dimpling at his sudden grimace of recollection. 'For I'm sure it must be very difficult to live with such a paragon!'

'That, fortunately, is something neither of us is ever likely to find out,' he said with a wicked grin, as he once more lowered his lips to hers. 'You are about to discover that I can be quite as impetuous as you are, *my lady*!'

* * * * *

A Scandalous Marriage

by

Mary Brendan

Mary Brendan was born in North London, but now lives in rural Suffolk. She has always had a fascination with bygone days, and enjoys the research involved in writing historical fiction. When not at her word processor, she can be found trying to bring order to a large overgrown garden, or browsing local fairs and junk shops for that elusive bargain.

Also available this month –
Mary Brendan's fabulous new Regency romance
The Rake's Defiant Mistress

Chapter One

'What an extraordinary coincidence!'

William Pemberton raised his distinguished head at his sweet wife's acid tone. Blue eyes that had been solemnly contemplating the brandy warming within his broad palm now met a glass-sharp gaze. It was a glancing contact, for her attention was already slicing past his shoulder.

'Your old friend is again socialising with us, William. Suddenly we appear to share many mutual acquaintances with Lady Bingham. She looks a little disappointed… Ah, but she has now spotted you and looks far less glum.'

'June…' William's weary sigh accompanied his wife's name.

June Pemberton bestowed on her husband a fleeting, bright smile. 'I shall not hamper your fond reminiscences this time, I promise. I was about to find my sisters, in any case.' June made to sweep away, her ivory skirts held in fingers so tightly clenched the delicate silk was imperilled.

'I have had enough of this interminable innuendo,' William gritted with a fierce azure look at his spouse from beneath heavy lashes. An unusually masterful hand on the soft skin of her arm stayed her. 'Accuse me or have done!'

'Accuse you? Of what, pray?' June countered, her complexion becomingly flushed. She was already regretting revealing that the elegant brunette, who had just entered the Cleggs' ballroom, had unsettled her to such a degree. Three times this week they had socialised. Three times Lady Constance Bingham had arrived shortly after they did, and on each occasion the pretty dowager had contrived at some point in the evening to corner William, in order to engage him in quite an intimate and cosy chat about the old days when once they had been *close*. And what worried June was she had recently discovered that once, indeed, they *had* been close.

In the previous few months Constance Bingham had limited her interest in William to lingering looks when their carriages passed on an afternoon drive, or a coquettish glance when they found themselves browsing the same parade of shops. In those early days, an arch comment from June congratulating her husband on his new allure had rendered him amused, then thoughtful, then murmuring that he believed she must be mistaken over it all. He had reminded her of his reputation as rather a dull fellow. She must look to her dashing brothers-in-law for gentlemen cast creditably in the role of gallant, he had told her with a wry grin that melted her heart. Thus, initially, she had felt an amount of pride that her William was drawing the attention of such a well-connected society lady.

But that was a month or more ago and Lady Bingham's interest was becoming insistent enough for others to notice and remark upon it. Not within June's hearing, of course; she was well aware that conversations sometimes dwindled on her arrival in an elegant drawing room.

Recently she had been on the point of demanding to know whether she was invisible, so blatantly had Lady Bingham been flirting with her husband, but angry tears had been too close to the surface for her to risk challenging the woman and making a fool of herself. Lady Bingham was making it clear she found her quarry's wife of no consequence, and that was galling. Dwelling on that truth now made her snap. 'Is it not coincidence then that Lady Bingham materialises at every social function we attend? And am I to believe it was simply good manners that obliged you to escort her to the terrace when she complained of feeling faint earlier this week?'

'God's teeth!' The oath was so explosive that a lady and gentleman close by slanted curious eyes at William's taut features. 'I believe I explained that incident at the time.' The words were enunciated through lips that scarce moved. 'Lady Bingham said she felt faint and asked me to accompany her outside for some air. Would you rather I had acted the boor and allowed her to collapse at my feet?'

June's amber eyes glowed tiger-bright as she dulcetly demurred. 'Indeed, no, sir. I would rather you had recommended she used her salts or, better still, went home. But whatever you *did* do to revive her certainly worked. When you later reappeared together she looked quite red in the face...radiant, I believe your mother put it when she drew my attention to you both.'

William closed his eyes and a low curse scratched at his throat. 'I might have guessed my mother would have some part in it. Come. We are leaving. I have had enough.'

'Too late, I fear.' His wife darted a look across his broad shoulder. 'Lady Bingham is being escorted to meet you by your parents.' With a flick of the wrist June had opened her reticule. A cold metal bottle was extracted and thrust into her husband's hand. 'Here! Take my hartshorn. Feel free to offer it to your admirer should she be in danger of swooning over you. 'Twould prevent a trip to the terrace and her risking pneumonia. That scrap she has on is positively indecent and will provide little protection against the night chill.' Without another word June turned and walked away.

William watched the ripple and sway of cream silk as his wife gracefully fled from him. The cascade of berry-blonde curls that curtained her nude sculpted shoulders glimmered in candlelight, stoking his frustrated desire. With a low sigh he forced his hungry eyes away. He hadn't investigated the approach of the people June had warned were nearby and, with rare incivility, avoided them by moving in the opposite direction. He felt unequal this evening to receiving any of his mother's studied bonhomie or Lady Bingham's coquetry. And he knew both were his if he remained where he was. But a quiet chat with his father would have been welcome. With a scowl moulding his mouth, he finished what was in his glass and weaved a path through a throng of people, hoping to find some uncomplicated male company.

As he walked he thought. He hadn't wanted to leave the house this evening, sensing this situation might arise, but June, with a *faux* gaiety, had evaded his amorous persuasiveness that they have a quiet night at home, and insisted they come. They had both known for some weeks that a confrontation about Lady Bingham's peculiar attention to him was

imminent. A constant strain between them was up-
setting their conjugal harmony, and thus William's
equable nature.

William was coming to accept that his wife's suspicions were valid. Wherever they went, Constance
was likely not only to materialise, but also to hound
him. He knew too that June's mild annoyance at the
woman's stalking had turned to a stronger emotion
since they had become the butt of gossip. The fact
that his own mother was fostering Constance's
friendship and thus exacerbating the friction between
him and June was obviously intriguing the *ton*.
William, on the other hand, was well used to his
mother's hostility to his wife.

'Is June ailing? She looked quite sickly, I thought,
as she passed me a moment ago, with barely a
greeting, too, I might add.'

William closed his eyes and blew a silent curse
through his teeth on recognising the voice accosting
him. It was wrong to have supposed his mother would
give up pursuit quite so easily, even if Constance and
his father had. On the edge of his vision he noticed his
father leading Lady Bingham towards the supper
room.

Pamela Pemberton fussily hoisted a flimsy shawl
about her thin arms. 'Really, William! I think you
ought have a word with your wife about her manners.
Several years you have been wed; time enough by

my reckoning for her early breeding to have been polished a little by association with us.'

William Pemberton gazed glacially at his mother. 'Yes, several years married, ma'am, and still she suits me as well as ever she did.'

Pamela sniffed. 'Still your nursery is empty. Where is my grandchild?'

'You have a granddaughter, as I recall… Hannah's child.'

'I have no daughter. I have had no daughter since she married that heathen.'

'Your choice, then, to have no grandchild either,' William pointed out, his voice vibrating with disgust. 'Your loss, too, for the little girl is beautiful and I'm proud to call her my niece.'

'That is understandable.' His mother theatrically sighed. 'Perhaps, if your wife suits you so very well, you must resign yourself to doting on other people's offspring.'

'Indeed I shall, if that is how it is to be.' William turned away from the sight of his mother's bitter, pinched features. 'We are going home. June is unwell and is just gone to take her leave of her sisters.'

'Going home?'

William removed the tenacious fingers that had fastened on his arm.

'But you have barely arrived. This is one of the

most lavish parties we shall see this season. You cannot go! Constance is here and keen to come to you.'

'Why is that?'

'Why is what?'

'Why is Constance keen to come to me? There are other people here she knows. Why single me out as a person on whom to bestow such favour?'

'Perhaps she finds you amusing…' The innocent simper that accompanied the remark was belied by the flush staining Pamela's cheeks. 'Oh, how should I know?' she blustered.

'I just thought you might, ma'am…' was William's parting shot as with a curt nod he moved on.

'If she's on the prowl for a husband now she's out of her widow's weeds, the least she can do is find one of her own.' Rachel Flinte, Countess of Devane, cast a belligerent glance at the back of Lady Bingham's coiffure as she made the remark.

'And it shouldn't be that difficult to attract one either, if rumours are true about what old Charlie Bingham bequeathed her,' Mrs Isabel Hauke contributed to the debate. 'Etienne said that it is rumoured he left her properties in three counties and a brace of ships docked in Bristol. Quite a lure for a gentleman with pockets to let.'

June looked at her two older sisters and gave a wry smile. 'Thank you! I wish you hadn't told me that. She really is a catch. And besides…she is a very attractive woman, isn't she?'

Rachel shrugged dismissively. 'A person who favours Amazonian brunettes might think so.'

Isabel gave a toss of her mermaid hair. 'And William patently does not,' she roundly emphasised. 'The man's as besotted with you as ever he was. Since you left him moments ago his eyes have tracked you constantly. He looks…a little furious, June, not at all his usual suave self,' Isabel warned. 'And, now he's free of that witch of a parent of his, he appears to be heading this way.'

June unconsciously tidied her sleek blonde ringlets on learning that information. Her sister's description of the wealthy widow was rather uncharitable, she knew. Constance Bingham was attractively tall and willowy and her hair was a rich shade of chestnut. And June had recently learned that her husband *did* find Lady Bingham attractive…or once he had.

June's irritation over Lady Bingham constantly paying attention to William was transforming to jealousy since her mother-in-law had let her know that the couple had once been in love. But she found herself unable to challenge William over it, for had he not voluntarily mentioned his aborted betrothal to her himself several years ago?

William had been engaged to a Miss Palmer when he was twenty. He had told her that when first they met, and that Miss Palmer jilted him for a wealthier man. He had seemed philosophical about it all and reluctant to elaborate. It was just an inconsequential part of his youth, he had said on dismissing the affair. At that time June had not pressed him for further details of an alliance that had ended before they met, deeming it bad manners, and unnecessary. She had practically forgotten all about the matter, for why should it bother her? William had married her. William loved her. Just a few short months ago had he not told her so at least once a day, and again impressed it on her with sweet passion at night? But now a wedge of tension was nudging them apart.

Her mother-in-law had been good enough to satisfy her unspoken curiosity about the woman's past, and William's part in it. Constance Bingham, née Palmer, was returned to town from Devonshire and socialising again now her mourning for her late husband was done. Was June aware that William had almost married such a personable lady? Pamela Pemberton had asked with a satisfied twitch of a smile when her daughter-in-law's expression made it clear she was not. Since that time an icy feeling had been curdling June's stomach, for how blatantly the widow was parading in her face the fact that she still found her erstwhile fiancé attractive.

Isabel and Rachel exchanged a glance on noticing June's unhappy preoccupation. Her small teeth were sunk low in her bloodless bottom lip.

'If William wasn't such a perfect gentleman, I'm sure he would have by now made it clear that Constance Bingham vexes him.'

'Is he almost upon us?'

At her sister Isabel's discreet nod, June tilted her heart-shaped face. 'Well, smile, then. I won't have him thinking I'm a jealous shrew, even if I stupidly did act like one earlier this evening.'

'William!' Rachel greeted her brother-in-law and slipped a hand through his arm. 'Connor was looking for you earlier. I believe he went along to the card room thinking you might be playing at the tables.'

William gave his sisters-in-law a charming smile. 'Another time, maybe. June and I are leaving.'

June shot her husband a startled look. Her elfin face was animated by slashes of colour staining her cheekbones. 'How masterful you sound!' she playfully remarked. 'You will make Rachel and Isabel think I am to be taken home in disgrace. I would rather stay. We were about to find the supper room.'

As June made to link arms with her sisters and urge them on, William arrested her progress and drew her to his side. His head inclined intimately close to hers in the manner of a fond spouse. 'Most of these good people would love a little more reason to gossip over us, June,' was murmured into a delicate ear. 'Let us at least be in agreement over quitting this infernal place even if all else lately has us at odds. Here, make your malady look real and sniff your hartshorn, my love.'

June slid a look from beneath her luxurious lashes at her husband as he returned her the small silver bottle she had forced upon him earlier. Their eyes clung and his lips tilted in an engaging smile that mingled seduction and threat.

June felt her stomach tighten. She rather thought she knew how her husband would seek reconciliation once they were private tonight. Would she allow it? Her fair complexion tinged rose and her limbs were already a-tremble with anticipation. 'It seems I must be a dutiful wife then and oblige my lord and master.' Just a hint of sourness betrayed her lingering hurt.

William glanced at his sisters-in-law, who had diplomatically distanced themselves, before casting a trenchant look upon his wife. 'It would certainly be novel if you did, my sweet,' William drawled, with a significant irony that she understood and that made her blush deepen. 'It seems to me overlong since you obliged me in a solitary thing.' With his hand on her elbow and a nod for her sisters, he led her away.

A heavy frosty atmosphere that had little to do with the glittering pavements accompanied the couple homeward to Bay House in St James's. Once or twice June sought, with a fluttering glance, to decipher the expression on her husband's shadowy countenance. She had believed he might take her in his arms as soon as they were settled on the upholstery for the hand upon her waist, as he helped her into their carriage, had been wonderfully caressing. But, once seated, he had put his head back into the squabs and assessed the carriage roof as though stars were visible through it. Far from rebuffing his amorous advances, as she believed she would—until she had some reassuring answers from him over that shameless widow stalking him—she now found herself summoning the courage to slip on to his seat and cuddle up to him. June tilted up her chin. *She* was not at fault in this. Neither, she suspected, was William. But she felt fragile and vulnerable and in need of a little reassurance from the man she loved that she was cherished now, tonight, as surely as she had been a few months ago when Lady Constance Bingham, née Palmer, was blissfully unknown to her.

'It is a very cold night,' June remarked into the silence with a peek out at the quiet whiteness. When a grunt was all the encouragement she received for her attempt at rapprochement, she snuggled into the seat and wrapped her arms about her.

Her husband's face was still angled upwards, his

eyes half-closed, when she heard, 'Are you chilled?'

'Yes,' she eagerly answered.

William uncrossed his arms, opened them invitingly and with no further encouragement his wife hurtled gracefully into them.

William folded his great coat about June's slender body. Instinctively she curved against his side and was anchored there in a familiar way. Warm lips grazed across her cool forehead, while deft hands within the enveloping cloak warmed her silken limbs.

'What is happening to us, William?'

The sobbing little query made her husband groan and lift his petite wife atop his lap. A hand smoothed her cheek; his lips followed as he felt the wetness there. 'What is happening to us, June, is that we are allowing mischief-makers to meddle in our life. We must not allow them to succeed,' he whispered huskily. 'If that means choosing very carefully with whom we socialise, and where we go, then so be it.'

June nodded against his coat. 'You were right earlier; we should have stayed home. I have not enjoyed one second of the Cleggs' ball.'

'We need not become recluses, but you know how gossips thrive if one seems affected by their malice. What else have the bitter souls to do but try to spread their misery?'

'Why does she hate me so? I have tried hard to please her and be a good daughter-in-law…' June choked.

William cupped tender fingers over his wife's jaw. 'And *I* have told you not to try so hard. You do not have to justify your status as my wife. She is my mother, that I cannot change, but you, I chose. You, I want. You, I will always want, no matter you came to me with little dowry and no aristocratic relations. Your father and mother are fine people. All your sisters I'm proud to call my sisters. My brothers-in-law I'm happy to do business with and call close friends. You suit me perfectly. You always have.'

'And your mother resents it, I know she does. She would have had you marry a nobleman's daughter…'

'Then she is a fool for not recognising *that* is exactly what I have done. I have married a very noble man's daughter.'

Chapter Two

'I had not believed William capable of such unmannerly behaviour till I witnessed it with my own eyes this evening.'

Alexander Pemberton shot his wife an ironic look. He dismissed the hovering servant with a weary hand-flick and discarded his overcoat on to a chair. Next he helped himself to the decanter. 'I perceived nothing unreasonable in our son's behaviour. I expect William considered a lack of gallantry appropriate tonight.' Alexander helped himself to a generous measure of cognac.

Pamela Pemberton, shrugging out of her pelisse, swivelled towards her husband, her arms imprisoned and mouth momentarily motionless. 'I'm sure I don't know what you mean by that.'

'I think you do, Pamela,' Alexander said quietly before he sipped. 'And I shall tell you something else: I shall not be a party to your schemes. Please do not again manipulate me into dancing attendance upon Lady Bingham as though I, too, approve of her peculiar interest in my son…my son, who is happily married to a woman he adores.' With unaffected chivalry Alexander helped his wife to extricate her arms from her coat and laid it aside for her.

Pamela snatched her satin sleeves about her in a way that her husband recognised, for it invariably presaged a tirade.

Alexander held up a silencing hand. 'And before you say one word, I have several more of my own I would have you listen to. Do not treat William as you do me: as though he were still a green youth likely to be swayed by your nagging. It is very many years since I observed him doing as you say, simply for a little peace and quiet. If you continue to meddle in his life, you will drive him completely away. I would bet a florin to get a crown that he is planning with June to repair to the country for the rest of the season, just so they might avoid any further unpleasant atmosphere.' Alexander cast a glance on his wife's indignant countenance and, as always, part of him softened for part of him still loved her. Gently he said, 'Do not underestimate William; he will not take kindly to being made to look a fool, Pamela.'

'How dare you lecture me over my son! Do you think I know nothing of his character? Naturally I

want what is best for him. I have always wanted
what is best for him.'

'If that is so, why are you helping to put him at
risk of ridicule?'

'Ridicule? What are you talking about? *Ridicule*?'
She illustrated her impatience and disbelief with a
whirling hand.

Alexander slammed down his glass with unaccus-
tomed temper. 'Tonight I heard Harley and Darlington smirking over a wager they've made that
concerned our son and Constance Bingham. Lord
Harley has it that William will have her as a mistress
before Whitsun. Lord Darlington favours Constance
holding out for a better offer from him and thinks Michaelmas might be when there is talk of a divorce. I
am not saying their slander was sincerely meant;
rather they seek to be jesters. I would have had both
of them outside and told them exactly what I thought
of their pathetic jokes had there not been over a
hundred people present to witness the ensuing chaos.
I'm quite sure that our son and daughter-in-law are
aware they are being made the butt of hurtful gossip.
Harley and Darlington haunt all the clubs and parties.'

Pamela had the grace to blush and stammer. 'I…I
don't see how that is my fault. People have long
memories. Obviously, some have remembered that
William and Constance once were engaged…once
they were in love.'

'If that is so, they must then also recall how enduring was her love for him. My own recollection is that, within a few months of my future daughter-in-law slipping on her engagement ring, she was replacing it with that flashy bauble Charlie Bingham gave her. Within an unconscionably short time she was Bingham's wife. Let us not mince our words over this, Pamela: Constance Bingham was a gold digger. William was hardly a pauper himself at that time, yet she wanted more. He couldn't give her a title, so with disrespectful haste she married a man who could.'

'She was browbeaten by her family,' Pamela quickly championed the widow. 'I can understand their ambition. I own I was angry with her when the betrothal was broke. But she *is* a baronet's daughter. It was natural her family would have favoured a more advantageous match for her. Lord Bingham was very wealthy and influential…and a nice gentleman, of course. Naturally, at his age, he wanted a speedy marriage and a chance to sire a male heir. Unfortunately it was not to be, but he has left her a very attractive prospect, and a daughter to love.'

'There is no nicer gentleman than our son,' Alexander said exceedingly quietly. 'Constance Bingham has had ample proof of it. If William were not such a courteous and tolerant character he would not give her the time of day, no matter what attractiveness or prospects she has. Do not help manoeuvre him into a situation, Pamela, where he is forced to relinquish his good manners to prove his love to his wife.'

'If June Meredith were a lady of proper refinement she would not make him act with incivility simply to flatter and placate her. She is behaving like a jealous minx, storming off like that when she knew we all were approaching to speak with him…and her. Why can she not conduct herself properly?'

'She is acting in the manner of a wife who is being exposed to humiliation and scandal through no fault of her own. And William is acting, not before time, like a man who is done with seeing upset the wife he adores.'

Pamela's mouth pinched. She stalked to the table and splashed cognac into a glass. 'Wife he adores?' she mimicked tartly. 'Why should *my* son be saddled with such a barren mouse? Had he and Constance wed he would have had children. She has already borne a fine daughter. I would bet a florin to get a crown she has many sturdy sons in her, too. It is not to be borne that William might have no heir.'

'If he can bear it, my dear, I do not see why you cannot,' Alexander suggested drily. 'William and June have been married not yet four years; not so long when you think on it. Perchance they might prefer these early honeymoon years just for the two of them. They have plenty of time to start their family. In a decade they might have a sizeable brood.'

Pamela squinted at her spouse over the rim of a glass. 'What romantic drivel!' She gulped at her drink and coughed. 'Of course it is important to start one's family soon. She might first produce a quartet of daughters, as did her mother. She might need a half-dozen attempts before successfully producing a son. When one is well connected, one understands the great importance of continuing a noble blood-line,' she impressed on him, waving her empty glass.

'Ah, I might have known mention would eventually be made of the ducal connection. Your great-uncle on the distaff side might be a landed duke, but he is better known as a common sot. He has beggared himself in brothels and gaming houses, as well you know. The fact he has no male heir to inherit his debts and debauchery can only benefit society.'

Pamela, with tipsy gravity, smoothed her wispy hair, then licked the residue of alcohol from her desiccated lips. 'I have no intention of letting you rile me. You have long been envious of my superior lineage, I know.'

'You mistake the matter, my dear,' Alexander corrected quietly. 'What I have long coveted is my son's wisdom, for Lord knows how he did it with such wilful obstruction, but he managed to find himself the perfect wife.' Alexander caught up his coat in a smooth snatch and closed the drawing-room door quietly as he retired to his chamber.

Pamela stared after him for a long moment, her mouth compressed to a thin line. She went to the decanter and refilled her glass, then sought the warmth of the fire. The red in her cheeks had little to do with its glow.

Edgar Meredith took his wife into his arms. 'Come...come now, hush. I might have been mistaken. I wish I had not mentioned it to you at all.'

Gloria Meredith accepted the linen handkerchief proffered by her husband and dried her hot eyes, her leaky nose. 'I'm glad you did, Edgar.' She sorrowfully shook her head. 'I cannot believe it. It seems that the whole *ton* knows more about the state of one of my daughter's marriages than do I. I thought Constance Bingham just a silly fool. I thought her fawning over William nothing to worry about.'

'It *is* nothing to worry about, my dear—'

'How can you say that! There is gossip everywhere about a divorce, you say. And June and William looked to be at loggerheads this evening. At one point I'm sure they were arguing. Then they barely made time to come over and take their leave before they had gone. If they stayed an hour at the

Cleggs' I should be surprised.' Gloria pressed the damp linen to her freshly streaming eyes.

'I did not say the *whole world* knows of it,' Edgar cooed. 'I overheard a conversation between two gentlemen in Boodle's and they were denouncing Harley's malicious lies as absurd. Most sensible people will dismiss them thus.' Edgar paused, a thoughtful look putting a crease between his eyes. 'But William is bound to be rightly furious when he finds out he and June are being pilloried. I hope he does not call Harley out…and he might with such provocation. He is a quiet gentleman; but then a mild manner sometimes conceals quite a dangerous adversary. I know he can fence and, if he shoots a pistol as well as he does a shotgun—he bagged more pheasant than any of us at Michaelmas—Harley will regret ever opening his mouth.' Edgar's enthusiasm for his son-in-law's sporting prowess tailed off as he heard his wife's unhappy little gurgle. 'There, there…dry your tears. Harley and his buck-toothed crony are just risible idiots, everybody says so.'

Edgar continued patting comfortingly at his wife's fingers until the tears glistening in her eyes were blinked away. 'Harley has never forgiven us since Connor made out of him a laughing stock over that game of cards, when I staked Windrush at the tables.' At his wife's piercing look of accusation, Edgar hurried on. 'Of course I would never have let him have it. I would have sobered up well enough to cheat if necessary to keep our home. But I knew Connor wouldn't let me down. He won the estate fair and square.'

'It is as well *that* son-in-law is also a fine gentleman, for I doubt many people would return such an asset to a man silly enough to lose it in the first place.'

'Yes…well…all in the past, all in the past…' Edgar quickly changed the subject, for the one he had stupidly settled on was a contretemps best forgotten. He relinquished past disasters and returned to the current family crisis. 'Harley would love to concoct a scandal about one of our daughters that was plausible enough to do us all harm.'

Gloria scrubbed her wet eyes. Oddly, the mention of other problems that had beset the Merediths rallied her courage. They had seen off trouble before and grown stronger for it. She sat straighter, and tapped lightly at the hand that rested on her arm, indicating Edgar's soothing was no longer required.

Creakily her husband straightened from his position, squatting by her chair.

'I suspect Harley and Darlington are not alone in weaving this tapestry of lies. Perhaps a female hand is dabbling in it too,' Gloria said with a meaningful squint at Edgar. 'Tomorrow I will call on Pamela Pemberton and she will see me if I have to loiter in her hallway all day. She has never accepted June, yet June has been unwavering in her loyalty. Just the other day June gave Rachel a scold for calling her mother-in-law a mean-spirited witch—an accurate description if ever I heard one. Naturally, I told Rachel off too, for it doesn't do to be *blatantly* dis-respectful.' Gloria frowned in puzzlement. 'But then I wouldn't suppose she wished to expose her own son to scandal.'

Edgar expressed his bewilderment with a long face.

'Tomorrow I *am* going to see her.' Gloria blew her nose with some force and a pugnacious glint fired her bloodshot eyes.

'I think that unwise, Gloria,' her husband advised sagely. He took a turn about the sitting room, thoughtfully quiet. 'If William has heard the latest rumours, I dare say he is fuming. But to put your mind at rest I shall make it my business to see *him*. A little man-to-man chat is in order, I think.'

His wife appeared unconvinced of the success of that.

'Tongues would really start wagging if you ladies engaged in a cat fight over it all,' Edgar warned with a grin. 'And should Rachel insist in going along with you, that might just come to pass. You know what a vixen she can be when protecting her family.'

'I don't think she would do that, Edgar,' Gloria an-

nounced softly. 'Not now she is again increasing. I
have not yet had an opportunity to tell you my glad
tidings, so engrossed have we been in your bad news.
I learned from Rachel just this evening that we are
to be grandparents again. Catherine is to have a
brother or sister and Marcus and Lydia are to have
another cousin.' The mention of all their beautiful
grandchildren at last put a smile on Gloria's lips.
'Isn't that wonderful news?'

Edgar beamed. 'Capital!' he breathed. 'Little
wonder Connor is looking so uncommonly pleased
with himself of late. When is the babe due?'

'Rachel thinks about September.' Gloria's expression became wistful. 'I know June will be so very
pleased for Rachel and Connor, yet I fear to mention
it to her. I know she says little on the subject, but I'm
sure she would dearly love to announce similar
news.'

'And so she shall, so she *shall*, my dear,' Edgar
quietly, confidently assured his wife. 'All in good
time June will have her family, you'll see.' He sighed.
'Of course, the mischief Harley is brewing is hardly
likely to help at all with filling their nursery. It would
need to be a most harmonious couple who could
remain unaffected by learning there is a wager on the
time of their divorce.'

Edgar put a finger to his lips, deep in thought. 'As
I see it, the problem—if it is one—is that June and

William are two people too nice for their own good. June has always been determined to be kind to all and sundry, even the undeserving, and her husband is the sort of fellow who would oblige you with his last sovereign. Such sweet-natured folk are bound to frustrate those malcontents who thrive on ill will.'

Gloria nodded agreement. 'Well, you may speak to the men first, but if nothing is done I will pay a visit on Pamela Pemberton. I will not have my June humiliated. I like William very much but he ought show his mettle over this.'

'He is looking grim; I feel sure his patience is at an end over it all,' Edgar championed his son-in-law.

'I noticed this evening he looked irritable,' Gloria said. 'I hope they have not gone home early simply to quarrel…'

With a tender sigh June buried her head against her husband's neck. A small hand slid over the hard ridges of muscle on his naked chest. Sated with pleasure, she slipped one of her silken legs between the brawny strength of William's, then sensually caressed it up and down. The fond tribute to his artful lovemaking made her husband angle his head and place a gentle kiss on her small nose.

'I'm sorry I was disagreeable earlier,' June whispered against warm skin.

'I would have you disagreeable every day if this

is how you apologise for it,' William answered huskily. With gentle urgency he lifted her atop him and a hard hungry kiss reinforced the words. 'Why have we not done this for so long? Why have you made excuses for so long? I have been mad with desire for you.'

'I think you know the answer to that,' June muttered with a touch of acerbity.

'Constance Bingham is no threat to you, my love. She is probably desirous of a little flattery to boost her confidence now her mourning is at an end and she is again socialising. Soon she will be turning her attention to a more appreciative and unattached recipient. But…you would not have me act rudely towards her?'

'No! Of course not,' June said. 'It is just…I'm not sure she *will* turn her attention elsewhere. Besides, I rather think your mother might be disappointed if she did. I get the impression Pamela likes Lady Bingham. She regrets not having her as her daughter-in-law.' June pushed back from William, her fine hair draping his chest in a blanket of silk. 'I did not know that Constance Bingham is the Miss Palmer to whom you once were engaged. I would rather not have learned that from your mother. Why did *you* not tell me?' she demanded raggedly.

William smoothed a finger over a pale cheek. 'Why would I mention anything so insignificant?

You are talking of a betrothal that ended over a decade ago. Our relationship endured for less than four months…or perhaps it was five. I cannot now recall.' A careless grimace transformed effortlessly into a fond smile. 'In the fullness of time I found you and I married you. I have no regrets at all. I love you.'

'Once you loved Constance.' When silence was all the response she got, June probed. 'You did, didn't you? Or was it a convenient match?'

'I'm not sure there was love between us, but it would have been financially convenient…' He sighed and put a hand across his eyes. 'I don't see that there is any point in pondering the matter now, June. I was barely twenty…still a green boy. The matter is finished.'

'Perhaps Constance would like to revive it. Perhaps your mother would like that, too. Lady Bingham has a daughter. One of the reasons you mother is disappointed with me is because you are not yet a father.'

William sat up, lifting his wife with him so she was settled on his lap, enclosed in a warm embrace, while he rocked her soothingly. The memory of his mother's bitter words over June's failure to conceive had simply fired his disgust for her and his protectiveness for June. 'If—when, God willing, we have children, then it will be wonderful…for us.' He gave his wife a seductive smile. 'Perhaps it is just that we need a little more practice to get it right. I might let you persuade me to try again now…' He smothered his wife's laughing response with his mouth as he lowered them both back to the bed.

Hours later in the dark, June whispered, 'Are you awake?'

Her husband grunted a sleepy response.

'I have been thinking…we should not let malicious people intimidate us. We shall not scuttle away to Grove House,' she said, mentioning their country estate in Essex. 'We shall stay here, and enjoy the season and socialise with whomsoever we please. We have nothing to be ashamed of.'

William murmured assent and cuddled his wife against his shoulder before whispering, 'Very well… Now, unless you are prepared to practise again…go to sleep.'

Chapter Three

'That is wonderful news. Oh, Rachel, I'm so pleased for you and Connor.'

'You would have known last night when I told the others…but you and William left so early…'

'It is obviously but a tiddler at the moment.' June gave Rachel's flat abdomen a fond pat. But she felt quite a fraud for appearing so jolly and sincere, for behind her congratulations and her smile was an ache of envy.

Rachel and Connor had been married just a few weeks before she and William, yet already her sister and brother-in-law were fortunate enough to be awaiting the birth of their second child. A disagreeable self-pity was consuming her, and such base emotion made her ashamed. It was not her sister's fault that she and William had yet to experience the excitement of impending parenthood. Quickly June turned away to compose herself. She found the teapot and poured herself a cup, obliquely aware that her mother and her sister Isabel were discreetly gauging her reaction to Rachel's news. Their anxious sympathy increased her turmoil; her eyes filled with tears. Banishing the heavy silence with some light conversation might have helped her humour, but the lump in her throat made speech impossible.

June gulped at her tea, relieved of the necessity of searching her mind for some mundane conversation. Gratefully she settled on observing some people newly arrived in the room. Close behind her strikingly blonde sister Sylvie came two distinguished dark-haired men. Connor Flinte, Earl of Devane, and Colonel Etienne Hauke were her elder sisters' handsome husbands.

But it was Sylvie, at sixteen, the youngest of Edgar and Gloria Meredith's four daughters, who captured all eyes, as she made her chaotic entrance into the sitting room. Sylvie's sculpted little chin was tossed back, tumbling tresses glinting silver in sunlight as she angled her head away from an attack by the creature she had imprisoned.

Gloria's jaw dropped in horror. 'What on earth are you doing with that?' she cried, glaring at two glass-bright beady eyes and a pecking beak.

'It has an injured wing,' Sylvie explained, with a finger soothing a bony dome of a head. 'One of

Isabel's cures might help the poor thing. It beat off Tabitha.' It was announced in admiration, for the cook's cat was a hunter par excellence.

'Take it to the garden at once!' Gloria exploded. Her furiously flapping hand created a draught and the ruffled bird deposited ample evidence on her rug that it indeed ought to be outside.

Connor arched an amused eyebrow at his brother-in-law. 'Will you or shall I?'

'You…I insist…' Etienne answered, all rueful courtesy, and grinned as Connor gingerly extricated the jumpy pigeon from Sylvie's clutch and headed for the terrace with it.

'Oh, Connor! Don't put it back in the open!' the Earl's young sister-in-law wailed. 'Tabitha will easily search it out. And it is cold…it might perish.'

'I'll find Bruce,' Connor promised soothingly, nominating one of the young grooms who kept all manner of wildlife as pets. 'I am sure he can find somewhere snug and warm for it.'

'Probably his oven,' Etienne muttered to his wife with a wicked smile. Isabel gave him a warning frown, but couldn't prevent a low chuckle at the thought of the plucky fugitive ending in a pie.

'You must get ready to go out, young lady,' Gloria instructed. 'You need material for gowns. You need hats, shoes, all manner of accessories.'

'I don't want a début ball, Mama.' Sylvie sighed. 'I have said so enough times.'

'You *will* have your come-out, young lady, for I would rather you scandalise society with your antics after having at least been launched into it.' At her daughter's mutinous look, Gloria snapped, 'You're fortunate Rachel and Connor have offered to give up their afternoon to escort you.'

After a moment Rachel followed her sulky sister into the hall, muttering that she had best hurry her along for, left to her own devices, Sylvie would not be ready to quit the house before the warehouses were closing for business.

Gloria sank back into her chair as silence reigned. 'That girl jangles my poor nerves like nothing else. Why is she not as other young ladies approaching seventeen? Why is she not giggling with friends over handsome young men? She is happier visiting the circulating library than the newest fabric emporiums.'

June went to her mother's chair and held still her fluttery hand to fondly chafe it. 'She is the baby of the family, Mama, and we have all woefully indulged her. She is just a mite immature and does love her pets. Be thankful she has got over her phase of wanting to tramp the jungle in Africa as a missionary. Instead of a wood pigeon in the house, it might have been a snake or spider.'

'You are right,' her mother agreed, appalled. After a brief fidget, Gloria was again up on her feet. 'Oh, I shall not rest if I don't go, too. Sylvie is bound to cajole her sister into letting her have a fright of a hat or material for a gown that wouldn't disgrace a Haymarket strumpet. And I'd best find a servant to clear up that mess…' With wrinkled nose and a finger waggling in disgust she drew eyes to the stain on her carpet.

June watched her mother bustling from the room. The past few chaotic minutes had, oddly, lifted her depression. Inwardly she gave herself a little scold for having given way to resentfulness over Rachel's happy news. She then offered up silent thanks for her youngest sister's tomboy ways. Sylvie could always be relied upon to create a drama wherever she went, and to do so with an air of heedless innocence that somehow charmed all that came close.

June turned to the sister who remained in the room with her, and noticed a significant look passing between Isabel and her husband.

'I think I shall find Edgar and his decanter and beg a restorative. I need it after all the excitement,' Etienne duly announced with a grin.

Guessing that Isabel wanted to resume their last conversation about Constance Bingham, June sought for an alternative. She and William had left the Cleggs' ball looking quite clearly at odds with one another. It was no wonder that her family would be anxious for her happiness. But now that they had tackled the subject of the preying widow, and William had sweetly allayed her fears on that score, she didn't want to think about the wretched woman, let alone discuss her. 'Poor Mama,' June blurted, as Etienne shut the door and she and Isabel were left private in the serene, sunny morning room. 'She will insist on Sylvie having her come-out this season. I think waiting another year or so might benefit her… character…and her prospects, don't you?'

Isabel grimaced with wry amusement. 'I think our poor parents would rather find an obliging gentleman to take Sylvie off their hands as soon as may be. She might do something utterly outrageous and really ruin her chances. She shouldn't have too much of a problem attracting a dozen or more admirers with that face.'

'It is as well she is a beauty,' June remarked. 'She is seventeen this year, after all, and we must all correct her more and tolerate her less. It is bad of her to aggravate Mama so.' June paused and chuckled. 'How righteous I sound!' she mocked herself. 'I think Mama would say we have all been an equal worry, in our own ways.'

'Not you,' Isabel said softly. 'You, my dear, are widely known as the *sensible* Meredith girl. I'm sure our parents have always been content with your goodness and sweet nature. And you married

William without any hint of scandal attached to the match, which naturally they very much appreciated.' Isabel lifted an eyebrow, a wry hint at the shocking events that had besmirched her spinsterhood. Neither had Rachel managed to attain the married state minus notoriety.

'But that is the point, Isabel, I am *not* all goodness. My nature is *not* sweet at all,' June insisted. 'Sometimes, I hate myself, and my selfish thoughts.' Following a moment's indecision, June confided, 'I envy you and Rachel so much that it makes me quite unkind. I know I shouldn't be like that… But I would dearly love to be able to announce to our parents that *I* am to give them a grandchild. I felt horribly bitter when Rachel told me her wonderful news. You see, I can be very mean.'

With a murmured, 'No, not at all!' Isabel was up and out of her chair. June's shrinking figure was drawn comfortingly into an embrace. 'It is natural you would be upset. You must not feel ashamed that you yearn to be a mother!'

'I do feel ashamed,' June gruffly admitted, shielding her wet eyes. 'I long to tell William he is to be a father. I know it is news every husband expects to hear from his wife. I feel I have failed him—'

'You have not! He has not said so, has he? You didn't quarrel with William when you got home yesterday, did you?'

A secret little smile slowly smoothed June's melancholic countenance. 'No, he never blames me. And, no, we did not really quarrel at all…quite the reverse…'

'Well, that is a step in the right direction to getting your baby.' The insinuation and saucy smile that accompanied Isabel's remark put a bloom in June's ivory cheeks.

Her sister's sincere concern and sympathy prompted June to open her heart. 'William's mother despises me because I am not yet increasing. William's sister, Hannah, has given her a granddaughter but she won't have anything to do with them because her husband is related to Romanies. Why is she so unkind? Toby is very good to Hannah and their little girl. She is three years old and adorably polite.'

'Pamela Pemberton will never be content,' Isabel interjected pithily. 'I do not know her as well as you, but I imagine being miserable is the breath of life to her. She will always find some fault to pick on. If you had a brace of healthy sons, for her, they would be too dark or too fair, too tall or too short. It is in her nature to be contrary. You must not let her worry you, June. If you are tense and anxious, it will not at all help you get the baby you long for.'

'Sometimes I think I have got him,' June volunteered softly. 'Then my menses come late. Sometimes they do not come at all for a month or two. But always, eventually, they come.'

'Oh!' Isabel turned her eyes heavenwards in exasperation. 'It is a shame you did not share that news sooner. I could prepare you a herbal remedy for the irregularity,' she offered. 'It has been known to help in other ways too, as a tonic.'

'Yes…I thank you. I suppose there is no harm in trying it.' Isabel was a talented herbalist, yet June looked a little unconvinced. Nevertheless she smiled in gratitude.

Isabel gave June's arm an encouraging shake. 'I am sure it will help for it has an added benefit…as a love-potion. Take no more than I recommend or you will quite wear out poor William!'

Edgar took a turn about his study, pretending to read the documents in his hand. The paragraphs were a meaningless blur so he yielded to temptation and peered myopically over wire rims at his son-in-law. He ferreted about for a few appropriate words with which to launch into the delicate subject of this fellow's domestic tribulations. June was a beloved daughter, but she had passed into the care of this man several years ago and Edgar had never previously felt anything but gladdened by that arrangement. Yet he had promised Gloria he would speak to William, so speak to him he must.

William was stationed close by the window in Edgar's study. After sipping at the fine Madeira his wife's father had pressed into his hand the moment he arrived, William turned his cerulean gaze to drift over the lime trees just coming into bud along Beaulieu Gardens. A brief smile moved his mouth for he was conscious of Edgar's observation and his predicament. He knew his father-in-law had summoned him here, not to comment on the performance of the stock portfolio bunched in one of his fists, but to interrogate him over rumours he had heard. Edgar was concerned for his daughter's happiness, which was as it should be. William had always liked and respected Edgar. Connor would always be Edgar's favourite son-in-law but he treated Etienne and William with affection. However, even had they hated one another, William realised he would have still asked the man for his daughter's hand in marriage. Almost four years wed and June still had the power to stir his blood with her sensual-shy smile.

William turned abruptly from the window, making Edgar glance away swiftly. He shook the papers in his hand in a businesslike manner and brought them closer to his bespectacled vision.

'I'm glad you invited us here today. June has not seen her sister Sylvie in some weeks. It also gives me an opportunity to have a private word with you.

A ridiculous bit of gossip about June and me is in circulation,' William opened proceedings.

Relief was apparent in Edgar's face as he carefully extricated his spectacles from his ears. The pair of glasses and the sheaf of papers were dropped to his desk before he gave William his full attention.

'I imagine you have also heard the rumours and have refrained from commenting on them because such absurdity is beneath notice or contempt. Nevertheless, I want to put your mind at rest. I will do my utmost to protect June from the harm the instigator of such vile lies intends.' William's tone and expression were frank and sincere.

Edgar nodded sagely. 'I'll admit that I have heard some talk of a wager between Harley and Darlington...the two buffoons. Harley is too far into his cups of late. He was found in a gutter in Shoreditch just last week. He'd lost his cash and other valuables and, by all accounts, it was only his coachman's lucky arrival that saved the clothes disappearing from his back. It's a shame the miscreants spared his skin.' Edgar's tone was uncharacteristically vicious.

'He is not worth your anger,' William stated quietly.

'The blackguard needs horsewhipping,' Edgar spat, unappeased. 'He has antagonised too many people over too many years. It is not the first time our family have clashed with him. It makes my blood boil to let him get away with it.' Edgar sent a shrewd look flitting over William's pacific demeanour. 'Perhaps we ought to have a word with your brothers-in-law about it. Connor and Etienne have said nothing to me, but they must be aware of the gossip. They will not like it that June is being upset…'

'*I* do not like it that my wife is being upset,' William interjected. He had spoken exceedingly quietly, yet every word was clearly enunciated. 'Do you think I cannot protect my own wife from such as Harley?' The query was mild, a little short of amused.

Edgar had the grace to blush. 'No, of course I do not. I meant no offence. It is just that Connor and Etienne are military men. They are used to… umm…acting aggressively when necessary,' Edgar explained in a rush. 'You, William, have led a quiet and perfectly blameless life.' He endorsed his conciliatory compliment with a proud beam.

William's lips twitched in response. 'Thank you for the offer to find such assistance, but, quiet and blameless as my life might have been, I will fight this particular battle, should it come to that. At the moment I am loath to give credence to the gossip by challenging Harley over it. I think it best not to dignify absurd slander with any such attention.'

Edgar nodded agreement whilst subjecting

William to a penetrating stare. 'Do you think these rumours of a divorce have been fuelled by the fact that…?' He hesitated, stuck his fingers between his neck cloth and his bobbing Adam's apple. 'Do you think it has come about because your nursery is still empty?' he rattled off.

William frowned, and looked genuinely puzzled. 'It is a possibility, although I admit it had not occurred to me. But then I admit, too, it had not occurred to me that vicious-minded people would try to cause us trouble. I think I can honestly say that June and I have never knowingly made enemies.'

'You and June are fine people…fair people.' Edgar emphasised his admiration with a quivering fist in the air. 'Your good natures rankle misanthropes. How pitiful must their lives seem when they witness how happy and popular you and June are.' He took a turn about the room, slowing to stub a foot against the fender. 'This is not easy to say, for I know once you were close to her… Do you believe that Lady Bingham might have a hand in stirring this particular pot? It is obvious she…umm…she still likes you.'

William shook his head. 'I think such scheming would be beneath her. Constance simply hankers after flattery. She must be sadly disappointed in having wasted time on me.'

'Don't be too modest, my boy. She seems to me

a woman with regrets. Even without your mother's encouragement, I think Constance Bingham might still trail in your wake.'

William grimaced a sigh. 'I deduce that you think my mother is making mischief.'

'Perhaps your father will speak to her…just a cautionary word that it is being noticed how well she favours Constance.' Edgar refrained from saying that it was becoming common knowledge that Pamela Pemberton preferred the lovelorn widow to her own daughter-in-law.

'Perhaps he will,' William returned evenly, yet he was aware of what remained unspoken between them.

Edgar cleared his throat. 'Please don't think I am prying, but I would hate this gossip to propel you and June into constant arguments.'

William's head tipped back and he frowned at the ceiling. 'Naturally Constance's odd attention to me has not pleased June.'

Edgar frowned. 'Of how much is June aware? Has she heard that Harley is spreading rumours of a divorce?'

William looked sharply at his father-in-law. With uncharacteristic vehemence he blasphemed beneath his breath. 'I hope she has not. I'm convinced she cannot know or our household really would now be set on its ears.' He looked off into distance, his jaw set solid as stone. 'I shall tell her soon for I do not want her hearing of it elsewhere. It is very new tattle in the clubs, but it will soon spread to the drawing rooms.'

'Oh, yes,' Edgar concurred with heavy irony. 'Once those gentlemen's ladies get wind of it, it will spread like wildfire.'

William nodded. 'I'll tell her soon,' he repeated quietly.

'I just spotted Connor out of the window in your father's study. Why is he carrying about a fat pigeon?'

June gave Isabel a look and, simultaneously, they burst out laughing. Catching her breath, June said to her newly arrived husband, who was in the process of closing the sitting-room door, 'Come, let us take advantage of the sunshine this morning. You promised to take me to the opera this week and I haven't one decent shawl to match my blue gown. Let's go shopping in the landau and I shall tell you all about Sylvie's latest escapade.'

Chapter Four

'I recognise that fellow over there. I wish I could recall where I know him from.'

June peered through dim light in the direction that her husband had indicated and saw, in an adjacent box, a tall, dark-haired gentleman laughing with a rather showy and tactile female companion. June shrugged her ignorance of the man's identity and settled back. Within a moment, exhilaration had her once more on the edge of her seat, keenly observing a seething scrum of humanity in the theatre pit. She idly looked back at the person William thought he knew and noticed he was turned their way, his opera glasses raised, obscuring his eyes.

'I believe that gentleman has spotted you too, William,' she told her husband just as the strains of the orchestra filled the air.

A thousand conversations ebbed into silence as a

flow of pastel-clad dancers shimmered on to the stage. Entranced by the magic, the assault on the senses of sweet music, swaying bodies, June twined her slender hand into her husband's long fingers. The immediate welcoming pressure from William, the warmth of his familiar skin, had her snuggling back blissfully into her chair. Four years wed to this man and still with a look or a touch he had the power to twinge her insides with mingling excitement and longing. Her anxieties over Lady Bingham seemed just so much silly hysteria. Soon, she promised herself, every bad thing would simply melt away. So blissful did she feel that, just as the soprano swelled to sing, she whispered, 'Rachel is to have another baby. Isn't that wonderful news?'

William slanted her a lingering look that bathed her in adoration. A low-lidded smile and the increasing pressure of his hand on hers told her he was equally happy for the couple. At the second attempt he managed to drag his eyes back to the nubile dancers flaunting their charms.

'William Pemberton, if I'm not very much mistaken. And this, I take it, is your lady wife?'

William turned about as an affable cultured voice hailed him. An arm about June was keeping her close to his side, shielding her from the crowd clogging the corridors and stairs of the Theatre Royal during the opera's interval. After a frown, William's blond head tipped back and a bark of laughter was followed by, 'Adam Townsend! Hell and high water! It's been some years since I saw you! How many is it, do you think? Eleven? Twelve?'

'More than I care to count,' the man responded with a wry grin.

William turned to June. 'Here before you, my dear, is one of my old friends from school. We were at Eton together, then I went to Cambridge and this scoundrel defected to Oxford before going off to explore exotic lands.'

'Is he a scoundrel for choosing Oxford, or for exploring exotic lands?' June asked. 'Or perhaps he is simply a scoundrel,' she murmured archly. June smiled up at the tall gentleman, judging him rather nice and decidedly handsome, too!

'I must answer that, ma'am, for I don't want to be bad friends with your husband if he is too honest. As we haven't seen each other in more than a decade I'd like to have a chat with him over a good cognac rather than call him out. I must confess I've been a bit of a rogue, but only when in like company.' He clapped a hand on William's shoulder. 'Needless to say, I'm presently on my best behaviour. This fine fellow always exerted a civilising effect on us all. My mother used to like him very much. In fact, not that long ago, she asked whether I had set eyes on him.

Obviously she deemed me in need of his worthy influence.'

'How is Lady Rockingham?' The fondness in William's tone made June take a look at her husband.

'She is not in the best of health. But then she is still well enough to ride to hounds on occasion, so I accuse her of being a fraud.' Adam suddenly cast June an admiring look. 'If I'd known that you had married such a beautiful lady, Pemberton, I might have come looking for you sooner. You're a very lucky man. Has she any sisters?'

June blushed prettily at the compliment.

William drawled, 'When are you returning to those exotic lands, Townsend? Soon? I think you should.'

'Not just yet, I'm afraid,' his friend responded with an impenitent grin. 'By the by, have you seen Blackmore? I was astonished when I clapped eyes on him. Someone told me—can't remember who— that he had bolted for the Americas some years ago. But he is here, tonight, large as life and looking better than I remember he ever did.'

'Blackmore? Gavin Blackmore?' At his friend's nod, William turned to June with a rueful, 'I'm sorry, my dear. We venture out for a romantic evening at the opera and it turns into a school reunion.' To Adam he said, 'I haven't seen him either since we all went our separate ways. I'm not sure I would recognise him if I did.'

'Oh, you'd recognise him. He has a more affluent look, but his plebeian swagger is unchanged.' At the clatter of feet over the stairs that heralded the start of the second act he added quickly, 'I'd be obliged if you both would honour me with a visit soon. I'm staying at my house in Upper Brook Street for a while.'

At June's happy nod of assent, he gave a courteous bow. To William he said, 'Fancy a game of faro in Boodle's tomorrow? We could mull over old times.'

'I look forward to it,' William answered.

'Your friend appears to be trying to catch your eye,' June helpfully mentioned to Mr Townsend as she saw the flashy woman he had been conversing with earlier ducking this way and that to try and attract his attention.

Adam took a glance to his left. His eyes skimmed William's and a corner of his mouth tugged into a smile. He bowed again, all innocent politeness, and was gone.

June watched his imposing figure retreating until it was lost to view in the crowd. 'He seems an interesting gentleman. I have never heard you mention him, William, or that other friend—Gavin Blackmore, was it? In fact, you have told me little of your schooldays.'

William shrugged. 'My schooldays are a long

time ago. I can barely recall much about them. I'm nearly thirty-one, you know… almost middle-aged,' he lamented.

June gave him a sultry sideways look. As they walked back to their box her regard turned into strengthening subtle assessment. William had spoken modestly, as always. Yes, he had entered his thirties, and to her he looked ever more handsome. His eyes were still an intense blue and the fine lines the years had settled on his countenance gave him a charismatic worldliness. His fair hair shone with silver close to his ears and that too suited him. It was distinguishing rather than ageing. William's father, Alexander Pemberton, was one of the most handsome men amongst his sexagenarian peers. He had retained his tall stately bearing and his thick hair, once blond, was now a fine shade of steel. June imagined that William would look much the same as his father when in his sixties. An odd and forlorn feeling crept over her and analysing it made her catch her breath, for it was born of an uncertainty whether she would still be close to him to witness it.

At the touch of loving fingers caressing her neck beneath soft tumbling curls June's eyelids drooped. Instinctively she snuggled closer to her husband as they journeyed home in their comfortable carriage. 'Do you think we should have tarried a little after the performance for you to look for your other friend?'

'No.'

'Why not? Was he not a close friend?'

'I'd rather we went straight home.'

At the subtle seduction in his voice June peeped from beneath a luxurious fringe of lashes and asked coyly, 'And why is that?'

'Because I'm in the mood to again practise making a baby.'

June wanted to match his bantering mood, but found she could not. She turned her face away from the smouldering affection in his eyes. 'Stop it! It is not a game. Not to me,' she whispered in anguish. 'I know you are disappointed with me, however careful and kind you try to be over it all.'

After a tense silence William asked softly, 'Has it ever occurred to you, June, that perhaps I fret that *you* might be disappointed with *me*?'

'Disappointed with *you*?' June echoed, an odd mocking note in her voice. 'Disappointed with my perfect William? What could you possibly lack?'

William ignored her petulance. 'It takes two people to make a baby. Perhaps the fault is not with you. Do you think that has not occurred to me?'

June noticed a painful solemnity in the profile presented to her. She had moved slightly away from him to properly see his expression, but now wanted to have him hug her again. When William made no attempt to bring her close she stayed still, feeling awkward and guilty, with her head bowed and tears needling her eyes. Tentatively she slipped a solitary finger over the broad hand, still beside her hip. She expected him to turn his fingers, to clutch at her conciliation. The only movement was in his face as a muscle tautened close to his mouth. As the tense silence protracted June shifted to her corner of the carriage and watched the dusk through blurry vision.

'If you're waiting for my sister June, she will be an age yet. She has trod on the hem of her gown and torn it. It will take her an hour at least to decide what next to wear.'

Adam Townsend dropped the hand that propped his chin and turned to see who had spoken. The grubby goddess just inside the door ventured further in, staring boldly at him with an unbecoming inquisitiveness. Shifting position from where he had been lounging against the marble mantel, Adam summoned up a smile while thoughtfully studying the angelic chit. Her sweetly curving body proclaimed her a young woman; her dishevelled pink attire and her attitude proclaimed her just a precocious child.

'Ah, you must be Sylvie,' he said pleasantly. 'William said his wife had a younger sister who was visiting today.'

'It's not my proper name,' she informed him. 'My

real name is Silver. My mother named us all for what caught her fancy when we were first born. My eldest sister is called Rachel for Mama then read Bible stories. Isabel arrived at a time when she liked learning about the Spanish court. June Rose was born in the summer, naturally, and my mama's bed was close to the window…the ramblers are right up to the eaves at Windrush.'

Adam looked at a tumble of polished platinum tresses spilling almost to her tiny waist. 'And when you were born your beautiful hair caught your mother's eye…'

Her frown told him she was piqued at being deprived of concluding her tale of Meredith family eccentricity.

'Do you not like the name Silver? I think it rather nice.'

A shrug answered him. 'When I was little, I could only say my name as Sylvie. So I have always been Sylvie.' She walked further into the room and, head cocked to one side, looked him up and down. 'You came here a few days ago to take June for a ride. I saw you through the window. Is that your curricle? It's very flash.'

Adam nodded, confused, for he wasn't sure whether he would have the odd minx go or stay. There was something about her that fascinated him. Perhaps the fact that she was so easy on the eye explained it.

'Why isn't William taking June for a carriage ride? I hope they haven't quarrelled again.'

A small frown met that artless announcement. Adam answered diplomatically, 'William has urgent business with his attorney. I requested the pleasure of taking Mrs Pemberton for a ride in the park this afternoon.' He studied the exquisite features turned up to his. She met his stare unblinkingly. Suddenly he was blushing and the experience was so novel that he felt a further surge of blood to his head.

It was a unique experience to have such a perfectly beautiful young lady peer directly at him with no hint of coquetry. He was used to fans and eyelashes stirring in his presence, signalling a young lady's interest in his eligibility. Silver's candid curiosity made him fear that, not only did he not appeal, but that he might suddenly have sprouted horns. Feeling oddly unsettled, he shoved himself away from the mantelpiece and looked at the door. As if in answer to his prayer, it opened.

'Have you been keeping Mr Townsend company, Sylvie?' June asked as she stepped, perfectly attired in amber velvet, into the room.

'I explained you ripped your skirt. I thought you'd be ages yet. May I come for a ride in the curricle with you?'

'No, you may not, young lady. Mama is expecting you upstairs. Madame Bouillon is coming soon to give you a fitting.' June ignored Sylvie's laboured sigh. With a smile at Adam's expression—an odd mix of regret and relief—June indicated to her urbane escort that she was ready to go.

'Your young sister seems quite a... forthright young lady.'

'Oh, yes,' June concurred on a smile. 'She can also be rather...gauche at times.'

'I noticed,' Adam replied ruefully. 'How old is she?'

'Older than she seems,' June returned. 'I should warn you, when she sets her mind to it, she can be perfectly charming. Nevertheless, it is hard to believe that she has her seventeenth birthday in two months.'

The astonishment arching her companion's brows beneath his dark hair was almost comical to behold.

'Our parents are hoping to launch her into society this season. Sylvie is reluctant to relinquish her life as a tomboy. Hence her lack of interest in having her new dresses made ready. As the baby of the family she has been spoiled—I suppose it is unfair of us all to expect her to undergo a miraculous transformation on her seventeenth birthday and emerge as a demure débutante.'

Adam chuckled. 'Indeed, that would be a miracle...and not necessarily an improvement.'

June slanted him a curious look, dismissed the

notion as absurd and tucked a curl behind her ear. She ran a hand over the curricle's glossy green coachwork. 'It is such a mild afternoon for this time of the year.' After a few minutes of harmonious quiet she added, 'It was a piece of good luck that you and William met at the Opera after so long a gap in your acquaintance. But I'm glad you did. I have enjoyed our two excursions. I was hoping that we might also meet the other friend you mentioned that night...Jason Blackwell...' she suddenly burst out, pleased at having dredged the name from her memory.

'Oh, you mean Gavin Blackmore,' Adam amended lightly. 'If you really want to meet him, let us take another turn about the park for we passed him some ten minutes ago by Hyde Park Corner. I can't say I'd usually go out of my way to seek him out.'

June peered over her shoulder back towards the portals to the park. She recalled her escort had lifted a lazy hand to acknowledge an acquaintance as they drove towards the entrance. In her mind's eye was a gentleman who was fairly unremarkable, although he had looked at her with the sort of penetrating masculine interest that was complimentary, if a little stark. June gave Adam a quick look, for he had not sounded very enthusiastic about the fellow. She re-membered he had made a rather barbed comment about him when they first met at the Opera House. 'Do you not like him?'

Adam shrugged. 'At school he was the sort of person I found hard to like or dislike, being a rather insipid sort of show off. A scholarship gained him entry, for his family were not wealthy. The majority of us took up residence at Eton courtesy of our fathers' money or influence. I was never sure whether Blackmore deemed himself superior or inferior because his father was a country parson. Mostly I avoided him.'

June was about to say that sounded rather uncharitable, but a knowing chuckle from the man at her side kept her quiet.

Adam's lips twitched at her expression. 'I expect he had far more right than the rest of us to be at that noble establishment. He'd earned the right to be there and was definitely a studious fellow. His lowly background didn't colour my judgement of his character. There were other boys there from straitened circumstances, some of whom I still count amongst my friends. It was something else about him that rather grated on my nerves…' He shrugged. 'I never found the enthusiasm to discover exactly what it was.'

With expert handling of his perfectly matched black stallions, Adam smoothly turned the curricle and was soon proceeding back towards Hyde Park

Corner. 'If he is still there, I shall introduce you. You must judge for yourself his character. And just to prove to you that I have no quarrel with him I shall invite him to my little party next week.' He grinned. 'But don't blame me if you're disappointed and find him a dull fellow.'

'I have heard William described thus.'

'William?' Adam looked genuinely surprised. 'William? Dull? Never!'

Chapter Five

'Did you enjoy your drive with my friend this afternoon?'

'I did,' June enthused with a smile. She reached across the table to slide aside the flickering candelabra so she could properly see William. In between enjoying mouthfuls of creamy asparagus chicken she told him, with a fork employed to emphasise, of the crowds they had encountered out enjoying the early spring sunshine. Suddenly her cutlery dropped back to her plate. 'You will never guess who else we saw…*and* I sought an introduction.'

'Not one of Townsend's doxies, I hope.'

June blushed at the audible irony. 'As if I would…as if *he* would,' she squeaked, embarrassed. She brought her wine glass to her mouth and sipped demurely.

William gave her an apologetic half-smile that

did nothing to lighten the gleam of amusement narrowing his vivid eyes. 'If you had asked it, I expect he would oblige you. I told you he was a villain.' He paused thoughtfully. 'Did he introduce you to his mother? I have heard that Lady Rockingham is in town, although I have not seen her.'

June shook her head sending auburn curls, burnished by candlelight, to dance about her nude shoulders. 'It was someone else. We drove past your other school friend at the entrance to Hyde Park. At the time I didn't know it was he, of course, but strangely enough a little later I found myself thinking of Gavin Blackmore and told Mr Townsend so. Round he turned, quick as you like, with great expertise for the road was busy, and took me back to be introduced.'

'And how did you like Blackmore?'

'I'm not sure I did. But then I can't say I took against him either.'

June's full, wine-ruby lips pouted with unconscious sensuality at her husband as she considered that meeting. She recalled a gentleman clear of complexion and with regular features. His colouring was rather bland: light brown hair and eyes. In all she had found Gavin Blackmore…pleasant—but, as Mr Townsend had warned her, there was nothing greatly to either like or dislike about the man. His manner had been rather enigmatic; he had postured this way and that, yet in an oddly self-conscious way that made him seem keen to conceal his nervousness. His conversation had been hardly inspired and June had been aware of Adam's mild amusement as she endeavoured to extract more from Blackmore than a blunt one-syllable response when she commented on the fine weather and the amount of people out to enjoy it.

She was too fair-minded to make any harsh judgement of his character based on one short meeting. Possibly he was shy and that accounted for his awkwardness. Yet he had not been too timid to signal he found her attractive. With a woman's intuition she knew that beneath his discreetly brief, stabbing stares lay an intention to indicate his admiration. At the time, so aware was she of his regard, that for a while she wondered if her presence was overwhelming him and making him tongue-tied. Later, driving on with Adam Townsend, such conceited presumption had made her inwardly laugh at herself.

Compared to her three beautiful sisters *she* was fairly ordinary. Rachel had always scintillated with her golden looks and character. Isabel possessed an ethereal charm that drew endless compliments. Sylvie was blessed with classical features and hair the colour of moonlight. The most June, with her slight figure, hazel eyes and reddish-blonde hair, could claim was that she had been known as the sensible Meredith girl. Of course, dear William told her time and again that she was beautiful…but then he had married her, so he would…wouldn't he?

She glanced up at the man opposite, noticing his blue eyes warm with affection as he watched her grappling with her thoughts. She shrugged away the memory of Gavin Blackmore and her silly insecurities. This was her beloved William and he loved her. 'And how was your day? Did you finalise your business?' she asked. 'What was it all about in any case?'

'Just boring legalities over my grandfather's trust.'

'Oh?' Delicate brunette brows arched questioningly. 'I thought that was all settled many years ago.'

William cut into the food on his plate. 'It is just an additional codicil regarding a fund that will be set up for any children we might have.'

June looked up slowly. 'I see,' she murmured.

'My grandfather had wanted separate provision made for my heirs.'

'That was very good of him,' June said quietly.

'Our children will thank him. He was a fine man.'

'That's not what your mother says,' June interjected wryly.

William's lips tilted a smile. 'No…and to be fair to her, she has reason to be disappointed over it all.'

'Your father has more reason. Yet he bears it all with remarkable equanimity.'

'He refused to renege on a promise for a fortune. It was a noble and gentleman-like act.'

'Indeed he is a saint and it is a shame that…'

William raised questioning eyebrows, begging his wife to conclude her statement. After a moment she obliged him.

'It is a shame that your mother doesn't seem to acknowledge the great sacrifice that he made for her. Your father must have idolised her to cede his inheritance for her sake.'

'I believe once he did. Love can make people do strange things. I often wonder if he ever regrets his decision to do the decent thing. He was just twenty-three at the time, you know.'

June nodded, wondering, as she had many times before, whether the fact that William's grandfather had left his estate to his grandson rather than to his son was the reason why Pamela, if not Alexander, was so bitter at life. William had been very young, too, when he inherited the bulk of Sir Keith Pemberton's riches…nineteen. William's father had been bequeathed just personal mementoes by the parent who had cherished him.

When Alexander told his father he had proposed marriage to Pamela Castle, Sir Keith had been keen to meet her. He wanted his daughter-in-law to be a woman worthy of his favourite boy. On first acquaintance Sir Keith was prepared to give the *little madam* the benefit of the doubt. After a few weeks socialising in Pamela's company, Sir Keith had changed his opinion. He made it clear that, if the wedding went ahead to that *common gold digger*, Alexander must forfeit his inheritance.

Despite the enormity of the financial loss, Alexander had not budged and refused to breach his promise to a humble clerk's daughter…who was distantly related to a duke.

Alexander had an older brother, little favoured by his father, for Joseph's hedonistic lifestyle had besmirched the family's good name. Joseph would take Sir Keith's title but he had had no intention of the spendthrift also having his money to squander. From the moment William was born Sir Keith doted on his flaxen-haired grandson. When, at seventy-eight, Sir Keith was advised by his physician to put his affairs in order, he knew he was never likely to know more grandsons—even supposing either of his two middle-aged daughters-in-law managed to produce any. Lawyers were summoned and William was formally bequeathed the bulk of his wealth.

June could easily understand Sir Keith Pemberton's antipathy for Pamela. June had little liking for her mother-in-law and, much as she battled to overturn that opinion, it was impossible to warm to a woman who seemed to thrive on being mean. But she had always liked William's father and respected him for showing such devotion to the woman he loved.

June's thoughts dragged to the present as she heard fingers drumming steadily on the table. She glanced at William. He looked as preoccupied as she recently had been. She changed her mind about intruding on his thoughts and instead drew one of the young servants into a chat.

William watched his wife as she graciously instructed one of the young serving girls to convey her best wishes to her mother, who had just been brought to bed with her tenth child. How difficult it must be for June to send congratulations to a poor woman burdened with another mouth to feed when she yearned to nurture her first born.

He raked fingers through his hair and prepared himself to tell his beloved wife that there was gossip he might seek a divorce. It was too ludicrous to contemplate; yet he must actually voice it. He felt fiery rage again consume him, and a shiver of sheer impotence. What could he do? If he rose to Harley's bait, the blackguard would win. Harley would relish riling him into making people think there was no smoke without fire.

When the servants had filed out, William announced quietly, 'I have something to tell you, June. It is a subject I would rather not mention, for it is bound to hurt you.'

June pushed the silver candelabra further aside. It was an unnecessary movement, for she already had an uninterrupted view of her husband. 'What is it?' she asked, half-smiling. 'Heavens! Don't look so severe or you'll frighten me half to death.'

William thrust his spine against the chair spindles. His clasped hands cupped his scalp as he gazed up at the ceiling. A short bark of laughter preceded him saying, 'It is so ludicrous I feel stupid mentioning it at all, but I want you to hear it from me rather than from malicious tongues that are already wagging.'

June felt her heart plummet to her stomach. Carefully she laced her slender fingers, then settled her hands on her lap. 'It concerns Constance Bingham, doesn't it?'

When William was tardy in replying she repeated quite shrilly, 'Doesn't it?'

'Yes.' William rose and slowly walked the length of table towards her, one languid finger skimming the shiny walnut wood.

June was mesmerised by that long caressing finger. She watched it rise to smooth her cheek as, fluidly, he crouched down by her chair.

'Look at me.'

June did as she was bid, but a stubborn shaky twist to her lips told William this was not going to be in any way easy. She was angry merely that the woman's name was again being mentioned between them.

'Is there more talk of that widow pining after you

and regretting not marrying you when she had the chance? Is that it?'

'No...not exactly. A pair of idiots have been wagering that I will take her as a mistress.' William refused to let his wife flee from him and held her gently in her seat. 'There is more. A wager has also been made that I might seek a divorce to marry her.'

This time William had no need to restrain his wife. He felt her small, tense hands fall slack in his. He watched her angry flush seep away and inside he withered. But he made no attempt to soothe or cajole with pretty words. Quietly he demanded, 'Tell me you know how pathetic and ridiculous a lie it is.'

June's shocked gaze found her husband's stony features. Her tears were dammed behind fury and fright. What dominated her thoughts was the eerie recollection that recently she had wondered whether she would still be with William when he had silver hair.

William urgently shook the hands clasped in his. 'Do you not trust me, June? Do you think me capable of such behaviour?'

She shook her head wildly, her pale Titian curls flying about her fragile milky shoulders as her bodice slipped askew.

'What I want to know,' William said quietly, 'is if you would like me to run Harley and Darlington through for it? You only have to say and I shall call out both of them with every intention of striking to kill.' His voice was vibrating with repressed rage. 'Just for seeing you this upset, I would do it.'

June suddenly turned in her chair and threw her arms about her husband's neck. 'Why are they *doing* this to us?' she wailed.

'Simply to revel in the knowledge that they can,' he answered quietly. 'When I spoke to your father over it all, he said, quite wisely I thought, that contented people, such as we, rankle cynics. We must not allow them to bring us down, June.' His words were harsh with demand yet he stroked at her silky copper hair, thrusting his fingers deep into its warm mass to curve about her scalp and bring her face to his. 'I meant what I said. I will call both of them out if you want. At first I thought that we should not show those curs that they have the power to affect us. Now I'm not so sure. I hate to see you so sad.'

June managed a watery smile; again she enclosed her husband in a fierce emphatic embrace. 'Do you think I would risk my William to a cheat's tricks? Or to a gaol? That is where you would end if you were to succeed in putting those pathetic creatures out of their misery. No! I would never risk losing you. You will not call either of them out.'

She lowered her face to the handsome man gazing earnestly up at her. A soft, creamy cheek swept over the abrasive texture of his face. 'My papa has clashed with Benjamin Harley before. So has Connor. Both of them hate him. In fact, I have never heard anyone speak a good word about him. If he had no money and no influence, I'm sure he would not be received anywhere.'

A loving hand smoothed her husband's strained features. 'I trust you. I believe you. I love you and I know you love me. Harley and Darlington will simply have to find some other poor souls to torment. And Constance Bingham, I'm afraid, will just have to look elsewhere for her next husband.'

William rose to his feet, drawing June with him.

'Are we finished?' June said, looking at her unused dessert spoon. 'There is some syllabub.'

William smothered the rest of her words with a bittersweet kiss, hard as his desire, honeyed as his love. Without releasing her mouth, he swung her up into his arms, and headed for the door.

By the stairs June managed to surface long enough to choke, 'William! The servants will be back. Dessert—'

'The servants and the syllabub can wait,' her husband announced roundly as he took the first two treads in one stride. 'I'm not sure I can…'

Chapter Six

'I gather you rather like my roguish school chum.'

'He *is* very good company.'

'I'm sure. But he is a villain, June,' William emphasised with rueful gravity. 'A most charming and amusing fellow, too, I grant you. Adam springs from a very long line of fêted reprobates. The Rockinghams have long entertained society with their scandalous ways.'

'And you allow such riffraff to escort your wife? Shame on you!' June mocked with a flash of laughing eyes.

'I'm not sure why I trust a man I have not seen for so long and whom I know to be an inveterate womaniser. Yet I would vouch for him acting the perfect gentleman with you.'

'And very wise you are, for he does,' June endorsed softly. But she looked intrigued. 'Now you have whetted my appetite, you have to tell me more of his family than that,' she urged. 'Is the Fleet full of impoverished Rockinghams who have gambled away their last halfpenny? Are there mad relatives locked away in gothic turrets?' She gave a low chuckle as William's eyes narrowed in sultry humour at her teasing. 'In any case…' She playfully squeezed at William's arm and, going on her tiptoes, brought their faces close, her breath whispering warm and sweet past his lips. 'In any case,' she softly echoed, 'the Merediths are able to boast a scandal or two of their own. We are not fazed by notoriety,' she proudly announced.

A discreet caress welcomed the seductive pressure of her hip against his. 'True. But your sisters' youthful misdemeanours are as nothing compared to some of the Rockingham sons' sins.'

'Were some of those men pirates? Smugglers?' June was only half-jesting, for she was genuinely interested in finding out more about their host's intriguing history.

'All of that and more, I suspect,' William told her. 'I recall spending one school holiday with Adam when I was about fourteen. We spent an entire afternoon exploring the eaves' rooms of Rockingham Hall—' He broke off to digress. 'We were trespassing. All those rooms were out of bounds. The Hall is a draughty old medieval house and the thing I remember most about it is that it seemed an endless maze of icy corridors.' He resumed his tale. 'Anyway, in one locked room—of which Adam expertly picked the lock—there was a portrait of a barbarous-looking cove with lengthy black hair and a monkey crouched on his shoulder. Adam asked his father about him and was thrashed for revealing his intrusion and his inquisitiveness. Adam, being Adam, was undeterred by that and persevered with his investigations into the man's history. When back at school, he told me that he was a disgraced Earl who had turned to life as a privateer and had got rich again from sugar plantations. He was very bad even by Rockingham standards.'

June looked fascinated, but murmured, 'Perhaps they all have improved since. I expect the portrait might have been some centuries old.'

'It was relatively recently that his great-grandfather was gadding about in caves in West Wycombe, or so rumour has it.'

June's eyes widened. 'No! Really?' Her lucid amber eyes slipped sideways to target their handsome host and she cocked her head to one side. She had heard whispers of the tales of the Hell Fire Club, whose wicked members engaged in unspeakable acts whilst dressed in ceremonial robes. A shocked laugh bubbled in her throat. 'I'm sure Mr Townsend is much too civilised for such tomfoolery.

I might not know him as well as you, but even I can
see he would not look well in monk's garb.'

William chuckled. 'What a pity! No orgy
tonight!' A heavy-lidded suggestive look preceded
him saying, 'We could create our own diversion
later.' As his wife prettily blushed, and gave his arm
a punitive bang, William cast a discreet eye over her
shapely curves.

June was dressed in quite demure style, as ever.
She rarely opted for daring fashions that left little to
the imagination. But for him, she looked delectable
and desirable, however modestly she was garbed.
He knew other men must find her as attractive as he
did. Adam Townsend had told him more than once
he was lucky in his choice of wife. June had a beauty
of countenance and nature that made her seem
alluring yet vulnerable. It made him—and he suspected other men who escorted her—want to act the
hero protecting her. William took a glance to the left
at his old friend.

Adam and his mother, Eleanor, Lady Rockingham, were greeting guests at the stately entrance to
the vast ballroom of Number 20 Upper Brook Street.

William assessed his wife's suave admirer, noting
his muscular stature and dark thick hair, in the
manner of a man measuring a rival. Luckily he was
not a possessive man. He never had been of a jealous
disposition. When Constance Palmer had jilted him

in favour of a better catch, everyone praised him for being stoic and mature beyond his years. William could recall feeling a little guilty at the unwanted praise and sympathy. It had seemed to him to be churlish to point out that Constance had never captured his heart and soul and her defection was more inconvenient than inconsolable.

But June had his heart and soul and he wondered how her defection might have affected him. He imagined stoicism would have swiftly deserted him along with his lauded maturity. Losing her might have seen him howling like a baby. He brought his odd musings to an abrupt halt and frowned at his shoes. It had never before occurred to him to analyse his reaction to an imaginary separation from the woman he loved. Why would he? It would never happen.

'It is a shame the Marquess of Rockingham is ailing. I should have liked to meet him,' June hissed in a whisper. Her eyes continued to watch elegant ladies and gentlemen proceeding with much aplomb over polished wooden boards to mark territory in which to preen and peruse.

'I have not seen Adam in an age and he has certainly not broadcast the fact that his father has deteriorated mentally.' William grimaced as he said, 'He and his father have never got on. He dotes on his mother, however. I like her. She always made me welcome when I went to stay during school holidays.'

'Family feuds are horrible,' June said significantly. 'Was his father cruel to him? You said he beat Adam when he discovered that pirate's portrait.'

'I think a polarity of personalities causes them to be constantly at odds. I remember his father being a bit of a puritan. Despite his money and influence, the old Marquess has never cared to enjoy himself. That cannot be said for his heir. Adam was always very aware of life's pleasures. A pure Rockingham through and through—'

'Oh, look!' June interrupted and shook William's arm. 'Here is your other school friend. Mr Blackmore is just arrived.' June recognised him immediately, for it was only a week or so ago that Adam had stopped his curricle by the Park gates to introduce them.

William was staring at the gentleman being welcomed by Lady Rockingham and her son. 'By Heaven, it is him! Perhaps we ought go and talk to him.' He turned to June as Gavin Blackmore proceeded, alone, into the room. 'He looks a little forlorn over there on his own.'

As they picked a path through scented air and silk and satin to where Mr Blackmore stood—so close to a potted palm it seemed he intended shrinking behind it—June reminded herself how lucky she was to be married to a man of such philanthropy and sensitivity that he would immediately wish to make welcome an old acquaintance he had not seen in more than a decade.

'I always envied your husband, you know, Mrs Pemberton, even at school and years before I learned what a beautiful wife he has.'

June's cheeks bloomed rosily at the compliment and she smiled sweetly at Gavin Blackmore, but her eyes again scanned the room for William. It had been some while since he left her side. Summoned by his mother's urgently crooked and waggling finger, he had excused himself and strolled off, sighing, to see what it was she wanted.

June's sparkling amber eyes again alighted on the man at her side. In her husband's absence she was quite content to keep him company. Mr Blackmore might not be quite as tall or dark as Adam Townsend but, now she had had a chance to study him more closely, she thought his mild looks and diffident manner rather appealing. She had been correct in supposing that at their first meeting he might have been endeavouring to conceal his shy nature with a show of confidence.

This evening he seemed less inclined to try to impress. He also seemed overawed by his surroundings and constantly darted glances up and down and around and about at the magnificent appointments in Adam Townsend's mansion.

June attempted to put him at ease by reminding him of the one thing at which she knew he had excelled. 'I have been told that you were an exemplary student at Eton. No doubt there were many at school who envied you your intellect.'

'Oh!' Gavin twisted a smile and seemed a little disconcerted. 'I gather you have been informed that I was rather the poor boy at school. Did your husband tell you I scraped a place at Eton from a scholarship, or was it Townsend's doing?'

'It was Mr Townsend…I should say…his lordship's doing, for I keep forgetting that he is so seriously lofty. William says he has never much bothered about using his courtesy title. I never realised he was the Earl of Malvern.' A little smile followed that. 'And he was complimentary about your achievements.'

'Was he?' A slight sourness honed Gavin's tone and tugged down one side of his lips. 'I don't recall ever receiving a kind word from him at Eton. But he gave me a beating. And oh, yes, he is exceedingly lofty. He was always keen to keep lesser mortals firmly in their place, when he noticed they existed. I was astonished to receive an invitation to his soirée tonight. Or perhaps that was your doing. Townsend always liked to impress the ladies.' He gave June a boyish smile. 'I'm not complaining. I'm thanking you, for it is indeed a most lavish affair. Did you persuade him to invite me?'

June murmured, a trifle abashed, 'No…' but she knew her cheeks had tinted with guilt. Adam's intention in inviting this man to his party had been, so he had said, to prove to her that he harboured no animosity towards him. Her eyes strayed to where their splendidly sophisticated host was grouped with some ladies and gentlemen. He was a villain, she reminded herself. Even her William had warned her of that. But she baulked at believing him a pompous bully. 'I'm sorry to hear that Lord Malvern beat you.' She said no more for she didn't want to be drawn into blaming or championing their host. Neither did she want to be seen to be inquisitive enough to pry for further details.

Gavin's careless shrug demonstrated his willingness to let bygones be bygones. 'It was nothing, of course. Boys will be boys. Thrashings, boasts, all are just part of being at boarding school. It is a most hierarchical life.' A suitably brave smile accompanied the explanation. 'Of course, my griping might have a little to do with the fact that I was…still am…exceedingly jealous of him. Who would not be? He has everything.' A small gesture indicated the opulence all around. 'Townsend always had everything any man could want including, as I said, a most successful way with the ladies.'

'You said you envied William, too. Did my husband also have a successful way with the ladies?' June enquired with a teasing smile.

'Well, I'm sure such a personable man had his admirers, but I did not witness anything…anything excessive,' was Gavin's diplomatic answer. 'Your husband was an all-round good chap. I think everyone—even Townsend—envied William. He was incredibly popular, clever, a fine sportsman. It is no surprise to me that a man so blessed managed to persuade a lovely, charming lady to marry him.'

As June again coloured at his praise, Gavin looked momentarily apologetic. 'It is not insincere flattery. I mean what I say.' He paused, moved awkwardly from foot to foot. 'I am afraid I made rather a fool of myself when we were first introduced at the Park. I must have seemed to you a witless idiot to act so tongue-tied. The truth is, you rather overwhelmed me. But then I expect you have that effect on other gentlemen.' He gave a little nervous rub to the bridge of his nose. 'I'm sorry if my regard makes you feel uncomfortable.'

June touched his arm lightly, reassuringly. 'It does not. It is kind of you to be lavish with your compliments.'

June looked at Gavin's tense, proud features. She guessed it was in his nature to be bluff; no doubt he would feel rather out of place in such sophisticated company as this. Possibly he regretted coming at all and having revealed so much of himself to a woman he barely knew. June sensed a sudden surge of empathy. She was no stranger to feeling envious. Did she not sometimes consider herself unfortunately plain in comparison to her startlingly beautiful siblings? Had she not felt resentful and self-pitying on learning that Rachel was to soon have another baby? She could sense this gentleman attempting to repress similar emotions to those that had recently bedevilled her.

'Envy can stimulate us to try harder…or it can be a most destructive emotion,' she softly said. 'Sometimes it is difficult not to be angry when something you believe you deserve… something dear to your heart…is denied you. Life can be unfair in how it distributes its bounty.'

Gavin Blackmore gave her a grateful smile. 'You are perceptive as well as charming, Mrs Pemberton. But not too perceptive, I hope, for I sometimes worry I can be a bore and I should like your good opinion.'

'And you have it. I do not at all think you boring. I have enjoyed our chat.' June glanced about and said, 'I suppose I ought go and rescue William from his mother. She can be quite a…tenacious lady.'

'I think William has managed to extricate himself,' Gavin said with a flicker of a smile. 'I'm sure I saw him go outside…just a moment ago.'

June felt her insides tighten, for something about Gavin's attitude made her sure he immediately regretted telling her so. She sensed he also did not want to disclose whether William had stepped alone on to the terrace.

'I must not keep you from your husband or take up any more of your time.' He executed a polite bow for her.

Having said farewell, June turned away to begin her search for William. After a few steps she pivoted back in a rustle of cream silk to see Mr Blackmore had not moved and was watching her. 'Did my husband go alone on to the terrace?'

Gavin cleared his throat, frowned over her head as he gripped his hands behind his back. 'I believe he was with Lady Bingham...and some others,' he tacked on quickly, perhaps too quickly.

A constrained smile met that news. June tilted her chin. Following the latest outrageous gossip, perhaps her perfect husband ought to know he was acting rather rashly by being seen again in the company of that woman. June strove to sound insouciant as she asked, 'Do you know Lady Bingham, Mr Blackmore?' She came towards him again as she spoke.

'We come from the same part of the country...Devonshire. Not that I socialised much with Lady Bingham and her late husband. I might have been lucky enough to secure an education at Eton, but even my father's best efforts could never gain me an entrée into such circles.'

'Constance and William were once engaged, you know. Then she chose to marry Lord Bingham instead.'

'Yes, I knew of that. I'm sure William is glad that it all turned out for the best. I'm sure, too, he would never knowingly snub anyone, however tempted he might be to do so.'

'I gather from your tactful response that you are aware of gossip concerning my husband and Lady Bingham. You need not fear embarrassing me. William and I have dismissed it. We will never let malice ruin our happiness.'

Gavin gave a relieved sigh. 'Very sensible too! I feared that I might inadvertently disclose what I knew and that might make you angry—'

He suddenly fell silent and frowned, making June suspect he had been about to say more.

'I must go now. I did not mean to stay long. But I am glad to have again had an opportunity to talk to you, Mrs Pemberton.'

June put a light hand on his arm. 'Must you go so soon?' There was just a suspicion that he had been about to disclose something else…something, she sensed, that she didn't know.

With a look that told her how easily she could sway him, Gavin drew June slightly behind the potted palm he had sought as company when first he arrived alone. 'Perhaps you would do me the honour of allowing me to take you for a drive one afternoon…with your husband's permission, of course. I shall call next week, if that is convenient.'

Having gained a small nod in response, he bowed briefly and was soon striding away.

'You seemed very deep in conversation with my old friend. I was loath to interrupt. His manners are still sadly lacking. He has dashed past me with barely a farewell. Have you given him a well-deserved set-down?'

June turned to see Adam Townsend smiling at her. He looked outrageously handsome in his excellently tailored dark clothes. 'I hope I have not,' she said, struggling to find a smile. 'I think Mr Blackmore simply felt a little…left out of it. I have the impression he knows few people here this evening.'

Adam's shrug was indifferent. 'Where is William? I was looking for him earlier.'

'So was I,' June announced a trifle tartly. 'I believe he might be outside on the terrace.'

Adam gallantly proffered an arm. 'Let us see, then, if we can find him.'

After a stroll in the chill moonlight and no sign of William, they returned to the supper room, and it was there that William found them. He drew his wife away from Adam, who relinquished her with a theatrically regretful sigh.

It took but one long look for William to sense his wife was angry and hurt. 'What is it?' he demanded with a fierce look at their urbane host some way in the distance now. 'I saw you come in from the terrace with him. Has Townsend at last disgraced himself with you?'

'Of course not!' June looked up into her husband's face. 'Have *you* disgraced yourself...or me? Did you accompany Lady Bingham outside a little while ago?' she accused bluntly.

William's face darkened. 'I went to the terrace with Isabel and Etienne. Constance Bingham, I believe, was right behind us with several other people. There was talk of a shooting star having been seen in the night sky. In all, twenty or more people ventured outside, hoping for a glimpse of it. It grew so crowded that I was soon again inside and looking for you.'

June stared up at him, blatant angry suspicion still firing her golden eyes.

William suddenly captured her soft arm in a firm grip and drew his wife close to a marble pillar so they could talk more privately. 'When we spoke of this the other evening, I thought we had agreed to ignore the gossip and act normally. It would have seemed exceedingly odd had I turned around and fled as soon as I noticed that Constance Bingham was in the vicinity. I thought you had told me you trusted me. Is that not so? Am I going to have to beg permission to go out, and justify my every movement to you, June? Do you want a husband or a lap dog that will never leave your side? If you wish it, I will be your pet, you only have to say, my dear.' He struck a hand over her head to lounge against the pillar. Only a keen observer would have seen his knuckles whiter than the marble they gripped as he strove to shield their discord from prying eyes. 'Is there ever to be any trust and harmony again in this marriage?' The reprimand was blasted through teeth that looked set perilously tight.

Over one of his broad, bunched shoulders, the pale oval of June's face was just visible. Her complexion was stark white against the black cloth of his jacket. Her teary tawny gaze focussed on a woman who was watching them...watching them intently. Aware of June's eyes on her, Constance Bingham tilted her head slightly to one side then with triumph flaring in her eyes she turned away.

Chapter Seven

'We will pack today and leave for Grove House tomorrow.'

The bluntly delivered instruction brought up June's chin. Over her raised coffee cup she challenged her husband's edict with brilliant tiger eyes.

So far this morning they had breakfasted in total silence. A little over ten hours earlier they had returned from Adam Townsend's ball in much the same icy atmosphere. June knew that a depressing pattern was emerging in their lives. Invariably they set out happily in the evening to socialise with friends and family, yet returned home in low spirits with a wall of tension between them.

Yesterday at midnight, they had wordlessly entered their cosy house in Mayfair and stiffly gone their separate ways. June had headed for the stairs and her chamber. Her husband had stridden immediately towards his study. The sound of the door slamming shut had disclosed his unabated frustration. She had no need to move closer to that room to know the brandy decanter would be in use. Nevertheless, with a sad sigh she had retraced her steps down the stairs with the intention of offering an olive branch. They could then at least retire for the evening with the prospect of some sleep, if no raw, healing passion.

In the event as she came closer to William's study, what she heard was a string of muttered oaths pouring forth. She had returned to the stairs and to the knowledge that it would be a very long and sombre night.

When the door to William's chamber was quietly shut in the small chill hours of the morning she was still restless. Now as she discreetly studied him, she noticed a pinch of tiredness to his features and dark beneath his eyes. She guessed he had found no more repose than had she last night. But one thing she *had* decided upon while she tossed and turned, feeling one moment entirely blameless, the next hideously at fault, was that she was glad she was close to her parents and her sisters. Never before had she realised just how much she appreciated their comfort and support.

'I have no wish to go to Essex. I want to stay by my family in London. I thought we had agreed that the malicious people who wish to torment us would not drive us into hiding.'

'So did I,' her husband said quietly. 'But after last night I am prepared to admit defeat on this. I have no intention of enduring any more of your sulks and accusations. We must leave London.'

'I have not been sulking!' June snapped. 'And I think I was perfectly entitled to enquire whether you had been seen in the company of Constance Bingham. Considering what gossip has been bandied about, it was rather…rather ill advised of you to go outside with her, even if other people were also present.'

William gained his feet so abruptly his chair clattered on to its back. His eyes flicked distractedly as though in search of something on which he might vent his anger. Five fingers dug trenches straight through his thick fair hair. 'Instruct your maid, Verity, and choose a few other servants you would like to accompany you to Grove House. The arrangements have already been made. I want to leave by ten in the morning.'

June smartly set down her cup on to its saucer. 'And *I* have no intention of being carted off to the country. Are you going to abandon me there and return at your leisure so you may do as you please without me witnessing it and thus nagging you?'

William slanted June a fierce low-lidded look.

'Do you really think that is what I would do?' When she refused to answer him, he bellowed, *'Do you?'*

'No.' Her hands flew to cover her face. 'I'm sorry. That was a stupid thing to say. It seems so easy lately to say stupid things.' When her husband made no attempt to placate her with words or touches—and how she yearned that he would cuddle her—she proudly raised her head. With a subtle touch the tears weighting her lashes were dashed off. 'I want to stay here with my family. I need to see my sisters…my parents. Can't you understand that I need to be close to people who care for me whilst we deal with this awful situation?'

After a silence that throbbed, seemed laden with tension, William enquired with cool politeness, 'Do I not care for you then?'

June gripped the table with both her small hands. 'I hope so…I *do* hope so. But just lately I should like a little more hard proof of your feelings for me, William.'

William's cold blue gaze was unwavering, yet a glimmer of amusement was far back in eyes that were becoming sleepy.

June flushed and looked at her breakfast plate as it dawned on her how indelicately she had phrased her needs. She thus missed the smile softening the hard edge to her husband's mouth.

Slowly William withdrew his watch and studied

it. 'Well, I have fifteen minutes to spare before I'm due at my attorney's…'

June shoved away from the table and was, in a whisper of sprigged muslin, halfway to the door when he caught her and whirled her about. Off balance, she tipped straight into his welcoming arms.

'Just a joke…I've all morning…all day…all the time in the world for you. You must know that.'

'There is other proof, you know!' June didn't persist for long with her feeble attempts to extricate herself. She allowed him to hold her, for moments before she had pined for this comfort. Half-heartedly she scolded, 'There are other ways you might show me you care; that you love me and cherish me and…'

'I know,' her husband answered softly, a finger tracing a curve of her cheek, soothing her pique. 'But that way seems to work best, and I confess I like it. Don't you?' He gave one side of her mutinously strict lips a soft kiss. When she refused to respond he enclosed her tightly and rested his chin atop a crown of glossy Titian hair. 'How then shall I show you I love you?'

Indifferent shoulders lifted, then slumped within his embrace.

'Shall I pen Constance Bingham a note informing her she is a hag and dispatch it forthwith?'

June's choke of laughter and frantic shake of her head had him moving loving hands over her slender spine, drawing her imperceptibly closer to undeniable proof of his desire for her. 'I've already offered to meet Harley and Darlington at dawn and risk life and limb for you in a misty glade.'

June tipped up her head, looked into the warm cerulean gaze that roved her face. She was already won over. She yearned for the touch of his mouth on hers, the cool sleek sensation of his velvet skin moving on her body.

'I know what you'd like: the diamond rope bangle we saw when out last week. I noticed you linger by it.'

Swiftly June put up a finger, placed it over her husband's lips.

William kissed it, turned his face so the soft digit smoothed his cheek. 'No? You don't want it? I know you'd rather I made your arms tired with the weight of our baby but it seems, much as I love you, that gift is beyond me…'

June wound her arms tightly about his neck. Abruptly she released him and was soon by the door. 'In five minutes come upstairs. More than anything I long for such proof of our love and it is not beyond you…or me.'

'It is an outrage too far! Are you certain?' Edgar Meredith's bluish lips virtually disappeared, so grimly were they set.

Etienne looked to Connor to respond to their father-in-law's hoarse demand. Connor sighed and nodded his head. 'We both heard what was said.'

Edgar dragged off his spectacles and, in shock, let them carelessly clatter to his desk. A mottled hand covered his eyes, massaged wearily as though to ease away strain beneath straggly brows. Eventually he said, 'Do you think this is yet more of Harley's mischief?'

'I've no idea,' Connor told him truthfully. 'White's was crowded, but I don't think Harley or Darlington were there. The conversation we overheard was not malicious. It was just a bit of ribald banter between a few young bucks. They looked to be still wet behind the ears. When they noticed we seemed annoyed at what they were saying, they made a swift exit.'

Etienne sighed pessimistically before joining in the conversation. 'William won't take this as philosophically as he has the other rumours, that's for sure.'

'How do you think my June will react to it all?' Edgar exploded. 'She and William are looking more and more as though a rift is opening wide between them. They quit Townsend's party the other evening looking morose. It is being noticed that all is not well. More than once recently I've had to deflect impertinent inquisitiveness on the state of their marriage.' Edgar frowned at his sons-in-law. 'Are Rachel and Isabel aware of this? Have you yet told them? I know they will not want to hurt their sister but they will not want to conceal anything so vital from June either. They would hate her to hear it when out and unprepared for such devastating news.'

Etienne and Connor, with a simultaneous shake of dark heads, denied having had an opportunity to tell their wives about this episode. Edgar scooped up his spectacles and nodded in meagre satisfaction. 'Well, that gives us a little time I suppose to sort out what must be done. And I fear that *we* must do it, for even a fellow as placid as William will feel it his duty to call out whomever has so maligned him. And he might shoot to kill the devil.'

Etienne frowned. 'There is something else that occurs to me; with respect, sir, we are all men of the world. Do you think that perhaps we ought to speak urgently to William before we act, in case there is a possibility a grain of truth exists in it? William and Constance Palmer were betrothed for some months, after all…'

Edgar stared, and as the full implication hit him, he squeezed shut his eyes and gulped back the outrage that had been on the point of blasting forth from his puckered lips. What did emerge eventually was a muted oath followed by, 'I must be older than I think, for I admit that had not occurred to me. And yet it should have, for now I ponder on it, that infernal woman did jilt William, then go on to marry Charlie Bingham with indecent haste.'

'Supposing it to be true…do you think perhaps the lady might bizarrely feel she has a valid claim on William? Has she got a hand in it all?' Connor elevated his shoulders, indicating it was no more than a suggestion.

'Bingham's first wife died childless…' Edgar muttered almost to himself.

'There were rumours before that, which seemed unfounded, of course, when he married for the second time and started his family,' Etienne added cautiously.

The three men looked at one another. Edgar slowly sank into his desk chair. 'If proven, what an awful irony it would be! Please God it is not true, for I fear it might transform those other lies to truth. Divorce! It ought not be uttered in the same breath as June's name, yet it no longer seems outlandish. Indeed, in my opinion it would be unendurable for June to stay with William should it be proven he has sired Constance Bingham's daughter.'

'I am going to be on my best behaviour this afternoon and say nothing that might easily embarrass you.'

'What makes you think I am easily embarrassed?'

Gavin Blackmore slid June a teasing grin. 'You blush every time I compliment you.'

June put a pale hand to a pink cheek. 'I have a naturally high colour,' she fibbed on a shy smile.

'You have rosebuds in your cheeks. And I am glad that I am able to put them there, for it suits you very much.'

'You promised to be on your best behaviour this afternoon.' The reprimand was followed by a coy cluck of the tongue. 'I'm not sure such praise lavished on a happily married lady *is* good behaviour, sir.'

Gavin let the reins slacken in his fingers and the modest equipage he had hired to take them for an afternoon drive slowed to a sedate pace. 'I think you know I would rather die than offend you.' The words were vibrant with sincerity and a look mingling apology and adoration bathed her face.

'I'm not at all offended,' June reassured lightly and, after a smile, turned her head. During the following quiet minutes they spent inspecting passing landmarks, June was aware of Gavin taking sidelong peeks at her profile.

It was the third time they had taken an afternoon drive together while William's commerce kept him closeted with his men of business in Cheapside. Now June had got to know Gavin Blackmore better, she had discovered he could be amiable and amusing. He was a good mimic and satirist and several prominent figures had, earlier in the week, been wittily subjected to the sharp side of his tongue. She had, between chuckles, scolded him and warned that he risked being incarcerated for sedition if he carried on so.

Assuming a humble pose, he had promised to desist and changed the subject. And the subject he again settled on was her. The constancy of his compliments was quite alarming, for it was unlike the practised gallantry that Adam Townsend casually bestowed on her...and she imagined many other ladies of his acquaintance. Yet June was not displeased by Gavin's attention. It was flattering for the *sensible* Meredith girl to be the object of such ardent admiration from a man who, despite his mature years, was obviously a novice at flirtation.

June was unpractised in such arts, too. She had never before had much opportunity to test her feminine wiles for she had married young, to her one and only love. And she was sure she didn't regret any of it...

At her débutante ball William had appeared to notice her at the same moment she saw him. An unspoken bond seemed to forge between them and, shortly after she wished he would, he had come to her side. They had danced together perfectly, talked together as though long acquainted. Before the evening was over she had known with a sense of serenity that he would offer for her in the morning. Equally, she knew she would readily consent to be his wife. They were engaged before her first season had got properly under way. She had never before pondered on whether she missed the thrill of enticing men to notice her, whether she regretted acting mature for her years when barely out of her teens. For, eager to please her acid-tongued mother-in-law, June had conducted herself with modesty and decorum from the outset.

'I feel we are becoming friends, so I hope you will not mind me saying that sometimes you look a little...wistful. I hope it is not due to spiteful people, for I am quite afraid you will choose to escape to your retreat in the Essex countryside. I hope you do not. I shall miss your company and our little outings.'

'William and I will not be driven from our home by those nasty tattle-mongers,' June confidently told him.

At Adam Townsend's ball she had had an instinct Gavin was nervous of inadvertently revealing something sensational. June had decided not to probe but heed her husband's quiet wisdom, bestowed after their passionate reconciliation earlier in the week. 'Let us avoid even thinking of any of it, sweetheart,' he had impressed on her. 'In that way we will certainly frustrate those fools who think they can torment us.'

With a secret smile, June thought further about that delightful time; she thought of how very easily she had persuaded her husband to change his mind about going to Essex. He had groaned as she covered his face with tiny kisses and pressed home her suit, but then within a pleasurable while she had groaned too, so loud he had had to stop her with his kiss covering her mouth and with a whispered scold that she would startle the servants…

As she felt her face flame with her reminiscences she brightly blurted out those other valid reasons for staying in London. 'My family is in town for the season. We must make the most of our times together. Soon Rachel will be returning to Ireland, and Isabel will go to Suffolk. If Sylvie does not attract a husband—and Heaven knows I don't believe she is even ready for one—she and my parents will journey back to Windrush, my childhood home in Hertfordshire. We all adore Windrush. We spent some very happy childhood days there.' She gave Gavin a smile. 'Enough of me and mine…you have told me nothing about your family.'

Immediately he averted his face as though she had mentioned something disconcerting.

June persevered. 'Do you have brothers or sisters?' In response June received a brief nod. 'I believe it was Adam Townsend who informed me your father was a clergyman. You must have spent your early years in a rural vicarage; or perhaps you lived in a town in Devon…'

'I lived at The Rookery, which was the parsonage in Maybury village. I wish I could say they were happy days,' he informed quietly. 'My mother died in childbed when my younger sister was born. My father was a cold and brutal man who would preach damnation at us with the same zeal he addressed his congregation.' He gave June a taut smile. 'I am sorry but I have no pretty pastoral tales of romping through meadows or of sunny days angling in a clear stream. My father found chores for us every day. His favourite quote was, "The devil makes work for idle hands". Mostly my childhood was unremittingly bleak.' Gavin slid a wary glance at June as though ready to flinch at her disgust at such unsavoury reminiscence.

June's expression radiated sympathy as her eyes implored him to continue.

'My father treated my sister little better than he did me. In truth, I think he blamed Bethany for our mother's demise. Time and again I shielded her from a beating by taking the blame for some prank of hers.'

Gavin suddenly whipped the horses into faster pace, indicating he hoped he had said enough to satisfy June's curiosity.

'You must have missed your mother dreadfully. Were you still quite young when she died?'

Gavin looked resigned to her perseverance. He reined in the horses to a more sedate pace. 'I was seven. And, yes, I missed her dreadfully. When my father was remarried to his housekeeper—I think he married her simply to save himself her remuneration—things were worse for us. In her new position she became as harsh as he. I think she hoped to have children of her own and usurp us. But fortunately we were not burdened with any of their offspring. Bethany and I had no step-siblings to contend with.'

'Does Bethany still live in Devonshire with your father and stepmother?'

'No. They are both dead, and good riddance to that. I know it is a terrible thing to say about one's parent, but my father showed us no love and little attention, unless it was to bend us to his will.' He paused for a moment and at last turned his head to look at her. 'Bethany has endured a hard and cruel life. I have helped her as much as I can, but I am not a wealthy man. Bethany was married quite young to a man who was not worthy of her. I think she accepted the first offer of marriage that came her way simply to escape from the hell that was our home. My stepmother was delighted to be rid of her. My brother-in-law had a small importing business in Bristol. But Bethany, bless her, leapt from the frying pan into the fire with that cur. He regularly beat her and kept her short of food and other necessities. She absconded as far away as possible with what funds she had. She is here in London, but in grave trouble. One of the reasons I came here was to try and help her. I do what I can.'

June dropped her eyes from his. A light hand rested on his sleeve. 'I feel very sad for you. I wish I had not mentioned my happy childhood. It must be galling to have had to listen to my speaking of Windrush.'

'I enjoy hearing of your family. Please don't pity me; I could not stand that…not from you. I have been pitied as the poor boy all my life.'

'You mean at Eton?'

Gavin nodded.

'At least your father did one good thing for you and helped you gain a scholarship.'

Gavin's top lip curled in a sneer. 'He did it for himself, not for me. He wanted to associate with distinguished families in the neighbourhood. He hoped to gain an introduction to the wealthy and influential. My stepmother was scathing of my inability to make many friends at school. No rich lord's son ever invited me to stay with them during school holidays.'

'But I think…I guess from what you have said that you are close to your sister. I imagine you are a comfort to each other,' June said carefully.

Gavin nodded and his tight lips softened. 'Yes, Bethany and I are close and a comfort to each other.'

'I should like to meet her. As she lives in London, perhaps we could pay her a visit. It is still early.'

Gavin gave June a lengthy look in which he appeared to be considering her request. 'That is very good of you. I should like you to meet, but I'm not sure you would still want to should you know where she presently resides.'

June masked her incipient alarm as she calmly enquired, 'Is she now living in a different sort of rookery? Is she in a slum?'

'No, she's in a gaol,' was Gavin's bleak response.

Chapter Eight

'In a gaol?'

The horrified demand was barely audible and elicited from Gavin a rueful smile. 'I am sorry if I have shocked you with tales of my abysmal family's woes, Mrs Pemberton.'

'You have not shocked me…' June protested, then sighed in defeat. 'I own I am shocked, and very sorry that your sister has suffered such trials and tribulations. You, too, it seems, have not had an easy life,' she added in a tone resonant with sympathy.

'Bethany has suffered far harsher treatment than have I. She is in a debtor's prison. I expect you have heard of the Fleet. Please God you never see its accommodation, or come within range of its stench.'

June gazed at the rigid profile presented to her. Gavin simply kept his eyes on the road and the horses trotting. 'Is it not possible to gain your sister's release from that awful place?'

'I could never find enough to pay what she owes. As I have said, I am not a wealthy man. I have bribed her gaoler to make sure she has at least some edible food each day. And he brings her washing water. I have tried to scrape her a few comforts—' He broke off to bark harshly, 'Comforts! How stupid to use such a word. Of course a human being ought be entitled to such basic necessities.'

'I should like to help…'

It seemed Gavin did not hear June's offer, for he continued in a tone of repressed rage, 'Bethany has fled from that monster she married only to be hounded by the cost of freedom. If only she had waited just a little while longer, I would have made arrangements for her escape. I told her that. But she can be impulsive. She hired a rig and a driver and was charged an extortionate price. Then, when in the city, she needed somewhere to stay and the friend she thought she had found turned out to be no friend at all but a procuress. Bethany immediately sought her own lodgings elsewhere, but she has never been able to haggle. She would always give over whatever amount was asked of her, fearing her dignity would be compromised should she tender a shilling less.'

He shook his head in despair. 'What dignity has she now? She weeps away the day and night. By the time I had caught up with her the duns were hot on her heels. Within a few days they had brought her up before the magistrate. If only I could pay off her debts!' His fist was slammed in frustration against a solid thigh, and June noticed his lips tighten against his teeth.

'You should not have hired this rig to take me for a drive. Not today or earlier in the week. That expense would have been better spent helping your sister.'

Gavin acknowledged that truth with a short, uneasy laugh. 'I do not regret indulging my desire to see you. I have enjoyed our drives. There! I confess I am a selfish beast. Bethany, of course, tells me I do too much for her. She scolds me for wasting my money on bribes given to a pig of a gaoler. I'm quite sure the oaf could do more for her for what I pay him.'

'It must be dreadful for her!' June cried softly. 'I shall speak to William and…'

'I beg you will not do that.' The demand was gritted out in such a harsh and authoritative tone that it startled June into staring at him.

Quickly Gavin steered the rig to the side of the road and brought it to a halt. He turned to June and his expression was calm and yet implacable. Gently he took her hands into his. 'I thank you very much for the offer to speak to your husband on my account,

Mrs Pemberton, but I cannot allow it. Indeed, I would be grateful if you would not repeat what I have told you today to anyone at all. I hope I am not a proud man, but neither do I want charity or pity from my peers. I had my fill of being patronised in my youth when sent to school with people who considered me an upstart. I shall strive to bring this right for Bethany, and I know I can trust you to keep what I have told you to yourself.' He suddenly smiled. 'I am grateful to you for your condolences, and for allowing me to unburden myself. I feel quite isolated at times and it is nice to have a friend to talk to.'

June squeezed his fingers, then gently extricated her own. Suddenly her problems seemed rather trivial. Malicious gossip was unpleasant, but it could not injure her physically. She guessed that Bethany Blackmore was younger than herself and in her tender years she had endured much hurt and hardship. 'Has Bethany enough clothing to keep her warm? It has been quite bitter cold at night. I imagine the damp in such a place must seep into one's bones.'

Gavin dropped his chin. 'I brought her a blanket and a warm shawl, but one of the other women stole those.' He choked a laugh that petered out and was followed by a rueful shake of the head. 'My Bethany is an intrepid character. She attempted to get her things back, of course, and has quite a shiner to show she has no talent as a pugilist.'

June unwound the soft silky scarf from her neck and drew off her calf-leather gloves. 'You must take these to her. I insist!' she ordered when he made to immediately protest. 'If she wears them at all times no one will be able to steal them. I shall get more for her. Warm stockings and…under-things…' She barely blushed as she mentioned the unmentionables.

Gavin carefully, reverently, folded the items that she had given him. 'Thank you.'

June said brightly, 'And next time we go for a ride we must use my transport. Perhaps later this week we should meet again. I shall bring those garments for your sister, and you must tell me how she fares.' Absorbed with the intriguing nature of it all, she added, 'Also, I shall rack my brain for a money-making scheme to help pay off the debts.'

'I have spent many a sleepless night doing just that. There is nothing I can think of other than to be lucky at the tables, or perhaps to put a wager on a boxing match or the Epsom races.' Gavin sighed dolefully. 'But such luck has always eluded me. Perhaps you might attract good fortune…'

'It is time for me to return home, and I *shall* speak to William.' She put out a reassuring hand at Gavin's immediate disapproving frown. 'Never fear that I will disclose what you have told me. Although I do not like having secrets from William, I will respect your reasons for privacy. I shall simply quiz him over where good odds are likely to be had.'

To an observer, William's profile could have been carved from granite, so solidly was it set. Fortunately, most gentlemen in the vicinity were too engrossed in watching the card game in progress—for it seemed a sizeable fortune was about to change hands—to ponder on his stony expression. His savage fingers made to cursorily crumple the letter, recently delivered to him by a steward; instead they crisply folded it and stuffed it into a pocket.

He made a brief excuse to Adam Townsend, who slid up at him a thoughtful look before shuffling the cards in his hands and flicking them precisely about the green baize. Moments later William was making for the door of Boodle's. He was at the exit when he caught sight of his father-in-law's stocky figure striding along the pavement with the intention, it seemed, of entering the club.

Edgar Meredith quickly approached his son-in-law and, from his inferior height, glared up at William. 'Thank God you are here. Connor and Etienne have been scouring Cheapside for you; they thought you were attending to your stock portfolios this afternoon.'

'I was until recently. I have not long ago arrived here. Now I must leave.' William surfaced from the mire of anguish that dulled his mind to appreciate that his father-in-law seemed equally distracted. He wiped a hand across his chin, settling it within the comfort of thumb and forefinger. 'I hope I am wrong…but does your urgent pursuit of me mean you have already got wind of this?' William withdrew from his pocket the note he had recently received, whilst drawing his father-in-law into a convenient alcove between the buildings where they might be more secluded. Blue eyes steadily watched Edgar above the hand curled into a fist at his grimly set mouth.

Anger surged through Edgar's body and attempting to contain it made his fingers rigid. He thrust the vibrating paper back at its owner. 'Is it true?' he barked without preamble.

William beckoned curtly for his carriage and had assisted Edgar to climb in and got in himself before he uttered a reply. 'I hope to God it is not true. But if you were to ask me if it were possible…I would have to say, yes,' he admitted hoarsely. He ignored Edgar's blaspheming groan at that and again withdrew the message from his pocket. He rested it on a knee and read the few lines of boldly printed script.

I know that you have a by-blow in Devon. I expect you know who the mother is, for she makes

*her attentions to you plain enough. A barren
wife might be insulted good and proper if this
got out. Pay me a thousand guineas and nobody else will know of it. Take the money to
Saul's Pawnshop in Houndsditch and never
fear but it will reach me.*

William had reread the note a dozen or more times
when Edgar's voice penetrated the deafening fury
pounding in his ears.

'The rumour is out in any case, so that blackmail
note is not worth a jot. Connor and Etienne were in
White's and overheard some macaronis crowing that
Bingham was not the man he would have had people
believe. There were rumours before that he was
lacking spunk when his first wife died childless. Her
four sisters had produced a score or more offspring
between them.' At his son-in-law's lack of response,
aside from his face tightening to a masklike stillness,
Edgar added, 'Those prating dandies went on to
mention you by name as the prime suspect.'

At that information William's blond head fell
back against the squabs and he stared at the carriage
roof.

'Do you think that Constance Bingham has
anything at all to do with this? Would she scrape the
barrel in her effort to entrap you?'

A mirthless laugh scratched at William's throat.

'Hardly! It is common knowledge that Bingham left her a very rich woman. She might want a husband to replace him and she might have stupidly set her sights on me, but I don't see why she would resort to blackmail. That amount would be to her pin money. The mode of writing is hardly a lady's style, although I confess it is not difficult or novel to attempt to conceal one's true identity with such a trick.'

'Perhaps the rumours are her work, if not the note. An opportunist might simply have dashed that off, thinking to make himself a tidy profit before the tale became common knowledge.'

'If Constance, for some odd reason, now wanted to inform me that a decade ago I impregnated her, she would have found a private way to do it. Her reputation will suffer from this gossip…'

'I couldn't give a tinker's cuss what either of you suffer! It is my June *I* am concerned for. How do you think that poor innocent will fare when it comes to her hearing that you have sired a child out of wedlock? And June so desperate to be a mother herself.' Edgar had shifted forward on the seat in his agitation and his fists were wobbling close to his contorted features.

William's icy gaze quit the coach roof to cool Edgar's boiling countenance. When he spoke his voice was silky with politeness. 'I am glad that there is at least one thing on which we agree. My wife is, of course, also *my* first concern. She is to be protected at all costs from any more scandal. With that in mind I would ask you to act moderately and not create a drama where perhaps none exists. I will sort this out. There is no proof at the moment that I am guilty of any more than failing to confront Harley and Darlington sooner.'

Edgar stared, slack-jawed, at his son-in-law. This was a side of William he had not known existed. He warily eyed the blond gentleman opposite. He seemed a stranger with that ruthless set to his mouth and his blue eyes boring ferociously into a spot close to his head. Edgar had a mind to look about and see if a hole was opening in the coachworks. Edgar moistened his lips, undecided as to whether maintaining dignity required him to blast back a reprimand of his own. Inquisitiveness got the better of pride and he demanded, 'So you believe it is their doing. Will you call Harley and Darlington out?'

William shifted his eyes a fraction so they encompassed Edgar. After a moment of intense concentration he answered, 'I have some investigations to make. It is probably best to say no more than that at present.'

'I gather you are telling me to mind my own business. Don't you think your wife's father has a right to know what is going on?'

'No,' William replied tersely and, glancing through the coach window, noticed the vehicle was pulling into the kerb at Beaulieu Gardens. He had alighted in a trice and courteously helped Edgar out. With barely a farewell for his indignant father-in-law, the coach was soon again bowling down the road at a pace that looked perilous.

Pamela Pemberton was arranging some daffodils in a vase, pulling the stalks this way and that, to her dissatisfaction, when her son strode into the small salon of her neat townhouse. As always, Pamela was pleased to see her favourite child. The yellow trumpets were soon abandoned on the table and she exclaimed, 'William! Have you heard I have had a chill and come to see how I do?'

'No, ma'am,' William bluntly disabused her. 'Naturally, I am pleased to see you are not still ailing.'

'I am a mite improved.' Pamela sniffed, having hoped for a little more sympathy than she had got. She whipped a scrap of lace-edged linen from her skirt pocket and dabbed delicately at her dry nose.

'I have come to speak to you about Constance Palmer...Lady Bingham,' William crisply corrected himself.

Pamela gawped at him, taken aback. It was not at all a topic of conversation she would have imagined her son would broach. She slanted a nervous look at the door in case Alexander might appear, for he had forbidden the woman's name to again be mentioned in his house. And Pamela was chary of displeasing her husband, for he had been uncommonly sharp with her of late.

As if on cue, Alexander strolled in and greeted his son with a clap on the back and a brisk, 'Is June not with you?' Alexander suddenly noticed his wife was quiet and her expression was stunned. An enquiring look was shot at his son.

'I apologise in advance for the unseemly nature of what I must disclose,' William commenced gravely. 'But it is as well you hear this from me. Soon there will be new gossip about Constance Bingham and me joining that already entertaining the *ton*. My brothers-in-law have overheard a conversation in one of the clubs that I sired Constance's daughter.'

'How ridiculous!' Pamela burst out on a scathing laugh. The silver salts bottle she had withdrawn as a precaution was airily wafted beneath her nostrils before being dropped back in her pocket. 'How could it be true? You were no more than betrothed to her…' Her voice dwindled and, aghast, she darted a glance at her son. 'You surely would *not* have… Constance is gently bred… She is a lady…'

'I am not guilty of seduction and abandonment,'

William stated in a tone devoid of defensiveness. 'Constance might then have been young in years, but she was an experienced woman and knew her own mind. It was her decision to end our relationship.'

'You mean she was not… She had already…with *another*?' Pamela blurted, outraged.

William strode over to the window where he stared sightlessly out. 'I hope I am a gentleman, even when behaving as one is a trial. Consequently I have nothing more to add to what I have already told you. Other than perhaps if I had been more mature at the time, I would never have got involved with her at all.' As he turned back into the room, his eyes skimmed his father, digesting that Alexander's reaction to it all was to pinch his mouth whilst shaking his head.

'You and Constance seem friendly,' William addressed his mother. 'Has she ever hinted that her late husband was not the father of her daughter?'

William ignored his mother's amazement at such plain speaking. His sympathy for her was scant; she had been mean to June throughout their marriage and his patience with acting tactfully in it all to keep a harmonious relationship with his parents, especially his father, was at an end. Blinkers had been lifted from his eyes and he saw himself as a coward, not a diplomat. At some time before the day was out he had to tell his beloved wife of a devastating possibility.

Had he not considered himself too dignified to bite at the tormenting bait Harley had been dangling, perhaps the rumour mill might not have ground on this long. The first whisperings from Harley and Darlington, making a mockery of his and June's domestic bliss, should have been nipped in the bud, in the time-honoured way of a man protecting the woman he loved. His passivity made his stomach churn with self-disgust and he flung his head back to combat the bile rising in his throat.

By the time his mother again had his attention her complexion was as grey-tinged as was his own. 'What is it? Have you remembered something?' William demanded.

'No, I have just thought of something. That shameless hussy might have foisted on you a bastard had you married her. How do you know she was not already increasing when you were betrothed?'

'It hardly matters now. I did not marry her, thank God!'

'To think *she* had the gall to reject *you*!'

Alexander seemed to surface from his brown study in a passionate mood. His perspiring face gleamed as ashen as his hair. Usually a man of impeccable etiquette, he exposed his uncontrollable anger in emitting an audible oath in the presence of his wife. It was followed by, 'I knew that woman was no good. She has never been any good. Why in damnation did she ever come up from Devon? All of the troubles started when she arrived in town.'

'I know,' William said bleakly. 'But I hope she would not attempt to drive June and me apart by resorting to spreading such spite.'

'Do you, indeed?' Alexander said quietly. 'I'm not convinced she is innocent in all this. She has ever had a sly look about her.'

As Pamela paced to and fro, alternately crushing her hanky in a hand, then stuffing it to her mouth, William stabbed a significant look at his father. Alexander nodded imperceptibly before saying to his agitated wife, 'There is nothing more to be done just now, my dear. Why do you not have a rest before dinner? You look to be overset.'

'Of course I'm overset!' Pamela shrieked. 'I have no grandchild to call my own. All I have is a rumour that my son might have fathered a bastard—'

'There is no proof the child is mine!' William thundered across his mother's hysteria. 'If Constance is now out to cause mischief, she will find it will not work—'

'Oh, it is working very well,' Alexander interjected with great perception. 'I wonder, you know, whether Harley and that woman have cooked this up between them for some reason best known to themselves.'

As Pamela stifled a sob with her crushed scrap of lace, William said coolly, 'Heed good advice and take yourself off to rest, ma'am.'

Once Pamela was from the room Alexander gave his son a long look that mingled censure and sorrow. 'Have you told your wife any of this?'

William shook his head and a hand rose slowly to cover his face. 'No. And God knows I don't relish the prospect of doing so. But I must.'

'Indeed you must. It will reach her eventually… the poor mite,' Alexander said quietly.

William spun on his heel, shoved his hands deep into his pockets. 'My father-in-law knows, he thinks the attempt to blackmail me is of no consequence.'

'*Blackmail?*' Alexander exclaimed, throwing his hands up in despair.

William realised he had forgotten to mention that particular aspect of the disaster. He withdrew the note from his pocket. 'Edgar thinks this is the work of an opportunist. Possibly he is right.' He handed over the note for his father's perusal. 'First he thought that Constance Bingham might be the culprit.' A bleak laugh lodged in William's throat. 'She doesn't want for money. I imagine she could buy and sell the lot of us with what Charlie Bingham left her.'

Slowly Alexander raised his pewter head. His face was grimly set as he said ominously, 'Charlie Bingham was not the man he would have liked us all to believe in that respect either.'

Chapter Nine

It was mid afternoon, not yet four of the clock when William entered his Mayfair townhouse. His demeanour was forbidding and all Herbert, his old retainer, received by way of greeting was a concise question.

If Herbert noticed that his response caused his master's tense countenance to relax, the butler was too professionally detached to betray his curiosity as to why Mrs Pemberton's absence was a relief. But as Mr Pemberton passed by, his rapid footsteps cracking against polished oak, his pace uninterrupted by their dialogue, Herbert's rheumy eyes followed the tall figure until it disappeared within a doorway. Then he shook his sparse-covered head.

Had William witnessed Herbert's sad gesture, his sombre mood would have darkened, for it surely indicated that not only was the *ton* whispering about his domestic problems, but his servants were too.

Once within his walnut-panelled study William prowled restlessly from desk to fire to window, all the while despising himself for a caitiff. June was still out on her afternoon drive with Gavin Blackmore, and he was thankful of the reprieve afforded him by another man paying attention to his wife. He gazed steadily through glass at swaying hornbeams, as though their graceful dance had entranced him. With a strangled oath he shoved away from the wide sash and in a moment had slumped into a leather wing chair positioned in a corner of the room. His head had barely appreciated the comfort of antique hide when, with a groan, he sprang up and was again tracing a triangular path across thick carpet.

A tumult of agonising thoughts was constantly battering his mind, but what gnawed at his sanity most was that shortly he must inflict on the woman he loved similar torment. He didn't want to be the one to cause her such anguish. Yet if he did not disclose today's distressing news, someone else most certainly would.

If he were too craven to admit to his youthful lechery, and its possible outcome, June's father would tell her simply to save her the humiliation of hearing it from the town tabbies. And William knew it was his place to protect June from such hurt. But by protecting her with that knowledge, he must also wound her deeply.

First he had to recall that particular incident and

it was not something he could gladly do. He had banished the episode from his mind years ago. Had he exercised a little more self-control during his betrothal to Constance Palmer, he could have now dismissed this latest gossip as malicious fantasy. Instead he could not be sure that he was innocent of the latest accusation laid at his door.

There had been a single occasion when he and Constance had been intimate. His fiancée had hinted as soon as the betrothal contract was formalised that he need not wait for a plain wedding band to join the fancy gem he had given her before she act the wife for him.

It was no love match between them, but at the outset he had found Constance attractive in looks and character. He remembered feeling surprised and flattered that she should desire and trust him strongly enough to make such an offer. Virile and tender of years perhaps, but William had been brought up in his father's image. He had thus done the decent thing and an oblique refusal had been offered, couched in phrases containing honour and respect. Thereafter, when his chaste kisses were met with her teasing tongue and her body openly pliant against his, he began to reconsider his position. Her lowered eyes might have seemed demure, but her inquisitive fingers nudging close to his groin persuaded him she was insisting he accept the challenge.

So he did and soon fully understood why she had tempted him. It was not his desire she wished to slake, but her own. Beneath her pretty, girlish exterior was a woman of rapacious passion. It was no selfless demonstration of her loyalty or consideration that made her disrobe on a sultry August afternoon when they were, at her orchestration, alone, away from the other people enjoying a rout at her parents' mansion, and deep in lush Kent countryside. He was, at twenty, no novice in sensuality, having kept a mistress for several years, but no woman had ever played the whore for him with such tireless enthusiasm as Constance. He recalled he had felt at one and the same time fascinated and repulsed by the violence of her endless frustration. Time and again he had brought her to shrieking ecstasy, but it wouldn't do. Finally he had collapsed in long grass, exhausted and sated, and laughing in defeat. She had laughed too, scornfully, and tongued the vermilion welts on his chest, as though savouring that she had put them there, before determinedly straddling him again.

He understood many things after that, not least why Sir Timothy and Lady Palmer seemed keen to quickly marry off their daughter, for doubtless her lusty appetite had previously threatened to disgrace them.

But William was a gentleman. The uneasiness

over their future together had obsessed his mind during their quiet ride back to the Palmers' Kent mansion that sticky afternoon, yet he had not seriously considered betraying Constance by ending their betrothal. By the time he and his fiancée were again in company, William had resigned himself to several facts, one of which was that he had not taken his future wife's virginity. Miss Palmer was an insatiable wanton and he'd accepted that even his best efforts to hose the fire in her loins were likely to be unsuccessful. He'd expected to be, early in their marriage, a cuckold. Precociously cynical, he had reasoned that so were half the gentlemen of the *ton* who were, themselves, adulterers, regularly servicing another man's wife. He had decided it would be no real hardship to continue the *beau monde* tradition of marrying for convenience and forming a discreet attachment elsewhere.

Once his heirs were born, he would have allowed his wife her liaisons, so long as she was reciprocally discreet. Like his father before him, William decided to do the decent thing. The contract had been signed and sealed. He would have allowed himself to be led by the nose, straight down the aisle…and into a life of hell. For such it would have been, now he knew what a marriage could be.

Thankfully Constance and her parents had other ideas. They were not so troubled by conscience over a deal brokered with a young man of affluence but little influence. A nobler prospect had presented itself and William had been summarily dismissed. Lord Bingham had married Constance and made her a lady. But it transpired she had little else than her title to succour her in widowhood. Before he left his father's house this afternoon William had learned from Alexander that the city was now abuzz with some startling news.

It was widely known that Charles Bingham had speculated in overseas commerce prior to his death, but what had not been broadcast was that he had managed to conceal the spectacular extent of his portfolio's losses. Hoping to recoup some resources, he had then turned to an occupation destined to divest him of what little assets he retained. Charlie Bingham had privately wagered himself and his family into vast debt. The banks involved in loaning him money to shore up his foreign investments, and his reputation, were now impatient for repayment. Finally it had emerged that, far from leaving his wife rich, practically every piece of stock with which Constance Bingham was saddled was mortgaged to the hilt.

'Where are the best odds to be had, William?'

The soft melodic voice, the hint of teasing husking the words, dragged his blond head down in shame, for shortly he must dash that mellow mood. William stared at his white knuckles gripping at white marble as a rage of emotion threatened to sway him on his feet. The temptation to turn and crush his wife to him, beg her not to hate him, was not easily vanquished. But first there was much to be said…

Moments later, when June hugged him affectionately around the waist, William flinched. So deep had he been in his ravaging thoughts that he had not even heard the door open. He was unprepared and unequal to deal with the most daunting duty of his life.

June withdrew a little way from her husband's rigid back. She stepped a few paces to his right so she could study his profile. It was an unnecessary repositioning, for within a moment William had swung about and was gazing down into a pure sweet expression. June smiled, but as her husband's eyes jammed shut and an unsteady hand brushed his chin on its way to concealment in a pocket, her small teeth gripped her lower lip.

'What's the matter? Are you unwell?' June took in, with anxious hazel eyes, his pallor and the dark partings his agitated fingers had tunnelled through his fair hair.

'I will not gamble if you do not want. It was just that Mr Blackmore and I were talking of where we might get good odds and win some money. Horses or a boxing bout? Which to choose?'

'Gambling is for fools!' Her husband choked on a bitter laugh.

June eyed him with a dawning suspicion of the reason for this odd mood of his. 'You have not played at the tables this afternoon and lost heavily, have you?' It was a waspish nag, yet doubtfully uttered, for William had never been much of a gamester. 'Is that why you look so haunted? Are you feeling guilty?'

A bleak sardonic smile confirmed her correct. 'That is exactly how I do feel, June. God knows I'm feeling guilty.'

June felt an icy shiver at his raw irony, for it sounded so unlike her William's usual confident drawl. She put out her hands to hold him, but he caught at those two small comforts and held her rigidly at arm's length.

I'm feeling frightened, too, June, was a soulful whisper in his thoughts as his unwavering gaze drank in the sight of her beautiful topaz eyes and rich honey hair.

The ice stalking June's spine shivered tendrils to squeeze her heart. She had returned home determined to set her mind to helping Bethany Blackmore. Her first thought had been to find William and quiz him over sporting venues. Now, to her shame, Bethany's predicament was less important. How easy it was to lose charitable intentions when under threat oneself.

With sinking heart, she instinctively knew who might be the menace. 'Is it new slanderous lies about you and that woman?' An increased pressure on her slender wrists curbed her movement to free herself. She allowed him to hold her, his thumbs grazing rhythmically over the translucent skin of her inner arms. After a deep breath, June said calmly, 'Well, you must tell me, William. If you do not, be assured someone else will.' When her husband seemed to struggle with inner decisions that aged his brow, she said on a sigh, 'Perhaps you were right. Perhaps we should have moved away from town. This constant anxiety over spiteful gossip is exhausting and stressful.'

William threw back his head, and sought solace from the ceiling, while attempting to conceal a spontaneous sheen in his eyes.

June observed it and, with a soft cry, launched herself against him. He allowed her hands, still imprisoned in his, to coil about his middle so she could cuddle him. 'Oh, William, what is it you must tell me this time?' she whispered against the muscular strength of his chest.

'I love you. I've always loved you. I have never in my life loved anyone else.'

The simple, hoarse declaration drew an enquiring little smile from his wife and she sought to gaze into his brilliant blue eyes.

'I want you to remember that. Whatever I tell you, that is the truth.'

June nodded and waited.

William suddenly withdrew from her embrace and walked away. By the window he turned, and seemed primed to speak. He hesitated, to put a hand against the sash. It had barely rested there a moment before it joined the other behind his back.

'The latest gossip is that I sired Constance Bingham's daughter.'

The declaration took barely a second to give out. There followed a hollow, seemingly interminable silence. Eventually, as though the gist of her husband's words had finally penetrated her mind, June fluttered a hand to her chest. It was a gesture of relief and a bubble of laughter erupted. 'Is that *all*?' A contemptuous cluck of the tongue was followed by, 'Harley and his cronies again, I suppose? How very silly these people are.'

'I am not sure whether Harley or someone else is to blame,' William said hoarsely. His voice was tinged with a betraying self-disgust that fired the first glimmer of suspicion to shock his wife's golden eyes wider. With a ragged indrawn breath William confessed, 'Much as I pray it is not so, I cannot dismiss it as impossible. The only way to know for sure if I justly stand accused is to go to Constance Bingham and demand the truth.'

June's complexion, already pale with strain, turned chalky. Slowly she moistened her lips then, as though in a trance, glided to the wing chair and put out a hand to clutch its back and steady her.

Watching her, a knife twisted in William's stomach and his hands clenched into fists. He wanted to rush to her to comfort her. Selfishly he also wanted her to succour him. Forgiveness, reassurance that she still loved him—he was prepared to beg on his knees for those things. But first there was yet more to say. He had not mentioned the blackmail note; as he remembered it two fingers pinched the paper in his pocket. He had thought Constance Bingham too wealthy to need such a paltry sum! With what he now knew of her financial circumstances he could draw no comfort there.

'It's a lie!' June whispered fiercely, splintering his feverish reflections. 'It's a ploy by that…that hussy. She has started this rumour because she knows you must then visit her and talk intimately before you can scotch it. She wants people to think it true. She intends you should abandon me and go to her. She is a scheming trollop!'

She got no further, for William strode across the carpet to take her into his arms and curb her hysteria. With a slap and a punch from two small fists clubbed together June freed herself. 'Don't you dare touch me!' she hissed. 'You say you have only loved me, yet you might have made a baby with Constance Bingham. You have made love to her.'

'I have not.' Realising how ridiculously inept that sounded, William added desperately, 'It was nothing like what we have together, June. It wasn't like that.'

'What was it like?' June shrilled.

William's fingers sank into his fair hair, momentarily clenched there as though he might rip some hanks of it out. 'It was…a long time ago. It's pointless talking of it, sweetheart,' he inadequately explained. His intention of calming his wife was thwarted by his inability to eloquently convey his regrets. His mind had been dulled with longing to have her back in his arms. June had so recently held him, looked at him lovingly. He wanted more. His arms stretched out, inviting…pleading with her to try a little conciliation.

June's response was to, with great deliberation, lift the heavy tome on the table close by and hurl it, with good aim, straight at him.

Despite his anguish, excellent reflexes had William ducking out of danger and the book smashed into the mantel behind, knocking a Dresden falcon off its perch and into smithereens.

'No, you are right. It is pointless talking of it to *me*,' June concurred in a low quavering voice. 'You must go and talk to that woman and find out if she is indeed the mother of your bastard.' She tossed back the red-gold curls that were sticking to her wet cheeks. 'What will you do if she says it is so? Are we to be a *ménage à trois*?' June faced him with bitter challenge in her eyes. 'A *ménage à quatre*, I suppose it would be, if she brings the girl too.'

William strode to her and, gripping her by the shoulders, pulled her with a shake against him.

In a trice June had slapped and squirmed in his arms enough to make him let her free. 'I think I hate you. Yes, I do. I hate you very much.' Her shaky fingers wiped the moisture from her eyes.

'Listen to me!' William pleaded desperately. 'There is no proof I am guilty. What is indisputable is that someone intends us grave harm. The rumour could be concocted mischief. Many people know that Constance married Bingham with indecent haste after she jilted me.'

'After you were indecent with her, you mean? Did you seduce her? How, I wonder, did Lord Bingham take that? How did that poor gentleman like discovering that you and his bride already had…had…' She stared violent-eyed at him. Part of her wanted to run and hide from the horror, yet another part desired to extract from him every sordid detail of his time with a woman who seemed to have the power to ruin her life. 'Was the child born soon after they married? Was it deemed to be a honey-moon baby?'

William nodded slowly. 'Yes. I recall that people congratulated them on soon starting their family,' he answered, with searing honesty.

A hand flew to cover June's mouth as though the escalating proof of what might be was nauseating.

Immediately William started towards her with such a determined step and look on his face that June fled to the door. 'I am going out,' she gasped. 'I have to go out,' she echoed in a whisper. 'I have made no arrangements yet for dinner. Perhaps you ought to dine at your club or ask cook to get you something.' Not once did she glance back before quitting the room.

'It will seem a little better in the morning.' Isabel was rocking her distraught younger sister in her arms, a hand stroking against June's silky berry-blonde hair. At an explicit look from his wife, the gentleman hovering uncertainly by the fireplace gratefully exited from the room. Shaking his head sadly to himself, Etienne sought the sanctuary of his study, where he sat pondering on how best he might help remedy the latest troubles afflicting the Meredith family.

June disengaged herself from Isabel's embrace. A pale hand went to smear the tears from her eyes. 'I feel as though my world is crumbling down about me.'

Isabel put an arm about her sister's shoulders and drew her close to drop a sympathetic kiss on June's brow. 'I know. It is a shock, but do not hate William too soon.'

'I do hate him!' June cried on a sniff.

'At the moment you think you do; but you must approve of his honesty. Would you rather he had tried to conceal this from you? Only think how you would have felt had you learned of the rumours when out and unprepared to deal with it.'

As that wisdom registered there was a softening in the tight line of June's mutinous mouth.

'William has not lied to you.' Isabel pressed home her advantage. 'He might have tried to deny any wrongdoing. In fact he is not yet judged guilty of any wrongdoing. He has acted decently, June, as he always does. The fact is, there is no proof that he has fathered the child.'

'But he has admitted that he and that woman were lovers! There is every likelihood it is true!' June choked. 'I am his wife and I yearn for his child, yet he might have made a baby with a woman who rejected him.'

'I know,' Isabel soothed. 'If it is true, it would be a very cruel twist of fate. But if it is not true, you are no worse off than you were yesterday. Your husband loves you and you love him.'

'I hate him!'

'You do not!' Isabel chided on a soft laugh. 'You are indignant because you have discovered he is human. It is as well you do not know all that Etienne got up to in his youth or you would brand him the veriest rogue.'

June looked at her sister through watery vision. 'Etienne is a good man. I like him very much.'

'I know. And I like William very much. And I would like it if you did not blame him for something he did before he even had met you.'

'He *is* to blame!' June raged, then closed her eyes for she knew how petulant she sounded. 'I am acting like a shrew,' she confessed on a wry laugh. 'I expect he will be glad to be rid of me.'

'I know he will be glad to have you home. William must be worried where you have got to.' Isabel took a glance at the clock in the corner as it chimed out ten.

June had arrived at their home in Eaton Square some two hours ago and had, at first, been too distraught to talk much at all about her troubles. Isabel had let her be until she had quietened, for she already knew what prompted her sister's distress. Earlier in the day Etienne had returned home to tell her worrying news of what he and Connor had overheard in White's. Beneath Isabel's charming air of serenity was simmering fury directed at the woman who seemed central to all June's woes. Isabel knew her sister, Rachel, was also of the opinion that it was high time Lady Bingham was on the receiving end of a tongue-lashing.

'I cannot go back there…not tonight,' June said, interrupting Isabel's thoughts. 'I cannot face William. I think I will not be able to act rationally in his company until some hours have passed. I suppose he must contact that woman. And if what she tells him is not good news…will I ever be rational again?'

'Indeed you will! No brass-faced baggage is about to ruin your happiness! And of course you must stay here tonight and very welcome too,' Isabel said briskly. 'I can soon find you some of my night things, then in the morning everything will seem better… you'll see…'

Chapter Ten

'Are you looking for Harley?'

The familiar male voice close behind barely penetrated William's consciousness as he strode into the hectic atmosphere of the Palm House gambling den. Certainly it did not slacken his unwisely rapid pace into a dim environment wreathed in aromatic fumes. William collided with a man holding a freshly replenished glass of whisky and, as the fellow muttered an obscenity, William returned him one more volubly.

Undeterred by this undeniable example of a foul mood, the gentleman pursuing William tugged at his arm to gain his attention. He succeeded in making his quarry swing about to reveal a gleam of bared white teeth. 'If you are looking for Harley, he is not here. He has gone to ground.' Adam Townsend was not rebuffed by his friend's snarl; indeed, he gripped

William's shoulder in a show of sympathy and support.

Aware that his arrival and this conversation were under surveillance, William indicated a more private spot by brusquely dipping his head at an empty alcove.

'I take it everyone knows why I'm here,' William said sardonically. A score or more pairs of eyes were now covertly observing their dialogue in that murky corner.

Adam nodded. 'Word has got round that you're likely to be riled enough to be out for blood. Harley is denying he had anything to do with this latest rumour. I have to say, much as I detest the weasel, I think he is telling the truth this time. He is not long returned from Brighton, and Darlington is yet there. The rumour mill started grinding when they were out of town.'

William gazed intently at his friend. 'I still want to talk to him. Do you know where he is?'

Adam grinned. 'I expect I might manage to find him…if that is what you want.'

'That is what I want.'

With a nod towards the door, Adam indicated he was ready to go.

'I've always wondered why you are such an in-adequate, pathetic little man. Now I know.' With a frown of distaste and contempt curling his lip, William gathered the tumbled clothes from the threadbare chair and hurled them. 'For God's sake, put something on or I'll not know whether to laugh or commiserate. And it's certainly not for either of those reasons that I'm here.'

Harley snatched his breeches to his puny chest. Its grubby pallor looked as unhealthy as his facial complexion. He was infuriated by the disturbance, yet his black eyes slid nervously between the two men lounging inside his current paramour's tawdry boudoir. In his mind he was already beating an explanation out of the slut of a landlady who had allowed them to gain entry. No doubt the hag was so far in her cups she had forgotten her mistress already had a client. He slid a look at the comely doxy. She looked to be little older than nineteen, yet she was posing with professional ostentation behind a sheet clutched to her quivering white bosom.

As Adam Townsend glanced her way, Violet Smith lowered her eyes, and her linen.

Harley observed her at her tricks with sour interest. He was just a short while out of her bed and had received little satisfaction during the ten minutes he had spent in it. Already the little whore was soliciting for new company. 'How did you get in here?' Harley snapped sulkily, keen to soon get back to business and show Violet he was not a man to take short shrift.

'Same way you did,' William told him silkily. 'By crossing a palm with silver.'

Harley stomped behind a flimsy screen daubed with erotically entwined figures. Within a trice, peppered with expletives, he emerged, doing up his breeches. 'What do you want?'

'To talk to you.' William's tone was deceptively humouring.

'I've paid for sport, not conversation.' The bluster emerged from tight lips and with a slit-eyed threat for the languid woman on the bed he was soon sidling to the door in bare feet.

Benjamin Harley's bombast soon withered once they were out in the cold musty corridor of Number 12 Brick Lane, where Violet plied her trade along with a number of other enterprising young women with nothing to lose but their looks and desperation.

The hostile scrutiny of two pairs of hooded eyes soon had Harley unwisely scraping his soles on rough timber. 'I know why you are here and I had nothing to do with any of it.' It was a querulous announcement issued while he hopped away from splinters. His colour heightened as William's eyebrows rose quizzically.

Although they did not socialise in the same circles, Harley had thought he knew Pemberton. Here before him was not the placid chap he had carelessly pilloried, safe in the knowledge that the man was too nice to retaliate.

For some while he and Colin Darlington had happily fabricated tales about this man's renewed attachment to Lady Bingham without drawing repercussions. Too late he recognised, with awful clarity, that he had overstepped the mark and prodded a restful tiger to life. The William Pemberton confronting him was an unpredictable stranger and the way he was steadily watching him was making the hair on his neck eerily stir.

'It's true that Darlington and I made a joke and a wager about you and Constance Bingham being… affectionate. But there was nothing malicious in it.' A whine of entreaty purred in Harley's nasal tone.

William's look of scepticism turned sardonic.

'And we wouldn't have taken it that far but for the lady making it plain she still pined after you. If Lady Bingham don't mind us being funny, why should you?' Harley shot an appealing look at Adam Townsend and received nothing but a stony stare in response.

'You thought what you did was funny?' William asked quite gently.

Harley managed to scuttle closer to Violet's door. Once he had the security of the handle turning within his grip, he recalled the pleasure awaiting him within. Emboldened by frustration, he jeered, 'I'm not frightened of you, Pemberton. You've never had the stomach for a fight. Have you brought along your friend to throw your punches for you?' He didn't want a response and had no intention of waiting for one. He was already sliding a leg through the aperture in readiness to dart neatly inside. A powerful hand spanning his throat, then leisurely closing on it, denied him his escape. Harley just had time to peer longingly at the crack of enticing yellow light before he was hauled away.

William, arm outstretched, his fingers an iron hasp on flabby flesh, took a casual pace closer to the man squirming against the wall opposite Violet's door. He lowered his head so his mouth was close to a side of Harley's blotchy, bloated complexion. 'I asked you a simple question that requires a simple answer. Do you think it funny to invent scandal about us and distress my wife?'

Harley just managed to shake his head, at which point William released his grip and the man caught a hoarse breath.

'Good,' William said brightly. 'I'll expect your full apology to us to be gazetted before the end of the week.'

Astonishment and fury mingled to make a comical study of the unlovely sight that was Benjamin's florid physiognomy. To submit to such a course of action would be unendurably humbling. He glowered at William whilst massaging life into his vocal chords. 'Apology?' he wheezed. 'You must have an attic to let if you seriously think I will—'

William turned back to inform the man with a traitorous amity, 'Be assured I think you will. Gazette an apology or ask Darlington to stand second for you and we'll settle this less lawfully. You may choose the secluded spot on which to expire and the manner of your despatch. In fact…let's do that. I'd like you and the rest of polite society to discover just how deadly serious I am.'

Benjamin Harley swiped his mouth with a hand that quivered. Never before had he, or anyone else, considered William Pemberton a man of action. Now he feared he could be a lethal adversary if he chose. 'I'll do it,' he muttered darkly and crept out of sight.

It was close to midnight when William wearily trudged into his chamber. His fingers loosened buttons as his eyes went immediately to the door that gave access to his wife's bedroom. A hand, unsteady at his mouth, betrayed his indecision whether to enter and recount where he had gone tonight in an attempt to start salvaging their marriage. He didn't want to waken her and see anguish return to haunt her tawny eyes. Worse still, he didn't want to see the hint of disgust that had made her retreat from him as though he was an adulterous monster.

Throughout their marriage he had been faithful and the idea that he might take a mistress was as alien to him as he knew it was to her. That he might contemplate divorce was laughable. June was all he had ever wanted; in her shyly sensual way she was far more erotic than Violet Smith or any such mercenary practitioners. As for Constance Bingham, her rampant sexuality might excite some men, but dogged fornication was not to his taste. June expected kindness and affection as a prelude to passion. She wanted to be wooed and he courted her now as tenderly as he had in their early honeymoon days.

Two hesitant paces were taken towards her room then, in a rush, he swept up the candle from the washstand and turned the handle.

A familiar floral scent wrapped about him like loving arms as he walked in the teardrop of golden light shed by the taper. Once close to the bed a draining sadness engulfed him as he gazed steadily at the undisturbed covers. The candle was deposited on her bedside table and, planting hands on hips, he bowed his head. An awful realisation swept over him that it was to be the first night of their marriage that he would sleep alone. The candle was snatched up, and so rapidly did he stride back the way he had come that the light was extinguished before he had fully retreated.

* * *

'You look in better spirits.'

June helped herself to toast and coffee from the sideboard and sat down at her sister's elegant dining table. 'You were right last night when you said I would feel better in the morning. I am now more rational.'

Isabel didn't look totally convinced by either her sister's smile or explanation. Nevertheless she nodded, and after a moment enquired, 'Have you been taking the herbal tincture I prepared for you?'

June wrinkled her nose as she complained, 'I have, and foul it tastes too! Yet despite you trying to poison me, I have persevered.'

Isabel sent her sister a significantly enquiring look.

June placed down her cup. 'Nothing to report, I am afraid, other than my menses last month arrived precisely on time, so that was a benefit of sorts, I suppose.'

"Tis often the case that the restorative must be taken for a while before a pregnancy results. But I know it can help. When I lived in York a local woman conceived a daughter after ten years childless and three months of swallowing the brew.'

'It will take a little more than just the potion to get me pregnant. I need a husband to help too.'

'And you have one.'

June's smile was brisk and courageous. She took a bite of her toast. 'Are you going to the Sandersons' *musicale* tonight?'

Isabel nodded. 'And you and William must go too.'

June tossed the toast crust to her plate at the mention of her husband's name. 'Yes, I know. We must go and put on a brave face. I had already decided that, if William is in agreement after the terrible argument we had, we ought to act civil and pretend nothing is amiss.' She sighed. 'William has ever been a private man. He will not want it known the troublemakers have succeeded in separating us.'

It sounded so easy now. The simple, sensible statement betrayed none of the turmoil that had kept her a sleepless guest in her sister's house while the insufferably long hours ticked away and she longed for the release of dawn light and a troublesome new day.

'I don't think you are as right as you would have me believe,' Isabel said softly, perceptively. 'I think the June who arrived here in high dudgeon last night was the right June.'

June drew her slender fingers through her autumn-gold hair. 'Oh, I still feel murderous,' she said with wry melancholy. 'But I am no longer sure who it is I must assassinate. And I accept that I still love William, although I would like to hate him…hurt him…as he has hurt me. And if it is proven that the child is his, I expect he will act honourably and not neglect his duty, although I would rather he ignore the hussy and her brat.'

'You would not have him act mean, June, and you know it.'

'No…I would not have him act mean. Not my Perfect William,' June said softly sour. 'The merry widow is wealthy, so I have the comfort that she will not be importuning at our door for money to keep a roof over her and her daughter's head.'

June noticed that comment prompted her sister to quickly chew her lower lip. 'I take it from your expression that even that small comfort is to be denied me. What have you heard?'

Isabel poured her coffee as she said gently, 'I'm sure it is not significant, but apparently Constance Bingham has no wealth. In fact, she has been saddled with her husband's debts. Far from coming to town with a fortune to lure a husband, it seems she is here to find herself a meal ticket.'

'So! It all becomes clearer. William will be distraught to know it is not him but his cash that is attractive,' June sniped caustically. She rose in a swish of skirts from the table and stepped to the window. 'I am not going to say another word on the matter, for what will be will be,' she announced quietly. 'William must do what he thinks best to sort it out, and I am going to do what I had planned to do yesterday, before I learned I had married a stranger. A certain cure for one's own woes is to reflect on a worse misfortune endured by others.'

Isabel's expression made it clear she required an explanation for such philosophy. June obliged with, 'Gavin Blackmore and I have become good companions. He was telling me just yesterday how terribly his younger sister has suffered. Neither he nor Bethany had a very happy childhood in the parsonage where they grew up. Now his sister's plight is so much worse. Yesterday I was determined to help her, for the poor woman is incarcerated in the Fleet prison.'

Isabel's green eyes widened with shock. 'Gavin Blackmore? He is an old school friend of William's, is he not?'

June nodded. 'He gained a scholarship and excelled academically, although he seems a little defensive about his origins as a clergyman's son.' She sighed impatiently. 'How bad of me! I promised Gavin I would not repeat what he told me about Bethany's plight to anyone at all.'

'Your secret is safe with me, June,' Isabel said a trifle indignantly. 'I would not break your trust.'

At June's small grimace of acceptance, Isabel continued, 'How on earth did a gently bred lady get into such a pickle?'

After just a brief hesitation at disclosing more, June concisely recounted Bethany Blackmore's history.

Having listened to the woman's hellish ordeal, Isabel simply raised her eyebrows in disbelief. 'And her brother does not have the wherewithal to purchase her freedom?'

June shook her head. 'Gavin has told me little about his circumstances and I have not liked to pry, for I fear it might embarrass him to admit he has not done as well as his peers. He seems a proud man but, despite his fine education, it seems Gavin has not prospered as well as he ought. I believe he has made a career brokering insurance, for he mentioned attending to such a business in Devon. I'm sure William would loan him the money needed to free Bethany, but Gavin will not hear of it. He became quite sharp with me when I hinted at such. As I said, he seems independent and will not accept charity under any circumstances. But I gave him some clothing to take to his sister, for Bethany has had her possessions stolen by rowdy women in gaol.'

Isabel shook her head, sending her pretty curls rippling about her shoulders. 'For a lady to endure such treatment…oh, it doesn't bear thinking about.'

'Tonight at the Sandersons' *musicale*, I shall keep myself occupied at the card table,' June announced.

"Twill give me something to do and if I am lucky enough to win some money, I shall put it aside for Bethany Blackmore.'

'You are back then.'

'Of course,' June responded in an equally cool tone as that used by her husband. 'Did you expect I might have run away from home?' This was added with a slanting flash of topaz eyes as she stripped off her gloves, then whirled about to fully face him.

'Where did you stay last night?' William curtly interrogated.

'I stayed with my sister Isabel.' June found it easier to keep her tone light as his grew harder.

'And you didn't think to send word to let me know where you had gone or that you would be out all night?'

'There are many times when you are abroad and I have no idea where you have gone. I have not before thought it necessary to check on your where-abouts. Perhaps I have been regretfully naïve.'

'Only once have I stayed out all night and you knew I was with Etienne at my club. So what in damnation is that supposed to mean?'

'It means that if I were more sophisticated, I might cope better with knowing I have married a libertine...'

His hand slammed against a wall, abbreviating June's further censure. William closed his eyes and two fingers momentarily pinched at strain between them. 'Am I to be condemned as an insufferable rake because I once was intimate with a woman to whom I was engaged?'

June felt a tightening in her throat at the mention of the horrible fact. A part of her mind recognised she was being unfair, but it was impossible to control the pain of knowing that she was childless yet her husband might already be a father. 'You might have made Constance Bingham pregnant…' Her voice was raw with accusation.

'I know…'

His voice was husky with apology, but its soothing tenor only stoked her angry frustration and she hissed, 'My husband has a daughter with his former fiancée and I am supposed to just *accept* that?'

'June…' William sighed in the exasperated tone of a man unsure whether to be authoritative or supplicating. He walked closer to her and pulled her against him, curbing her resistance with strong arms. 'I don't want it to be true. I'm sure it is not true,' he crooned gruffly through the lump in his throat. His hands cradled her head, tightened in emphasis. 'I love you.'

June pushed at his shoulders, looking into his distraught face through blurry vision. 'You have not yet been to see Constance Bingham?'

'No. I wanted first to speak to Benjamin Harley to find out if he has fabricated more gossip.' He sighed his disappointment. 'Unfortunately I think he is telling the truth when he says this latest rumour is not his doing. He admits to spreading those other lies about a mistress and a divorce and is to gazette an apology to us.' As June's eyes widened in surprise a hand gently cupped her cheek. 'Oh, he is not genuinely sorry. He would be pleased to know his scheming has had such a profound effect on us.'

June's soft mouth hardened. 'One thing I did decide upon last night was that I would hate to give our tormentors the opportunity to gloat over how they have broken us.'

'I feel just that way. There, we still suit,' he said with wry humour in his tone. When a side of her tight lips involuntarily tugged into a small smile he dipped his head to steal a quick kiss, pursuing her and defeating her evasion.

Uncaring of the fact that they were in full view should any of the servants wander into the vestibule, William slipped his hands inside his wife's coat and moved her closer to him. When he kissed her this time it was no gentle salute. His mouth captured hers, moulded to hers with a fiery urgency that made June's blood throb at her temples.

'I missed you so much last night!'

'Yet you didn't think to come and find me?' June returned archly, her lips still pulsing from the heat of his kiss.

'I did come and find you. I knew you stayed at Isabel's for our carriage was stationed outside their door. Did you want me to come in and get you? I nearly did.'

Isabel quickly looked up into her husband's sultry low-lidded gaze. 'You knew I stayed there?'

'As soon as I realised you were not at home I scoured the streets of every conceivable place I thought you might be. I went to your parents' address first, of course… Oh, they didn't know,' he reassured on seeing her immediate anxious look. 'I stayed outside and would only have let it be known you were missing had I not managed to locate you somewhere. I have not had a wink of sleep all night,' he complained.

'Neither have I!' June retorted with asperity.

'We are both tired then and ready for bed.'

William's sultry suggestive tone made his wife blush and just for a moment laugh. Oh, how skilfully could her husband manoeuvre her into submission!

'Come,' William invited huskily. 'Let's go upstairs…'

'No,' June said quietly but in a voice that quavered with resolve. 'Can't you see it won't do? No!' She turned her head as he made to kiss her again. 'It solves nothing, William…' Her tone was raw with despair.

'It does for me,' William said bluntly before he turned and left her.

Chapter Eleven

'I am not surprised he is grown bored with her.'

'Neither am I. That gown she has on is as prim as the one my mother is decked in. She dresses so matronly, yet has no babe-in-arms as an excuse for it. What did an attractive man like him ever see in her?'

'I have always thought he could have done better for himself. His mother makes it plain that she thinks so too.'

'He once wanted to marry a woman who does herself up in scraps of muslin.'

'Wanted to? He did marry her…in all but name. If the gossip I've heard is true, perhaps she has their daughter to prove it.'

The disembodied dialogue was replaced by the sound of two women tittering. Their shrill amusement finally broke the spell that held June shocked

and unmoving at the entrance to the ladies' withdrawing room. She took a hasty step back from the
threshold, remaining unseen.

June and Isabel had moments ago been on the
point of entering this sanctuary set aside by the Sandersons so their female guests could rest and refresh
themselves. Isabel had diverted to speak to an old
friend and as June loitered, lost in her own thoughts,
waiting for her sister to return, she had paid little attention to the snippets of conversation that had
drifted to her ears. Over some minutes she had as-
similated the significance of what was being said.
She had tensed, straining to listen through infuriatingly deafening blood pounding in her skull. Even
had she not heard William's name being mentioned,
other clues would have indicated that she was the
object of scorn.

She recognised her detractors from their voices.
Julia Lake and Monica Dawson were spinsters in
their early thirties. Neither had managed to lure a
husband in their prime and now they were united in
feeling particularly sour towards well-married ladies.

June would have liked to burst in and tell those
spiteful spinsters a few bald truths, but she hesitated.
Not so very long ago she might have remained non-
chalant on overhearing her appearance judged and
her husband pitied for his choice of wife. With the
rift between William and her widening inexorably,

she felt vulnerable to doubts and picked over what the vinegary misses had said, wondering if perhaps there was truth in their criticism.

A quick glance down at her turquoise silk gown confirmed it was modest in style, yet this evening when she had descended the stairs, William had steadily watched her from his vantage point, propped against a doorframe. Acutely aware of his low-lidded appreciation she had felt almost triumphantly alluring. There might be friction between them, they might be conversing shortly, but William could not conceal his admiration. In his eyes she was beautiful.

June proudly raised her chin and, seeing that Isabel was still engaged with her friend, gathered up those dowdy skirts in tight fists, summoned up a smile, and went to join the company.

'I say, steady on, Pemberton. That's the third glass of champagne you've downed in half an hour. If you carry on like that there'll be none left for the rest of us. I thought you steady chaps favoured small beer.' The jovial gentleman who had spoken grimaced disappointment at the cards he'd been dealt and discarded his hand.

'I recall a time when he had a partiality for warm lemonade. He was a stalwart at Almack's every Wednesday when he was courting. My nieces regularly graced that noble marriage mart while poor old Edgar regularly moped about the pillars like a wall-flower, looking miserable as sin.' Edgar's brother-in-law, Nathaniel Chamberlain, had introduced that humorous anecdote about the *ton*'s premier match-making assembly before lounging back comfortably in his chair and winking with pleasure at the monarchs fanned in a hand.

'So would you have looked miserable,' Edgar moaned to the happy gamester, 'with the prospect of all those débuts paring down your bank balance. Not to mention the prospect of all those nervous chaps pacing back and forth in your drawing room, wearing out your carpet.' He shook his head to himself. 'It's not to be recommended. Oh, no. Not to be recommended by me at all.' He glanced fondly at William. 'Of course, we were more than happy with the outcome for our girls. Fine husbands so far…every one of them,' he added with emphasis.

William sipped at his champagne and inclined his head in acknowledgement of Edgar's compliment. 'From a nervous chap's point of view, it's a relief when his courting days are over. Luckily I won't again need to enter Almack's.'

'Don't be too sure of that,' Edgar warned his son-in-law. 'You might yet have a brace or more of daughters to settle, and be again fed bread and butter and warm lemonade, while you observe the sweet chits fluttering about in their finery. Take my word on it, with every single one of 'em, you won't know whether to encourage the scoundrel who's caught her eye or to call him out.' He shuddered at the reminiscence. 'In truth, I didn't like losing them, you know.'

'You've still got Sylvie to keep you company in your dotage,' William ruefully reminded him.

Edgar smiled. 'Yes…my Sylvie can stay home and keep her old papa happy. She's not in a rush to grow up. Sensible girl.'

'I'll put down a wager that in ten years' time we see Pemberton's chit in the marriage mart. Why, she will be all of eighteen by then.'

In the wake of that smirking aside settled an uneasy silence. Colin Darlington sauntered closer to the table. Benjamin Harley, another new arrival at the Sandersons' *musicale*, hurried closer, glaring an explicit warning for he had sensed a dangerous atmosphere fomenting. Darlington was only recently returned to town and Harley had not had an opportunity to bring him up to date with what had transpired in his absence.

'Ah, Darlington, back from Brighton, I see,' William drawled. 'Sea air quite chill, was it? Come and join us. Sit down and warm up your brain.'

The speaking stare Benjamin Harley was directing at his crony became pronounced enough to crane his neck. Finally he resorted to beckoning frantically. Darlington stabbed a poisonous look William's way, but allowed his friend to steer him away without countering the insult. The retreating men were so engaged in their hissing conversation that they didn't notice the woman they passed or the dismay they had caused her.

June had been on the point of joining William and her father at the table in the hope of winning a tidy sum to hand over to Gavin Blackmore for his sister. Twice this evening her progress had been halted on overhearing hurtful gossip about her or William.

She watched her father glaring at Harley and Darlington before he reached over and grasped William's arm in a show of support. As June's misty eyes focussed, she realised William was looking at her. After a heady heartbeat in which she felt engulfed by the strength of his regret and sorrow at what she had witnessed, he smiled. His whole demeanour exuded a plea that she would not allow this paltry incident to worsen things between them.

'Are you ready to join the gamblers?'

June pivoted about to see Adam Townsend just behind her, mischievous laughter in his eyes.

He took her hand and placed it on his arm. 'Let's see if we can relieve these gentlemen of a few sovereigns.'

Having taken a deep, inspiring breath, June rose

to the challenge. 'Yes, let us do just that. I have a good cause for a few spare sovereigns.'

'Ah, let me guess,' Adam said with a twinkling smile. 'You have seen an indispensable something in the modiste's that's newly opened in Starling Street.'

About to shyly chide him for his chauvinistic levity and declare she had a less selfish use for her winnings, June changed her mind and simply laughed. 'How *did* you guess?' She had promised not to repeat what Gavin Blackmore had told her of his family's misfortunes and, although she implicitly trusted her sister Isabel, she felt a little guilty at having revealed even to her Bethany's plight.

Adam chivalrously ejected the nearest fellow from his seat at the crowded table to offer it to June. The young buck goodnaturedly waved away June's apology with a stuttered, 'My...my pockets aren't dee-deep enough anyhow...'

Once settled, June bestowed on her father a fond smile before acknowledging the other gentlemen with a gracious dip of her burnished blonde head. Then she looked at her husband. But the appeal and apology that she had seen in his eyes moments ago, which had wrenched at her heart, were gone.

With a woman's intuition June knew he was still smarting from her rejection earlier that day. With a wife's intuition, she also knew that she was right to want a more permanent solution to their problems than an hour or so of amorous abandonment...even if it was delightful. The memory of a mere kiss from him made an involuntary little *frisson* tingle along her skin. His artful hands could move and smooth away her anger and hurt and insist she forget everything but what pleasure would come next...

With a quick lift of her head she gave William a scintillating smile; it caused him to quirk an indolent eyebrow at her.

William was not fooled by her *faux* gaiety, but eventually his sardonic expression mellowed and a reciprocal slow smile tugged at his lips. His wife blushed prettily beneath his sultry regard, but her eyes defied him beneath a web of lashes. It couldn't have been plainer had she clearly said, 'The answer is still no.' William's fingers tightened on the cards he held before he dropped them to the baize. As a small growl of mirthless laughter gazed his throat, his father-in-law, seated next to him, sent him a quizzical look.

William observed that the gentlemen about the table were exchanging knowing glances. He could guess what they were thinking and the irony was not lost on him. *They appear fond even if it is gossiped he has a love child in Devon.* The words seemed to hover unspoken in the atmosphere and, looking at June's contained composure, he sensed she knew it too. William felt irritated enough at the sham to want to shove back his chair and walk away. But his wife was where he wanted her, close to him, and they were united in wanting to appear harmonious. Why fret that the subterfuge was working? 'Shall I deal?' he suggested.

'What are we playing, gentlemen?' June asked. 'Faro? *Vingt-et-un*? Oh, some cash, please, William…' she sweetly tacked on to the end while airily extending a slender white hand towards him.

Adam Townsend, who had stationed himself behind June's chair, leaned over a demurely bared white shoulder. A pile of coins was deposited on the table. 'Allow me…I insist, for I know the lady has in mind a good cause for any winnings,' he amiably explained to June's flint-eyed husband.

'You were lucky tonight.'

'Yes…wasn't I…' June replied and chinked the coins held inside her glove. She continued gazing at the night scene as the carriage moved along although she could feel the strength of her husband's stare singeing the side of her face.

'I didn't mean your winnings,' William advised with mild irony. His eyes drifted over June's moonlit profile. 'What I mean, my love, was that had you and Townsend flirted just a moment or two longer I might have had to intervene. Blackmore has a serious rival, it seems.'

June tilted her head, stripped off a glove and let warm coins drop, one by one, on to her palm. 'I never flirt, William, you know that. I was married before I learned that art. And Gavin Blackmore is your friend and amiable and courteous to me, nothing more. You surely aren't jealous? Whatever for? I'm the sensible Meredith girl…modest and demure, everyone knows that.'

'Of course I'm not jealous. I'm a dull, peaceable chap. Everyone knows that, too. But I could change.'

June's eyes flicked to her husband, for the tone he had used chilled her. Their shining eyes tangled in the gloom. She cocked her head and countered slowly, 'Yes…I could change, too…'

Gavin Blackmore looked at the small curled fingers close to his chest, then up at a sweet expression. 'I take it from your happy countenance that I'm not in danger of a punch from that fist.'

'Guess what I have for you…or rather for Bethany.'

Gavin shook his head. 'I don't think it is a pair of woollen stockings concealed in there.'

Laughing, June took one of his hands and dropped with a chink and a glint four half-sovereigns on to his palm.

Gavin looked at her with amazement then bowed his head. He made to return the coins, but June quickly foiled his reluctance to accept the money by curling his large fingers over the gold. 'I was lucky last night. Adam Townsend and I were partners at cards. Had he not partnered me I expect I might now be offering you a farthing, for I have always before been bad at playing. Adam is a fine player.'

Gavin twisted a smile. 'As I said before, Townsend is blessed in lots of ways.' Almost thoughtlessly the sovereigns were slipped into a pocket while he chuckled. 'How satisfying that the money has been donated in a roundabout way by the high and mighty Earl of Malvern.'

June frowned at him. 'I think Adam seems… nice…not at all high-handed.' The praise was muted, but made Gavin shoot a measuring look at her.

'As I said before, Townsend has a winning way with the ladies, too.' Gavin shrugged his indifference. Gathering up the reins, he shook them over the sleek and supple backs of William's matched greys. 'This is a fine equipage. Do you drive it? Does William allow it? I know more and more ladies are driving their own carriages. Some of you young women are quite daring in your sporting exploits.'

'I've never been of a daring disposition.' June grimaced a laugh. 'But I had a try at taking the ribbons once on a piece of common land. I can't say I was very successful. In fact, but for William's help

I might have turned the thing over. William said I ought to try again.'

Gavin looked mock-horrified. 'Did he indeed? Your husband is a brave man. I would have imagined he might have banned you from trying a second time in case you came to some harm.'

'William can be surprisingly liberal. He is not at all as sober and predictable as people think.'

Gavin was quiet for a few moments, then mentioned, 'I think you are an uncommonly understanding wife to deal so well with the recent scurrilous gossip concerning your husband. William is a fortunate man to have your loyalty, no matter there is no truth in any of it.'

June's lips twisted wryly. 'We do our best to carry on regardless, but it has not been easy. I cannot honestly claim not to have been shocked and upset by it all but... Oh, enough of it! Come, you earlier promised to tell me how Bethany is doing. I should like to visit. I am not daunted by the thought of entering the Fleet to see her. Will that money I have given you help bring her closer to being released?'

'Her debts are heavy.' Gavin's answer was shortly given. 'And I would not dream of letting you set one foot inside that hell-hole. Your husband would kill me should he ever find out I had taken you there.' A hand was put up to silence June's protest. He continued with a sad shake of the head, 'Her gaolers demand bigger bribes. But I must keep her properly fed or she will succumb to disease. Dysentery and consumption are constant threats.'

Gavin turned to look at her with a sheen enhancing the brown of his eyes. 'Bethany asked after you. When I took her those things you had donated she wept. She sends all her best wishes to you and her grateful thanks.'

'And I send her back equal good wishes. I know those coins won't release her…but if they buy her some meagre privileges and her health, it is something.'

Gavin nodded. 'What you have donated so far has been a great help and so very well received. Once the turnkeys have their bribes she feels a little safer. She need not huddle the day and night away in a corner trying to stay inconspicuous.'

'Does she need their protection? Is she frightened still of the other women? Do they still steal her things?'

'The women she is incarcerated with are of the vilest nature, but the gaolers are a worse menace. Bethany is a pretty girl. It is not a place for a genteel lady to be. Those lecherous swine have no respect for virtue or good breeding.'

As June understood his meaning colour flooded her cheeks. 'We must get Bethany free as soon as we can,' she said earnestly.

Gavin urged the horses to a faster pace. 'Indeed we must…' he murmured.

Gloria Meredith poured her son-in-law's tea with a hand that shook. The emotion causing her ague was anger, not a nervous disposition. Etiquette decreed it would be unseemly for her to take William to task over yet more gossip that had come to her ears. But, if there was truth in it, she had no intention of letting William escape without he took with him a flea in his ear. With that in mind she was hoping to keep him here until her husband returned and decided whether he deserved to be hauled over the coals. With a forcefulness that slopped liquid into the saucer, William's cup was banged down on the table at his side.

William glanced enquiringly at his mother-in-law, for he had sensed in her an unusual hostility as soon as he entered her house this afternoon.

His reason for visiting was a hope that he might come upon June here. His wife was rarely to be found at home during the day. His friends were allowed to escort her on shopping trips or drives in the park whereas his efforts to take her out were coolly rebuffed. Her sisters and parents were regularly treated to her company, yet she stayed out of his. He now knew June was being squired about town this afternoon by Gavin Blackmore. He had prised that much information from his mother-in-law's pursed lips before, with seeming reluctant duty, she insisted he have some refreshment and swept away.

William took a sip from his cup and took stock. Momentarily his eyes closed. He was out of favour everywhere it seemed. Even Adam Townsend had had a prior appointment with his mother and had tarried but a little while to talk in Boodle's.

Only one individual had made it clear they would welcome his company today and it was someone he wished to avoid seeing at all costs. The infernal woman causing problems in his life had responded coyly to the note he sent her demanding an unequivocal answer to a single question contained therein. A simple yes or no would suffice, he had suggested in his second letter, when the first had prompted Constance Bingham to return him a missive spanning two lengths of parchment that revealed nothing other than her desire that they meet privately to talk.

William glanced at Gloria's stern profile, wondering whether her aloof attitude was due to the fact that she had already got wind of his visit to Lady Bingham's residence in Park Lane. In view of the fact that he had come here straight from there, it seemed unlikely she would know of it, but then the speed at which gossip travelled no longer amazed him.

The fact that his erstwhile fiancée would not confirm or deny the rumours until he danced to her tune and visited her had vastly exasperated William. He knew that June would hate to discover he had paid Constance a visit. Yet equally he knew that their wounds would never heal until it was discovered whether he had sired Constance's daughter. On receipt of Lady Bingham's response that morning he had at a respectable hour in the afternoon gone, unannounced, straight to see her, only to find her already abroad. Oddly he had felt vexed rather than relieved that she was out. Having taken his courage in both hands and forced the dreaded visit upon himself, he was immensely peeved to find the effort squandered.

'I wish Edgar were here to speak to you,' Gloria suddenly burst out, shattering William's moody introspection. 'But as he is not, there is something *I* must say…for enough is enough…'

William was frowning in bemusement at his mother-in-law when a servant entered and announced that Lord Malvern was waiting in the hall and wished an audience.

Gloria looked surprised, but instructed the servant to show him in.

In the event it was Edgar Meredith who ushered Adam Townsend into the cosy room, having returned home just minutes after his visitor arrived. 'How opportune, both of you are here together. Just the two *gentlemen* I wanted to see,' Edgar snarled in greeting.

Chapter Twelve

'Have you now a taste for scandal?'

Having bellowed out his opening salvo, Edgar cast a frown at the door. His wife had excused herself so he was not anxious for her delicacy. Besides, Gloria was aware of the nature of William's alleged crime. What worried Edgar was that his raised voice might bring the servants to queue at the keyhole. In a low hiss he continued, 'I have to say that I am now heartily sick of having my family— my daughter June in particular—made the butt of gossip because of the way you have conducted yourself. William Pemberton, the quiet man, the steady fellow…hah!'

'What is that supposed to mean? What in damnation is going on now?'

William's tone was weary, but the speed with which he lithely unwound from his chair alerted

Edgar to the fact that his son-in-law's temper was as volatile as his own.

Without waiting for his father-in-law's reply, William enquired sharply of his friend, 'Are you here to meet my wife?'

'Not specifically, but I believe she might soon arrive.'

'What makes you think so? Have you seen her? I believed her to be shopping with Blackmore this afternoon.' William knew he must sound tediously possessive, but June's preference for any company other than his was deeply irritating him, and he no longer felt inclined to feign nonchalance over it all. Yet how could he blame her for withdrawing from him? She was the innocent in it all. She did not deserve to have her contentment stripped away. They could have coped with the gossips and Harley's malice. It was the regrettable liaison in his youth that was the stumbling block to regaining happiness. And he shouldn't seek to deprive June of her gallants. At least if she was out socialising it might keep her spirits up and her worries at bay. The fault was his. The blame was his alone. He sighed.

Adam gave his beleaguered friend a disarming smile. 'There is no intrigue, I promise. A few hours ago I was escorting my mother about the shops in Regent Street when we ran into your wife and Blackmore. My mother invited Mrs Pemberton and her sisters to an impromptu gathering she arranged this morning for five o'clock this afternoon. I believe there are to be other débutantes present with their mamas and your wife thought it would be an excellent opportunity for her youngest sister to socialise. I expect they will all be attending the same balls and assemblies. As time is short I am here to convey the invitation to Mrs Meredith. Your wife has gone to speak to her married sisters about the invitation.'

Adam hesitated, looked quizzically at his friend. 'Do you mind?' The query was laden with mockery. 'I assure you they will like it. My mother is a capable hostess.'

A capable hostess? Lady Rockingham was known to be one of the *ton*'s most popular and influential ladies. If Sylvie were to be taken under her wing, the success of her début would be assured. William muttered on a sigh, 'Of course I have no objection to your mother's invitation.' A hand illustrated his apology.

'Well, this is all very nice!' Edgar huffed. 'The two of you discussing respectable ladies' tea parties when I have the task of speaking of women of a very different class.'

Edgar drew himself up, his head waggled on his neck as a haughty glance whipped between the two cultured gentlemen. 'Lord Malvern is single and thankfully his conduct is of no consequence to me or to my family. You, sir, are married to my daughter and your morals and behaviour have an impact on us all.'

'God's teeth!' William snapped impatiently. 'Am I to ever be advised why I stand accused this time?'

'Indeed you are!' Edgar retorted. He inclined closer. 'And quickly, before June arrives, for I do not want this tawdry tale to reach that innocent's ears. She has been hurt and humiliated enough.'

William strode in exasperation to the window while he waited to be advised of his crime. 'Gentlemen, you were both spotted in a place frequented by low life. If you must go there, sirrah,' his son-in-law received a narrow-eyed glare, 'perhaps you ought to be more discreet.'

William, whose thoughts were cluttered with many things, still looked baffled, for he detected few clues in the homily to jog his memory.

'It would not be quite so bad if you had not been spotted entering together the strumpet's bedchamber. One at a time would have been preferable, for better to be thought lechers than deviants.'

William and Adam simultaneously made sense of Edgar's lecture. Adam's expression showed he was undecided whether to laugh or protest. His friend's latent amusement simply darkened William's scowl.

'And don't think to deny it.' Edgar dismissed anticipated excuses with an airy gesture. 'I have the information first-hand from a reliable source. Unfortunately, my wife was, unbeknown to me, in the vicinity when the gentleman spilled the beans, so she knows too.' Edgar shook his head. 'Gloria is again agitated. She is gravely worried for June's health and happiness. How much more can that poor mite take?'

'There is nothing at all about that incident that need disturb my wife.'

'You might think so, but women don't see it that way,' Edgar philosophised, having taken a sophisticated view of his son-in-law's remark.

William gave Edgar an exasperated look, but decided against further explanation or defence.

'I have a curiosity to know the identity of your friend who frequents a Brick Lane whorehouse,' Adam mentioned while studying his nails.

Something in the way his lordship speared a stare at him from beneath his dark brows made Edgar redden and bluster, 'Well, I hope you don't think it was me! A hovel like that!' A hand dusted his coat sleeve as though a mere thought of the place might contaminate him.

'It doesn't matter who it was,' William interjected impatiently. 'My reason for being there had nothing to do with any doxy or the services on offer. We went there—unwisely, now I think on it for God knows everything I do seems to be under surveillance—to find Harley. With hindsight I admit it was rash to go to a bawdy house, but at the time I was irate and set on extracting an immediate promise from that weasel that he would make a public apology to us. He has kept to his word. *The Times* carries the piece today if you care to check on it.'

'Are you stalked wherever you go? I feel guilty for having revealed where Harley was. I can vouch for his innocence,' Adam told Edgar.

'Harley? Does *he* go there too?' Edgar sounded shocked. 'I imagine Nathaniel doesn't know *that*!' he muttered to himself.

'Nathaniel Chamberlain?'

Edgar turned florid on realising he had inadvertently betrayed his informant as being his sister's husband. He had always got on famously with Nathaniel, which was more than could be said for his overbearing sister. 'Well, we are all men of the world. My sister's health is not good and Nathaniel is a considerate chap...' He mumbled that out in his brother-in-law's defence before he strode two paces back and forth. 'The point is that, with the gossips out for blood, it was not wise to have been seen in such a place. Popular she may be, but it is not as though Violet Smith could boast a certain...*distinction*...' he chose the word carefully before adding on a sly nod '...as can those demi-reps who like to keep company with this fine fellow.'

Adam Townsend remained impassive in the face of that compliment.

'I am conscious of the difference,' William said in an exceedingly dry tone.

'What is a demi-rep, Papa?' Sylvie Meredith had slipped inconspicuously into the room.

Edgar visibly winced at the untimely intrusion by his youngest daughter. He cleared his throat and mumbled in embarrassment, 'Umm, well, never you mind. You should not barge in, but knock first, you know, young lady. Did you not hear me talking to these gentlemen?'

Sylvie flushed slightly at the rebuke, but her chin lifted and her violet eyes searched a sternly handsome face as though she might detect an answer there.

'Sylvie!' Edgar chided as his daughter remained where she was and continued to gaze boldly at his aristocratic visitor. 'Now come along, my dear, go from here! I was having a private talk with your brother-in-law and his lordship. They will think your manners sadly lacking.'

'Why? All the time I am told I must improve and grow up, yet when I ask a question I get no answer. How will I learn things?'

'The expression refers to a lady of doubtful character,' Adam quietly satisfied her curiosity.

'Thank you, sir.' Sylvie smiled at Adam. 'You see, I am not about to swoon on knowing it, Papa.'

'Sylvie!' Edgar sped to his daughter's side and, snatching her arm, firmly steered her to the door. 'You will have Lord Malvern think you the silliest girl—'

'*Au contraire*…I don't think that at all. Besides, it is on Miss Sylvie's account that I am here.'

Sylvie swirled about, freeing her arm from the parental grip. 'You are here to see me?'

'Yes,' Adam said in voice that had become husky.

'Are you going to take me for a ride at last?'

Aware that her father and her brother-in-law were watching him curiously, Adam added crisply, 'I ought speak to your mother. Naturally you are both invited out. Would you find her for me?'

Sylvie nodded her brilliant blonde head and in a moment was gone.

'This is most unexpected…but very welcome, sir.'

Adam smiled politely on learning that Mrs Meredith gladly accepted his mother's invitation. His eyes involuntarily veered towards the woman's daughter. The angelic chit seemed only interested in teasing her papa over his failure to beat her at chess the previous evening.

Gloria had also noticed Sylvie's indifference to this precious opportunity. In common with William, Gloria recognised that Lady Rockingham's patronage, once gained, would be of invaluable help in making Sylvie's come-out a triumph. She could think of several acquaintances, with daughters to be launched this season, who would give their eye-teeth for such influential backing.

Suddenly aware that Lord Malvern looked ready to depart, Gloria quickly said, 'Oh, my apologies! How remiss of me. You must take tea, sir.' Feigning deafness to Adam's excuse that, on the contrary, he must take his leave, Gloria hurried to summon servants and refreshment.

'I did not expect to find you here.'

'I'm sure that now you have you are pleasantly surprised.'

June ignored the hard irony in her husband's tone and the frustrated desire that darkened his blue eyes to gleaming jet. She had only recently arrived at Beaulieu Gardens, having sped through Mayfair to convey to Rachel and Isabel Lady Rockingham's invitation. Both had been pleased to receive and accept it.

'It seems you have a hectic programme today. Shopping with Blackmore this morning and a visit to Lady Rockingham planned for this afternoon. Am I to book an hour of your time to dine later?'

'I welcome keeping busy. I do not want time to think at the moment. I'd far sooner have too little time on my hands than too much.'

There was a pointed reference to their troubles in her answer that froze the air between them.

'Why are you here?' June asked after a short silence.

William shrugged casually, about to say he had just popped in on passing. Instead he settled on telling the truth. 'I came hoping to find you here.'

Immediately June sent him a sharp look. 'Have you some…news for me?' she asked in a low voice that mingled hope and trepidation.

In truth, all the news William had was that he had no news. His efforts to extract the truth from Lady Bingham had been fruitless. But, if he had something to impart, now would not have been the time to do it. He wanted some time alone with his wife away from the constant cautious observation of friends and family.

He shook his head and, because her disappointment made her half-turn away, he sought to keep her there with idle conversation. 'How is my friend Blackmore? Well, I trust? I have not seen him myself for a while.'

'He seems very well,' June replied. 'He sends his best wishes to you.'

'In that case you must convey mine to him. Shall we dine together later?' William asked. A plea was in his eyes, if absent from the lightly spoken enquiry.

'I…I don't know whether I shall be late back from

Lady Rockingham's salon. I shall not mind if you do not wait. You might get hungry.' June was very conscious of blue eyes boring into the side of her face.

'I am able to curb my appetite…'

His slow sardonic drawl brought a beautiful blush to accentuate June's high cheekbones. Her head tilted up and her tawny eyes challenged the mocking humour in his face.

'Do you never get hungry, June?'

'Of course I do,' June breathed. 'But a fast can be cleansing…and necessary. Perhaps at some time you might appreciate its benefit.'

'Perhaps I shall…but the memory of a banquet is not easily forgotten. I am human and tempted to seek sustenance.'

'Then eat when you like and with whom…' June hissed.

'Do you mean that?'

June swung back towards him, having angrily backed away a few paces.

'Do you mean that?' William repeated in a growl, his eyes capturing hers.

Simultaneously they became aware that they were drawing attention from the other adults in the room. Only Sylvie seemed oblivious to the tension between her sister and brother-in-law.

June flicked a glance sideways and, with true diplomacy, Adam's eyes shifted effortlessly to his cup and he lifted it to his mouth. It hovered there, tea untasted, as he noticed the seductive *ingenue* was strolling his way. Sylvie halted in front of his chair.

'I am not sure I want to go to your mother's house party, although, of course, it is kind of her to ask me. I imagine those twins Deirdre and Diane Mortimer might be there. They think they're so grand and have planned a flash come-out ball for May.'

Adam's intense appreciation of her exquisite features went uninterrupted, although he managed to tilt his mouth in a mildly sympathetic smile.

'A few of your ladies of doubtful character might be better company.'

That bright observation had the effect of making Lord Malvern choke on a sip of tea. The coughing fit that ensued slopped wet from his cup on to his breeches.

Sylvie tutted concern, found a napkin on the table, and immediately set to mopping up the damage.

As though scalded, Adam shot back in his chair, sending it skidding on the parquet. The teacup clattered on to a table and his long fingers gripped and held rigidly, at arm's length, the small hand clutching a cloth that, seconds before, had been solicitously dabbing his lap.

June and William exchanged a glance of amused horror.

With a slender hand shielding her smile, June murmured, 'I think it is time we got ready to go out.'

'And it is time I took my leave,' William said softly. 'I shall wait dinner for you…till midnight if need be.'

June turned to look at him. 'You will be ravenous by then.'

'I know. I'll wait anyway,' he said.

'I said you would enjoy yourself, young lady,' Gloria happily told her youngest daughter. 'And I believe that Lady Rockingham took a particular shine to you. Those twins were quite put out by it.' Gloria Meredith sank back with a contented smile. It was eight o'clock and coming on to dusk as Gloria, June and Sylvie journeyed home together from Lady Rockingham's salon, having left Isabel and Rachel to be collected and driven home by their husbands.

'Lady Rockingham seems very nice and the food was delicious,' Sylvie agreed, for in particular she could recall the tiny pastry cases stuffed with sweet and savoury fillings.

'Yes, it was all very tasty.' Gloria hesitated and frowned. 'But I have to say, Sylvie, that you must learn not to partake of the buffet quite so heartily. There is a certain merit in appearing abstemious, especially when in company with the gentlemen. It is not very charming for a young lady to be seen with her jaws constantly chomping and spotted with crumbs.'

'There was so much it seemed a shame to waste it. Besides, there weren't any gentlemen there,' Sylvie reasoned, unperturbed.

'Yes, I know. But on other occasions there will be.'

'I wish that Lord Malvern had been there. I think he likes me.'

'Did he say so?' Gloria demanded after a moment in which she and June had locked eyes.

A reflective frown hovered between her brows as Sylvie cast back her mind. 'Well, I know he keeps company with ladies of doubtful character. I suppose that means they must improve as I must.'

'And how do you know that, pray?' Gloria demanded stiffly, a dangerous maternal glimmer in her eyes.

'I overheard Papa talking to William and Lord Malvern about demi-reps.' She flushed on remembering being rebuked in front of the gentlemen by her papa. 'Papa was cross that I had joined them and wanted me to go away. His lordship was kinder, and satisfied my curiosity. *And* he didn't think I was wrong for wanting to know. *Au contraire*, he said when Papa said I might be thought silly…'

Gloria sent an anxious look at June, for she guessed that what Sylvie had overheard was her husband giving William a dressing down over his visit to a brothel.

As soon as they had had an opportunity to be private, Gloria had learned from Edgar what had prompted their son-in-law's visit to such a dive. She now felt a little guilty at ever having doubted William might not have a proper motive for being spied in such a place. But then he had been accompanied there by one of society's most notorious rakes. It was hardly surprising she had thought the worst.

Edgar had even produced *The Times* newspaper and shown her the paragraph that contained Benjamin Harley's apology to Mr and Mrs William Alexander Pemberton. It was adequate, if imprecise, and had served its purpose. When at Lady Rockingham's several ladies of her acquaintance, who had developed a distinct *froideur* towards her family once the rumours started, had thawed enough to make a point of greeting her warmly. Naturally Gloria had virtually ignored them.

'What was William's contribution to this debate?' June asked her sister in a tight voice.

'Nothing,' Sylvie replied. She wound a pearly curl about a finger. 'William didn't say very much at all. Perhaps there was an argument. I heard Papa shouting, that's why I went to find out what was going on.'

'And this is what happens when people eavesdrop,' Gloria retorted. 'You, young lady, would be well advised to do as you are told. When your father tells you to go away, you must obey him.'

Sylvie's indignant retort that she wasn't eavesdropping and a person in the street could have heard the commotion barely registered with the other occupants in the coach.

'You *knew*,' June accused her mother in a shocked little whisper. 'You and Papa knew that William and that reprobate had been…had been keeping company with harlots.'

'Harlots?'

'Be quiet!' The command issued simultaneously from two voices.

Sylvie shrugged and sighed.

'Do not jump to conclusions, June,' Gloria quietly advised. 'William has explained his reasons to your papa and your papa has told me.' Gloria sighed. 'Please don't ask me to repeat any of it, for I fear I might inadvertently make things worse. Besides, it is your husband's place to tell you. I know all this taken together must be so hard for you to bear, my love.' Gloria's voice was shaky with tears. 'I hate to see you unhappy. William is a good man and lately he looks so terribly sad too.'

'Well, I must not complain then,' June said acidly. 'Perhaps he went there to cheer himself up.'

Chapter Thirteen

'You're home early.'

William's husky welcome brought June to a halt just before one of her dainty slippers stepped onto the bottom tread of the stairs.

'I'm glad to see you. My stomach has been protesting this past hour or more,' he added on a slow teasing smile. 'It was a brave promise I made to wait till midnight. May I tell Herbert that we are ready to dine?'

June turned towards him, unable to speak for the rage of violent emotion that was clogging her throat. She had intended to go straight to bed and avoid a confrontation. Once before at Isabel's home she had used those long, lonely night-time hours to blunt her anger against him and sharpen her reason. She gripped the banister in an attempt to control an urge to speed across the hallway and beat at him with her fists.

'I can wait a little longer. Do you want to refresh yourself before we eat?'

'I want to retire,' June managed to force out in a voice made querulous from distress.

'And I want to take that as an invitation for us both to have an early night.' His affectionate tone was already lost to irony. 'But of course, it isn't.'

He strolled closer and June noted obliquely that he had dressed for dinner with great care. His dark clothes were immaculate, his hard angular cheeks freshly shaven. Her husband looked heartbreakingly handsome and the more conscious of it she became, the more painful was the ache within. She stared at him as though entranced by his presence. Of course, she knew she was envied because she had married well. But why had she never before fully appreciated the thrill of his virility? A nearby sconce flickered, highlighting the silver at his temples to mock her. The idea of another woman tangling her fingers in his hair, tantalising her palm with the rough edge of his jaw, was too much to bear.

She was tortured with images of her husband giving another woman those intimate pleasures that were hers alone. The thought of him with a mistress of some refinement was harrowing; imagining him lying with a common prostitute sent nausea to scald her throat.

Suddenly he was close enough to catch her arm

and prevent her bolting. 'What is the matter?' he asked softly, then grunted a mirthless laugh. 'That was a stupid thing to say. Obviously I know already what is the matter. But...' his eyes scanned her strained face '...there is something else...something new. What is it?'

June tilted her chin and her fierce eyes darted to his. 'Very well, I shall tell you. I am disgusted that you have allowed your friend to speak of loose women with my young sister. She is only sixteen and not yet out. I do not think she needs to have the term demi-rep explained.'

William shoved his hands in his pockets and his head tilted at the ceiling. 'As you know that much, you must also know that your father was present at the time of the incident. Direct your righteous anger at him, not me.'

'That is for my mother to do.'

'I agree. And if your mother has not taken him to task over what occurred, perhaps that is because she knows the full story and is aware of mitigating circumstances. I think Sylvie is not your main concern at all. I think what irks you is not knowing why I was involved in a conversation about demi-reps.'

'I think I can guess the answer to that,' June sweetly snapped. 'Sylvie heard my father shouting when closeted with you and Lord Malvern. I imagine Papa had accused you of keeping company with harlots. Are you about to deny that is why he was angry?'

'No. That is exactly why he was angry.'

A small hand immediately cracked hard on a fleshless cheek. June back-stepped up one stair. 'I am sorry. I should not have done that.' The words vibrated with such fury it made nonsense of the apology. 'I now recall having given you permission today to slake your appetite elsewhere. You obviously guessed earlier in the week that I would do so and lost no time in gorging yourself.'

William simply stared unflinchingly at her with eyes that looked as black as ebony.

His composure simply heightened June's vexation. Suddenly instead of wanting to flee from him, she was determined to stay long enough to prod from him a vehement response. 'You admitted your friend is disreputable. Mr Blackmore has called him a villain too. And you…you will simply say you are human and have succumbed to temptation. Despite your boast earlier, you cannot…will not curb your appetite.'

June gripped the banister and glared at him with tawny eyes that threatened stormy tears. 'Why so quiet? Have you no pathetic defence? No lies to tell me?'

William's smile chilled her heart. 'You are not sure what has gone on, are you?' he said quietly.

'Yet you would rather believe your overwrought imagination than ask me why I was in a bawdy house with Townsend, and believe what I tell you. What happened to trust and loyalty, June?'

'How dare you try to make *me* feel guilty! Why should I believe what you tell me after all that has gone on?'

'When have I lied to you?'

June swallowed, chewed her lip and frowned. His cold, contained anger was unexpected and unsettling and doubts infiltrated her mind. Her mother had advised her to ask William for his version of events and not jump to conclusions. Her jealousy and pride had made her deaf even to her mother's counsel.

'When have I lied to you?' William bellowed, making her jump and clutch at the spindles for support. 'I imagine Sylvie has innocently repeated to you fragments of an overheard conversation. Would you like me to tell you the rest?'

'I do not for one moment think I could stomach more.' With that hurled defensively over her shoulder, June had twisted about and retreated another step up the stairs when a brawny arm girdled her waist and her husband hauled her back against him.

His lips closed with her small ear, spreading a sensual heat at her nape that made her shiver yet seek its comfort. 'You will listen to this whether you want to or not.' His voice was thick with violent determination. 'I am perhaps guilty of fathering a child out of wedlock, but I am not guilty of adultery or falsehood.' William spun her about and, with her slender wrist manacled by his brutal fingers, pulled her, unwillingly trudging behind him, towards the dining-room door. 'Come, sweet, let me show you what benefit I got from visiting that whorehouse. Then you may go alone to bed.'

The magnificent walnut table that spanned more than twelve feet was set for two to dine cosily close together. Crystal and silver glittered in firelight; shiny china reflected shapes like ghostly morsels. William snatched from the table *The Times*, then sent it skidding along the polished wood towards her. 'Harley has gazetted an apology to us for *any misunderstandings that could be misconstrued as slanderous*—I think those are the weasel words he employs. He agreed to do it when at a distinct disadvantage: Townsend and I had found him naked in his doxy's bed. I don't feel the slightest remorse at having humiliated him into giving his word to make this public announcement. What I do regret is not having chosen a better time and place to browbeat him.'

June looked at the paper and then at her husband. William managed half a sardonic smile. 'Take it with you. A little bedtime reading might delay your slumber, but never fear that I will.'

June picked up the paper in quivering fingers. She was being summarily dismissed, but her indignation was swallowed by shame. Her husband's wrath wound about her like a stifling cocoon until it seemed too late to salve her conscience with a few conciliatory words.

With her head high but her voice low, June quickly called to William before he could quit the room. 'If I have judged you harshly, I'm sorry. I hate to be suspicious, but there is so much horrible uncertainty. All I yearn for is an end to not knowing.'

'Not so very long ago all you yearned for was my baby,' William returned in a voice that was harshly melancholic. The door closed quietly as he left.

If many a true word was spoken in jest, the same philosophy could apply to words launched in anger. With that maxim circling her weary head, June rose unrefreshed from her jumbled bed. Pulling back the heavy curtains she watched with wistful entrancement as the dawn became a blush on the horizon. For an unknown reason, and one she was too exhausted to investigate, the flamboyant view settled on her a calm determination to put an end to not knowing…

As soon as a reasonable hour to visit approached, June donned her most stylish walking gown and went out alone without her maid, Verity, accompanying her. She walked some streets away before hailing a hackney cab and instructing the driver to take her to Belgravia.

'Will you take tea?'

'I thank you, no.'

Constance Bingham shifted her shoulders. It was an approximation of a shrug intended to convey her indifference. An elegant white finger indicated a gilt-framed chair. 'Please sit down, Mrs Pemberton.'

'Thank you.' June's polite acceptance sounded as aloof as had the offer.

As she settled herself June was peripherally conscious she was being subjected to a discreet appraisal. Her chin flicked up and she boldly invited her hostess's inspection.

Lady Bingham blinked and looked away, but not quickly enough to conceal the glint of jealousy narrowing her eyes.

A month or so ago such an explicit display of rivalry from this woman might have toppled June's confidence. Now she simply felt irritated and emboldened enough by it to immediately open proceedings. The sooner she might discover the truth and thus return home the better she would like it. 'I must thank you for receiving me without a prior appointment.'

Lady Bingham graciously inclined her head, acknowledging that indeed it was a generosity on her part.

There was a subtle slight in the gesture that was not lost on June. If the woman thought she might cow her with a superior attitude, she was mistaken. Constance Bingham might be the daughter of a baronet and the widow of an earl…she might even have once been William's chosen wife, but June had so far detected nothing other than unpleasantness in this woman's character. She would not despise Constance for deviating from society's constraints and losing her maidenhood before marriage. Perhaps it had been a selfless act of love for William, or perhaps it had been seduction…

Quickly June drove away such painful thoughts and concentrated on the woman's more recent aberrations. She had certainly made an unseemly spectacle of her interest in a married man. It was hardly conduct of which to be proud. With that thought bolstering her determination, June again attempted to start a conversation.

'There is no point in making any pretence over the reason for my visit, Lady Bingham. You must know I am not here to curry friendship. I am sure you are also aware that objectionable gossip is circulating concerning the Binghams and the Pembertons. The point of my visit is to ascertain whether you will assist us in putting an end to the rumours once and for all.'

June paused, giving the woman an opportunity to comment. Constance Bingham simply lifted her teacup to her delicately rouged lips. June had her suspicions confirmed by gleaming eyes insolently challenging her. Constance Bingham was glad... triumphant that her name was being linked with William's.

'As the gossip concerns your child I imagine you must be greatly angered by it. I'm sure I would be,' June reasoned mildly. She stripped off a glove and let the supple leather fall to her lap.

Constance put down her cup. 'Then you must be glad your temper will ever remain unprovoked, Mrs Pemberton. I understand William still has no *male* heir...' The sarcasm was purred at June and Constance lowered her eyes and allowed a tiny sly smile to tug at her lips.

June felt the blood rise in her cheeks, but swallowed her ire. She was more annoyed at herself for having stupidly uttered something that would make her vulnerable to such an attack.

'Naturally I am concerned for my daughter's wellbeing,' Constance continued while rhythmically smoothing her satin skirts with the backs of her fingers. 'I cherish her and am glad she is too young and too far away to be affected by any malice. When she is old enough I will disclose to her those important facts she ought know.'

'Which are?' June immediately regretted that her impatience to cut to the chase and gain some proper answers had made her sound impertinent.

Lady Bingham cocked her head and her amusement skewed her mouth into a vermilion slash. 'Do not look so crestfallen, Mrs Pemberton. I understand that inquisitiveness can make people act indecorously. With an empty nursery yourself it must be galling for you to hear it said that your husband has a child with his first love.'

'I have not come here either for pity or for scorn,' June said with quiet pride. 'Neither have I come to defend or to accuse my husband. The rumour is thus far unsubstantiated. You were the wife of a well-respected gentleman. I imagined that you would want to scotch insinuations about your child's father to honour your husband's memory. I have come to discuss how matters can be made better for all concerned. That is my purpose in visiting you.'

'I think you are only concerned for yourself, Mrs Pemberton. I think that because you are childless you want to persuade me to deny how intimately I once knew your husband, simply so you might save face.'

'Are you saying that my husband sired your daughter?' June immediately whipped back in a whisper.

'I am saying that if I were to discuss such a delicate matter, then I would naturally do so with the person who is central to the drama...*not* with his wife.'

June felt an icy embarrassment needle her skin. Yesterday her husband had summarily dismissed her from his presence. Today it was the turn of his— what was Lady Bingham to him? Forgotten fiancée? Mother of his child? Nothing at all? June felt her stomach heaving in anguish as she realised she simply didn't know.

'I am aware of your straitened circumstances, Lady Bingham, and I am sorry for you, but if you think to fuel these lies simply to find in my husband a meal ticket, you will be sadly disappointed. He is a gentleman, not a fool.' June gained her feet. 'I will waste no more of my time, Lady Bingham, and bid you good day.'

'Past folly can come back to haunt one...as your husband now knows. But do not look so anxious, Mrs Pemberton.' Constance's light tone could not disguise that June's frosty speech had affected her deeply. Her powder-pale complexion was burning bright spots of colour high on each cheek. 'William has been keen to keep in contact with me. He was here earlier this week.' Constance announced this with a fierce triumph that tightened the pit of June's stomach and persuaded her it was true. 'Soon the time will be right for him to tell you the truth about us.'

'You are lying!' June said in a low, vibrant voice. 'William will never let an unfortunate liaison in his youth come between us. He has said so.'

'I would expect no less of him. He was ever gentlemanlike.' Constance's tone hinted at a husky sneer. 'It is amazing, is it not, that beneath his sobriety is a man of such…energetic passion? Perhaps a virtuous little madam like you has no lover…no comparison to make. But I have comparisons, so many… Believe me when I say that William is hard to forget…hard to forgo… Everything about him is so hard…hard…hard…'

'Good day.' June struggled blindly to find the doorknob, struggled to block out the sound of lewd laughter that accompanied her into the marble-flagged hallway. It was only when she was close to the noble portal of the house that her temper surfaced from beneath the shock of being subjected to such coarse talk. Lady Bingham, widow of an earl, a member of polite society, had just acted like the wanton June had suspected her to be. Suddenly June was bedevilled by an urgent need to race back and tell the woman how vile she thought her. She didn't succumb to the urge to act as vulgarly as had her tormentor and, in her eagerness to breathe clean air, barely acknowledged the aged butler who politely held the door for her.

The fresh morning air cooled the sprinkling of

warm tears on June's cheeks and, once aware of the moisture, she dashed it away. After taking a deep, calming breath, she scoured the street for a hackney to take her home. She spied one at the junction with Waverley Street, but it pulled away from the kerb with a new fare before she had taken more than a half-dozen paces in that direction.

June spun about and noticed that, almost opposite the townhouse from which she had recently fled, another vehicle had stopped to allow a portly lady to alight. She hurriedly retraced her steps, hoping to secure a ride back to St James's.

She stood on the pavement, staring at the elegant façade of that hateful house which was visible through the windows of the cab, deaf to the demands of the driver. Eventually his raucous impatience penetrated her shock and she glanced up at his weatherbeaten countenance. June managed to shake her head, simultaneously shrinking back into the shadow of a budding lime tree.

As the conveyance pulled away she had an interrupted view of the distinguished gentleman she had just spied mounting the steps she had so recently descended. He was now rapping on the door while looking about. Suddenly he threw back his head, stared up at the sky as though impatient for admittance.

The elderly butler opened the door and then the

lady of the house was there too. June watched, her face a chalky mask, her bone-white knuckles grazing the trunk of the tree as Constance Bingham stepped on to the stone step and promptly slid her arms about William's neck and kissed him.

Chapter Fourteen

'What the hell do you think you are about?'

The rebuke was gritted out with tooth-shattering ferocity as William strode through the door with Lady Bingham still an appendage. He removed her limpet fingers from his neck and immediately put distance between them.

'I do not know what game you think you are playing, madam, but I have not come here for you to make a public spectacle of us. Why did you insist I come in person rather than send me a letter? Was it simply so you might throw yourself at my head on your doorstep and thus incite more gossip?'

The butler had closed the double doors and was now hovering. The elderly servant had been in Lady Bingham's employ only the few months since she came up from Devon for the season. In his prime he had presided over far grander vestibules, and taken far better remuneration. Never, in all his years of service, had he witnessed a lady act quite so outrageously and he hoped that, for the pittance the hussy had persuaded him to accept, she was not expecting his duties to include ejecting gentlemen who didn't appreciate her being shockingly amorous. A wary glance scanned the muscular frame of the vexed fellow and he shrank into his shoes.

'Go about your duties, my good man,' William instructed quite kindly, having noticed the manservant's uneasy stance. Without waiting for his employer to sanction his dismissal the butler gratefully hobbled away. William's attention reverted to the brunette sullenly peeping at him from beneath a web of dark eyelashes. 'Lead on to somewhere private where we might talk.'

That snapped command elicited a petulant look, but Constance swished about and, hips undulating with every step, glided to a nearby door.

Once within the room, where a short while before she had received this man's wife, Constance turned to William. A scornful stare met her bold invitation and she put a hand to her throat as though to stay the rash of colour spreading there. 'I beg you will not be angry with me, William. I…I could not control myself just now. I did not want to simply pen a letter. I have yearned to see you.'

William slung her a frown of disbelief. 'You have

yearned to see me?' he echoed. 'Why? You have seen me often enough. My wife and I were recent guests at Lord Malvern's party. You were also present and we exchanged pleasantries.'

'Pleasantries? I do not want pleasantries! You must know why I have wanted to meet you privately,' Constance cried huskily. 'I have never managed to put from my mind the incredible passion we shared. I know there is gossip about us. I do not wonder at it. My mourning is finally at an end. People have remembered that once we were in love. We were to be married, but stupidly I listened to my family instead of my heart…'

'What nonsense is this?' William interrupted on a brusque laugh. 'You are harking back to events that occurred a long time ago when we were both adolescents. You chose someone else and I married a woman I adore. I'll allow that there is gossip about us and also that once we were betrothed. But that is all that is honest in what you have said.' He paused and looked at her for the first time with a modicum of sympathy. 'I can only imagine you are prey to loneliness and nostalgia now Charlie Bingham is gone.'

'It is nothing to do with him!' A contemptuous flick of a hand dismissed her late husband as inconsequential. 'But there was something between *us*…we were lovers,' Constance insisted, a glitter hardening her eyes.

'Our relationship was misguided…a *mésalliance*.' William's tone made it clear he deemed her attitude absurd. 'Had we gone on to marry we both would have been dissatisfied with our lot.'

'I would not! You satisfied me more than any other man I have known. I cannot forget that wonderful occasion when you proved so many times how much you desired me—'

'This is madness.' William curtly cut across her explicit flattery. He strode to the door as if he would leave. 'I think, madam, you are deluded and ought seek the help of a physician. Perhaps you are afflicted with melancholy.'

'I am afflicted with a broken heart,' Constance called theatrically. 'Why will you not admit that there was something between us?'

'Very well, if you insist on candour, I concede there was something between us,' William drawled in irritation. 'Lust.'

Constance hurried after him as he jerked the door ajar. 'Are you going? Before we have discussed my daughter? From your letters I know you suspect that you sired Cissy.'

William shut the door again and with straining patience turned back to her. 'Then I'm sorry my prose can be misconstrued,' he returned in a weary tone. 'By my recollection I implied nothing of the sort. I asked you to confirm that the rumours, not the child, were spurious. I am still awaiting your response. You must have known your reticence would incite more speculation.' William narrowed his eyes on a downcast face. 'I am here now, willing to listen. Still you seem reluctant to be specific.' He paused, allowing her time to rectify matters and finally tell him what he wanted to know.

Constance bowed her head and dabbed at her face with a scrap of lace.

'Damnation! I believe you are a good enough actress to tread the boards at Drury Lane.' The chuckle that scratched at William's throat was nearly amused. 'There will be no more letters and no more visits. Do not contact me again except through my lawyers. With or without your help I hope to soon bring an end to this farce. I have sent private investigators to Devon.'

'What do you mean by that?' Constance dropped her handkerchief away from her flawless complexion and sent him a sharp look.

'I thought that news might dry your tears,' William said sardonically. 'Not to put too fine a point on it, madam, when we consummated our betrothal it was obvious to me, even at a tender age, that it was not the first time you had bestowed your favours. I would wager a tidy sum that even before the engagement was broken you had other lovers. I had no illusions about you then. I am certainly not about to be gulled now. In short, I know there are other candidates for the deed.' William smiled inwardly at the calculation narrowing her eyes as she endeavoured to guess his intentions. 'I accept that the child might not be your late husband's, for it was rumoured Charlie might lack in that respect…'

Constance's lips slanted in sly disappointment. 'He was of no use at all in that respect.'

'But you soon found someone who was. Are his pockets to let? Is that why you have come up to town? To find a sap willing to bail out your swain now you can no longer do so yourself?'

Constance swiftly averted her face, but not before William had glimpsed her dismay. He paced back into the room. 'My God,' he said slowly. 'That is it, isn't it? You hoped to play on my conscience and attempt to extort money from me to give to him. In which case I assume this pathetic attempt at blackmail is your work.' He withdrew from a pocket the note he had received and thrust it at her.

Constance scanned the script and frowned. A scoffing smile turned down her lips, but there was a wary look haunting her eyes. 'You can't seriously think I would bother with such a paltry sum?' She flicked the note back at him. 'If it was my work I would have demanded ten times as much.'

'Yes, I must admit that had occurred to me,' William drawled damningly.

Constance peered at him over an arrogantly elevated shoulder. 'You are a fool to reject me because of that barren mouse you married. I did not expect you to divorce her. In fact, I have no desire to again be a wife. I am a far better mistress. Are you sure you do not want a little sample of the ecstasy you miss?'

William simply stared at her, his eyes brimming with disgust.

Constance brazenly came closer and circled him. Suddenly a white finger was raised and a sharp nail tickled one of his cheeks.

William disdainfully flicked his head to one side at the same moment Constance drew blood. She backed away, smirking. 'Go! Go away…explain my brand to your sweet little wife.'

William put a hand to the thin welt on his cheek. 'God help your daughter if she favours you,' was all William muttered as he quit the room.

Lady Bingham mouthed an obscenity at the closed door and her simmering anger erupted, manifesting in her hurling to the floor the closest ornament to hand.

She then flew over the broken shards of porcelain to a small desk in the corner and scribbled a note. The bell was rung with violence until her butler, in a limping gait, arrived to find out what was causing the commotion. 'An urgent letter to be hand delivered,' she snapped at him. 'Quick! Do it now, you goggling old fool!'

'I want to talk to you, June.'

June froze momentarily to the spot with a hand on the banister, and a foot hovering over a tread. Quickly she resumed her graceful descent of the sweeping curve of stairs. 'It must wait. I cannot stop now,' she breathed with barely a tremor to her voice. 'I am on my way out…a prior engagement with Gavin…Mr Blackmore.' *William had something to tell her.* In her mind's eyes June could see the gloating look in the eyes of that preying widow as she had crowed, *'Soon the time will be right for him to tell you the truth about us.'*

Earlier that afternoon she had been so anguished by the scene she had witnessed between her husband and Lady Bingham that, had William soon come upon her she might have succumbed to hysteria or aggression. But, of course, she'd had no need to fret her husband might soon be home. She had no need to guess why he had been so long abroad or how he and Lady Bingham might have occupied their time together. If the woman were confident enough of her allure to blatantly kiss him on her front step, once within doors she would have still fewer inhibitions. Perhaps it was during pillow talk that she had persuaded William that his wife should be told about the two of them.

Had Constance Bingham regaled William with all that had gone on when his wife had called earlier in the day? Would he take her to task over that? June knew she should confront William, but she could not. She felt unprepared to deal with the anguish he might inflict on her. Her husband seemed increasingly to be a stranger to her, yet still the thought of losing his love was unendurable.

June gasped in a silent sob of a breath and steadied herself with the banister. She must not jump to conclusions, she inwardly impressed on herself. She must not allow hurt and humiliation to give rise to feverish imaginings. There might be a reasonable explanation why a vulgar wanton had kissed and embraced her husband in public.

This time there were no malicious tongues to blame for inventing a scandal. It was a truth she had witnessed and could not deny. She came down the few remaining stairs. She knew she must get away for a while. A little distraction might help her until she could be sure of controlling her emotions enough to discuss matters reasonably.

William caught at his wife's arm as she made to slip past him on her way to the street door. Blue eyes slowly looked her up and down. 'It is the first time I have seen you wear that outfit. As I recall, it was put away in your clothes' press because you did not like it.'

June glanced down at a fitted bodice of flimsy peach muslin that was scooped quite daringly low across her breasts. An equally light skirt floated tantalisingly about her body with little more than a cobweb of underskirt veiling lissom limbs.

'I have not worn it before,' June answered with some asperity, walking backwards while speaking to him. 'When first I had it made, I regretted it. I did not think it fitting. Now I have changed my mind. I think I do like it and it suits me very well.'

William stalked her retreat, while passing a lazy gaze over her revealingly attired lush little figure. 'It is not very clement today. Do you think you ought go abroad in nothing more than a camisole and petticoat to spare your blushes and keep you warm?'

William took her cloak from her grip and settled it with slow sensuality about her slender shoulders.

'Oh, this cloak is wool and I shan't blush, William.'

June felt her husband's hands tighten on the fastening under her chin. She cocked her head, her whole demeanour challenging his restraint. Soon her expression softened, for her eyes were drawn to the scratch on his cheek. With instinctive frowning concern one of her hands was soon raising to soothe it. Within a hair's breadth of his skin her outstretched fingers shrank into her palm. 'You have had an accident...' she murmured.

William rubbed the mark with a careless finger. 'It is nothing…nothing at all.' He looked at the small fist close to his face. 'Are you intending to add to the damage?'

William immediately regretted the remark as he saw his wife's eyes dart back to the wound. The expression in her soulful eyes had changed from sympathy to suspicion. With his unwitting help she had recognised it for what it was: a woman's brand. 'We need to talk, June. It is important,' William cajoled throatily.

So sadly sure was June that they were pondering on the same person at that precise moment that she choked out, 'I have no time and no inclination to discuss Lady Bingham with you.' Within a moment she had freed herself and passed him.

'How have you been, my dear? Well, I trust? It is *so* nice to meet you unexpectedly.'

June looked curiously at the person who had greeted her. The woman was not a stranger, but her affable attitude was definitely foreign.

June and Mr Blackmore had just been on the point of taking a stroll about the lake in Hyde Park to talk of his sister's plight when a smart carriage drew alongside and one of the occupants hailed them.

'It is good to see you too, ma'am,' June told her mother-in-law while wondering curiously why she now pleased Pamela Pemberton.

June tilted her head, including her father-in-law in her cordial smile. Alexander returned her a courteous nod whilst fiddling with the carriage ribbons. Conscious that William's parents were not intending to immediately move on, June continued politely, if not wholly truthfully, 'William and I have lately missed seeing you. We expected you might attend the *musicale*…'

'We have not been out very much at all,' Pamela disclosed, with a pointed look at her husband.

Alexander missed his wife's wordless rebuke, for he had politely responded to Mr Blackmore's comment on the fresh weather they were experiencing.

'Shall we take a stroll to the lake while the gentlemen have a chat?'

June nodded, while still puzzling over what might have prompted this unexpected bonhomie. June's bemusement escalated as Pamela linked their arms in a cosy fashion.

They had barely gone a few yards towards the water when Pamela sighed. 'It won't do! I must eat humble pie while I think I can.'

June slanted her a look of frank enquiry.

'I have wanted to visit you at home,' Pamela started her explanation. 'But Alexander would not allow it. He said I must stay away in case I caused trouble between you and William. He does not trust me, you know. See! He watches me now…' Pamela hissed, peering over her shoulder.

June obediently turned her head as she received a light dig in the ribs reminding her to check on their audience. Alexander Pemberton indeed appeared to be observing them rather than giving Gavin Blackmore his attention.

'He fears I might meddle, even though I have promised not to! You would think, would you not, that after more than three decades wed he would trust me to my word.' Pamela's wide-eyed look begged an ally.

June kindly returned a neutral smile.

'I have told him of my regrets, but he blames me still. He implies it is partly my fault that you and William seem at odds.'

At her mother-in-law's muffled tone, June inclined her head to look beneath Pamela's bonnet brim. She spied downcast eyes and a nose ready to drip. 'I concede that in the past I might have seemed…cool to you. It was simply a disappointment I felt that William's first engagement came to nothing.' Pamela snuffled. 'Only now do I realise it was a double blessing that he was jilted and then was fortunate enough to marry you.'

June swallowed, about to speak, but found she could not immediately think of a single thing to say. This, then, was her apology for the several years of poor treatment she had received at her mother-in-law's hands. Not so long ago she might have felt indignant that it had been so long in coming and was so inadequately delivered. Now, with far greater troubles occupying her mind, she simply squeezed her mother-in-law's arm in comfort and murmured, 'Do not distress yourself, ma'am.'

'I thought Constance genteel and charming…but she is not,' Pamela finished on a hiss, her eyes and lips tightening. 'I have it on good authority that the woman is a scheming hussy. She has been left a pauper by Lord Bingham and it serves her right.' Pamela barely paused before continuing, 'She is not at all the lady I believed her to be. She would have humiliated our son by marrying him when already she had—'

June was sent an intensely meaningful stare that sent Pamela's head to one side and her eyebrows winging into her hairline. 'It is outrageous! When I think that she might have tried to pass off a bastard as our grandchild! You understand my meaning, don't you?'

June knew exactly what her mother-in-law meant. It was why she felt an urge to mention that just this afternoon Lady Bingham had yet again been acting the scheming hussy with their son. June simply nodded.

Pamela took a glance through misty vision at her

daughter-in-law's tense features. 'You must not let that…that creature come between you and William. You are right for him… demure and ladylike…' The flimsy skirt floating about June's ankles received an inspection. 'That is a pretty gown you have on, my dear. It is…unlike the style you usually favour… Oh, look! Alexander is on his way to take me away lest I upset you. I have not upset you, June, have I? He will scold me if I have.'

'No,' June reassured her. 'You have not upset me at all, ma'am.'

'He seems pleasant…'

'What? Who?' June asked on a frown.

'Mr Blackmore.' A nod of the head indicated June's escort. 'He seems nice, but it is being noticed that you have spent a lot of time with him lately and very little with your husband.' Pamela squeezed her arm. 'Now we are friends I know you will not mind me saying so, for it was brought to my attention by Phyllis Chamberlain.' Pamela sniffed derisively. 'Of course, I told her to mind her own business, even if she is your father's sister. But I thought I would just mention it to you…

'Why, Alexander, I was just saying to June that we have missed seeing her and William. It is time, is it not, we had a little get-together?'

'Yes…' Alexander said without enthusiasm. 'Come, my dear, it is time we started home, for I think it is coming on to rain.'

'Nonsense!' Pamela contradicted. 'It is but a cloud.'

'It seems we are not to have an opportunity to talk of your sister today,' June mentioned wryly to Gavin as she waved at her in-laws departing, and then at some newcomers drawing up in a different coach.

'There is nothing good to report in any case,' Gavin responded flatly.

June frowned and slipped him a small bag of coins. She shook her head as he made to protest. 'William makes me a very generous allowance. It is only money I might have spent on fripperies. I would sooner you put it to good use. Come and say hello to my mother. And Sylvie is with her. She is my youngest sister. I shall introduce you to her.'

'We were just taking the pretty route home with our purchases,' was Gloria Meredith's answer to June's enquiry as to what brought them into the park. 'Sylvie has chosen some rather fine Brussels lace to edge the pink muslin Madam Bouillon is making up.' Gloria looked at her youngest daughter for a comment.

Sylvie simply jumped down from the landau to stroke Mr Blackmore's horses. 'Is this your phaeton?' she asked him.

'Alas, no,' he said on a rueful smile. 'I have borrowed it from a friend of mine.'

Sylvie was peering in at the hint of a spring

poking through cracked leather upholstery. 'Have you seen Lord Malvern's grand curricle?' she asked.

'Oh, indeed,' Gavin replied drily.

'I would have liked a ride in it.'

'It is mean of him not to oblige you,' Gavin said.

'I think so, too,' Sylvie agreed with a firm nod.

'Manners, Sylvie!' Gloria chided. 'Come, it is time to get along home. You have a fitting with Madam Bouillon.'

At Sylvie's glum look, June and Gavin exchanged a glance. 'We shall give Sylvie a ride about the park in the phaeton and bring her home shortly,' June said, with a smile of thanks directed Gavin's way.

Sylvie beamed at her mother and got a heavy sigh in return.

'Oh, very well. But don't be an age, young lady. Here, give me the bag with the lace.'

'Look!' Sylvie exclaimed as Gavin helped her alight. 'Lord Malvern is over there! I expect that is a demi-rep with him.'

June choked on an embarrassed chuckle. 'Sylvie! That is Lady Forsythe. She is very nice.'

'It is an easy mistake to make where Townsend is concerned,' Gavin muttered before proceeding to show Sylvie how one must hold the reins.

June stepped over to speak to Adam Townsend and Lady Forsythe.

'I see your sister is already drawing admirers.'

Adam watched Gavin Blackmore threading reins in and out of small, graceful fingers. 'I seem out of favour with her today,' he added ruefully on noticing Sylvie had barely glanced his way.

'That is because you have not taken her for a ride in your curricle.' June included Lady Forsythe in her wry smile. 'My young sister can be fickle-hearted as well as adorable.'

'Ah, sisters!' the middle-aged dowager said on a knowledgeable nod. 'I have one and *she* can be a trial! But I must not complain for I would not want to be without her. That poor gentleman must miss his sister dreadfully.'

June glanced warily at Lady Forsythe. 'You know about Bethany Blackmore?' she asked hesitantly.

'My sister knew of their family, oh, some many years ago now, when she lived in Devon. I understood the girl was named Laura, but I might be mistaken. Perhaps that was the mother's name. But it is a shame the youngster died.'

Chapter Fifteen

'Died?' June's astonishment was gruff with disbelief.

She glanced at Adam for his reaction, but he was engaged with a lady and her daughter who had succeeded, on their second stroll by, to catch his attention.

'Diphtheria…or perhaps it was smallpox… I cannot now recall for my sister told me about it a long time ago.' Lady Forsythe started to nod her head in sympathy. Suddenly she stuck out a hand to test the air. 'Come along, Townsend! Get us moving! It is starting to rain. My new style will suffer, you know.' Her elaborate coiffure received an anxious pat.

Adam suavely saluted the disappointed ladies. June received from him a genuine smile. Finally, with a frown Sylvie's way, he sent his coal-black stallions into a trot.

A slow spatter of raindrops began dotting black into the blue silk of June's cloak; still she stood dazed by what she had heard. Sylvie's laughter finally broke through her confusion and brought her back to the phaeton.

Gavin was pulling up the creaky hood with Sylvie's eager assistance. As June joined her on the seat her sister, still giggling, covered their laps with a travelling rug.

Gavin was breathing hard from the exertion of forcing into position the dilapidated rain cover when the pouch of coins June had given him dropped from his pocket with a chink. Sylvie picked it up, rattled the money, then made to mischievously hide it behind her back. Immediately the purse was snatched from her and stuffed back whence it came.

Gavin's eyes met June's and for a moment his impenitent scowl frightened her. The questions she had been ready to put to him, about what she had heard concerning his family and Bethany in particular, withered on her lips.

Within a moment Gavin was smiling with his usual diffident charm. 'That was rather rude of me,' he mildly apologised. 'I must get you both home before I am in trouble with your family. William will ring a peal over my head if either one of you catches a chill from being out in this weather.'

Neither June nor Sylvie responded, for both were

still shocked by his spontaneous boorishness. Just moments before he had been acting the impeccable gallant.

'And you must be home in time for your seamstress's visit.' Gavin persevered in his attempt to restore an air of harmony. A casual look slanted up at the leaden skies. 'I think it will be quite a downpour.'

Sylvie was unimpressed by his smooth talk and glared reproachfully at him. 'It was just a game. I would not steal from you, you know,' she muttered and slid along the seat towards June.

'Of course; I am sorry,' Gavin muttered. Being reminded of his incivility clearly irritated him, but, as though in an effort to finally banish the episode, he offered, 'Would you like to drive a short distance? I shall help you handle the ribbons.'

Sylvie shook her head and instead tossed her face to the driving rain. A flicker of resentment tightened Gavin's features despite his easy shrug. He made to whip leather over the horses' backs; instead, the reins fell slack.

Increasingly uneasy, June searched about to see the reason for the delay. She was regretting having suggested taking Sylvie for a ride in the phaeton and had a powerful instinct to quickly get her young sister safely home. She soon spotted that Mr Blackmore was staring at a youth weaving a path towards them whilst keeping beneath the dripping trees to shelter from the worst of the rain.

The young fellow, on spying the phaeton, ran the few remaining yards to the vehicle whilst jamming his hat protectively low on his brow. He thrust up a note and, once it was taken, left his expectant palm extended. His reward was only terse thanks. The youth slunk off, a sullen stare slung back at them.

'He is my landlady's son. A surly enough fellow if ever there was one.'

Gavin's excuse for his meanness did nothing to alleviate June's disquiet. 'It must be an urgent message for him to come out looking for you to deliver it.' She barely paused before adding, 'Let us quickly get Sylvie back to Beaulieu Gardens, please. My mother will be worrying about her.'

June's eyes darted here and there, assessing the environment. The park was emptying of carriages now the rain had properly set in. A few promenaders who had lingered under the trees, expecting the shower to pass, had given up that hope and were dashing away to find better cover. She fidgeted on the seat. 'Mr Blackmore, we must go!' she implored.

June's demand had little effect. Gavin did not look up from breaking the seal on his note. A low, driven oath followed a perusal of its contents. June felt Sylvie slip her hand through her arm and hug closer.

Her young sister was not of a nervous disposition, but was obviously also sensing a queer atmosphere.

The letter was stuffed into a pocket. Catching up the reins, Gavin sent them snaking over horseflesh. His swift sideways glance took in June's fretful expression. A boyish smile ensued, but June was not tempted to feel reassured. She suddenly understood that the careful attention she had been used to receiving from this man was not so much born of his interest, but his calculation. As though seeing him properly for the first time, she realised he was gauging her reaction so he might adapt his own.

'I must beg your pardon if I have seemed short-tempered, but I have been most anxious to receive that communication. I expect you have realised the letter is from Bethany.' It was the same grave tone he always used when speaking of his poor sister. 'It has got speedily to me via my landlady's kindness, for she knew I waited on it. Unfortunately, it confirms what I suspected, but dreaded knowing. Bethany writes that she is ill again. I must purchase some laudanum for her with the money you have kindly donated. I cannot bear to think of her discomfort.'

June did not reply as they proceeded from the park, for her mind was in turmoil. She was glad they were at last on the way home, yet depressed that what had seemed a pleasant interlude in an unpleasant day was actually turning into nothing of the sort. Again her thoughts circled back to what Lady Forsythe had said.

If Mr Blackmore's sister was dead from disease, how could she write to him from gaol complaining of feeling ill? It seemed absurd to suppose that Bethany might be a fictitious character in a plot Gavin Blackmore had concocted. But June felt compelled to discover whether the gentleman she had considered a friend considered her a gullible fool, who would simply swallow whichever yarns he fed her. Was he really so desperate for her sovereigns that he would stoop so low to get them? He had certainly made it clear that the money she donated was important to him by so churlishly snatching it from Sylvie's hand. Indignation prompted her to blurt out her suspicions.

'I fear that something is not right, Mr Blackmore. I have heard an odd tale that your sister died of an illness many years ago. If that is so, how can Bethany now be incarcerated in the Fleet?'

Gavin didn't even turn his head to look at her. His profile looked skeletally tight and so clumsily did he steer past a lumbering cart that the trio were jerked sideways by his ineptitude. Unbelievably, once round the obstruction, he urged the horses to a greater pace. June struggled to find her balance on the precarious seat and pulled Sylvie protectively close.

Finally, when the vehicle was racketing along straight, if not safe, Gavin uttered in a tone of sombre resignation, 'It is a shame. I had hoped that things might come good for me before you found out. Who told you? I know it was not your husband or Townsend. My fellow scholars knew little of my home life. I made sure of that.' He turned her way and June noticed that the fall of light brown hair over his eyes was darkly sleek with rain. Tear-like rivulets ran down his cheeks. 'You are fortunate, Mrs Pemberton. You have lived a charmed life. You have no idea, have you, what it is like to be without, to be deprived of what others, less entitled, take for granted?'

June ignored his self-pity and said coldly, 'It does not matter how I have found out. Why on earth would you fabricate such a tale? If you have striven to keep your past a secret, I imagine everything else that you disclosed to me about your parents and so on is a lie, too.' June was no longer interested in his reply for she had become peripherally aware that something else was wrong. 'Where are we going?' she demanded as she noticed they had turned towards the suburbs rather than towards Mayfair. 'Take us to Beaulieu Gardens immediately,' she ordered.

When he made no reply, but sent the horses into a perilous canter on the glistening cobbles, June lunged at the reins. Gavin elbowed her roughly off and growled, 'Sit still, Mrs Pemberton. I warn you to sit still! Do as you are told and you will come to no harm.'

'Take me home, you brute!' Sylvie, squashed between them, immediately took over attempting to grapple the reins from Gavin's grasp, and added a fairly hefty punch or two to his shoulder for good measure.

'Stop this carriage at once and put us down,' June yelled breathlessly, restraining Sylvie lest she got injured.

'I can't do that, I'm afraid. You know too much and are thus a liability…unless I can discover some value in you…' His eyes half-closed in consideration and a crafty smile suddenly tilted his mouth.

June cuddled Sylvie to her, stroking away straggly silver tresses from her rain-damp face. 'I beg you will listen to me! Let us take Sylvie home and I shall remain with you,' she reasoned desperately, yet in a voice shrill with panic.

The plea earned her nothing other than a derisive laugh. 'I really would be a dolt to agree to that! Do not try to humour me, Mrs Pemberton. I am not a madman, rather a desperate man who is infinitely ambitious…'

June leaned forward, watching slick grey ground spinning past.

'I would not attempt it. But it is your choice

whether you jump and break your neck,' Gavin mocked. 'But then I don't imagine you would risk leaving this comely maiden at my tender mercy…'

Gavin turned a lascivious eye on her young sister. June instinctively enclosed Sylvie in a fierce protective embrace that sought to shield her from his view. To distract him, June asked desperately, 'Why are you doing this? Why have you lied and invented someone called Bethany?'

'I have not invented someone called Bethany. You asked to meet her, did you not? I am an obliging soul, Mrs Pemberton. I shall take you to meet Bethany.'

Sylvie struggled free of June's restraint. 'I'm not going with you! I hate you! Take me home!' she shouted and let fly with a small fist. The blow landed with a crunch just behind one of Gavin's ears, wobbling him on the seat. Without hesitation he instantly retaliated. A short jab to Sylvie's chin rendered her immediately unconscious. June supported her gracefully crumpling form, preventing her from falling.

'You vile beast!' June screamed as they thundered on and swerved east so the driving rain slanted further beneath the hood to drench them. 'Stop and put us down now. Or I swear I shall jump.'

Gavin put back his head and guffawed. 'Go ahead and jump, if you dare. You can't carry your sister and you certainly won't leave her with me, I'm sure of that. I got no enjoyment from hitting the sweet innocent, but she would certainly provide other pleasure…'

June's face became chalky and her arms tightened about Sylvie's limp form. What he'd said was infuriatingly true. She could probably escape herself, should she dare to risk life and limb. But how on earth could she leave Sylvie behind?

'They are dead in a ditch, I know it!'

Edgar Meredith rocked his hysterical wife in his arms and whispered soothingly to her but his face, visible across her shuddering shoulders, was ashen. 'I shall just go and see if William is back with any news. Sit here by the fire…' He led Gloria, tottering on nerve-racked legs, towards an armchair and gently forced her into it. Before he had reached the door she had sprung up again.

'You must search for them! Find everyone you can! Every servant must be taken to scour the roads and hedgerows. That phaeton didn't look safe. I didn't want to let Sylvie ride in it.'

Edgar returned to his wife as she whirled feverishly about the room with a hand gesturing here and a foot stamping there. 'There might be nothing so calamitous to it all, Gloria. The rig might simply have lost a bolt or one of the nags might have thrown a shoe…'

The door bursting open at that point curtailed Edgar's desperate mitigation for June's failure to bring home her younger sister. He rushed towards the man striding into the parlour.

'Is there any news?'

The exact phrase that Edgar had been about to utter was in fact barked at him by his son-in-law. As Edgar shook his head, William swiped a hand across the bluish bristle on his chin. 'I have spoken to Etienne and Isabel,' he concisely informed them as he paced back and forth like a caged animal. 'They have not seen June and Sylvie today. But Isabel recounted something that I did not know. Gavin Blackmore has told June he has a sister in the Fleet. June has been charged to keep the information confidential for Gavin did not want pity or charity. Nevertheless he has allowed June to donate money and clothes to take to his sister to help her.'

'Is that significant at all, do you think?' A glimmer of hope elevated Edgar's heavy brows. 'Would June have asked to visit her? Have they been silly enough to go there?'

'June would never take Sylvie to such an establishment, no matter how charitably inclined she was feeling towards Blackmore's sister.' William's defence of his wife emerged through lips that were white and bracketed with strain. 'But I'm hopeful they have gone somewhere on impulse and are unavoidably delayed by the rainstorm. One of the horses might have thrown a shoe on a slippery road…'

'You see, my dear, William is of the same opinion. We must not think the worst.' A faltering smile accompanied Edgar's reassurance.

'But you must search!' Gloria wailed. 'You must take everyone and search for them in case they are injured or lost. If Mr Blackmore is hurt and cannot protect them, they might be set upon by thieves or…'

'It is dusk. By the time we assemble it will be full dark,' Edgar soothed.

'Get flares…and lanterns!' Gloria screeched.

'Do not upset yourself so, ma'am.' William's tone was kindly heartening, despite the fact his mother-in-law had voiced the same perilous thoughts that were running amok in his own mind. William knew his father-in-law also was gravely worried, for his brave face was becoming florid with tension and his old eyes were suspiciously moist. 'I have already arranged with Herbert that footmen scour the immediate environs of Hyde Park,' William told them both. 'They will be out in full force now, looking for any sign of an abandoned vehicle. Everything will be done that can be done…'

His determined promise tailed off into a quiet that seemed thick with unspoken fears. 'If they were intending to simply take Sylvie for a ride about the park before returning, then there is only one route of travel to cover. I will join the search party once I have exhausted all other enquiries with family and friends.'

'They would not stay out visiting without sending word!' Gloria insisted. 'June would not worry me so.'

'I know,' William said simply. 'But they might be marooned and unable to get a message to us.' William knew the excuse was feeble. But every fibre of his being resisted pondering the unthinkable: his wife and sister-in-law might be lying dead or injured in an overturned high-flyer. 'I have come directly here from quizzing my parents. June didn't mention to them where she and Blackmore might go next. Do you recall seeing any other people they might have talked to in Hyde Park?'

'As I was leaving them Lord Malvern came by. I expect, as he is a friend of yours, he would have passed the time of day with them. Lady Forsythe was out with him in his curricle.' The words tripped over each other as Gloria frantically imparted any snippet that might be of help in finding her daughters.

'I shall speak to Adam at once,' William said. He then addressed Edgar. 'Etienne has said he will go and check whether Rachel and Connor have seen them. Will you go and see any other friends and relatives you can think of who may have tempted them away somewhere?'

Upon Edgar's nod, William immediately took his leave of his parents'-in-law and was soon striding from the house.

'Missing?' The single word was expelled in disbelief.

'You and Lady Forsythe were possibly the last people to speak to June before she and Sylvie set off with Blackmore. Did June give any hint where they might go next?'

Adam Townsend shook his head. 'I barely had an opportunity to talk to your wife. Lady Forsythe was conversing with her while I fielded Mrs Prothero's invitation to her chit's ball on Saturday. I saw Blackmore demonstrating how to handle the ribbons to your sister-in-law, then it started to rain…' He shot an aghast frown at William. 'My God! You don't think he would have let her drive in that perilous weather, do you? They might have had an accident.'

William's face slumped into his hands and he gritted out, 'Do not say that! They are simply delayed. One of his infernal horses might have taken lame.'

Adam came around his desk and gripped William's shoulder. 'You are right, of course,' he encouraged quietly. 'They are probably sheltering somewhere. We'll search until we find them.'

'I have a search party out. They are concentrating

their efforts about the park. Do you know where
Blackmore has been lodging? I asked him once and
got no more information from him than he'd taken
rooms close to Greyfriars. Stupidly I didn't perse-
vere. I imagined he was reluctant to be specific
because he was embarrassed that he couldn't afford
decent accommodation.'

'He was always reticent about his circumstances.
Personally I didn't bother to ask where he lived. In
any case, I doubt they will be there.'

'Every possibility must be investigated!' Immediately William dragged fingers through his hair and
a shrug and a sigh were offered in apology for his
raised voice.

Adam twitched a smile at him. 'We *will* find them
very soon.'

William nodded, yearning for such arrogant confidence to be his. To keep at bay the tormenting demons
that sneaked terrifying images into his mind he concentrated on facts. 'Blackmore was forthcoming about
his personal life with June, but made her promise not
to repeat what he confided…even to me. June unin-
tentionally let slip to Isabel Hauke that Blackmore's
sister Bethany had been hounded into the Fleet for her
debts. June has been giving him money to take to her.'

'Stranger and stranger…' Adam murmured. 'I had
no idea he had a sister. He never spoke of siblings;
I assumed he was an only child.'

'As you say,' William said, 'he was secretive about his circumstances.'

'Why would he choose your wife…a woman he barely knows…as a confidante? You say June has given him cash and been charged not to tell you about it?'

William and Adam exchanged a long look. 'What are you thinking?' Adam finally asked in a voice that was rather hoarse.

'The same as you, I expect,' William said with a hint of anger overcoming his anxiety. 'I'm thinking that perhaps there is something queer in all this.'

'I know he has a way of inveigling that is admirably successful. Percy Carstairs was gulled just before we quit Eton. He gave over fifty guineas to Blackmore for contraband. The geneva and cognac were, according to Blackmore, not forthcoming because The Revenue had confiscated the lot. Carstairs was too credulous to challenge him over it. My investigation turned up that Blackmore had sold the entire stock elsewhere and kept all the profit.'

For the first time in many hours a ghost of a smile curved William's strained lips. 'I would not have had Blackmore for such an enterprising fellow.'

'Neither would I. I had to admit to admiring his audacity. But Percy Carstairs was a friend. We kept it quiet for Percy felt a numbskull to have been so easily duped.'

'We? Why were you involved in it?'

'I felt compelled to help,' Adam drily explained. 'After all, the fifty guineas were mine. Carstairs borrowed the money.'

'I recall you gave Blackmore a hiding. No one seemed to know why and Blackmore just acted the martyr over it.'

'If he has put your wife and Silver in jeopardy in some sordid scheme, I'll make sure he really suffers this time.'

'Not before I do,' William countered with deadly softness. So deep were William's troubled thoughts now that it didn't occur to him to enquire how his friend knew young Sylvie's true name was Silver.

'I shall go to Lady Forsythe's and find out if she has any light to shed on matters. Your wife might have told her something relevant about their plans for the afternoon.'

William nodded his gratitude. 'And there's only one way to know if Bethany Blackmore has benefited from June's benevolence: go to the Fleet prison and ask her.'

Chapter Sixteen

'Open this door at once!' June's shouting and hammering were to no avail, her efforts mocked by branches strumming on the window and wind piping in the chimney. The mournful concert made June spin about and watch an eerily quivering curtain. Then once again the locked door had her full attention. She banged repeatedly on the paint-peeling panels until her wrists ached.

'Where are we? Has that fiend gone and left us all alone?'

'Thank Heavens you have woken up!' June sped back to the bed and, leaning over her shivering sister, put a hand to Sylvie's clammy brow. 'How do you feel?'

'I'm cold and my head aches,' Sylvie grumbled, but none the less she struggled upright, still snuggled into the bed quilt.

June cupped one of her sister's icy cheeks and, by the light of the small stump of candle Blackmore had stuck on a shaky shelf, carefully scrutinised her appearance.

'Do I look a mess?' Sylvie asked in a tone that was curious rather than anxious.

'Your hair is like a bird's nest and you have a bruise on your jaw.' June combed back the platinum tangles and touched the purple blotch with fingers that were infinitely gentle. Quickly she took off her cloak and used it as an extra cover for Sylvie.

'Where are we? Are we prisoners?'

'Hostages, to be more accurate,' June told her. 'Blackmore let on, when he was carrying you up the stairs to this room, that we shall be held until a ransom is paid.'

Sylvie attempted to smile, but winced as it caused her injury to twinge. 'Is it still raining? Shall we jump from the window and get away?' she rattled off. 'I suppose I ought try to escape and save Papa the expense. He is already moaning about the cost of my come-out. Of course, that *is* a waste of money.'

'Papa would give everything he has to keep you safe and never begrudge a penny piece.' June went to the casement, rubbing briskly at her arms to ward off the chill air. She peered into dismal blackness whilst trying to fathom where on earth they might be.

During their hectic flight out of London, dying

light and drizzle had blurred woods, fields, villages
into a bolt of brown until June, hampered further by
tears, no longer had any idea in which direction, or
how far, they had travelled. It had been dusk, with
wind coursing the rain clouds to the horizon, when
Gavin Blackmore finally turned the phaeton off the
road and on to a sludgy track. June had watched a
ghostly outline solidify into a lime-washed lodge as
they moved closer over the ruts.

With his arms occupied carrying Sylvie's
comatose form, their captor had aimed urgent kicks
at the door until an oafish-looking man had let them
in. Blackmore had addressed the fellow as Cursley
with an abruptness that denoted him as a menial.

There had been little time to look about the
interior for Gavin had ushered her straight to the
stairs, forcing her to mount them and enter this spar-
tanly furnished chamber. June judged they had
probably arrived less than an hour ago, yet the
minutes seemed to have dragged interminably until
she felt sure she had counted each stitch in the bed
quilt and every nail in the door that barred their
freedom.

Now she focussed on an impenetrable dark beyond
the window. She could just detect the outline of the
phaeton and horses still tethered to it. If only they
could reach that vehicle and have a few minutes' head
start, she would soon grasp the knack of steering the

contraption. She sighed on realising how futile was any hope of escape. If they managed to hoodwink Blackmore, there was still the gigantic Cursley to dodge.

But for a taper in a window below pitching yellow on to the ground, and an occasional murmur of voices, they might have been alone in the house. June let the curtain fall back into place. 'We certainly cannot escape through this small opening. Besides, I am not sure where we are and it is so dark now we might wander into a bog or ditch or get set upon by thieves.'

She returned to the bed to sit beside Sylvie and chafed her freezing hands between her palms. 'Daylight and providence will be needed to get us away from Blackmore and his toady.' At Sylvie's enquiring look she explained. 'It seems our abductor has an accomplice. But no sign of Bethany, whom he promises we shall meet!' June suddenly hugged Sylvie to her. 'I'm so sorry to have got you embroiled in all this. If only I hadn't been so foolish as to have been taken in by Blackmore's cock-and-bull story.'

The purpling mark on Sylvie's jaw made her look poignantly vulnerable and only served to heighten June's feelings of guilt. 'But we shall not try to escape unless there is a good chance we might get clean away in the phaeton. We must be sensible. If we risk fleeing on foot, we might be prey to thieves or the elements.'

'There are worse hazards in you attempting to drive that rig.'

It was cheekily said, but June noticed that some of her sister's buoyancy was flagging. Sylvie was wrapping herself into her blanket, her eyes huge and luminous in the candlelit dusk. June stroked her face encouragingly. 'If we do not get an opportunity to bolt, you must be my brave girl until William comes for us and takes us home.'

'How will William know where we are?'

June made to utter some empty reassurance, but she swallowed the platitude. Her sister might be young, but she was no fool and June would not treat her as such. 'They will even now be searching for us. We must hope that Papa and William and our brothers-in-law make investigations and find out Blackmore is a villain and which places he frequents. I'm sure eventually they *will* trace us to this house.'

'It is not your fault that I am here.' Sylvie smiled kindly on sensing June's self-torment. 'I could have gone straight home with Mama, but I didn't want to. I know you were being nice by letting me ride with you. I wouldn't have minded if you had escaped on the road and left me behind, for you could have raised the alarm.' A whimsical look misted Sylvie's eyes. 'I'm not frightened, anyhow. Lord Malvern is coming to rescue me. Before I woke up just now I dreamed he would.'

'Well, I hope you are right,' June said.

'So do I,' mocked a voice from the door. Gavin Blackmore sauntered into the room…but not too far. He stood close enough to the exit to prevent June slipping through it. 'How marvellous it would be if Townsend came here begging me on his knees to spare you. Unfortunately, I doubt an innocent maid would tempt that reprobate into acting the hero. You're pretty enough, but Townsend likes his women seasoned. Of course, if your father fails to meet my demands, I will personally ensure that before you leave here you have all the experience you need to keep his lordship besotted for a year or more.'

June stepped in front of Sylvie so she was screened from view. 'What demands? What have you done? Have you sent word to William where we are? He will kill you for this outrage.'

'If he is foolish enough to defy me, your family will never see either of you again. My man Cursley is on an errand to deliver letters to William and your father. I'm sure your husband will act the loving spouse and give me what I want to recover what he wants.'

'And what is it you want?' June demanded angrily.

'I want you. But, against my will and my instinct, I haven't told your husband that. I know you still love

William, despite the rumours of adultery and my efforts to turn you against him. So I'll act the martyr and instead settle for five thousand of his pounds.' Blackmore mentioned the sum impenitently.

June echoed the amount in astonishment.

'Indeed. It should get me to the Americas before the duns find me again.'

'So it was *you* who had run up debts, not the fictitious Bethany Blackmore?'

Gavin adopted a hurt look. 'Why do you persist in thinking she is a figment of my imagination? Be patient a while longer and you will meet Bethany in the flesh, I promise.' He strolled closer to the sisters. His finger managed to idly brush the bruise he had given Sylvie before she recoiled and smacked away his hand.

'But you are right,' Gavin said, unperturbed by Sylvie's disgust as he stationed himself close to the door again. 'I have been hounded by those curs, Bethany, too, and she *was* in the Fleet for her misdemeanours. You cannot accuse me of telling *only* lies, Mrs Pemberton, for I have simply tailored falsehood with truth to fit my needs.'

'I cannot believe that once I regarded you as a friend,' June flung at him contemptuously. 'What a fool I have been!'

'Don't rue your kindness,' he said with an unexpected sincerity. 'I'm grateful to you, and so is

Bethany, for she did receive the fine clothes you donated.' His interest again became intimate. 'William is a very lucky man to have such an alluring wife. If I did not hold you in such high regard, I might be tempted to…' A low-lidded gaze lingered lustfully on her.

Suddenly he laughed. 'Enough! Of course we are friends and as such I respect you too much to take advantage of your position as my prisoner. I hope your family do not force me to act the brute with either of you.' Another smouldering look was slanted at June. 'It is fair the tables are turned, for you captivated me from the start. With a little more manipulation I'm confident you would have agreed to us becoming lovers. Then, of course, there would have been no more need for subterfuge. As my mistress you would have willingly paid my debts. Perhaps you would have come to America with me…'

June darted a quizzical look at him. 'You are obviously deluded to think so.' Suddenly her amazement transformed to suspicion. *A little more manipulation…turn you against him…* were phrases filtering back into her mind. 'In the ridiculous belief that you might bring about such a fantasy, did you instigate some of the scandal that was circulating simply to drive us apart?'

Gavin chuckled. 'Lord Harley and his friend had already succeeded in causing discord between you and William. I was unaware of their intention to make mischief, but gratefully exploited it. I hoped you would be suspicious and hurt and would eventually turn to me for solace. But you seemed determined to love your husband no matter what scandals were bandied about. Of course, I had heard talk that you wanted children. I thought that, if you believed William had already sired a child with another, it might be the final straw and kill your devotion to him. I confess I sowed that seed. I'll admit that Bethany sought to benefit from it, too. She can be a greedy minx when she scents money, rash and incautious too. We argued over that.'

'What do you mean…over that?' June demanded.

'She was too impatient and sent William a blackmail note. It was a silly attempt to make a quick profit, for there was no longer a secret to keep from you. The rumour I started was already in circulation, I made sure of that.' He gestured in emphasis. 'Besides, had Bethany known William as I do, she would have realised it was a wasted effort. He might be a quiet man, but your husband is too strong a character to bow to blackmail.'

Blackmore sighed his disappointment. 'It is a shame things have gone awry. I'm sure I would have won you over eventually. You are quite right for me, generous and sweet. And I know you understand my torments…how envy can burrow deep within a person and rot their soul. We are kindred spirits, you and I.'

'We are nothing of the sort! Don't you dare say otherwise.' June gulped a breath, attempting to stifle her anger, for she knew there was a grain of truth in his ramblings. He had recognised in her disposition flaws that made her ashamed, flaws that had made her compassionate and blind to a swindler's true nature.

She also understood quite clearly the threats lurking in his compliments. He was desperate for cash; should the ransom demand not be met swiftly enough, he would, without compunction, act the abuser out of revenge. If he attempted to perpetrate such horror, she would fight him tooth and nail and she knew Sylvie would too. The thought of Sylvie defiled and beaten made her blood alternately boil, then flow cold. 'You are insane, not disadvantaged,' she hissed. 'The only way you could prove otherwise would be to set us both free immediately. If you do that, you also will have time to abscond before the authorities catch up with you. Kidnap and extortion carry high penalties. I promise to speak in your defence and will say you treated us well.'

'Bravo! A fine attempt, but, alas, it will not work.' He smiled ruefully. 'I am not sure how Bethany endured being incarcerated. I would rather kill myself than go to such a hell-hole. That is why I have

striven to keep the duns at bay through your generosity, but they will be back.' He tilted his head to
assess her. 'You are becoming quite…bold and confident. I am not sure I like that, June. I shall call you
June now, for there is a special bond of intimacy
between us, you cannot deny it. I must say that I'm
also disappointed you no longer seem as keen as
once you were to meet Bethany. Ah…' He cocked
his head, excitement glittering in his mild brown
eyes. 'How timely! I expect that is her now. I suppose
she will have brought with her that tiresome…'

June missed the rest of his speech, for she too had
heard a vehicle outside. She rushed to the window
and, lifting the curtain, squinted out. Through wind-
tossed branches she saw that a carriage had stopped
by the door. A woman in a hooded cloak stepped
down into a lantern-lit pool of light, then a diminu-
tive figure, similarly swaddled against the elements,
followed. The carriage immediately pulled away
again. The key scraping in the lock curtailed June's
curious peering at the intriguing silhouettes. She flew
from the window to the door and yanked at the
handle, shouting, 'Come back, you beast, and let us
out!'

'I have discovered something very odd.'

'So have I,' was Adam's concise response to
William's unceremonious greeting.

The two men had just arrived back, with timely precision, at William's elegant townhouse. In unison they took the front steps two at a time.

Once inside William's walnut-panelled study, Adam strode to the fire and held out his palms to the blaze. 'Did you find this Bethany woman at the Fleet?'

'I did not, but a couple of sovereigns soon oiled the tongue of a gregarious cove by the name of Tommy Barr, who was happy to tell me all he knew about her. He confirmed Bethany Blackmore was recently detained there. Her debts came about when she rented flamboyant premises in Mayfair for her business as a bawd, then absconded without paying the landlord. She tried to intimidate him and the other turnkeys into giving her privileges by threatening them with dire consequences should they not be forthcoming. When that didn't work, she resorted to payment in kind for favours.'

Adam grunted a laugh. 'If she *is* a relation of Blackmore's, it's little wonder that he keeps his home life private.'

'Those were my thoughts. I asked about her visitors. A gentleman fitting Blackmore's description brought her some clothing, for her own had been torn when she was attacked by another bawd who thought she was acting above her station.'

Adam stuck his warmed hands in his pockets. He

arrowed a slanting glance at William's haggard features. 'It's welcome news. The more intrigue we uncover, the less likely it is that the phaeton has come to grief in the storm.'

William nodded, his eyes wide and desperate. 'Bethany fed her gaolers some salacious titbits about her influential clients when attempting to wheedle favours. She stopped short of naming names, but bragged about a secluded hunting lodge in Finsbury Park where a talented courtesan—a friend of hers and a society lady—discreetly entertains Quality. I know of White Lodge in the vicinity. Some years ago now I went there on a shooting party. It belongs to the Carlisle estate.'

'Robbie Carlisle had a reputation as a whoremonger. Is the decrepit old fool dead yet?' Adam asked.

William shrugged. 'I haven't seen him in a while.' Recalling Adam had some news to impart, he asked, 'What did you learn from Lady Forsythe?'

'In light of what you have just told me, I have discovered something very peculiar. Lady Forsythe's sister once lived in Devon quite close to the Blackmore family. By all accounts there were only two children born to the Reverend and Mrs Blackmore. The mother died when the daughter was born and the daughter died of illness when she was a youngster. Lady Forsythe said that she and June were talking about that just this afternoon.'

'June would not have hesitated in challenging Blackmore if she thought he had been intentionally duping her.' William stared at his friend, his face ashen with anxiety. 'I can't think straight any more. Would he resort to violence or crime to keep safe his secrets?'

Herbert's appearance on the threshold prevented Adam from giving his opinion on Blackmore's capacity for evil. 'There is a gentleman here to see you, sir.' The butler stood aside to reveal a figure dressed in a dun-brown travelling cape standing just behind him in the hallway.

Before Herbert could return to his duties, William asked urgently, 'Is there any news from the search party?'

'No, sir,' Herbert said. 'I'm sorry…' he added softly before his slight, dark figure melted into the shadows.

The newcomer immediately doffed his hat and stuck it beneath an arm. 'H'I'm sorry to call late, sir, but h'I have taken it upon myself to suppose rightly or wrongly that what h'I have uncovered in the county of Devon—from which h'I am just returned—appertaining to the background of a certain lady and her child might be so important to you as to make you angry should you wait till tomorrow when in fact h'I could have brought you the news sooner, for it might be—'

'For pity's sake, tell me what it is you know, man!' William bawled with uncustomary churlishness. 'And be quick about it, for there is much work to do.'

The detective flicked a glance between the two gentlemen and sucked his teeth before saying in a deeply cautioning tone, 'H'it's news of a sensitive, shocking nature…'

'Be assured we are braced and ready,' William said with a sigh.

Chapter Seventeen

'*This* is Bethany?' June's voice, when she finally found it, emerged in a breathless squeak.

So much that was preposterous had occurred recently that June felt sure she was inured to the bizarre. But the sight greeting her, as Gavin ushered them into a snug parlour, rendered her transfixed.

'Of course it is not,' Blackmore mockingly chided. 'It is Lady Bingham…or Celeste as she calls herself professionally. You cannot have forgotten her; I know you visited her just this afternoon. I learned that from the letter I received, for it was her work, not Bethany's.' In an under-breath he muttered, 'I apologise for her presence. I have little liking for the bitch either.' Turning, he beckoned to someone else. '*This* is Bethany.'

June had overlooked the slight cloaked figure as that of a child. But as a woman's head emerged from the confines of an enveloping hood, a pair of dark cynical eyes challenged her. 'It is unlikely she is your *younger* sister.' June was no longer interested in knowing how Bethany was related to Gavin. In a daze, she was attempting to comprehend how a gentlewoman—even one as indecorous as Lady Bingham—might be in cahoots with the Blackmores. Her memory dredged up a single fact that might link them—they hailed from the same part of the West Country.

'Bethany is my stepmother and *very* wicked,' Blackmore introduced the woman with a grin. 'My father rued the day he married her, for then she was no longer the God-fearing Christian she had seemed while keen to remain employed as his housekeeper.' A sly look that made June's skin creep passed between the two. 'We have always got on famously for the most part.' Blackmore sauntered away to the inglenook and poked at a small grate until orange lights sparked amid the embers.

While his back was turned June urgently addressed Lady Bingham. 'I have no idea why you are here, but I'm sure you cannot know that we have been kidnapped and threatened with violence. You must help us. Make him see sense and set us free immediately.'

Constance's only reaction was to narrow her eyes in consideration.

'Why do you hesitate?' June demanded. 'Do you want to be thought a party to such an evil crime?' She watched Constance slide a look of furious despising at Gavin. Desperately she repeated, 'Why do you hesitate? You must know your reputation will be tainted by your association with this madman.'

'I do know that very well!' Constance finally responded in a voice made husky with contempt. 'You lily-livered blockhead! You have panicked and ruined everything.'

'*I* have ruined everything?' he sneered. 'If you could control that infernal itch between your legs, we would still be cosy in Devon and with cash in our pockets.'

'But for me you'd still be working dawn till dusk in a musty clerk's office for a pittance! The cash you had in your pocket was put there by my efforts! And you repay me with stupidity!'

'It is not all Gavin's fault! Mind your tongue or you will have me to answer to!' Bethany barked in a rough voice that belied her tiny stature. With her hands planted on her hips she studied the assembled company whilst pacing back and forth.

June assessed Gavin's stepmother with a female eye. So this virago was Bethany, the delicate soul on whom she had squandered her compassion and charity. She might have been about forty-five years old, yet she had the wiry slenderness of a much younger woman. There was silver shining in her dark coarse hair and some crinkles about her eyes that betrayed her age, but she was certainly handsome if extraordinarily petite.

'You cannot deny he has acted stupidly,' Constance reasoned, illustrating her exasperation with a flick of a hand. 'Since he started that absurd rumour about William Pemberton siring Cissy it is all gone awry. William has sent detectives to Devon to investigate. I made it plain in my letter we must proceed with caution. Caution! Hah! Just look what he has done!'

'You were not above conniving when you thought it would get you Pemberton's protection,' Gavin sniped. 'You could have quashed the gossip. You have only decided to despise the idea since he rejected you out of hand.'

Constance glared at him, with indignant colour bright as rouge on a marionette spotting her cheeks. 'I can have any man I want...when I want,' she hissed.

'I beg to differ, my dear,' Gavin drawled. 'Pemberton and myself are just two gentlemen I know who are disinclined to dally with a tawdry jade.'

'That is just *one* gentleman and a eunuch who would be fortunate to ever again get such a chance,' returned the lady with acid sweetness. She smiled with vicious triumph as her insult blanched Gavin's complexion.

Constance intercepted the brooding look he shot at June. 'Has he threatened to violate you? You have little to fear…' An elegant white hand raised and a small finger wiggled in lewd belittlement.

'You bitch, I'll kill you!' Blackmore suddenly lunged across the room at her but was prevented from lashing out as Bethany sprang between them.

'Enough of this!' The roaring baritone would not have disgraced a navvy. 'You are *both* imbeciles!' Bethany sent threatening stares between them, pacing backwards. She turned her shrewd eyes on the blonde sisters.

Instinctively June had cradled Sylvie against her side as though to protect her from the violence in the room. Now the combatants had quietened, yet so keenly did June sense an air of menace that she pushed Sylvie behind her back.

Bethany Blackmore crept around their fused forms as though playing a game, but all the while she was seriously intent on investigating the adolescent beauty in June's shadow. Suddenly she took a tress of platinum hair, stroked it across her palm while testing its silken weight.

Sylvie snatched herself free of the woman's impertinent touch and in doing so fully exposed her face and figure.

'Gavin's got us treasure all right! Spirit as well as looks!' Bethany chuckled contentedly. 'Waiting for ransom money will take too long and bring the dragoons as well as their kin down on our heads.' She looked slyly at her stepson. 'Save your lechery for the elder, the younger is out of bounds. There are several gentlemen who would gladly pay a king's ransom to feast a while on such pure honey. But we have no time for an auction. There is one close by, and I know he would willingly pay tonight, whatever I ask, to be first.' Her rising excitement was evident in the glitter in her sly eyes. 'By this time tomorrow we could all be at Newhaven. Then, once safe in France, we can arrange passage to the Americas.'

Listening to their foul plan to barter Sylvie's virginity made June tense with wrath. William would be searching for them, she was sure, but equally she realised it would now be a miracle should he find them before Sylvie was sold to a disgusting debauchee.

Waiting for a good chance to escape now seemed absurd rather than sensible. Getting Sylvie immediately away from these vile people was imperative. But to do so they must employ some daring and cunning of their own. Quickly she pivoted about and, before hugging Sylvie, strove to convey her wordless instructions to her sister with her eyes. 'You have made my sister ill! Can't you see she is about to be sick after listening to your diabolical scheme?'

Sylvie's acute mind immediately comprehended her role. Her arms crossed her middle as though she had a cramp and she bent forward with ballooning cheeks.

Constance Bingham looked askance at Sylvie's bobbing throat. 'For God's sake, quickly, get the girl some hartshorn. I hardly think Lord Carlisle will relish taking his pleasure of a chit who stinks of vomit.'

'I must take her upstairs to rest. If she becomes hysterical she might have one of her seizures.'

'Seizures?' Blackmore echoed.

'She is prone to fits brought on by extreme fear or excitement.'

'Indeed?' Bethany Blackmore's smirk said she guessed the indisposition was dubious. 'Luckily I have a cure. A dose of my laudanum will calm her well enough for Carlisle to have his fun.'

'I must take her upstairs!' June shrieked and imperceptibly nudged at Sylvie's ribs for her to intensify the drama. Sylvie obliged by groaning and clamping her hands over her mouth.

'For God's sake, take her away before she *is* sick!' Lady Bingham cried, with a look of sheer distaste creasing her features.

A flick of Bethany's head at the door was enough permission for June to steer her sister towards it. A backward glare at Blackmore as they mounted the stairs showed that he was observing them from where he had astutely stationed himself in the hallway.

Once the chamber door was shut, June whispered urgently, 'We must escape, but not in the phaeton, for Blackmore is suspicious and will be upon us before we are able to move it a yard. You must be my brave girl, Sylvie, and get away first. Run for your life once you are outside. I will follow shortly and find you. Secrete yourself somewhere till daylight and I promise I *will* come and find you. Put on my cloak.'

Sylvie did as she was bid, but her large blue eyes were wide and fearful. 'How will we escape? That monster is downstairs guarding the door.'

'I know, but there must be a way!' June sent searching glances about the chamber, desperately looking for something, anything, that might serve as a weapon. The empty china pitcher, should she smash it, might provide sharp shards, but how would they overcome three adversaries? A diversion was needed... By the light of the candle-stump she peered out of the window as though for some inspiration. A draught flicked an edge of flimsy curtain towards the flame and instinctively June cupped a hand about the wick. A glimmer of an idea came to mind.

'It would be a perilous risk...' Sylvie ventured, a natural acuity having alerted her to June's thoughts.

'Yes, but there is a perilous risk if you stay here,' June uttered softly. She said no more, for she did not want to panic Sylvie with examples of depravity. Her mouth had dried with terror at the thought of her sweet sister's fate should either Blackmore or Lord Carlisle get their hands on her. Forcefully she said, 'It is the only way, Sylvie! You must be ready to flee. Never fear that you will be hunted down. They are three cowards who will only be interested in saving their own miserable skins once they know the house is afire.'

Sylvie nodded, unblinking, as she drew courage from June's confidence.

Quickly June tore a strip of linen from her petticoat and held it to the candle. As soon as it was alight she made a nest in the quilt, coddling the flame with her breath until it smouldered and opened a circular hole from which down drifted like snow. As the fire took hold, June quickly embraced Sylvie, then determinedly put her from her. In a fluid movement she smashed the pitcher against the bedstead, muffling the sound with the blankets. She gave Sylvie the sharpest shard she could find and took one herself.

'I don't want to go without you,' Sylvie uttered on a sob.

June put a hand over her sister's quivering mouth. 'I shall be soon with you, I promise. You must run and run and never look back. When it is daylight I *will* find you.'

Sylvie nodded.

With a deep breath and a glance at the flames dancing on the bed, June flung open the door. 'Quick! Come at once!' she called in a husky hiss so Blackmore alone would be summoned. Sylvie might slip past one of their enemies; she would not evade three.

When their guard did little more than glance quizzically up at her, June sped to the top of the stairs. 'You fool! There is a fire! The candle is overset!'

June's silhouette suddenly acquired an amber aura. After a second of stupefaction, during which his reaction was limited to an open-mouthed goggle, Blackmore pounded up the stairs whilst spitting out a string of oaths. Once he was in the room, the sight that confronted him had him baring his teeth in frustration. He rushed to the washstand where once the water jug had rested.

'Go!' June propelled her sister through the door. 'I will not let him come after you, I promise.'

Sylvie opened her mouth to protest, but her sister's fierce look and rough push had her fleeing silently down the stairs, through the door and into the night.

'What in damnation is that?'

The two riders reined in. Adam pointed off to the distance. 'Over there!'

'It looks like a fire,' William said, peering at a nebulous yellow light arcing into the night sky. He turned in the saddle. Through the dusk his eyes gleamed wide and alert at Adam. 'We must be close now. It could be a signal. Please God, if that is White Lodge and they are there, don't let it be anything other than a signal.' He kneed his horse forward and was soon thundering towards the burning building with Adam close behind.

'And what the hell was that?' Adam reined in so hard his stallion pranced and pawed at air. A shadowy cloaked figure started, then darted into the trees close by.

'Show yourself!' William roared, taking his horse in a wide circle and thundering back towards the fringe of woodland that had swallowed up the fugitive. 'Who is there?' he bellowed again as he peered through barring trunks.

'William?' a croaky voice called.

'Is that you, Sylvie?' William had dismounted in an instant.

Sylvie was soon running forward, her sobbing gasps shaking her body as she launched herself at her brother-in-law's chest. 'June is still Blackmore's prisoner and she said I must keep running and she will follow me and find me…but I'm frightened…I don't want her to die in the fire.'

'June won't die!' The vow was forcefully expelled

in a tone so raw each word tore at William's throat. In seconds he was racing back to his horse. 'Keep her safe!' was slung back over his shoulder at Adam.

Adam encircled Sylvie's body lightly with an arm. She immediately plucked away the restraint. 'I must go back and help. I could not bear it if June should perish. I wanted her to come with me, but she made me go first…to make sure I got away.' Sylvie's soft bosom heaved in breathlessness against a barring forearm.

'Hush, William will get her.' Adam soothed and once more urged her back against his muscular torso. Gently he smoothed her moonlight hair. 'You must calm yourself. Your sister will be angry if you again put yourself in jeopardy when she has risked all for you. Your other brothers-in-law are bringing the dragoons. They are close behind us.'

Adam's wise words had little effect on Sylvie, who fiercely pushed and pulled in vain at his arm. Finally she pivoted about, kicking at him until she broke free. She had sprinted a yard or two when Adam caught her and, with an oath beneath his breath, swung her into his arms to protect his shins from further assault. When repeated reassurance and reason were to no avail, and his face became a new target, he hoisted her over his shoulder and strode back to his horse.

Having transferred the spitfire to his stallion, he

swung into the saddle before sitting her upright. He deftly dodged the proof that her hysteria was unabated and set off after William in the direction of the blazing Lodge.

'For pity's sake! There is still time for us to escape the flames!'

'I prefer death to capture, I told you that.'

'Well, I beg you will let *me* go.' June's voice was gruff with smoke and pleading.

Blackmore shook his head. 'I told you I wanted you or your husband's money. It is only fair I should get one or the other. Why should William have all? Do you believe in an afterlife, June? I do and should like you there with me. But might you go to Heaven and me to Hell, I wonder?'

June squinted through the turgid atmosphere at her executioner. Blackmore was standing with his back against the door, barring her escape to cool sweet air.

Constance and Bethany had already given up their efforts to persuade their cohort to flee with them in the phaeton. Gavin's stepmother had been the first to lose courage and bolt. Constance had hesitated a moment longer, endorsing June's frantic appeal that Gavin act rationally now the game was up. But the noise of charred timbers splintering had soon startled into flight Lady Bingham's humanity and her person.

June had listened, despairingly, as the carriage rattled away, bearing the women to safety. Now she was left alone, at the mercy of their crazed accomplice.

A burning beam crashed down on to the landing, sending sparks raining into the hallway.

'The thatch is burning! For pity's sake! The roof will collapse.' June's mouth was arid from terror and black motes that were suspended in the thick air. She felt her lungs ache and cupped her hands over her nose to try and filter each breath. *William, I love you...please know I love you...* chanted in her feverish mind as she watched flaming petals curving about the banisters in an inexorable descent towards her.

She pricked her finger with the shard of china in her pocket. Again and again she tested its sharp edge. But first she needed to get within striking range of him...

June took a step away from the searing heat at her back while conversing as calmly as she was able. 'Did you father Lady Bingham's daughter?'

'I thank God I did not. I would hate a daughter of mine to be reared by a whore.' Blackmore coughed as the heat and smoke attacked his throat. 'Now you think me a hypocrite, for I expect you have guessed that Bethany and Constance are alike. Both have catered to the basic needs of men. But Bethany is a businesswoman; Constance simply worships the work. We had a sweet trade in Devon, but she put it all in jeopardy with her insatiable appetite. We had fine gentlemen clients who paid well. They didn't take kindly to discovering that *Celeste* was dallying with the dregs of humanity. Quality make bad enemies. Even her daughter's father could not prevent her from acting like a bitch in heat... Enough!' he suddenly shouted. 'Enough of her and fornication! I should like *us* to be lovers before we die. I should like one last earthly pleasure.'

June stepped closer to him, feeling the heat of burning detritus beneath her shoes.

'If I kiss you would that be enough to save us both?' she said huskily.

He grinned, a strip of white in his soot-stained face. 'As we are friends I must be honest and say I doubt it, but it is a start, so please try to persuade me to be kind.' He held out his arms in mocking invitation.

June wondered whether her complexion was as grimy as was his. She touched her cheek and felt grit on her fingertips. Her face angled to his at the same moment one of her hands began withdrawing the weapon from her pocket.

A violent battering at the door put a split in the planks and a palsy in Blackmore's limbs.

He recovered quickly and sprang sideways. 'Pemberton, the conquering hero…' Gavin sneered, his teeth bared in frustration. 'What a shame! For me he is too early and for you he is too late.' He fastened an arm chokingly about June's neck, pulling her backwards and off balance, just as the door caved in and William burst through the aperture.

'I might have known perfect Pemberton would arrive at the eleventh hour to try and ruin things,' Blackmore screamed across the crackle and hiss of the fire as he dragged June up the stairs towards the inferno.

'Let her go,' William bellowed hoarsely as he paced into the stifling hallway. A hand elevated in supplication, formed an impotent fist. 'Let my wife go and you can go too. I'll help you get away.'

'Of course you will,' Gavin mocked. 'Then I shall be arrested at the coast and taken to stand trial. Do you think I would stay alive at any cost? Stupid! That is not my way. What I fear is a living death rotting on a prison hulk or swinging on a gibbet with the crows at my eyes while I still breathe. But perishing cleanly…ah, that is sweet…'

'Listen to me!' William roared as the hand about June's throat tightened, jerking her smoky blonde head back against her captor's shoulder. 'What is it you want? Money? Name your price.'

'Tell him what I want, sweetheart,' Blackmore whispered to June while touching his lips to her grimy cheek. 'Tell him if he comes closer I will warm your icy heart with the flames. Tell him I can make you burn for me.'

June gasped for breath for a violent heat was stealing the little air she could draw into her lungs. A hand fluttered to her pocket to withdraw the sliver of crockery. With all her strength she stabbed it hard against his thigh.

He howled in pain and surprise and loosened his grip to investigate the damage. The makeshift dagger plunged again and again as June squirmed her head beneath his arm. She stumbled and slid down the treads on collapsing legs while half-blinded eyes saw her husband's face as a mask of torment as he sprang forward to catch her.

Then there was a welcome chill for her scorching limbs and the scent of rain-damp earth to soothe her lungs. And she was sure it was Sylvie's tears that wet her face although she felt her body heaving with sobs. And it might have been a dream that brought horsemen close before again they pounded away. But safe in her husband's arms she had only to turn her aching head away to William's chest to rest a while and finally she allowed it.

Chapter Eighteen

'I am not an invalid, you know. I am just tired.'

At those gentle teasing words, William placed down the bowl of broth he had been clumsily pressing on his wife. 'You must eat,' he insisted, while stroking back grimy golden hair to tenderly place his lips on a mucky brow.

'Yes, I know,' June said with a wry smile. 'And I look forward to tucking into a good dinner later.' As she saw her husband's glistening blue eyes roving her face she asked, 'Do I look awful?'

'You look beautiful. You always look beautiful,' he uttered hoarsely and sat down carefully on the edge of the bed.

June removed a hand from beneath the bedcovers where, time and again, he had tucked it in. A soft palm glided over rough stubble on a gaunt cheek. 'Don't cry,' she whispered. 'I am fine…Sylvie is fine…'

William nodded, and taking that delicate dirty hand in his he dipped his forehead to it as though in obeisance. 'Your parents are below, your sisters, too. I have told them you are sleeping, but they will not go away. They want simply to see you. Are you well enough just to say hello?'

'Of course,' June said and pushed herself up on to her elbows. Ten ivory fingers were fanned out and, after a glance to either side of her, she tutted her dismay. 'Heavens! Look at me! The sheets must be black.' She took one of William's hands and turned it over, examining his long, firm fingers. 'Have you not had an opportunity to wash either?'

William glanced at his stained shirt and soiled skin. 'I don't know…I have stayed here with you. It did not occur to me…' He paused before adding, 'Your pretty new clothes are ruined.' He looked towards the chair where he had lobbed those flimsy scraps she had worn for the first time.

On returning to the house close to dawn he had refused to leave her side for a moment. Her maid, Verity, had thus discreetly withdrawn, visibly distressed by her mistress's condition. William had carefully removed the tattered muslin from his wife's limp form until she swayed drowsily against him in only her undergarments. He had put her beneath the pristine covers, then collapsed beside her with his eyes fixed on her still profile.

She had slept for more than ten hours as though dead, without movement, although the physician who had examined her in that time said he could find no damage other than minor blisters and scrapes, and a lock of singed hair. Her bruised mind was of prime concern and had sought its own cure, he had said with a respectful nod to the wisdom of nature. Handing over a pot of unguent, he had advised William not to fret and William had blinked and lied.

'Send them all up. Afterwards I want to bathe—so must you—and then I want to dine.'

William sniffed, swiped moisture from his nose and smiled diffidently.

'And then I want you to love me, William…I want so much that you love me before I sleep again.'

He nodded, his lips tightly compressed, and stood up with an indrawn breath that seemed to take an inordinately long time to fill his lungs. He went to the window, quietly appreciating a glorious spring afternoon until it restored his composure. 'I'll fetch your family,' he finally said.

'For a man who in the early hours of today rode for two-score miles on horseback, kicked down a door and rescued a fair lady, you still have a surprising lot of energy, sir.'

'And it's not spent yet,' William wolfishly warned

his wife as he lowered his head to hers and took her swollen scarlet mouth in a deep drugging kiss.

June flexed like a languid kitten beneath him while skimming her hands over the hard ridges of muscle spanning the breadth of his back. She revelled in the taste and scent of him, the sensation of his body moulded to hers.

At first they had made love tenderly, as usual, but when William would have cuddled her protectively against his side in a prelude to sleep she had tantalised his long, lean body with subtle fingertip touches.

'I am alive…and well, William,' she had whispered against his warm musky skin. 'Prove it to me… please…as never before…' The wooing sweetness of his next kiss was welcomed with a nip from her small teeth. Softly sensual caresses tempted her to dig her nails into the muscle bulging in his braced arms.

Alert to his wife's wordless plea, in every sense he had obliged her. Kisses of exquisite savagery had bruised her lips. Her breasts had engorged and ached from the torture of endless attention before rhythmic thrusts had ground at her pelvis, so hard and deep, that she was jerked, moaning, from mattress to wall. Still she imprisoned him with silken limbs coiled at his head and hips and artfully enticed for more vital knowledge of her existence.

Their violent passion had sent the damp bedspread to trail the floor and with a languid hand June now drew it up over William's back so it formed a shelter for their exhausted bodies.

Sated and warm and with her mind sensually drugged she was ready to know...

'Did the dragoons catch up with Constance and Bethany?'

'Yes. They were arrested and will stand trial for aiding and abetting. I expect, when all is laid open to scrutiny, other charges will be laid against them too.'

The unspoken question thickened the atmosphere until June burst out huskily, 'Is Gavin Blackmore dead?'

William eventually answered hoarsely, 'I tried to reach him, so did Adam, but he refused to live and walked into the fire. I wanted to see him swing, or kill him myself, but he got his way and perished cleanly.'

June saw the torment in his eyes. With a kiss transferred from a finger to his lips, she attempted to soothe his pain. 'You were not to know how sick was his mind. I chose to spend time with him and, despite all our troubles and arguments, you kindly did not object. You rarely object to what I want, do you?' she praised him softly. 'I have always deemed myself fortunate to have a husband who so readily bestows on me respect and independence.'

'Kind words won't do, June.' William shook his

head. 'You have suffered horribly because of my neglect. I might have lost you,' he uttered, so hoarsely the words were almost inaudible. 'You are the most precious thing to me, yet I allowed you to be escorted and befriended by a man I never really liked and whom I had not seen in a decade. I knew Blackmore at school and even then he was…different.' He caught at June's small hands as they moved to comfort him. 'No! I must declare it or my conscience will rack me my life through.' He paused before adding, 'Adam knew Gavin to be a liar who had attempted to swindle money from a fellow student. Now Townsend feels he must share the blame for keeping that intelligence to himself.'

'If we are all to unburden ourselves of guilt, then I have confessions to make too,' June said quietly. 'I enjoyed receiving Gavin's flattery.' She smiled wryly. 'Of course, I see now that he intended to impress me. But my own behaviour was not impeccable. I guessed that he wanted to be more than the friend I considered him, yet I did not put a stop to our outings. I encouraged his attention from vanity.' She touched William's face with loving fingers. 'And I allowed the gossips to poison my mind. I began to deem you capable of committing adultery, yet previously you had never given me reason to doubt your loyalty. I was jealous, especially when I saw Constance shamelessly embracing you on her doorstep.

I could have challenged you over it, and believed what you told me, but instead I rejected you and went out to meet Gavin.'

William lowered himself to lie beside his wife and took her in his arms. 'The mischief-makers did their work well. It was always their intention to corrupt our happiness.'

'I learned how wrong I had been when listening to that evil trio bickering amongst themselves. Bethany tried to blackmail you through greed... Gavin was angry about that, even though he insti-gated the rumour about you having sired Constance's child.'

William tightened his embrace to absorb her shud-dering with his body.

'It was horrible listening to their depraved schemes. Time and again I prayed you would come for us. But I despaired of you finding us in time,' June whispered against his cheek. 'How on earth did you know where to look?'

'Isabel recalled that Blackmore had confided in you about his sister languishing in prison. Thank God you did disclose that to her, for it was from one of the turnkeys at the Fleet that I learned Bethany had told him about White Lodge.

'I had also sent an investigator to Devon to discover what he could about Constance's daughter. He uncovered unbelievably sordid details about Con-

stance and the Blackmores. Bethany and Constance
were unlikely partners brought together by a mutual
dependency on vice. When details of their vile
business, and especially Constance's proclivities,
were uncovered the locals hounded them away. Poor
Charlie Bingham must be turning in his grave.'

'What of the child?'

'She lives with her father's family now.'

June rose on an elbow to look enquiringly at him.

'The local clergyman has a pronounced limp. The
girl has the same affliction. Apparently it has been an
open secret since the child's birth that the vicar had
cuckolded the lord of the manor.' He gave a short
laugh. 'Apparently the villagers hold their minister in
high esteem, it is Constance they despise for leading
him astray. The reverend's wife was Christian enough
to allow the child shelter in their home when her
mother absconded to London with her colleagues.'

'They must have realised that the scandal would
eventually catch up with them.'

'Oh, yes.' William choked an ironic laugh. 'They
knew that gossip and debt would catch up with them.
Bethany was the first to fall foul of the duns. I
imagine Constance was hopeful of luring a wealthy
gentleman's protection to ease her path to a new life
overseas.'

'And she chose you as her victim,' June said
simply.

'That was her prime mistake,' William said. 'I might have had a reputation as a mild-mannered fellow, but I hope I am not a dullard.'

'I doubt people will think you placid now,' June said with some asperity. 'I could not wish for a more heroic husband.'

'And I could not wish for a more courageous and wonderful wife,' William said huskily. 'Sylvie is telling everyone that she owes you her life. It is marvellous that she has been so little distressed by it all. I think Adam is more affected. I have had to dissuade him from seeking out Carlisle. I have no liking for the old goat, but he cannot be hounded simply because he was nominated to ravish Sylvie.'

'We must not praise ourselves too much or perhaps we will again be deemed smug,' June said softly.

'I don't care if our contentment irks,' William countered vibrantly. 'We have each other and that is all that matters. Never again will I let us be pilloried. I have no intention of changing for anyone.'

'*I* feel different,' June said in a tone that harboured a secret, and her hands slid down to cup her abdomen.

William felt the sensation of her small hands moving between them. For a long moment his eyes devoured her face. 'Are you sure?' he finally forced out.

'No,' June replied softly. 'As yet I have no proof…no absence to convince me, but I *feel* so different.' She took his hands and touched them to her breasts, to her belly, as though he, too, must sense the wonder.

His hands travelled on and he smiled against her mouth. 'Well, until you *are* certain, there is still need to practise…'

Epilogue

∽∾∽∾∾∾

'Lord Malvern, please come in. How nice to see you.'

If Edgar was unused to receiving such prominent members of the aristocracy at eight of the clock in the evening when well past the fashionable visiting hour, he admirably concealed his surprise.

Moments later when a track had appeared in the pile of his carpet and he learned the nature of the man's impromptu visit, his disbelief left him goggle-eyed for several long seconds. Finally he brought together his jaw well enough to burble, 'I'll fetch her mother.'

Gloria and Edgar Meredith exchanged glances. They looked at their eminent guest, who exuded a stubborn air of polished sophistication.

Edgar swallowed, then blurted out, 'You must not feel obliged, sir, to do this just because you and she were alone in the dark for a short while. Exceptional circumstances were in play, and besides, nobody knows but us…the family. Good of you, though… very good of you, sir…'

'I should like to speak to her,' Adam said.

'She has not yet had her début,' Gloria whispered.

'By all accounts she does not want it,' Adam countered. 'It is not strictly necessary.'

'No, it is not,' Gloria agreed. Slowly it was dawning on her that what was occurring was not a mockery, but a miracle.

Adam read her expression and a half-smile tilted his lips. 'May I speak to her?'

Gloria looked at Edgar and, gaining little assistance from that quarter, made the decision to nod eagerly.

'Come away from the door, Gloria.'

'It's too quiet! Should I go in? It is highly irregular you know. I *should* go in…she is young…I am her mother…'

'She is seventeen next week. And for days past much in our lives has been irregular. Anyhow, who will know anything of it but us?'

Suddenly the door of the parlour burst open and Adam strode out. Without slowing his pace he managed to bow to Mr and Mrs Meredith and exit the house within less than a minute.

Edgar and Gloria stared at the parlour door, but

their youngest daughter seemed determined to remain within. Tentatively they entered the room.

Sylvie was standing by the fire with her arms crossed over her waist and her soft lips under attack from her small teeth. On seeing her parents she stormed, 'He asked me to marry him. Why? All I expected was a ride in his curricle. I told him so and he said it was time I acted like a young lady instead of an infuriating brat. I don't even like him now.'

Edgar shook his head and blew out his cheeks. 'I'm going to my study,' he muttered.

Within a few moments of Edgar settling into his creaky chair and picking up his pen, Sylvie burst into the room, tears glossing her violet eyes. 'You must call him out, Papa. He said I was an infuriating brat. You must go after him now and tell him I hate him.'

Edgar took hold of a small, fidgety hand that was making disorder of his desktop. He gave it a calming pat before continuing to write in his ledger.

Sylvie stamped a small foot. 'You must! You must go after him and tell him I hate him. I want him to know.'

Edgar dropped his quill and looked up. 'In a year or two he will be back, my dear, then you can tell him yourself.'

* * * * *

Don't miss the last Meredith sister to marry!
Silver's story
The Rake and the Rebel
by Mary Brendan
is available next month in
Regency High-Society Affairs
Volume 2